Praise for

Jill Gregory

Thunder Creek

"A transfixing blend of fiery romance and spine-tingling suspense." —*Booklist*

"For tales of romance and adventure that keep you reading into the night, look no further than Jill Gregory."
—Nora Roberts

"A compelling tale that works on two levels, as a well-structured mystery and a first-rate romance. Gregory . . . writes the stuff that romance readers yearn for. If you haven't yet read her, you're missing out on a great treat."
—*Oakland Press*

"Fans . . . will be pleased by her treatment of the protagonists' relationship and drawn in by the book's cozy, small-town setting. . . . Once the action revs up, readers will gladly sit back and enjoy the journey." —*Publishers Weekly*

Once an Outlaw

"Gregory's sensitive characterizations . . . will drive a herd of new readers to pick up this heartfelt family drama. . . . The story escalates with fast-paced action, romance, and several surprises as the fiery attraction between Clint and Emily hits fever pitch." —*Publishers Weekly*

"Jill Gregory's western romances always pack a wallop. *Cold Night, Warm Stranger* is true to form. Strong characters that engage readers' emotions and an action-packed story with a powerful plot make this a not-to-be-missed western." —*Romantic Times*

Never Love a Cowboy

"A western version of *Romeo and Juliet* . . . This is a who-done-it with strong elements of suspense . . . but the emphasis is definitely on the romance. This book has wonderful, tender scenes. . . . Jill Gregory creates not only a very human hero and a likeable heroine but also very evil villains with interesting motivations." —*Romance Reader*

"Sensual . . . Enjoy *Never Love a Cowboy*. . . . A western, a suspenseful mystery, and a good book. Combining grit, sensuality, and a cleverly plotted mystery takes talent." —*Romantic Times*

Just This Once

"Refreshing characters, witty dialogue, and adventure . . . *Just This Once* enthralls, delights, and captivates, winning readers' hearts along the way." —*Romantic Times*

"Here is another unforgettable story that will keep you captivated. She has combined the Old West and the elegance of England into this brilliantly glorious tale. The characters are undeniably wonderful. Their pains and joys will reach through the pages and touch your heart." —*Rendezvous*

Always You

"*Always You* has it all. . . . Jill Gregory's inventive imagination and sprightly prose combine for another bell ringer." —*Rendezvous*

"Compelling . . . definitely a winner!" —*Affaire de Coeur*

"A surefire winner . . . remarkable . . . A delightful romance with both tenderness and tough western grit."
—*Romantic Times*

More Praise for Jill Gregory

"A wonderfully exciting romance from the Old West. The plot twists in this novel are handled expertly. . . . It's great from start to finish."
—*Rendezvous* on *When the Heart Beckons*

"A fast-paced western romance novel that will keep readers' attention throughout. Both the hero and heroine are charming characters."
—*Affaire de Coeur* on *Daisies in the Wind*

"A charming tale of dreams come true. It combines a heartwarming love story with an intriguing mystery."
—*Gothic Journal* on *Forever After*

Also by Jill Gregory

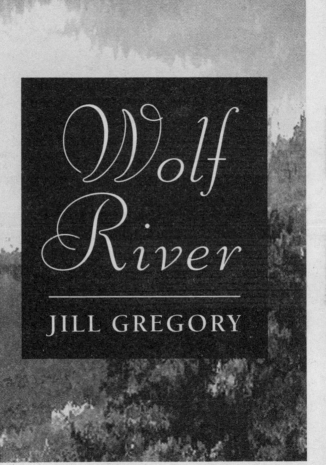

Wolf River

JILL GREGORY

Bantam Books

WOLF RIVER
A Bantam Book / May 2007

Published by
Bantam Dell
A Division of Random House, Inc.
New York, New York

Bantam Books is a registered trademark of Random House, Inc., and the
colophon is a trademark of Random House, Inc.

ISBN 978-0-440-24304-5

Printed in the United States of America
Published simultaneously in Canada

www.bantamdell.com

OPM   10 9 8 7 6 5 4 3 2 1

To my fantastic girl cousins—
Amy, Barb, Judy, Lynn, Paula, and Tracy
With lots and lots of love. This one's for you!

Wolf River

Chapter One

New York City

The phone call came at the worst possible time. Just as Erinn Winters was having lunch at Tavern on the Green with her new editor from hell. At precisely the moment the waiter set down their salads.

"Finally—great news, Ms. Winters," the calm male voice said at the other end of her cell line. *Cordovan*. In that instant, he had her full attention. She hadn't heard from him—or from anyone at Cordovan-Smith Security and Investigations—in more than two months.

"We've found her," Wayne Cordovan said. "We've found your sister."

In that instant Erinn forgot about Clare Bonham, frowning at her across the table. She forgot that she was planning to have a nervous breakdown later that day, and that if she didn't finish writing her latest Princess Devonshire book in very short order she was going to have to return every nickel of her advance and get herself a real job.

She forgot everything but the words Cordovan had just spoken in her ear. *We've found your sister.*

Her heart lifted and a dazzling relief rushed through her like golden sunlight in winter.

But then her gaze flicked to the subtly annoyed expression of her editor. Clare looked as if someone had superglued a lemon under her tongue.

Erinn knew she'd blundered by even answering her cell just as they were about to get down to business. Normally, she wouldn't have. But at the last second, she'd panicked and wanted to put off the central point of this meeting until she'd had time to gulp down at least half a glass of wine. So she'd impulsively scooped her phone from her bag, never expecting the call to be anything as important—and personal—as this.

"That's . . . that's very good news." She chose her words carefully and spoke as evenly as she could, flicking up one digit to signal Clare she'd be off in a minute.

No one in her present life knew anything about her search for Devon, or the truth about her own past. No one even knew her real name—except for Wayne Cordovan and his agency.

So she wasn't about to give anything away to the tall fortyish redhead in chic black sitting across the table, a woman who in Erinn's eyes represented the closest thing to a boss she'd known in a long time.

Erinn didn't deny she had a problem with authority figures. And Clare—with her protuberant brown eyes, air of breezy command, and repeated e-mails inquiring when the book would be turned in—definitely qualified as an authority figure.

It was therefore certain that Clare Bonham wasn't going to discover one thing about Erinn that Erinn didn't want her to know.

"I can't wait to hear all the details, but can I possibly call you back? I'm . . . in the middle of a business meeting."

"No problem." Cordovan didn't miss a beat. "Why don't you stop by my office sometime before three? I'm leaving for Rome, and I'm afraid I'll be gone for the next two weeks. If you can't get here before three, you can always schedule a meeting with one of my associates while I'm gone. But I have all the details right here on my desk, including some photographs, and I assumed you'd want to see the report on your sister as soon as possible."

"I do. Believe me, I do." The words flew from her mouth. She hadn't seen Devon in eleven years. Now the tiny chubby-cheeked four-year-old she'd kissed good-bye in their father's mansion that long-ago day was fifteen, a teenager herself.

And a runaway.

Just like me, Erinn thought.

But there was one big difference. Erinn had at least been eighteen, legally of age, when she'd fled Chicago and the stunning Lake Forest estate where Dane Stanton's word had been law.

Devon had vanished last year. When she was only fourteen. And no one in her family had seen her since.

Erinn's gaze shifted to Clare once again. The anorexically thin, cropped-haired editor was tapping a tomato-red fingernail on the snowy tablecloth.

Erinn spoke decisively into her cell. "I'll definitely be there in an hour. I want to see everything you've got."

Clicking off her phone, she slipped it into her bag and offered Clare an apologetic smile.

"I'm so sorry. That was important or I wouldn't have kept you waiting."

"I do hope everything is all right," Clare commented tartly, obviously waiting for further explanation.

But Erinn declined to oblige her. She hadn't even told Nancy Leonetti, her previous editor, who'd also become a close friend, anything about her past or her real identity.

She hadn't told anyone in all these years. So there was no way she'd discuss her family history with the woman who had reluctantly "inherited" the Princess Devonshire books from Nancy, and who had made it abundantly clear she hadn't a shred of sympathy for Erinn's writer's block.

"I know you're worried about my finishing the book." Erinn took the plunge, determined to get this discussion over with so she could grab a cab to Cordovan's office. "But you needn't be. I'll finish it soon. By the end of the summer."

"You don't know how relieved I am to hear you say that. But it's not quite good enough, I'm afraid." Clare raised her wineglass to her lips and tossed back a swallow.

"We've had to delay production twice, you realize— and it wasn't easy. But I managed to rearrange the entire schedule. Now I've snared you a lead slot for next April, but you must have the book on my desk by the middle of August. At the latest."

She eyed Erinn skeptically over the rim of her glass. "That won't be a problem for you, Erinn, will it?"

"Not at all." *Oh, God, what am I going to do?*

Erinn choked down a gulp of Pinot Grigio. Her successful series of children's books about a brave princess mouse, who happened to be a superheroine and rescued all manner of creatures in the Emerald Forest, had screeched to a grinding halt when she'd discovered three months ago that her control-freak billionaire father had died and that the little sister she'd left behind had disappeared a year ago.

Since then she hadn't been able to write more than a dozen pages of her book, which barely scratched the surface of Devonshire's latest adventure.

But nothing more would come. No ideas, no dialogue, no derring-do. The words were silent in her head. The characters and images frozen.

The magic gone.

"It'll come back," Nancy had assured her when in desperation Erinn had called in tears the day after her deadline passed.

"Hang in there and relax," Nancy advised. "I've worked with at least a dozen authors over the years who've had worse writer's block than you, and in each case the magic eventually returned. So count on it."

Erinn hoped she was right. There hadn't been much magic—at least of the good sort—in her life for a long time now.

And the last remaining drops of it had simply evaporated when she learned of her father's death—and that Devon had followed in her own footsteps and run away from home.

As Clare droned on about marketing plans, cover treatments, and publicity schedules, Erinn tried to swallow a few bites of her salad. But she scarcely tasted the delicate array of arugula, baby greens, grilled chicken, and sugared pecans gracing the china plate before her.

Her mind kept returning to the image of her baby sister the last time Erinn had seen her.

"I'll come back and visit you, I promise," she'd vowed, kneeling beside the golden-haired four-year-old with the fairy-blue eyes. They'd been in the upstairs hall near the curving marble staircase, while downstairs in the formal living room, Erinn's stepmother—Devon's mother—hosted a tea for the Chicago Art Institute's auxiliary board.

Devon had thrown her baby arms around Erinn's neck and held on for dear life. "Don't go, Tiffy," she begged. "I want you to stay. Stay *here*..."

"*Shhh.*" Erinn had hushed her, worried that either Annabeth—Devon's nanny—or her stepmother would come to see why Devon was crying.

"It's a secret, remember? I don't want anyone to know I'm gone until it's bedtime. Honey, quiet, please don't cry."

Her stomach had twisted like knots of twine at the sight of Devon's tears, at her pale cheeks blotching with despair.

"I'll come back, Devon." She smoothed her sister's baby-fine hair, the color of spun gold. "I'll come visit you and tell you stories and we'll ... we'll have a picnic in the garden on your birthday, just like we did last summer, remember?"

"P-promise!" Devon's voice had been a heartrending gasp that had filled Erinn with love and guilt and pain—all of it mixing with her own raw desperation to escape.

"I promise, sweetie. Every time you look out at the garden you think about our picnic and remember that I'm coming back. Okay, now, hurry—scoot back to your room and don't tell anyone I'm gone. Be brave, like Princess Devonshire. That's my good little mouse."

Erinn had smiled and waved as Devon scampered down the hall to her pink and white bedroom. Then she'd hitched her duffel over her shoulder, slipped silently down the stairs and across the vast ivory marble foyer, holding her breath that none of the Art Institute board members would look up from their tea and scones to notice her creeping out the door.

They hadn't.

She'd left her father's coldly beautiful three-story home, with its lush grounds and meticulous rose gardens, without a single look back.

And she hadn't seen Devon—not even once—since that day.

"Erinn . . . *Erinn* . . ." The annoyance in Clare's voice splintered through her reverie. "Did you hear what I said? *Good Morning America* has expressed interest in having you on during your next book tour. We need to start working on an itinerary soon, though I don't want to distract you from the writing, of course."

"I'll work with publicity on the schedule," Erinn promised, and tried to refocus on the discussion of her career. But she couldn't concentrate. She was ready to jump out of her skin.

It was nearly two and she had to get to Cordovan's office before he left for the airport.

"Shall we order coffee now?" She signaled the waiter

without waiting for a reply. "I'm sorry to rush, Clare, but this appointment that just came up—it's urgent."

"Obviously."

Tension knotted through Erinn's neck an hour later as she leaned back against the lumpy cushions of her speeding taxi, darting kamikaze-style through snarled midday traffic. Clare's displeasure was the least of her concerns right now. She wondered anxiously what she was going to learn about Devon.

Guilt whipped through her, not for the first time. *I should have gone back for her. Been there for her. I promised.*

But you did go back, a voice inside reminded her. *You tried to see her . . . you know what happened . . .*

She gritted her teeth, pushing away the memory of that disastrous July day, a little over a year after she'd run off. The day she'd returned to her father's house, determined to see Devon.

But the only person she'd seen had been Dane Stanton.

She drew in a breath as the cab swerved and braked for a red light, blocking her father's coldly contemptuous face from her mind. Blocking the acid of the words he'd hurled at her that day—words that seared and wounded like poison bombs.

She'd run away from him, from his house—*again*. And failed her sister.

I should have known Devon's life would be as awful as my own, even if she did have a mother to look out for her . . .

But one of the things she'd learned when the news of her father's death hit the network and cable news stations three months ago was that Dane Stanton's second wife had cheated on him and left him when Devon turned ten. And that the divorce settlement had granted her only a paltry twelve million dollars and the title to the house in Palm Beach in exchange for Dane Stanton being awarded full custody of their only child, Devon.

Erinn's first reaction had been horror. Horror for her sister, left alone at the mercy of the Great Dane, as she'd angrily nicknamed her father during her own teenage years. It hadn't surprised her that she'd felt nothing more than a momentary shock when she learned he had died. Dane Stanton had been as rigid and controlling as he was powerful, and those who crossed his path either revered him for his business acumen or feared him for his compulsion to ruthlessly dominate everyone and everything around him.

Erinn had ceased being intimidated by him long ago, but she'd never stopped hating him. She'd managed to escape, to make her own life, shunning both his fortune and his control. And somehow, she lived through it. But when the newscasters reported that Devon Stanton, Dane's now fifteen-year-old daughter, had run away from home and mysteriously dropped from sight a year before his death—following the same pattern as her older half-sister—Erinn had sunk into a chair, her legs too wobbly to hold her, her heart squeezing painfully in her chest.

Since then the enormity of her own failure had weighed on her every day. And each day that passed without Cordovan getting a lead on Devon's whereabouts, without discovering if she was even still alive, had taken its toll on Erinn.

As the taxi driver zigzagged across the financial district, she rubbed her temples and tried to prepare herself for the photos awaiting her, wondering with dread what kind of life her baby sister had found in the soulless chaos of the big wide world.

"Come in, Ms. Winters. I have your sister's file right here."

Wayne Cordovan, a tall and urbane man somewhere around forty, guided her to a wing chair opposite his sleek granite desk. The expansive office was every bit as polished and handsome as Cordovan himself. Cordovan-Smith Security and Investigations took up the entire seventeenth floor of the modern mirrored glass building.

Gleaming hardwood floors, high ceilings, modern Italian furniture, and massive contemporary paintings distinguished the reception area, conference rooms, and the series of plush offices that might have belonged to a prestigious law firm or Fortune 500 company. Instead they were home to one of the East Coast's most high-tech, high-priced, yet discreet security firms, one that boasted an elite clientele from major cities all over the world.

This was no shabby, nickel-and-dime private eye operation. It was a modern-day fortress of steel, glass, and smarts.

Erinn had hired the best and had invested a good part of her latest book advance in the initial retainer, and still it had taken Cordovan and his staff of investigators months to find her sister.

"Where's Devon? Is she all right?"

"She appears to be well. For the moment."

For the moment? Erinn felt a tug of panic as she read the somberness in the detective's eyes. "Tell me where she is."

"She's out West. We found her living on the out-skirts of a small town in Montana. It's just a speck on the map, in the shadow of the Beartooth Mountains. I doubt you've heard of the place. It's called Wolf River."

Erinn shook her head. *Wolf River.* He was right, she'd never heard of it. How in heaven's name had Devon ended up *there*?

"I need to see the photographs right away." Her throat was dry. "I have to see her for myself." Erinn pointed at the dark green leather folder on his desk. "Are they in here?"

Cordovan nodded. He flipped the folder open and slid it toward her. "Take your time looking at them." His tone was sympathetic. He cleared his throat. "Then I'll tell you how we found her."

Much later, Erinn gazed unseeing out the third-floor window of her apartment on 20th Street overlooking the gated darkness of Gramercy Park.

It was 2 a.m. and she couldn't sleep. Or work. Her laptop was open and booted up on the slim table across from her bed, but Princess Devonshire was still trapped in a giant sticky spiderweb on page twenty-two, as she had been for weeks. The pale champagne satin sheets on Erinn's bed were flung back, the pillows scattered, and today's *New York Times* had fallen unnoticed to the floor beside the five-foot-tall glistening bronze flower sculpture she'd bought to celebrate her first book sale.

The quiet one-bedroom apartment with its cream walls and champagne leather furniture was an oasis of calm and serenity above the pulsing energy of New York, but Erinn's spirit was far from calm, nowhere approaching serene. Emotion and anxiety churned within her and she was scarcely aware of her surroundings, of the beautiful sun-drenched paintings dotting the pale walls, or of the vases of tulips and calla lilies picking up the colors in the throw pillows and rugs, which gave the room a lovely glow of softness, color, and life.

Erinn saw only the girl whose face had stared back at her from the pictures she'd seen today—that pale, hard-looking teenage girl who'd borne scant resemblance to the dainty, doe-eyed child Erinn had known years ago.

A lifetime ago.

In most of the shots, Devon had been photographed alone, either standing, her gaze squinting at the sky, arms hugging herself, or sitting on the broken steps of a dilapidated shack. In each of the photos, she wore an expression of utter loneliness that stabbed Erinn like a blade to the heart.

For several moments, she hadn't even spoken. All she'd done was stare at the image of the sad, tough-looking girl who was a complete stranger to her.

The stranger was of medium height, small-boned, and far too thin. She looked like a strong wind would knock her to her knees, but her mouth was hard and defiant. The zoom lens of the camera had captured her hunched shoulders. Stringy blonde hair hung limply in her eyes, and the knees of her beat-up jeans were torn. She wore rubber thongs on her feet, Erinn had noted, as well as a faded black camisole that looked two sizes too small and barely reached her midriff.

But almost as disconcerting as her sister's appearance was the boy photographed in several photos alongside her.

The zoom on the detective's camera had captured them together, walking away from the same shack on a weed-strewn dirt road, mountains looming in the distance. The boy was wiry, and whipcord thin. He wore an untucked sleeveless flannel shirt and ripped jeans, and had a beer can gripped in one hand. Tattoos swirled over both of his shoulders and forearms.

"Who is he? And who's the other man?" Erinn had asked in alarm as she'd scanned eight separate photos, two of which also showed a scowling bull of a man with dark, close-set eyes.

"From what I've pieced together, the kid is Devon's boyfriend, Hank Wheeler. The other man is his older brother, Mick. There's some notes on them in the back of the folder, but I can summarize for you. They've both had trouble with the law. Mostly misdemeanor stuff— public drunkenness and disorderly conduct—meaning getting drunk and fighting," Cordovan explained. "But there was one more serious charge against Mick Wheeler. He was convicted and served a year-long prison term for assaulting a woman—his live-in girl-friend at the time."

"Oh, my God." Erinn's heart had skipped a beat at his words.

"Both brothers are now employed as ranch hands at

the Hanging J ranch in Wolf River," Cordovan had continued. "That shack you see in the background is
theirs. It's at the end of a dirt lane about thirty miles
outside of town."

"How did your people find her? And why in the
world is she living with these men?"

Her voice had trembled as she asked Cordovan the
questions, and his explanation—given patiently and in
detail—had done little to soothe the churning in her
stomach.

After months of fruitless searching, Cordovan's detective had finally managed to track Devon to Los
Angeles. More specifically, to a shelter for runaways.

But when he got there and started asking questions,
he discovered she'd left the shelter a few months earlier. No one there claimed any knowledge where she'd
gone, and at that point the trail had dried up.

But the detective had caught a break. He'd returned
to the shelter the following week and had come across
a volunteer who'd been out sick during his previous
visit.

The volunteer—a young social worker—not only remembered Devon when shown her picture, but recalled the girl spending time with another teen, a boy
by the name of Hank Wheeler. Hank had landed in
some minor trouble with the law, though, and had
been transferred to a halfway house several miles away,
sentenced to thirty days of community service.

Cordovan's man had probed deeper and learned that
both Devon and Hank had dropped from sight on the
same day—just two days short of his completing his
sentence. But fortunately, tracking the Wheeler boy

had not proved nearly as difficult as searching for Devon had been.

Hank had returned to his hometown of Wolf River, Montana, and was once again living with his older brother.

And that's where the detective had found Devon as well.

He'd done nothing more than locate and photograph her, per Erinn's instructions. There'd been no contact with Devon for fear that she might run again if she thought someone had located her.

And thankfully, someone had.

Erinn paced across the bedroom, her bare feet making only a whisper against the polished hardwood floor. Too bad she couldn't click her heels together three times and be in Wolf River right now, this very night. All she wanted was to wrap her arms around her sister and make things right.

But that would have to wait. At least until tomorrow.

Glancing at the packed suitcase sitting open on the floor near her vanity, she wished she had something else to throw into it, something besides clothes and shoes and underwear. Something she could bring to Devon, a gift, a memento, *something*.

But both of them had left their pasts behind and erased almost all remnants of their lives as Dane Stanton's daughters.

All she had left to give to Devon was herself.

And then she remembered.

She hurried to the bookcase, pulled down several slim volumes of her Princess Devonshire books, and tucked them beneath her bras and tank tops. Then she sank down on her bed, took two Tylenol PMs, and crawled beneath the covers.

Her flight to Billings left at 9 a.m. She needed sleep.

The vision came at dawn.

It tiptoed into her slumber like a spider and then jolted her awake like a stinger to the throat. It had been a long time since the last one, and she'd wanted to believe they were gone for good, but as the familiar sensations assaulted her, she jerked upright, heart racing, her dark hair tumbling over her eyes.

Waiting . . .

She felt sick to her stomach, just as she had that night, the night her mother died. Sick and scared and defenseless . . . and like something was wrong, terribly wrong. She shuddered in her bed, wrapping her arms around herself, trying to breathe, trying to stay warm. But her skin was ice cold and her chest burned and the air clogged in her lungs.

Then her apartment vanished and she was alone, hurtling down a long dark tunnel. All alone and cold. *So cold*.

The air was frigid and white as snow.

She tried to shut her eyes, to block out whatever was coming, but she couldn't. She *saw* it.

A body trussed, bound in the dark.

Who was it? And was he . . . she . . . dead? Or still alive? A man? Or a woman?

Please, God, not another child, Erinn prayed, as the vision filled her eyes, mirrored in her pupils, full of blood and darkness and fear.

Who are you? she shrieked. *Who did this?*

And then she heard it. The scream.

Her own voice. Screaming. Screaming again and again and again . . .

Light rushed in, vivid and blinding. She opened her mouth, gasping for air . . . for breath.

It was over. Gone. The vision and the dark vanished as quickly as they'd come, as they always did. Melting into nothingness.

She was alone once more in her bed with its pale sheets and peach-and-champagne-flowered comforter. Her skin was clammy, her chest heaving.

She staggered to the bathroom, filled a cup with water, sipped. Breathed. Stared at her reflection in the mirror, at her eyes wide and brilliant, her cheeks so ashen they looked like cardboard.

This wasn't the first vision and wouldn't be the last—but it had been so long since she'd had one. Nearly two years.

She'd thought they were gone.

Why is it happening again now? she wondered as she gripped the sink and stared into her own glazed eyes, ripples of fatigue rushing through her.

Why now?

Chapter Two

**Fortune's Way Ranch
Wolf River, Montana**

"Sorry, Jase. Damn, I hate being the bearer of bad news."

Ranch foreman Rawley Cooper spat a wad of tobacco into the dirt outside the barn and jerked his grimy thumb in the direction of the Fortune ranch house. He looked into his boss's eyes with deep regret. "I know how hard this is goin' to hit your pop. You plannin' to tell him?"

"It's not like I have much of a choice." Jase Fortune's cobalt blue eyes narrowed beneath the brim of his hat.

Five more bullet-ridden cows shot dead out on the range.

That was in addition to the pair found a month ago near Hawk Point, and the single calf that had been peppered with buckshot a week before that.

Someone was picking off Fortune cattle.

And whoever it is has to be stopped. And fast.

"Once I call the sheriff," Jase said, "word'll get out anyway. Clay might as well hear it from me."

The bandy-kneed ranch foreman nodded, his face somber. Beside Rawley, Don Culpepper listened with a glum expression. Sweat clung to the tall ranch hand's plaid shirt after the exertion of his and Rawley's furious ride back to the ranch.

But Jase wasn't really seeing either of the two men, or the lathered horses beside them. He was seeing another image in his mind—an image of his father going ballistic when he heard the news.

Jase could already see the rage rushing into his father's face. That kind of fury wasn't good for a man with high blood pressure and a bad heart. But Jase wasn't about to lie to him.

"Clay's going to Houston for the cattlemen's convention day after tomorrow. I want this dealt with by the time he gets back. Set up round-the-clock flyovers and extra patrols, Rawley. Starting tonight."

The foreman nodded, and Jase turned to Culpepper, skinny as a fence post, waiting for orders. "Check on the cattle in the south pasture, Culp. Take Stitch with you, and keep your eyes peeled. I want all our men on full alert until this bastard's caught."

"You got it, Jase."

Rawley scratched the stubble on his jaw. "You going to call the sheriff or you want me to do it, boss?"

"I'm headed into town—I'll talk to Farley in person. When he gets out here, show him where you found the steers."

"Will do." Looking grim, Rawley brushed two fingers respectfully against the brim of his gray hat. As he and Culpepper took off for the barn, leading their mounts, Jase turned toward the house.

He paused a moment near the corral fence, frowning, and let his gaze sweep over the vista of wild, splendid country that had been home to his family for generations.

What he saw had always filled him with pleasure and a sense of being exactly where he belonged. Lush grassland and meadows pretty as a painting. Foothills aglow with wildflowers. Distant waterfalls that glimmered like cascading diamonds. And mountains—mountains rearing up over valleys and gullies like mythic giants, bigger than life itself.

This was rugged land, open and bighearted—no place for the weak. Every way he turned there was sky, wide and fierce and endless, a massive canopy that dwarfed even the mountains.

From the spot where he stood, Jase could see summer sunlight speckling the cottonwoods that flowed alongside the creek bed. A dense fringe of fir and pine trees climbed the steep slopes and crested the ridges of mountains that seemed to poke the sky. The clean, tangy scents of pine and sage infused the crystalline air, calming and invigorating all at the same time.

This land was infinitely varied, as wild and tough as it was magnificent. It was as rich with menace as it was with beauty, though. Coyotes, bears, and wolves roamed at will.

But wildlife was an expected danger, as much a part of Montana country as the humans who'd made it their home.

Only now there was something...someone...out there who *didn't* belong. Someone playing a sick prank—or who meant Fortune's Way harm.

His jaw clenched, Jase bounded up the steps and let himself into the ranch house his grandfather James

Fortune had built more than fifty years ago for his own new bride.

His grandfather's original structure had been a simple one—a modest single-story dwelling constructed of solid timbers and designed with a sloping roof. But over the years, the Fortune family's cattle and lumber holdings had prospered beyond all of James's initial expectations. And the house had grown along with the ranch's good fortune.

Six months before Jase was born to James's son Clay and his wife, Penny, Clay Fortune had quadrupled the size of his parents' house, adding on a sweeping second story and two wide, graceful wings. With its covered porches, panoramic windows, and rustic high-beamed ceilings, the Fortune ranch house had quickly become the largest, most admired home in the county. Its nearest competitor was the Hanging J ranch owned by Holt Samson—but that property, a mere six thousand square feet on eighty thousand acres of land, didn't hold a candle to Fortune's Way.

Fortune's Way was the only home Jase, his younger brother, Colton, and his sister, Lily, had ever known. None of them were ashamed to admit that they loved it as much as they loved each other, that this house, this land—more than one hundred thousand acres of premium Montana grazing land and pasture—was in their blood. They all knew, had always known, that no matter how far they roamed, Fortune's Way would be there, proud and rooted and beautiful as a sunrise, when they decided to go home.

Jase had returned to Montana from Los Angeles

three years ago—after his marriage failed, after his father's first heart attack. He'd had no choice but to take on the day-to-day running of the ranch, to pry the reins from his father's grip for Clay's own good, and to keep the cattle and lumber operations running as strongly as they had for generations.

At first, the ranch work and his father's health had entirely consumed his time, his mind, and every drop of energy in his six-foot-two inch frame. Only later had he come to realize that the all-consuming workload had been a very good thing indeed.

He'd had no time to bleed over his failed marriage, over Carly and her lies. He'd been too busy taking over the mammoth business end of running the ranch and the lumber company, and of fighting his father every step of the way to get him to loosen control—even from the old man's hospital bed. Jase hadn't had time to give in to the rage and pain roiling inside him after Carly had cheated on him, raided their joint bank account, tried to steal his mother's pearls, and taken everything else that wasn't nailed down.

Including whatever he'd once had for a heart.

Entering the high-beamed entryway of the house, tossing his hat on the cherrywood table that gleamed as richly as the hardwood floor and brass chandelier, Jase's eyes turned cold as he thought of his ex-wife, with her seductive curves, highlighted blonde hair, and sweet smile as phony as a six-dollar bill.

Initially he'd been devastated by the end of his marriage. Now he figured that Carly had done him a favor. She'd opened his eyes, set him free. She'd made him into a man who was a hell of a lot tougher and smarter than the raw twenty-three-year-old who'd mooned over her and married her while they were both still kids, fresh out of college.

Carly and her lies had made him immune to any future pain. They'd ensured he'd never make the same stupid mistake twice—he wasn't about to give his heart away to a woman ever again.

He found his father in the walnut-paneled office at the back of the house, seated at James Fortune's big desk. Clay was scowling, writing rapidly in longhand on a lined yellow legal pad, his wide shoulders encased in a dark blue shirt, his gray-sprinkled brown hair catching the light that poured in through the wide window.

"Still writing that speech?" Jase entered without preliminaries. "It'd be a lot easier if you used a computer."

"That's what you think." Clay stared at him through shrewd blue eyes that could probe inside a man's mind like an X-ray. He was six foot two, the same height as both of his sons, and with the same powerful build, though now, at age sixty, the wide shoulders were slightly stooped and Clay's neck was thicker and creased with wrinkles. But like his sons, he still exuded power through every pore.

Everyone said he was the richest and the smartest and the toughest man in the state, and Clay prided himself on that being true. He also prided himself on his children. The boys were both different as could be, but they were every bit as hardheaded and clear-thinking as he was, each in his own way. Maybe that's why he admired them so much. And fought with them so much.

Clay wouldn't have it any other way.

Of course, his daughter, Lily, was hardheaded too, but she was more of a soft touch, having inherited the tender heart of her mother.

"I don't have time to learn all that word-processing crap. Ella can type it all up and print it when I'm done. I need to see the words on the page when I write, the old-fashioned way. But I hate writing. Don't have the patience for it. Oh hell . . ."

He suddenly tossed down his pen, tore off several pages from the pad, and ripped them in two. "I'll wing it."

He balled up the papers with a sly grin and tossed them into the wastebasket, then leaned back in his chair. "Tell me what you're worried about, Jase." Again, those keen eyes raked his son. "I know something's weighing on you. I can see it."

Jase met his gaze steadily. "If I didn't know better, I'd think you were looking for an excuse to skip the convention. Stage fright?"

"That'll be the day." Clay snorted. "Stop trying to change the subject. I saw you from the window, talking to Rawley and Culp. All three of you looked mighty worried."

When Jase said nothing, Clay scrutinized his son's face, but it was damned unreadable. *A skill he inherited from me,* Clay thought proudly.

"I can smell when trouble's coming." He spoke quietly now, bracing himself for the bad news he sensed was imminent. "And I know you better than you think I do. That poker face might work for everyone else in town, but not for me. Out with it, boy."

Jase had to give him credit. Clay still had it. The uncanny ability to read other men's minds. Well, then, so be it. Lying wasn't Jase's style, even to protect his father's blood pressure.

"Don't get all riled up," he warned, coming right up to the desk. "Rawley and Culp just found five more steers shot dead up near Hangman's Bluff."

Clay's neck muscles tightened. "Like the others— plugged with buckshot?"

Jase nodded.

"That's it, then." Clay slammed a fist down on the desk. "I want that murdering bastard caught yesterday—whoever the hell he is! You talk to Sheriff Farley yet?"

"I'm headed to town now. And I've already ordered extra patrols. Don't worry, we'll catch whoever's behind this."

"I don't suppose you've got any ideas who that might be."

"Nothing concrete. But I think we should increase our flyovers, see if we can catch anyone on Fortune land who doesn't belong, or spot anything suspicious."

"Do it then." Clay stood up and paced around the desk, scowling. "This is a hell of a time for me to leave. We need to end this, Jase—before we lose any more cattle. I'm rethinking attending this damned convention on Friday. I've already got my hands full, negotiating the contracts for the new lumberyard. I'm due to meet with Linc on the final legal changes next week. If I wasn't the keynote speaker, and Jeb Harper hadn't asked me personally to do it, I'd drop out of the damned convention and stay home to work."

"Give me the contracts and all the files on the lumberyard. I'll take care of it." Despite Clay's complaints, Jase knew he secretly loved attending the cattlemen's convention—probably because everyone there treated him like he was top bull of a vast and powerful herd.

"I'll call Linc in the morning and arrange to take the meeting in your place," Jase continued before his father could object. "Have you had your pills today?"

"What the hell does that have to do with anything?" Clay's bushy gray brows hurtled upward. "I don't need my own son looking after me like I'm some kind of baby."

"The way I see it, someone has to do it." Jase glowered right back, though his tone was even. "You know what Doc Stevens said. Now you either listen to him, start taking your pills every single day, or I'm going to call in Colton and Lily and the three of us will give you hell and set you straight."

"Like an intervention?" Clay laughed, a rusty boom that filled the office.

Jase nodded, his gaze holding his father's. "Whatever it takes."

Clay's face tightened. "Give it a rest," he said shortly. "I'll take the damned pills. But you need to stop worrying about me and find out who's killing our cattle. I mean it, Jase. No one harms anyone or anything on Fortune's Way and gets away with it."

"On that we agree."

Jase's gut clenched as he saw the concern in his father's eyes. Beneath the tough talk and the bluster, he understood what Clay was feeling. When Fortune's

Way was hurting, his father hurt. The ranch, the land were in his blood. They meant everything.

"I'll handle it, Pop." He spoke quietly. "You handle your health—and all those cattlemen. Need anything in town? I'm headed out now."

His father shook his head and stomped out of the room, his boots thumping up the stairs. Jase hoped he was going to his bedroom to take his pills.

Stubborn old coot.

It was a twenty-minute drive into Wolf River and Jase made it in just over sixteen. After parking his Explorer in front of the municipal building that housed the sheriff's department, Jase spent the next half hour filling in Guy Farley about the cattle on Hangman's Bluff.

Guy was old school—in his fifties, with a stout, beefy physique, graying hair shorn in a blunt crewcut, his lawman's eyes cool and observant.

He wrote everything down, and promised to go out that very day to the site of the shooting and start the forensics work, trying to find the slugs and determine what kind of gun had been used in the crime. If they matched the type that had been used before, the sheriff could then link this shooting to the previous attacks.

"How's Clay taking this, Jase? Bet he's fit to be tied."

"You got that right. You know how he is. He wants this bastard caught yesterday. So do I."

"I hear you, Jase. I'm on my way. How about I give you a call after I take a look?"

Jase headed down the street to the Saddleback Grill. The owner, Ginny Duncan, glanced up when she saw him and her crooked grin widened across her entire tanned and freckled face.

Then he saw LeeAnn—sitting at a table drinking coffee with Frank Wells, his former ranch hand. Culp's sister caught his eye over the rim of the cup, then quickly sipped and looked away. Not even a wave hello.

Damn, Jase thought. *She deserves a hell of a lot better than Wells. What's she thinking?*

No way he'd ever figure *that* one out. He didn't have a clue how women's minds worked. He hadn't understood Carly, and he didn't understand LeeAnn.

But he understood one thing—Wells was trouble.

Ginny set down two plates of burgers and fries before a couple of hands from the Sugar T ranch and came straight toward him.

"Don't you look all serious—for a change," she greeted him, and slanted him an appraising glance.

Ginny Duncan had been cook and housekeeper at Fortune's Way for a good many years while he and Colton and Lily were growing up. She'd been hired after their mother died—when Lily was four—and she'd become almost a second mother to all three of them— every bit as much a part of Fortune's Way as Rawley and Stitch and even Reese Murphy, his grandfather's foreman, who'd died a few years back. Ginny was as integral as the ranch house's wide sunny windows and hardwood floors, as the quarter horses Colton trained, and the yellow pines that fringed the garden out back.

She'd worked for the Fortunes until Lily turned twelve—that's when she told Clay she was quitting.

Ginny's lifelong dream had been to own her own restaurant, and old Charley McCabe, of the run-down Charley's Grill at the far end of First Street, was retiring and eager to move to Arizona to live near his daughter and grandchildren. She planned to buy the place—she had the money saved for the down payment. It would take her awhile to save up enough to redo the small restaurant the way she wanted, but she could wait for that.

Jase had felt like the breath had been knocked out of him when he heard she was leaving. Lily had begged her to stay, promising to be good forever and to eat all of her peas. Colton had hugged Ginny hard around the middle, as if holding on to her would keep her at Fortune's Way.

But none of them could blame Ginny for doing what she'd wanted her entire life—she was forty years old and felt it was now or never to make her dream come true. And after stomping around his office for a while, swearing up a storm, Clay hadn't been able to blame her either.

No one outside of the family knew—their father had expressly forbidden Ginny or anyone to tell—but on the day she left the ranch, Clay had given her a bonus of twenty-five thousand dollars toward renovating Charley's Grill. And every other Sunday she still came out to the house, fixed supper for whoever happened to be at home, and sat with them around the big table in the kitchen, still part of the family.

"Of course I'm feeling serious," Jase told her as she led him through the homey diner with its bright blue upholstered booths and white and blue striped walls decorated with dozens of saddles and outdoor Western prints in mahogany frames.

"I'm worried. My stomach's in knots, thinking you might be all out of lemon pie, when that's what I've got a taste for."

Ginny chuckled, her long, faded brown ponytail flipping back and forth as she shook her head. "In that case, Mr. Jase Fortune, you can just smile until your teeth hurt, because I've got a whole lemon pie left, and you can have as much as you want."

"One slice ought to do it. And coffee."

"Coming right up." She regarded him a moment as he slid his tall frame into the booth with the lithe agility of a born cowboy. "You missed all the excitement. Lynette Spencer went into labor right here not a half hour ago. You remember she's having twins? Well, Joe hustled her out of here faster than I can crack an egg. Her water broke just as he got her to the car." Ginny's eyes twinkled. "All of my regulars have a betting pool going—two boys, two girls, or one of each. Guess we'll have the answer soon."

"Stan Miller hit me up at the Redrock last week. I put in my ten bucks. Bet on one of each . . ."

His voice trailed off. Ginny saw him gazing at the door, and turned her head even as it opened.

A woman, a stranger, stepped into the restaurant. She looked around as if unsure if she should wait to be seated.

"Sit anywhere you want, honey," Ginny called out and the woman smiled, then slipped into a booth near the front.

"Whoa. Pretty thing, isn't she?" Ginny murmured.

Jase didn't answer. The woman who had walked into the Saddleback was gorgeous. Willowy and sleek, with thick dark hair the color of sable. It tumbled down her back in loose, sexy curls, framing strong cheekbones and soft features. Even the way she moved was pretty—smooth and graceful.

But that's not why he'd lost his train of thought when he'd seen her. It had more to do with the way she carried herself, the way she was dressed, the simple cropped white pants and yellow shirt, the low-heeled wedge sandals, even her purse, which didn't look like anything you'd find in Wolf River, or even in Billings or Helena.

Simple elegance. It was a look Carly had striven to perfect, to imitate, but never quite had. Perhaps that's why he'd stared at her—even though they looked nothing alike physically, she reminded him of Carly, or rather, of what Carly had wanted to become. Sophisticated. Refined. And citified.

"Want me to find out who she is? Introduce you?" Ginny whispered, gazing at him with both amusement and hope.

"Forget it." He tore his gaze from the beautiful stranger and leaned back in the booth, resisting the urge to pull his hat down over his eyes. For some damned reason he couldn't fathom, his sister and Ginny were set on finding him another wife.

It wasn't going to happen.

But he couldn't seem to get it through their heads that his first wife was the only one he planned to ever have.

Marriage and commitment just weren't in the cards for him. Not anymore. Even his uncomplicated, no-strings relationship with LeeAnn had gone south about a month ago. Somehow he'd hurt her. And he'd never meant to.

She was Culp's sister and the three of them had been friends for years. When he and LeeAnn had started hanging out together at the Redrock, Jase had thought they were clear, that they both wanted the same thing—friendship. Dancing and laughs at the Redrock, an occasional dinner of pizza and beer, a Saturday night movie in Crystalville now and then. Nothing more.

Until the day she told him different.

"All I'm hungry for today, Ginny, is some pie and coffee. How about it?"

"Yeah, yeah, in a minute." She placed one hand on her hip and spoke in a quiet tone that only he could hear. "I been holding this in for a while, Jase, and I just need to say it. You know darned well that you deserve more from life than the hand you're dealing yourself. There—I said it."

One eyebrow cocked. "Yep, you said it. Now can I have my pie?"

"No! I'm not done yet." She wagged a finger at him. "And I don't want you to take this the wrong way." Her voice dropped. "Don't think I'm saying anything against LeeAnn. Cuz I'm not. You know I've always liked her just fine—" She glanced quickly over at LeeAnn and Frank Wells, immersed in flirtatious conversation in the booth, then leaned in closer to Jase.

"But it was clear to anyone with eyes in their head that you were never in love with her and never would be." Ginny straightened, but kept her voice low. "There *is* someone out there for you, though, and it's time you thought about finding her. Don't you want something more from life than running Fortune's Way, riding herd on your family, meeting with lawyers nearly every day of the week? And I don't mean branding cows!" she added with a snort.

"Sure thing, Ginny. I do want more. I want some lemon pie."

She narrowed her eyes at him, her hands plopping at her waist. "You're only thirty. And just because you got your heart busted wide open once, that doesn't mean—"

"Excuse me, Ginny. *Pie*. Remember? P-I-E."

"Oh, all *right*." She blew out her breath in frustration. "I'll get your damned pie. And I won't say one more word about your being hardheaded and difficult, especially when it comes to—" she bent down and huffed in his ear "—marriage. At least not *today*."

Jase leaned back in the booth as she stomped off to the kitchen. He stretched his long legs out under the table and turned his attention to figuring out who in Wolf River would bear the kind of grudge against his family that they'd start picking off Fortune's Way cattle.

By the time Ginny whisked back with his coffee and set down a white plate with a huge slice of lemon pie in the center, he had it narrowed down to a couple of prime suspects.

Crime was rare and generally minor in the town. Wolf River was a friendly, decent place made up of ranchers, farmers, small business owners, and their families and kids. There weren't more than a couple of dozen storefronts and businesses, besides the several bars. These included a bank, a gas station, a few clothing stores, May's grocery, Scoop's ice cream parlor, and a hardware store.

There were also some antiques shops, a camping

outfitter, and Wanda's Bait and Tackle, all on Main Street, and servicing the occasional tourist who passed through on his way to camping or fishing in the national park grounds.

The highlight of Wolf River social life, aside from Saturday nights at the Redrock Bar and Grill, was the monthly barn dances held throughout the summer under the stars.

All in all, the town was pretty damned peaceful. And even though the Fortunes were the wealthiest and most prominent family in the county, no one seemed to resent them much for it.

Except two men. And one of them was right here in the Saddleback.

Jase glanced sideways at the table where LeeAnn was patting her napkin to her shiny pink lips.

Frank Wells slurped his coffee and stared at her cleavage.

Wells had worked as a ranch hand at Fortune's Way for seven months before Jase learned he was skipping out on the job and not following through on tasks assigned him. So he'd followed the ranch hand one day when Wells was supposed to be repairing a fence post. Instead, Wells had driven over to Crystalville and sauntered into the Tin Star Saloon, where he'd plunked himself down on a bar stool at one o'clock in the afternoon.

Jase went in after him and fired him on the spot. Wells had been cursing the Fortunes every which way to Sunday ever since, but no one paid any attention.

Could be he's looking for some different kind of attention, Jase thought as he finished the last forkful of pie.

He pulled out his cell phone and called Farley, reminding the sheriff quietly about his firing Wells. "Either you question him or I will," he said curtly as Wells leaned forward toward LeeAnn and said something Jase couldn't catch. But it made her giggle.

"Better let me handle it, Jase. Wells hates you, that's for sure. Best we keep this professional and not personal."

"Fine. And while you're at it, don't forget about Mick Wheeler. He picked a fight with Colton one night at the Redrock about five months back. Colton got in a few good shots before Pete and the waitresses broke it up. Wheeler's not used to anyone fighting back. So it didn't end there." He frowned at the memory. "Wheeler cornered Lily the next time he saw her in town. Warned her that Colton better stay out of his way or he'd be sorry."

"What'd Lily do?" Farley grunted.

"She slammed her purse into his gut, stomped on his foot, and warned him that if he didn't stay away from her brother she'd do a lot worse."

Guy Farley chuckled. "I gotta hand it to her. She's pure Fortune, isn't she?"

"In a lot of ways, the fiercest one of the lot," Jase replied dryly, thinking of his slender, exuberant sister who had the temper of a she-dragon.

"I'm on your property now, turning onto Cedar Road," the sheriff reported. "Thanks for the leads. I'll let you know what I come up with."

Jase paid for his coffee and pie and headed toward the door just as the teenage waitress bounced toward the dark-haired woman's table with a tray of food. As she started to set down the tray, she stumbled, losing her balance. The tray slid sideways onto the table, hitting the woman's coffee cup and sending it careening onto her lap.

The woman gasped as hot coffee splattered her pants, burning against her thighs.

"Oh, my gawd, sorry!" the waitress screeched. "Ginny! Bring a towel," she yelled. "Hurry!"

Jase moved instinctively. He was at the table in an instant, grabbed up the glass of ice water that had escaped being knocked over by the tray, and dumped its contents on the woman's lap to offset the burning coffee.

She gasped again, gazing down at the icy water soaking her pants. The cold instantly mitigated the scalding coffee, but she was sopping wet, and when she lifted her head to gaze at him he saw astonishment in her eyes, mixed with anger.

"You all right?" Jase asked.

"H-hardly . . ." the woman sputtered.

Ginny rushed over with a towel and pressed it into the woman's hands.

"Here, blot it up, honey." She bit her lip with concern. "I'm real sorry about that. Are you burned bad?"

"I don't think so . . . I think the cold water helped . . ."

Erinn gazed ruefully at the older woman for a moment, then at the impossibly handsome man who had poured ice water on her pants.

He was breathtaking—*if you liked the type*. Rugged and lean, he was well over six feet of hard muscle and sinew. Scorching blue eyes, dark blond hair, and the roughly dangerous allure of a fallen angel.

Not to mention the reflexes of a race car driver, she thought, remembering how quickly he'd seized the glass of ice water and tossed its contents over the scalding coffee. Directly onto her lap.

He was every sexy inch a cowboy, there was no doubt about that. From the wide shoulders filling out his pale gray shirt, to the well-worn jeans that slithered down long, powerful legs, ending at the leathered gloss of polished cowboy boots, he looked like he'd be perfectly at home riding hell-for-leather across a prairie, or shooting train robbers from behind a rock. Thick dark blond hair spilled out beneath his black Stetson as he gazed grimly down at her, and for a moment she couldn't catch her breath.

His eyes were an even darker blue than the brilliant Montana sky she'd marveled at during her drive down U.S. Highway 310, south of Billings Logan International Airport.

She ordered herself to stop staring into them.

"Sorry about the dunking, but it seemed like a good idea at the time." He glanced at the older woman, one eyebrow lifted. "Ginny, she could likely use some more ice."

"Right." Ginny jerked a thumb at the young waitress who wore too much eyeliner and low-rise jeans. "Mandy, quick, bring more towels and an ice pack." Then she cocked her head at Erinn.

"You want me to take you to the hospital, honey, get you checked out for burns?"

"That's all right. I doubt my pants will ever be the same but I think I'm fine."

The tall cowboy strode toward the door, and she bit her lip. "I guess I should thank you for your quick action," she muttered.

"No problem, ma'am." He spoke over his shoulder, dismissively, with only a flickering glance from those searing blue eyes, then the door slammed with a thud behind him.

Erinn suddenly became aware of several other diners glancing curiously over at her. A small woman with auburn hair and a pointed chin whispered something to the lean, black-haired man she was sitting with and he snorted with laughter. As the pair got up to leave, the young waitress reappeared and offered Erinn several flowered kitchen towels and an ice pack, then hurried off to bring menus to another table.

"I'm Ginny Duncan, I own this place." The older woman had returned with a mop. She swiped it expertly across the wet floor, even as Erinn dabbed at her ruined pants.

"Got a fresh burger for you coming right up—and it's on the house. Mandy's a good little waitress, but she hurries too much like most kids and gets clumsy," she added. "Last week she tripped and dumped a mess of ribs on poor Stitch Nolan's head. The boys at the Fortune Ranch will be joshing him for a month on that one."

"It's okay. Don't bother with the burger." Erinn slid from the booth, setting the towels and the ice pack on the table. "I think I'd better get back to my motel and

change. I have an important meeting this afternoon."
And there's no use putting it off any longer, she thought.

In some ways she couldn't wait to follow the directions Wayne Cordovan had given her out to the Wheeler brothers' cabin on Whistle Road. On the other hand, part of her dreaded actually seeing Devon—seeing what had become of her little sister with her own eyes, facing her for the first time.

Hi, Mouse, it's me, your big sister. The one who let you down big time. You remember me, I promised I'd come back for your birthday. Yeah, that *big sister.* She shook herself from her thoughts, realizing that Ginny Duncan was speaking to her.

"Well, then, you come back here anytime and your meal's on me," the woman told her. "Hold on, let me get you some of my chocolate-chip cookies for the road. You staying at the Watering Hole?"

"I hear that's the only motel within fifty miles." Erinn looked at her hopefully. "Unless my source was mistaken. Do you know of another one?"

"Nope. The next closest one is in Crystalville, fifty-two miles east." Ginny regarded her sympathetically and set the mop aside, returning a moment later with a bag filled with three large chocolate-chip cookies. "Maybe these will help. I know the Watering Hole is pretty much a dump. Old Lester Harp's owned the place for a million years and doesn't much care about anything since his wife passed on seven years ago. The thing is, we don't get many visitors in Wolf River— most folks just pass through on their way to the parks. So anyone who does want to stay ends up having to

take the Watering Hole—or leave it. Unless they want
to camp out."

"I guess I'm stuck then. Seems I've left my pup tent
at home."

That earned her a chuckle from the woman. "You going to be in town long?"

"I don't think so." Erinn slung her purse over her
shoulder. She had to get out of here, change her clothes,
then quit stalling and face Devon. But her stomach was
doing backflips.

Would there be tears, shouting, accusations? Or
would her sister fall thankfully into her arms?

She prayed for the latter, but a sense of foreboding
told her it might not be that easy.

"Thanks for the cookies—and the ice."

"Hey, come again—on the house!" Ginny called out
with a wave. Erinn glanced back as the screen door
thumped softly behind her, and saw the woman striding back to the counter, pausing to stack dirty plates
along one arm, and scooping up a basket of rolls in the
other.

Her stomach growled as she drove her rental car
away from the curb and headed north of town to the
Watering Hole motel off of Highway 310. She'd
stopped there only long enough to check in and dump
her suitcase and laptop in the dingy room before heading to town for sustenance.

And look how well that turned out. She reached into
the bag of chocolate-chip cookies on the seat beside
her, and munched as she drove, trying to quiet her restless stomach and to alleviate the nerves that felt like
they were poking right through her skin.

The countryside was gorgeous here—rolling hills dotted with black cattle, gullies strewn with rocks and wildflowers, mountains looming like giants in the distance. Overhead, the sapphire sky was almost brilliant enough to make her forget about her damp, stained pants and the fact that Devon was only thirty miles away—living in a shack with two men.

When she reached the Watering Hole she dashed into her tiny room with its worn beige comforter, thin pillows, and peeling pea-soup-green walls. Trying not to think about the horrid surroundings, she stripped off her pants and threw them into the chipped bathtub to soak in a swirl of shampoo and cold water, then tugged on a pair of jeans.

In under two minutes she was on the road again, Cordovan's directions on the seat beside her as she nibbled the last of Ginny Duncan's cookies.

Her former editor, Nancy, had subscribed to the theory of positive imaging—visualizing what you wanted to happen, sending out only positive vibes and helping to make that image come true.

It's worth a try, Erinn thought as she drove. Gamely she tried to convince herself that this reunion would be happy—and pictured herself driving out of Wolf River with Devon smiling beside her, heading toward the airport and civilization.

She saw herself and Devon in her mind's eye—boarding a flight to LaGuardia, stopping by her apartment to get Devon settled, then taking a taxi together to dinner at Georgio's tomorrow night.

They'd order minestrone soup and gnocchi, chicken Vesuvio, garlic bread. They'd get to know each other all over again. Devon would take to New York as quickly as she had herself and would have a fresh new start. They'd share everything—the apartment, meals, their lives, their pasts . . . it was all going to work out.

And George Clooney's going to invite me to be his date for next year's Academy Awards, she thought wryly.

The road began to climb as she turned onto Buckhorn Point, twenty miles west of town. Thick towering pines flanked the dirt road and clusters of delicate pink crocus peeked up here and there as it sloped upward. A red fox darted across and vanished into the dark shade of the trees. Her rented Jeep took the turns evenly, and at last the road forked left onto an even narrower dirt track—Whistle Road.

The Jeep jolted downward now, two miles farther, across a desolate stretch of scrub and rock.

And then she saw it—the cabin from Cordovan's photos.

It sat squat and ugly as a bug in a weed-strewn clearing backed by a belt of pine trees.

A dented old blue pickup was parked in front of the cabin, but there was no sign of life in the dusty yard, not even a rabbit or squirrel. No birds sang in the trees, nothing moved.

Only silence greeted Erinn as she parked the Jeep and climbed out, her feet thudding against hard-packed earth.

A sense of utter desolation filled the clearing, heightened by the loneliness of the rising hills beyond, by the encroachment of the tall weeds, by the cracked and faded shutters at the cabin windows.

The cabin looked even smaller and grittier in person

than it did in the photos—a stark contrast to the huge blue expanse of Montana sky.

As she walked toward the door, Erinn was fully aware that her own footfalls were the only sound that reached her ears. She lifted her hand, hesitated, then knocked. The sound seemed to boom across the clearing and her heart rushed into her throat as she waited for the door to open.

It didn't move. She knocked again. *There's a car here,* Erinn thought. *Someone must be inside . . .*

Suddenly the door swung inward with a creak that seemed to echo through the clearing. Erinn startled—and stared into the pinched, pale face of her sister.

Chapter Three

For a moment Erinn couldn't speak.

She could only stare into the dull blue eyes of the stranger before her, watching the shifting emotions of surprise and wariness flitting across the girl's face.

"Who are you?" she demanded. "What do you want?"

"Devon, it's me. Your . . . sister." Erinn forced a smile, but her lips felt as if they were cracking like plaster.

Devon stood rigid in her ripped Levi's and tight red tee with a tear in the shoulder seam. She wore no makeup, and her fair skin looked dry and sallow; her hair hung in limp, tangled strands around her face. There were two ear piercings in each of her ears, as well as one in her left eyebrow, and cheap black stone studs poked through each one.

But worse than anything else was the sense of hopelessness that clung to the girl like an unseen second skin.

"T-Tiffany?" The blue eyes stretched wide. For an instant, Erinn thought she saw a flicker of wonder, then something else clamped over it—rage. Pure red-hot rage. A moment later it merged with a flash of fear.

"What're you doing here? How'd you find me?"

"It wasn't easy. But if you'll invite me in, I'll tell you." Erinn spoke steadily. But as she glanced beyond Devon into the shack, her stomach took an unpleasant bounce.

The place was a pit. Filthy, dim, and dingy, it reeked of cigarette smoke and beer. She caught a swift glimpse of broken floorboards and dark cheap furniture that looked like it had been carted off from a secondhand shop. There were beer bottles everywhere, scattered across the floor, littering the wooden crate that served as a coffee table—and laundry overflowed from a grimy plastic basket in the corner. She caught a whiff of something sour wafting from the tiny kitchen in the back, and nausea filled her throat.

This was Devon's home? Guilt and horror surged through her.

"Invite you in? Nah, I don't think so." Devon's face twisted with fury. "Go away!"

She tried to slam the door, but Erinn gripped it firmly with both hands and slipped inside before her sister could stop her. "I've been looking for you for a long time, Devon," she said quickly. "And I'm not leaving without you. I know I let you down, but we have to talk. Just hear me out. I want to make it all up to you—"

"Kind of late, aren't you?" the girl sneered. Before Erinn could answer a rumbling male voice called out from behind the closed door near the laundry basket.

"Who's there?"

As both Erinn and Devon started, the door swung

open and the brawny man with the close-set eyes Erinn had seen in the photos glared at them.

"Who the hell are *you*?"

Mick Wheeler was big and coarse in person, with large ears and too much brawn for any one man. He had some nasty white scars zigzagging across his cheek, and mean slitted eyes the color of black beans. He came barreling toward her, smelling of onions and sweat, his hands clenched into beer-can-size fists.

"She's no one, Mick," Devon said quickly. "She was just leaving—"

"No, I was not." Erinn stared at the man bearing down on her and stood her ground. "My name is Erinn Winters. I'm Devon's sister."

Wheeler froze, his close-set eyes boring into her face.

"Yeah? She never told me she had a sister," he growled, flicking a dark glance at the girl.

"Well, I just did." Erinn tried to ignore the stench of the man. "Perhaps you're not aware that Devon is underage. She's only fifteen—and she's a runaway. I've traveled a long way to find her and now she's going to be coming with me. If you try to stop her," she added, "you could get yourself into a lot of trouble."

He looked dumbfounded. And furious. He swiveled toward Devon, his eyes narrowing. "Is she telling the truth? She's your sister?"

"*Half*-sister. But . . . I don't want to go with her. She's nobody to me now."

"Devon." Erinn kept her tone calm, even though her palms were sweating. "Please. Come outside and talk to me. I want to help you—give me just ten minutes—"

"No. My boyfriend's coming home soon—I have to go wash my hair. *Leave.*"

"I'm not leaving without you." Erinn's heart twisted at the misery in her sister's eyes and the anger flushing her pinched cheeks.

"Wanna bet?" Mick Wheeler took a step forward.

"Come with me, Devon. I'm staying at the Watering Hole motel. Let's go back there, just for a little while. We can talk—I can explain—"

"Get out of here! Why would I want to talk to you?" Sobs choked from Devon's throat. "You...you never came back, never called me, nothing. I h-hate you...as much as I hate *him*...our *father*!" she gasped, as tears streamed down her cheeks. "Just go back where you came from and *leave me alone!*"

"You heard her." Wheeler shoved Erinn's arm, his voice rough. *"Out."*

Erinn's heart pounded. She ignored the man glaring at her.

"I called you, Devon," she said quickly. "I did. Didn't Annabeth give you any of my messages? I wrote you several times, as well. And I did come back... once."

"Get out! I hate you!" Devon's voice rose to a shriek and Mick Wheeler swore, grabbed Erinn by the shoulders, and shoved her backward out the door.

"Don't come back here—she don't want nothing to do with you," he yelled, then he stepped back inside and kicked the door shut with his boot.

Erinn had a final fleeting glimpse of her sister's face, tears spilling down her cheeks, her eyes glittering with pain.

Then Erinn found herself staring only at a scarred wooden door.

As the sun slid across the softening Montana sky and a hawk circled high above, Erinn clutched her arms around herself and listened to the anguished sound of her sister's sobs.

Chapter Four

Erinn was too shaken to do more than sit in the Jeep with the engine running. Her heart squeezed tight in her chest, making it difficult to breathe without a clenching pain. She didn't want to leave here—not without Devon. Guilt wracked her as her sister's accusations roiled through her head, and the rage etched in Devon's face flashed over and over in her mind.

Oh God. What was I thinking all those years? How could I have been so self-absorbed . . . so busy going to school, making ends meet, writing my books . . .

Forgetting all about my sister.

Self-recrimination burned through her. She'd only tried to reach Devon a handful of times . . . not nearly enough . . .

Leaning forward, she rested her head against the steering wheel, trying to block out the memory of her sister's agonized sobs within that squalid, pitiful shack.

Finally, she wiped the tears from her cheeks and took a tight hold of the steering wheel. She managed to back the Jeep and turn it around, her stomach still churning. But after she drove up Whistle Road, then

turned once more onto Buckhorn Point, she glanced
about for Cordovan's directions.

Where were they?

She hit the brakes and searched the passenger seat,
then the floor, and finally, her purse. But there was no
sign of them. With a sinking heart she realized they
must have somehow fallen out back at the cabin.

*Damn it. I'm not going back there—not yet—not until
I've had a chance to come up with plan B.*

Cursing her carelessness, Erinn concentrated on trying to remember how she'd reached this desolate dirt
road, and how to retrace her trail back to town.

All she had to do was drive farther along Buckhorn
Point, she told herself. She'd recognize the place where
she'd turned onto it, wouldn't she? Something along
the route would have to look familiar.

She drove forward again, trying to mentally summon
Cordovan's instructions, but as the pines rolled lazily
by, their sameness began to induce a lulling effect on
her. Her thoughts drifted, roaming back to her past, to
her own frantic break for freedom on the day she
turned eighteen and escaped her father's house.

From that day on, Tiffany Erinn Stanton, eldest daughter of banking mogul Dane Stanton, had ceased to exist.
She'd legally changed her name to Erinn Winters,
boarded a Greyhound bus for New York City, and struggled to survive like a puppy running lost in a zoo.

Now that she looked back on it, she realized that
God only knew how she *had* survived. The first six
months had been pure hell. She'd pawned the pearl
and amethyst ring her father had given her for her six-
teenth birthday, and the diamond Tiffany necklace he'd

gifted her with on her seventeenth, and used the money for a security deposit and several months' rent in a rat-infested walk-up in Queens.

It had taken weeks before she found a job as a waitress in a Brooklyn diner and began working six days a week. Then she'd begun working weekend nights as well—running her legs off at an always-packed froufrou French restaurant on the Upper East Side.

At first just making ends meet had taken up most of her time and energy, but even so, she'd managed to send Devon a birthday gift and a card that first year, mailing them from a New Jersey post office. She'd called several times, but Devon was never in, and now she knew that either Annabeth had never given her sister any of the messages, or else Devon—so young at the time—hadn't remembered them for long.

By the time Erinn had worked her way up to hostess at the French restaurant and started taking classes at NYU, she'd been so busy and so intent on getting her degree in English lit that she'd almost forgotten the hell of living with her father's controlling rules and criticism. Each day away from Dane Stanton's house had brought her closer to her goal of attaining a college degree and a life all her own.

But there'd been one thing she hadn't been able to forget. Or escape. One thing that had kept its grip on her, even after she fled to New York.

The visions. The sight. The *gift*, if one could call it that.

It had come to her the first time the night her mother died, the night Evangeline Stanton killed herself in the master bedroom of the house on Everett Lane as her eleven-year-old daughter watched in horror.

Erinn's hands tightened on the steering wheel as the memories whirled across her mind, still vivid despite the passing of the years.

She'd been the only witness to her mother's suicide, awakened by an icy sense of dread she didn't understand, padding barefoot in her pink nightgown to her parents' bedroom, standing frozen as she witnessed the unthinkable.

She bit her lip in the Jeep, trying to shove away the image of her mother pressing her father's antique gun to her head—her mother with eyes closed, mouth shut tight, beautiful and delicate in an ivory peignoir as she stood alone beside the brass king-size bed, pulling the trigger of Dane Stanton's gun . . .

No. Erinn willed her mind to bar the vision of splattering blood and flesh. She'd slumped to the floor, unconscious, right after her mother's fall. A child's escape route, blocking the horror from her mind.

But she'd never forgotten, and the image of her mother pulling the trigger had remained forever engraved upon her brain. Yet something more had happened to her that night—something she hadn't realized until several years later.

A door had opened in her soul, a psychic door as nebulous as a shadow, but a door nevertheless.

She never knew when it would summon her, when she'd be whisked in dread across that murky threshold. Just as she never knew what she'd see at the end of that long terrifying tunnel of vision.

A white-tailed deer bounded across the road directly

in her path and Erinn gasped, slamming on the brakes. As the animal vanished unscathed into the safety of the pines, she sucked in a long shaky breath.

Concentrate on getting back to the motel, she told herself. *Forget the past . . . again. Just because you've found Devon doesn't mean you have to keep going back and reliving everything.*

You moved on before. You can do it again—this time you just have to find a way to do it with Devon.

Unfortunately, at the moment, she wasn't exactly in a position to move on anywhere. Staring around as she sat at a standstill in the midst of the winding, two-lane dirt road, she could see only trees, scrub brush, and the sky, now tinged with the luminous rose-gold of impending sunset.

There wasn't a single landmark that looked familiar. She hadn't a clue if she'd somehow missed the turn, if she was still on the right road, or even if she was still driving in the right direction.

Good move, Einstein, eating all the cookies, she thought uneasily, glancing at the empty bag Ginny Duncan had given her. *That sun's going down pretty soon and you could end up lost out here in nowheresville all night. With no food. No water. Not to mention, no directions.*

And eventually, she thought uneasily, glancing at the half-empty gas tank, *no gas.*

Shoving her hair out of her eyes she tried to gauge how far she'd come from the cabin—and wondered uneasily if she could possibly find her way back. Maybe she should try to call the Saddleback Grill on her cell phone . . . ask Ginny Duncan for directions. Or maybe the Watering Hole . . .

She was just digging her cell from her bag when a shiny red Explorer barreled around a curve up ahead and zoomed toward her in the opposite lane.

Erinn blared the horn, and frantically waved her hand out the window. To her relief, the Explorer slowed and then stopped on a dime alongside her.

A strikingly pretty young woman with high cheekbones and long honey-blonde hair swept up in a ponytail leaned out the open window of the SUV.

"Car trouble?"

"Direction trouble. I'm lost." Despite the tension knotting every muscle in her neck, Erinn managed a smile. "Can you tell me how to get back to the Watering Hole motel?"

"No problem. It's about fifteen miles due east. Keep on this road and when you come to the—" She broke off, staring.

"You look familiar," she murmured, eyeing Erinn with interest. "But I can't . . . oh!" The girl's face suddenly lit up. "You're Erinn Winters—the author!"

Erinn gaped at her. "And here I thought I didn't look anything like my publicity photo," she murmured. She'd worn a sleek cream-colored turtleneck and wide black pants with killer stilettos in the photograph taken on a bench in Central Park. Today, though, tired, distraught, and lost, she didn't feel anything like the confident-looking author in the photo. She felt like a complete and utter failure: as a sister, a decent human being, and a traveler without the vaguest notion where she was going.

"I read your latest Princess Devonshire adventure to my kids last week," the girl told her. "Well, not *my* kids," she amended with a grin as Erinn looked startled.

The girl didn't appear to be much older than eighteen or nineteen—how many kids could she have?

"I mean the kids at the day-care center." She laughed. "I'm working as a teacher's aide over the summer. In the fall, I'll be in my third year at Montana State, working toward my teaching degree—elementary ed."

Her hazel eyes sparkled as she gazed at Erinn as if she were Julia Roberts or Serena Williams. "I love all your books. Is Smogul the Goose ever going to make friends with Devonshire? All the kids yell *boo* when he calls her a rat, even after she saves his neck. I'm sorry, I'm talking too much, aren't I? My brothers tell me that's a habit I have when I get excited about something."

The girl leaned out the window, extending her hand. "I'm Lily Fortune—it's a pleasure to meet you, Ms. Winters."

"Erinn, please."

"What in the world are you doing in Wolf River? Your bio on the back cover said you live in New York—" Lily caught herself in midsentence. "Sorry. That's really none of my business, is it?" she asked wryly. Then sailed on without waiting for a reply. "It's only that . . . well, I was just wondering . . . if you're going to be in town for a few days, maybe you'd be willing to come in and read one of your stories to the kids at the day care? They'd be thrilled to meet a real author."

Erinn nodded. "Why, yes, of course. I'd like that."

She hadn't expected an opportunity to promote reading here in Wolf River, but that was one cause she could never turn down. "As it happens, I'm going to be here for a few more days."

At the very least. Who knew how long it would take her to get through to Devon?

"If you give me your number, I'll call you and we can work out a time for the reading," she told the girl, opening her bag and fishing for a pen and paper.

"Great. But... did you say you're staying at the *Watering Hole*?" Lily looked incredulous. "Why would you want to stay at a dump like that?"

"From what I hear, it's the only game in town. I didn't want to travel all the way to Crystalville."

Lily's lips suddenly curved upward in a broad smile.

"I have a much better idea. Why don't you stay at my family's ranch? We have plenty of room and I promise you that Fortune's Way is much nicer than that ratty old dump off the highway. Not to mention a good deal cleaner," she added with a shudder.

Erinn shook her head. "I couldn't impose—but thank you—"

"At least be our guest for dinner tonight," Lily interrupted. "I'd love to show you what real Western hospitality is like. Believe me, it's nothing like the grungy rooms and leaky faucets at the Watering Hole."

"It's very kind of you, but—"

"A home-cooked meal," Lily pressed, smiling. "You won't be sorry, I promise. I learned how to fry chicken from the best. Please say you'll come."

Erinn hesitated. A home-cooked meal with this

charming young woman and her family *did* sound much more appealing than a solitary meal in a strange town.

Besides, perhaps she'd be able to steer the course of the dinner conversation to the Wheeler brothers and learn something more about them. It wouldn't hurt to discover exactly who—and what—she was up against.

"Thank you." Erinn smiled. "I'd love to join your family for dinner."

"In that case, just turn your car around and follow me," Lily directed with a grin. "We're only a few miles from Fortune's Way."

This definitely beats being lost, Erinn thought moments later as she trailed the SUV down one lane after another until Lily turned onto a wider paved road that cut a swath across open grazing land. As the sun sank lower in the sky, they reached a vast fenced pasture where wildflowers rose amid lush grass. Then they stopped at a whitewashed gate, which Lily hopped out to open. She closed it after Erinn's Jeep passed through.

"Right up here," the girl called with an airy wave of her arm before she vaulted back into the Explorer.

Erinn followed her to yet another road, this one flanked by spruce and aspen. As the sun glowed a deeper lavender-rose in the painted sky, they passed beneath an archway adorned with a white-painted sign. It read *Fortune's Way* in thick black lettering.

A quarter of a mile farther, the sprawling ranch house came into view.

Erinn had expected an ordinary neat frame building—but she saw instantly that she was wrong. There was nothing ordinary about Lily's home.

The house was big, sprawling, and beautiful, as grand as the land that surrounded it. It had to be at least ten thousand square feet, she estimated, all of it polished stone and rough-hewn timber. It looked both proud and powerful amid foothills that rolled west, riotous with flowers.

Nearby, barns and stables and sheds flanked the magnificent house, and the two large corrals and long sloping fenced pasture were alive with horses romping or grazing in a paradise of high grass.

Parking in the circular drive, she slipped out of her rented Jeep and gazed with instinctive pleasure at the graceful porch and spotless wicker chairs, and at the tall oak double doors as Lily ran lightly up the porch steps.

Her own home, for all its beauty, had never felt welcoming to her. This house was not only spacious, but possessed an inviting aura.

"Come on in." Lily held the door wide. "I'll fix us some iced tea. I can't wait for you to meet my father and my—oh . . . Colton—speak of the devil."

The girl paused as a handsome, lanky young cowboy in a wide-brimmed hat, fresh pressed jeans, and fancy boots appeared at the end of a long hallway that stretched the length of the house.

As Erinn stepped inside the high-ceilinged hall the cowboy sauntered toward them, his boots thumping along the gleaming hardwood floor.

His stride was easy and unhurried. He had a rangy frame and glinting eyes beneath his hat.

"Colton, guess what? This is Erinn Winters. She's

written some of the best children's books ever—we have a copy of every single one of them at the day-care center and she's agreed to come read to the kids. How cool is that?"

Lily flashed her quick, vibrant smile and drew Erinn forward before the young cowboy could speak.

"This is my brother Colton. He's the easygoing one. Jase is the oldest and he's more . . . well, you'll see when you meet him."

"Pleased to meet you." Colton spoke hurriedly. His lightning smile quickly faded, replaced by a frown of concern as he focused on his sister.

"You haven't seen Pop, have you?"

"No, I just got home. Why?" Lily searched her brother's face. "Is he all right?"

"Hope so. Jase gave him some bad news today and now I can't find him—"

"What bad news?" Lily demanded.

"Five more steers killed out on the range. Jase went to town to talk to Sheriff Farley. In the meantime, Pop's disappeared. He's not here, not in the barn—he isn't answering his cell phone—"

"Have you checked the entire house?" Lily asked, a frown creasing between her slim brows.

"I've checked everywhere. His truck's gone. I've sent some of the hands out to look for him, but— *Pop!*" Colton was staring past Lily and Erinn as heavy footsteps thudded up the porch stairs.

Erinn turned in time to see a big man with ruddy cheeks and frown lines at his mouth charge through the doorway.

"Where did you disappear to?" Colton demanded, his gaze trained on his father's flushed face.

"Since when do I answer to you? To any of you?" The older man brushed off his son's question with a glare. His daughter went to him and gave him a hug, lifting a hand to the older man's weathered cheek.

"We were worried, Pop. I just heard about the steers—"

"Lily, we've got company," the old man said sternly, pulling away. "This is hardly the time to be talking about business. Or fussing over me. You're not my mother hen," he admonished her, eyes narrowed, and the girl squared her shoulders.

"I'm your daughter," she fired back. "I care about you and so do Colton and Jase, not that you deserve it most of the time," she added with a rueful laugh. "And if you don't like it, that's too damned bad!"

Erinn's stomach clenched. Lily's imposing father with his burly build, shock of gray and brown hair, and ruggedly good-looking features looked nothing at all like her own smoothly sophisticated father had, with his slim athleticism, immaculately groomed black hair, and impeccable European business suits. But the brusque, angry tone of his voice struck a familiar chord in her—and it wasn't a pleasant one.

She braced herself for him to turn on Lily with a withering retort, to rip her to shreds for her rudeness, or to simply, icily, turn his back.

Instead, to her surprise, he merely grunted. "Is Jase back yet?"

"No," Colton said. "But where'd *you* go off to?"

"Took a ride out on my own land, if that meets with your approval."

Suddenly, Erinn felt a sharp chill sweep through her and the room spun like a tilt-a-whirl. *Oh, no. Not now. Please . . . not now . . .*

"I wanted to see those steers for myself," Lily's father was saying, but his voice sounded far away. Erinn felt the chill wrap itself around her chest and spread outward, engulfing her. She was shivering . . . slipping away . . . toward the darkness and the cold . . .

No . . . no . . . get out . . . go . . .

"Met the sheriff out there—now where do you think you're going, young lady?" The old man rounded on Erinn as she backed toward the door.

"See what you did?" He glared at his son and daughter. "You're scaring a guest right out of our home. Did I raise you to behave like that?"

"No, it's my fault," Erinn said breathlessly. The darkness was descending, swirling across her vision . . . the cold pierced her bones like a snowman's breath. *Hurry . . . get out . . .*

"Don't blame Lily. I've come at an inconvenient time," she managed, and bolted out without giving anyone a chance to argue.

Why now? she wondered desperately, dread knotting inside her. The visions come at night . . . almost always at night.

She raced down the porch steps—and collided with someone. The force of the impact nearly knocked her backward, but strong arms shot out, steadying her shoulders and keeping her from tumbling to the ground.

"Whoa," he said, then broke off in surprise. "I . . . it's *you!*"

Oh, God, it was him. That magnificent cowboy of few words and quick action who'd dumped ice water on her in the diner had his strong hands planted on her shoulders and was gazing down at her in amusement from beneath the brim of his Stetson.

"You . . . you're the other brother," she murmured in shock, struggling against the cold, the darkness swirling before her eyes.

But both whirled closer, gaining hold. For an instant, she was caught up in the intensity of his blue eyes—darker than either Lily's or Colton's—or their father's.

Then, as the second wave of dizziness broke over her, she jerked free of his grasp. "I . . . have to . . ."

She was running, running toward her car, fighting to hold the vision at bay, fighting to get away before . . .

The darkness claimed her, scooping her into its midst, sending the world askew, knocking her legs out from beneath her.

She clutched at her Jeep, her nails scraping at the paint as she slid down, down, down . . . and the tunnel claimed her.

"Stop bawling." Mick Wheeler glared at Devon as she huddled on the lumpy couch and covered her wet face with her hands.

"How come you never told me you had a sister?" he shouted. "Answer me, damn you."

He stalked toward her and Devon glanced up fearfully, the sobs choking in her throat as she recoiled on the sofa. "She's only my h-half sister. And it doesn't matter, Mick, cuz she's not any kind of s-sister anymore." A sobbing shudder wracked her shoulders.

"I haven't seen her in y-years," she gasped. "She won't be b-back."

"She'd better not be back. You hear me, girl?" Wheeler scowled at her, his nerves frayed thin by the sound of female crying, by the kid's blotched, red little face. Man, he hated having this mewling brat living here. If it wasn't for Hank, he'd never have let her in the door.

"If she comes back here, you don't let her set foot inside, got it? She sees anything, so much as a sheet of computer paper, she's never getting out of here again."

Fear knifed through Devon as Mick towered over her. He seemed to fill the tiny run-down cabin the same way her father had filled the grand mansion that had once been her home.

But no place she'd ever been had felt like home. Nowhere had ever felt safe. Except maybe, at first, the shelter, after she met Hank.

"She won't be back, Mick," she repeated desperately as fresh tears spilled from her eyes. "Forget about her."

He glared at her, his eyes so black and soulless that the tears only fell faster.

"You forget about her too," he snarled. "Don't talk to her. Don't tell her a damned thing about you, Hank, me, Wells, this place. *Nothin'*, you got that?"

"Yeah, I g-got it. I wouldn't . . . I'm not ever talking to her again. Don't worry."

Mick grabbed her hair and yanked her head back,

just to make sure. He ignored her gasp of pain. "You're the one who should be worried. Don't forget that."

He let go of her hair with a grunt and watched with satisfaction as she again covered her face with her hands and fell back against the sofa, crying.

Didn't take much to keep this brat in line. Especially since she knew he meant every word he said.

Chapter Five

Her bones were like icicles, her skin slick and clammy. The tunnel was darker and narrower than ever before as she hurtled through it, barreling so fast her breath was trapped in her throat.

Then she glimpsed something ahead, and she clamped her lips tight to keep from screaming. *A figure, slight and huddled, lay prone in a small space . . . a space enclosed on either side, on top and bottom . . . a coffin?*

Erinn could see right through it.

The figure's hands were bound. She knew that without seeing them. White mist like cobwebs obscured the face and the body.

Hurry, Erinn told herself, *hurry.* She willed herself forward, closer, desperate now to see more. To lift that swirling curtain of mist and glimpse the face in the coffin.

Who is it? Let me see. Please—let me see . . .

Instead, she heard something. A cry. Low and keening and full of despair, it wailed from its confining box. Man or woman or child, she couldn't tell. It was an unearthly cry, one of hopelessness tinged with . . . *death.*

Death hovered there in that cramped misty space . . . waiting, watching, ready to sponge the life from that slight, unmoving figure . . .

Erinn's senses whirled. She tried to stay, to see more, *know* more, but blinding pain pierced her skull as she was hurtled back up the tunnel at a speed so swift it churned nausea in her stomach.

Her hands lost their grip on the Jeep. She slid to the ground, falling hard, falling fast . . .

He caught her just before her head struck the pavement. His arms clasped around her as her body slumped like a sack of sugar.

Then her eyes flew open and she stared at him, not seeing him, still seeing that prone helpless figure in the darkness.

"Is it happening now?" she whispered in a voice raw with fear. "I have to stop it."

"Oh, my God, Jase, what's wrong?" Lily reached him first but Colton drew up right behind her. Before Jase could reply, his father stalked up, took one look at the slim woman lying in his eldest son's arms, and spoke in clipped tones that brooked no argument.

"Bring her inside. Lily, get some water. Colton, you call Doc Stevens."

Jase lifted her with ease and carried her into the house. She was still staring straight ahead, those gorgeous dusky green eyes unfocused. But a haunted expression of fear lingered on her face and he could feel her shivering in his arms as he carried her through the hallway, shivering as if it was February and not June.

He took her to the small sitting room near the back of the house, the one that had been lovingly furnished by his mother, and that now had become Lily's favorite place to curl up with a book. Carefully he set her down across the overstuffed floral chintz sofa, frowning as her eyes closed again.

An instant later, they opened, and this time, she gazed straight at him with perfect clarity and recognition. Bright color stung her cheeks.

"I'm all right. I'm f-fine."

Her voice shook a little as she swung her legs to the floor and sat up. Jase didn't budge. He stood over her, his brows knit.

"Easy. I wouldn't jump up if I were you—not until the doctor checks you out. He's on his way—"

"There's no need for a doctor." In alarm, Erinn pushed herself to her feet, just as Lily rushed in with a glass of iced tea.

"Oh, good. You look *much* better." The girl expelled her breath in relief. "Please, sit down and drink this. Give yourself a minute or two," she urged.

Not altogether a bad idea, Erinn admitted to herself. The visions always drained her, more so each time. The image of the figure in the coffin still filled her mind, and the coldness in her bones hadn't yet eased. She sank down on the sofa and accepted the glass Lily pressed into her hands.

"Thanks. I'm all right now." She took a sip of the sweetened tea, trying to think of how she could possibly explain what had just happened.

"I didn't eat much today, what with traveling . . . and everything. I guess it made me a bit light-headed."

Light-headed? It sure looked like more than that, Jase

thought, but he kept silent as Lily murmured something sympathetic and the woman with the unforgettable green eyes kept her gaze lowered as she sipped the iced tea.

He noticed her fingers, long, slim, and graceful—like the rest of her. Her nails were delicately oval, painted the shell pink of a Western sunrise. And ever since she'd come to, her cheeks had been flushed the same color.

Is it happening now... I have to stop it, she'd said. What the hell did *that* mean?

"I don't think I caught your name." His voice sounded rougher than he'd intended and Lily glanced at him sharply.

"This is Erinn Winters—she's a famous author of children's books, Jase. She won the Newbery Award. She—"

"I asked her, not you."

Colton poked his head into the room.

"Doc Stevens is on his way. Pop said she's to stay put until he checks her out—"

"No—I don't need a doctor." Erinn stood up again, handing the glass to Lily with a quick, firm smile. "I'm sorry to have caused so much trouble, but honestly, Lily, I'm fine. I need to get back to the Watering Hole—and I've disturbed your family enough for one day. Please call me there tomorrow and let me know when to stop by the day-care center."

Jase watched curiously as she brushed past him, quick as a shadow passing in the night. Lily bit her lip and Colton stepped aside as Erinn hurried past him into the hall.

She ran lightly to the front of the house, relieved that there was no sign of the elder Mr. Fortune. She was dimly aware of the sound of her sandals clicking on the polished hardwood floor, of the scent of lemon wax and oranges, of the bleeding sun partially obscured by cotton-puff clouds as she hurried outside and toward the Jeep.

All around her was a peaceful silence, except for the whinny of a horse from the corral, but inside her head a chaotic tension thrummed. Then she heard running footsteps and turned to see Lily racing toward her.

"I almost forgot—directions. Go straight to Cedar Road and then turn left," the girl said breathlessly. "That will take you to Weeping Rock Road. Follow that to the second fork—you'll go to the right and keep on until you see the sign for the Watering Hole. It's just before the highway."

"Got it. Thanks."

She accelerated down the long drive, trying not to floor the Jeep. She couldn't get away from Fortune's Way fast enough. As if the unpleasant vibes she'd gotten from Lily's father weren't bad enough, she'd actually had a vision right there in front of all the Fortunes. In the *daytime*.

Her cheeks burned. The visions were her secret. They were private. They almost always came to her when she was alone. Usually in the deepest hours of night.

Trying to concentrate on the road, she couldn't block out the image of that bound figure still imprinted in her mind. Cold sweat moistened her palms as she clutched the steering wheel. She knew the headache that always followed the visions would come on any moment.

Damn it, wouldn't she ever get accustomed to them? They'd been part of her life for a long time now, but it had been two years since the last one. In that case, she'd seen a boy locked in a basement. His terror had been palpable.

Erinn had awakened in her bed when the vision was over without a clue where that basement was. She hadn't known if what she'd seen was happening right at that moment or if it had taken place a long time ago. Even more chilling, she didn't know if it was something *about* to happen, something she could prevent if only she could see *more*.

Of course, as always, she'd gone to the police. Detective McKindrick of the NYPD had thought she was crazy the first time she'd gone to him eight years ago, haltingly telling him about the tunnel and what she'd seen in her mind. But then he'd found the body she described, dragged out of the Hudson River. And after checking her out, he'd started asking questions—and writing down her answers.

Unfortunately, Erinn's visions weren't filled with detail and she never seemed to see the victims' faces clearly. But she'd known it was a middle-aged man who'd been killed and dumped in the river, and after the body had been found, McKindrick had asked her to accompany him to the morgue. It was the very last thing she'd wanted to do—but she had.

And though she'd only glanced at the dead man for an instant before turning away and pressing the palms of her hands to her eyes, two words had burst into her brain and out of her mouth.

Ivan Berberro.

McKindrick had stared at her as if she'd just dropped from the moon. Then he'd made several phone calls.

It turned out that the man dragged from the river had been a police informant who'd recently leaked incriminating information about a drug lord named Ivan Berberro. Because the body was found quickly, the police were able to identify the informant and trace the events of the previous forty-eight hours, finding evidence that linked Berberro's organization to the murder.

McKendrick had become a wary believer.

And through the years, he and Erinn had developed an alliance of sorts. Two years ago, after her visions of the young African-American boy tied up in a basement, McKendrick had linked her vision to an Amber alert that had gone out hours before in Detroit.

Erinn had been flown in by the police, and driven to the small well-kept house on the city's east side—the house from where eleven-year-old Damone Knox had vanished while his mother was at the grocery store.

At first nothing had happened. But after she walked through the house, with Damone's parents looking on with desperate hope, she'd stepped outside and circled through the grass of the postage-stamp-size yard.

Still nothing.

But when she returned to the cement steps of the front porch, the vision had swooped in and grabbed hold of her, sucking her down the tunnel, flooding her with terror. When she'd awakened, stretched out on the stoop, with three Detroit police officers crouched over her, she'd pushed herself up to a sitting position and riveted her gaze on a house across the street, four buildings down.

"There." She'd pointed at the house with the crumbling roof and dirty windows. "He's in *there*."

And he had been. He was alive.

All the while a nationwide alert was going out for information on Damone Knox's whereabouts, a twenty-two-year-old registered sex offender had been holding him captive in a locked basement no more than thirty yards from his own home.

Not all of her cases had turned out so well. Sometimes her visions were too late. Sometimes the police couldn't link them to a crime.

But one thing was certain. They weren't going away. They were, however, becoming less and less frequent. Steadily so.

Until now.

Now she'd had two similar visions in the past two days. That hadn't happened before, except in the rare instances when she was very close to the victim.

Like the little boy in the basement.

Why now? she wondered as she followed Lily's directions back toward town. *Why a second vision today?*

Uneasiness prickled down her spine. And so did a quiver of frustration. There was nothing to go on. She'd caught no glimpse of a face. She didn't even know if the person she'd seen was a man or a woman, or, God forbid, a child.

Only one thing was clear. Death was very near . . .

As Erinn parked in the lot behind the Watering Hole,

her head began to throb. She called McKindrick the moment she reached her room.

He questioned her for a good fifteen minutes before ending the conversation with instructions to call him back if anything else came to her. He was a sergeant now in the 69th Precinct—grayer, heavier, and even more seasoned by the brutalities he encountered in his profession. But he'd become a believer.

And a friend of sorts.

One of the few friends Erinn had allowed herself to have.

She threw herself down across the faded bedspread and tried to still the frantic hum in her head. The vision, the tunnel, the sense of death. The sight of Devon in that cabin, shouting at her to leave. The tears shining in her sister's eyes.

And the humiliation of succumbing to the vision outside the Fortune ranch house. With Jase Fortune staring down at her as she awakened, cold, scared, and at her most vulnerable.

He'd carried her inside with such ease. Such strength. Though still dazed from the vision, she'd been achingly aware of how effortlessly he'd lifted her and carried her through his house. Even now, warmth tingled through her as she recalled how firmly those powerful arms had cradled her.

A man like Jase Fortune wouldn't understand what it felt like to be vulnerable, out of control. At the mercy of a supposed gift that always arrived unexpectedly and brought with it fear and violence and death.

But Erinn did.

Frustration made her turn restlessly to her side,

sleep sliding impossibly further away. At the age of eighteen, she'd seized control of her life, but now she felt like she was losing that control again. She couldn't control the visions, what they revealed to her, when they might come. And now one had come to her for no apparent reason—the second vision in two days.

This afternoon a man she barely knew had been there when the vision took hold. He'd seen her helplessness, her weakness. Her secret.

Unacceptable.

She came off the bed, rubbing her fingertips against her temples. She didn't want to think about Jase Fortune. Those cobalt eyes of his seemed to burn right through her, and it wasn't a comfortable feeling. The man was far too confident, too good-looking to be anything other than a player of the first order. He was probably used to women melting if he even glanced their way. As for his irritable father—well, she didn't want to think about him either.

And she couldn't bear to think about Devon.

Too much was clashing in her brain, all of it jarring.

She knew only one possible way to escape. Pulling her laptop from its case she propped it on the scarred desk that looked as if it had been dragged from a junkyard.

Peering desperately at the screen as the laptop powered up, she tried to concentrate on Devonshire. The poor mouse was still trapped in a spiderweb.

It was time to figure out how she escaped. Time to lose herself in the private world of a heroic mouse and a hapless squirrel and a cocky chipmunk . . .

For nearly an hour Erinn typed and then deleted one

page, one scene after another. There was no escaping the truth.

Her imagination was in lockdown. And so was her brain.

At last she shut down the monstrous machine and pushed back her chair.

It's eight o'clock, she realized dazedly, *and I don't have anything to show for it. Not a single new page.*

Nor had she eaten a bite of food since she'd devoured Ginny Duncan's chocolate-chip cookies.

Feed the stomach, feed the brain, she told herself wearily. Pausing only long enough to brush her teeth and tug a comb through her hair, she grabbed up her purse and fled the ill-lit confines of the Watering Hole motel, stepping out into the cool vast darkness of the Montana night.

Chapter Six

"Damn."

Erinn gripped the steering wheel and stared in dismay at the shuttered blinds of the Saddleback Grill. The printed sign announced that the diner closed each night at eight and opened for business each morning at seven.

Now what? she wondered, her stomach growling with unladylike ferocity.

Ruefully, she scanned the empty street, wishing she hadn't waited so long to think about eating.

The growling of her stomach was turning into a roar.

Streetlights shone amber beneath a wide inky sky, but the shops were all dark and First Street looked like a ghost town.

I guess a big breakfast tomorrow will have to make up for skipping dinner. She drove on past the Saddleback, trying to resign herself to the idea of waiting until morning for sustenance. It occurred to her that there might be a half-eaten Milky Way at the bottom of her purse, and reaching for her bag, she groped around inside it with one hand while steering with the other.

Suddenly a burst of music blared through the car's open window.

She followed the sound to the intersection. First and Main. And there, down the block, she saw a big frame building ablaze with light and noise.

A huge neon sign told her it was the Redrock Bar and Grill.

Salvation.

Erinn made a right and stepped on the accelerator, noticing that the bar was flanked by a small parking lot where nearly every space was full.

Which wasn't surprising, considering that the din coming from the place suggested it was packed.

I hope that means the food's good, she thought, sliding into a spot between a pickup and a motorcycle. She guessed the Redrock would be all about the beer—and that was all right too. A cold one would go down nicely right now. It might take the edge off the nerves still prickling like sparkplugs through her body.

Pushing through double pine doors, she entered a smoky, low-ceilinged cave vibrating with life, color, and laughter. The aroma of chargrilled hamburgers and chicken wings pervaded the dimness that loomed before her. Men and women were crowded around the bar and lounging at big and small square tables. Country music oozed from a jukebox near a large dartboard, and as she maneuvered her way past a row of pinball machines near the entrance, she recognized the rough wail of Johnny Cash.

Several couples danced exuberantly across the dark-stained wooden dance floor, while all around them people talked, joked, and drank.

A man shouted as he banged on a pinball machine, then a woman's throaty laugh rang out from the bar. At one of the tables near the dartboard, three young cowboys were tossing back shots, one after the other.

Erinn spotted a smaller, out-of-the-way table in the corner beneath a framed poster of a young John Wayne on horseback and headed toward it.

A moment after she slipped into a chair, a breathless waitress in her early forties breezed up. "What can I get you, honey?"

"The Cowman's Steakburger, ranch fries, and one of those." Erinn pointed at a bottle of Budweiser on the waitress's tray.

"Comin' up." The woman was gone by the time the last words were out of her mouth.

Settling back in her chair, Erinn glanced around—and froze.

Mick Wheeler was hunched at the bar—drinking straight from a whiskey bottle. She could only see his profile, but there was no doubt who it was, especially with that beefy physique she remembered.

Where's Devon right now? she wondered with a quickened heartbeat. *Is she back at that awful shack? Alone? Or is she with Hank Wheeler?*

Both possibilities made her stomach twist.

Devon was in way over her head. She was far too young to be mixed up with either of these men. Yet Erinn had few illusions about what could have already happened between Devon and her boyfriend, what might be happening even now.

If she and Hank were having sex, the boy could be arrested for statutory rape. And if the brothers continued to keep her under their roof, they could be charged with kidnapping.

I'll use every weapon at my disposal, she thought as the waitress returned, placed her basket of food on the table, then thunked down her beer. *If it takes legal action to get Devon away from them, then so be it.*

Yet even as she bit into her sandwich, she realized that kicking up a legal dust could backfire. Hank had run away from trouble before, according to what Cordovan had told her.

If he ran again . . . and took Devon with him . . .

I'd be back at square one. And how long might it take to find her again?

There was another problem, she mused, spearing a french fry. If she went to the police, or the sheriff, or whatever law enforcement they had in this town, she'd have to explain. She'd have to tell them who she was, who Devon was. She might even have to prove their identities, their connection. And their link to billionaire tycoon Dane Stanton might become known.

If the local press got wind of who they were—the long-lost runaway daughters of one of the most powerful men of the last century—it would only be a matter of time before the national press found out and the airwaves and Internet and news programs would explode with the story.

Devon had already been through so much. The last thing she needed was to be dead center in the eye of a media hurricane.

I have to protect her, Erinn thought. *Going to the police will have to be a last resort. If everything else fails . . .*

It won't, she told herself, taking a quick gulp of the cold beer. *I can't let it.*

She nibbled another french fry and then remembered something else—something Cordovan had told her. The Wheeler brothers both had jobs. They were ranch hands. Mick had been at the cabin when she arrived late this afternoon, but what if he'd just come home from work? What if he was usually gone during the day, along with Hank? Perhaps she could get to Devon, have a chance to really talk to her, when no one was around to interfere.

Hope sparked, then flickered.

What if Devon also had a job?

There's one way to find out.

Small steps, Erinn reminded herself as she sipped at her beer. That's how she'd made it all alone in New York City. That's how she'd put herself through school. And taking small steps—smart ones—might be the way to get her sister back too.

Still, she studied Mick Wheeler uneasily as she finished her burger. He was the only person at the bar who wasn't engaged in friendly conversation with someone. The others were all laughing and talking, bantering with the bartender, joking with the waitresses, but Wheeler sat apart at the end of the bar. Drinking alone.

"Hey, there, pretty lady, you look a mite lonely. Mind if I take a seat?"

Startled, Erinn stared up at the man standing beside her chair. He looked familiar . . .

Then she recognized him. The dark-haired man she'd noticed in the Saddleback earlier that day, sitting with the redheaded woman. His oily black hair was slicked back tonight and he wore a collared red shirt and jeans. And a smug little smile that made her think of a snake-oil salesman.

"No, thanks. I was just leaving." She pushed her plate away hastily, but before she could signal for her check, he grinned and eased into the chair beside her.

"What's the rush, sweet thing? How about another beer? I'm buyin'."

"I'm done," she said coolly. His aftershave was greasy smelling. Off-putting. And there was dried ketchup on his chin. Erinn scanned the cavernous room for her waitress, but the woman was behind the bar and not looking her way.

She stood up, ignoring the man as she reached for her handbag, but he grabbed her wrist, his strong, moist fingers clutching it tightly.

"Hey, now, angel face, don't get all huffy on me. I'm just trying to make you feel welcome. My name's Frank Wells, what's yours?"

Erinn jerked free, eyeing him with revulsion. His grin only widened across his sleazily handsome face.

"Pay attention," she said evenly. "I'm not interested in making any new friends. Go away."

Wells shoved the chair back and jumped to his feet, and for a moment she felt a lick of fear. "Fuck you, lady," he said softly, stepping in front of her as she tried to edge away. "I know your type and you're not as hot as you think you are."

"Get out of my way. Right now."

He laughed. "Yeah? Or what?"

"Or I'll wipe that ugly smirk off your face," Jase Fortune answered.

Erinn whirled toward his voice. She hadn't seen Jase in the Redrock when she sat down, but he was standing beside her now, his eyes cold as marble as they bored into Frank Wells's face. He looked tough, calm, and formidable, she thought as her heartbeat quickened. Wells tensed, a muscle pounding in his neck as he glared up at the taller man in the gray slacks and white polo shirt.

"Sticking your nose in my business isn't the best way to keep it attached to your face, Fortune," he snapped.

"If I were you, I'd be worried about my own face," Jase said tightly.

Wells glared at him, trying to outstare the rich son-of-a-bitch who had everything he'd ever wanted handed to him on a gold-plated platter. Wells hadn't had it nearly so easy, not by a long shot. He'd been handed off to relatives right and left after his ma croaked and his father ran off with the queen of the trailer trash and her five sniveling brats.

Wells hated men like Jase Fortune. And he felt vastly superior to them. He'd learned how to make money too—only he couldn't brag about how he did it. But it had taken more smarts and guts than any rich man's son could ever imagine.

Fortune had interfered with his own private business when he'd followed Wells to the bar in Crystalville and fired him. The bastard was too stupid to know that he hadn't been drinking that day—or any of the days he'd taken off from being a lowly Fortune's Way ranch hand. He'd been waiting for a meeting with some very wealthy and connected partners. Men who'd grind up and spit out their own grandmothers to make a buck.

Fortune had no idea who he was dealing with right

now. But Wells fought down the urge to show him how a real down-and-dirty fight worked. He knew better than to call attention to himself. His partner did enough of that and Wells had been warned by the men he worked for to see that he and his partner both kept a low profile.

Getting into a bar fight with Jase Fortune wouldn't exactly keep him under the radar.

Wells reluctantly dropped his gaze, shoved his hands into his pockets to keep from punching Fortune, and sent the dark-haired bitch a sneering grin.

"Hey, what can I say? You're just not worth it, baby."

Jase's fist shot out, slammed into Wells's stomach, and sent the other man doubling over, the wind knocked out of him.

Wells struggled for breath, fighting the overwhelming urge to leap at the other man.

As Wells staggered back, reining in his temper, Jase took Erinn's arm. "If I ever see you bother her again, Wells, we're going to pick up right where we left off."

"Better watch out for your new boyfriend, baby-cakes," Wells called to Erinn as she and Jase walked off. "He crumples women up like toilet paper and flushes them away. If you don't believe me, ask anyone in town."

Erinn's heart was thudding as Jase Fortune led her toward the front of the bar. "I really don't need you to keep coming to my aid," she said over the sound of cheers as someone at the dartboard hit a bull's-eye and a Lonestar song blasted from the jukebox.

"Really? You could have fooled me."

"If you'd given me a minute, I'd have—" She broke

off, sucking in her breath as one of the couples on the dance floor suddenly careened right into Mick Wheeler at the end of the bar. Wheeler's drink sloshed down the front of his shirt.

Then, as Erinn watched in shock, he roared in fury, sprang off his bar stool and loomed like a thundercloud over the smaller man in a bright plaid shirt.

The man was extending an apologetic hand, but Wheeler ignored it. As everyone in the bar watched, he shoved the man backward with one brawny arm, sending him crashing into the jukebox.

Even as the Redrock went silent, the smaller man straightened and charged at Wheeler, landing a solid punch to his midsection. The woman scrambled aside with a scream, and Erinn's breath caught in her throat as the two men went at each other like boys in a schoolyard.

People were cheering, yelling, as fists flew. She noticed Frank Wells had edged forward, and was watching the fracas with an intent expression.

He's probably enjoying this, she thought in disgust. Even from across the room, Erinn could hear the sickening crunch of fists meeting flesh. Then she gasped as the plaid-shirted man fell to his knees, blood gushing from his nose.

"Stop it! Damn it, both of you—stop!" the woman shrieked. The bartender, a stick of a man with a flowing brown ponytail, had raced out from behind the bar and was trying to tear the two men apart.

But Mick Wheeler had transformed into a human tornado—dark, furious, and a power unto himself—blind to everything but the rage and liquor pumping through him. As Erinn watched in horror he slugged the bartender, then absorbed a return blow to the ribs that would have felled a horse. But he staggered back only a step before lunging after the plaid-shirted cowboy again.

The bleeding man tried to block the punches, but several got through and sent him spinning to the floor. Beside Erinn, Jase swore and lunged forward as Wheeler threw himself on top of the other man, pinned him to the floor, and hit him again.

As the man's head lolled sideways, Jase reached Wheeler and hauled him off, while the bartender and two other men knelt beside the dazed and bleeding man on the ground.

"That's enough, Wheeler! You hear me?" the bartender yelled.

"Someone call Sheriff Farley!" the woman cried. She bent over the fallen man, struggling to help him to his feet. "I think he needs a doctor!"

Jase shoved Wheeler aside and hurried over to have a look.

"You all right, Chris? You want me to call the sheriff?" the bartender asked.

The plaid-shirted man shook his head, then wiped his sleeve across his bloody nose. Jase helped him up and back to his table, as the woman called out to a waitress for ice.

Wheeler stumbled toward the door.

"Damn that son-of-a-bitch." Erinn's waitress skidded to a halt beside her. "If he didn't get into a fight with someone every freaking week, it'd be a full-blown miracle."

"He has a short fuse?" Alarm was pumping through Erinn's blood.

The waitress flashed her a resigned glance. "That's an understatement, honey."

"Is he only violent when he's drunk?"

"Since he's drunk most of the damn time, who can tell?" The waitress shook her head and strode away.

Panic coursed through Erinn as she stood in the darkened bar, where conversation and dancing were already continuing as if nothing had happened. Jase was still with the injured man.

And Wheeler was probably headed back to the cabin right now. He was drunk, angry. *Dangerous.*

What if Devon was there all alone? What if Hank wasn't with her? Even if he was, the two of them would be no match for the wrecking machine Erinn had seen in action tonight.

She ran from the Redrock. But Wheeler's dented blue pickup was already peeling away down the street. She hadn't even noticed it when she'd parked her Jeep.

Bolting toward her car, she fumbled with the keys in the darkness. By the time she dove behind the wheel and switched on the ignition the pickup was out of sight. But Erinn knew the first part of the route to Whistle Road and jammed her foot on the accelerator.

Anxiety squeezed through her like an ever-tightening vise as she wove her way out of Wolf River and hit the open road. Cool night air rushed in through the window and her own heart beat in her ears, louder than the sound of the Jeep's tires grating over the road.

All of her senses seemed on fire. She smelled the sage and pine of the mountains, felt the clamminess of her palms gripping the steering wheel, even as the night around her sang with life, the life of unseen wild creatures humming, cawing, scuffling through the brush on either side of the road.

She stamped her foot down on the accelerator. She hadn't seen another car, not behind her or ahead. She had to get Wheeler in her sights soon or she'd get lost again and lose him . . .

Then she saw him. Actually, she saw his lights ahead and after a moment made out the truck. Her mouth was dry but she kept her foot steady on the pedal, keeping an even distance between them.

When he took a turn too fast she cursed under her breath. It was amazing he hadn't spun off and hit a tree.

She slowed for the turn and took it smoothly, then caught his lights ahead in the distance and accelerated to catch up.

In the blackness nothing looked familiar, but she knew they'd been driving long enough now that they should be reaching Buckhorn Point.

And then they did. A half mile later, Wheeler barreled onto Whistle Road. Erinn followed him down the dirt track, keeping a good distance between them. Her heart started to knock against her ribs as she wondered just what she was going to do once she reached the shack.

But there was no time to plan. She saw the clearing ahead and slowed to a crawl, killing her lights. Beneath the cover of the moonlit Montana night she eased to a halt and peered ahead into the gloom.

A light shone in a window, giving off just enough of a gleam to illuminate the pickup parked sideways in the

drive. As she watched, Wheeler staggered out of the vehicle and up the broken steps.

She eased silently from the Jeep as he disappeared
inside the shack. There was another vehicle parked
among the weeds—a Blazer.

That must be Hank's car. Her throat was dry. *He's inside with Devon . . .*

She bit her lip, trying to decide what to do next.
There was a chance she'd make the situation worse if
she went to the door, tried to speak to Devon. But she
couldn't leave without making sure her sister was going
to be all right.

I have to get her away from this place, Erinn thought in
despair. *I should've just dragged her out of here this afternoon.*

Carefully, she started forward. Suddenly, a shadowy
movement ahead made her freeze.

Two figures rose ghostlike from the grass by the
trees, their heads bent close together. It was Devon and
a boy. He had the same build as the boy in Cordovan's
photographs.

Hank.

The faint moonlight glinted off her sister's hair, the
fair strands tangled anyhow about her face. Devon was
tucking a tank top into her jeans and Hank seemed to
be buttoning his shirt.

Erinn didn't have to guess what the two of them had
been up to out there in the grass.

"Wait outside," she heard the boy say in a low tone.
She had to strain to hear him. "I'll be back in a few."

"No, Hank, he's okay, why don't you just leave him
alone?" Devon sounded nervous. She clutched the

boy's arm. "He's going to take it out on you if you go in there—"

"Yeah. So much for stayin' sober," he muttered. "If he doesn't get to work tomorrow there'll be hell to pay. The jerk. I gotta talk to him, Dev."

He hunched away from her and sprinted up the porch steps two at a time.

"Wait out here, no matter what happens," he shot back over his shoulder and then shoved at the cabin door.

Devon wasn't having it. She started right up the steps after him, but Erinn sprinted forward.

"Devon, no!" Her voice was a whisper but it carried across the clearing. Her sister whirled, looking incredulous in the faint light.

"Tiffany?" she breathed.

Suddenly from inside the shack they heard a crash. Erinn's heart jumped into her throat.

"Devon, you need to come with me right now." She eyed the Wheeler shack anxiously as a shouted curse boomed through the curtained window, followed by an ominous thud.

She grabbed her sister's arm. "Don't argue with me, just come!"

"No! Let go of me!" Devon wrenched away. "How long have you been hiding out here, spying on me?"

"Long enough. Mick Wheeler's drunk as a skunk and I just saw him beat a man whose only crime was accidentally bumping into him at a bar. I'm *not* letting you stay here with him—he's dangerous. And as far as your boyfriend is concerned—"

"You can't tell me what to do!" Devon's voice rose

defiantly in the darkness. "If you don't leave me alone, I'll run away. I swear I will! Hank and me, we'll run so far no one will ever find us!"

"You tell her, Dev."

They both spun toward the shack, where Hank Wheeler slouched in the doorway, glaring at Erinn.

He sauntered down the steps with the lithe, arrogant stride unique to a raw-boned sixteen-year-old male.

"Where's Mick?" Devon hurried to him, searching his face in the moonlight for bruises, but Hank merely shrugged.

"Passed out. He threw the coffeepot against the wall, that's all. Yelled something about some bastard knocking his drink over, then he tripped on the rug coming out of the can and fell flat on his face. He's out cold on the floor. Is this her?" he asked Devon. "Your sister?"

"Used to be." Sullen blue eyes flicked over Erinn. Erinn felt her heart crack.

It struck her then that the sweet little girl with the open heart and fairy eyes was really gone. Vanished. She'd disappeared forever, replaced by this lost, rebellious, angry young woman.

At that moment Erinn didn't know with whom she was more furious—her father, Mick Wheeler, this cocky boy who had one arm draped around her sister's shoulders—or herself.

"Devon's only fifteen." She gazed directly into Hank Wheeler's distrustful eyes. "I'm her blood relative. Her legal guardian. She's coming with me. Tonight—right now—"

"Yeah? Who says?" His lip curled insolently.

Erinn turned toward her sister. "Devon, give me

twenty-four hours, that's all I ask. Come back with me to the Watering Hole motel—"

"That fleabag? No way."

Erinn managed to refrain from pointing out that the run-down Wheeler shack made the Watering Hole look like a resort. She clenched her jaw and searched for a way to sway her sister. Intimidation, threats, anger wouldn't work. They'd both encountered enough of that back in their onetime home. If Devon was anything like she was herself, those tactics would only make her more determined to revolt.

She drew in a breath and tried again. "Devon, I was wrong for the way I abandoned you. I know that and I want to make it up to you. All I ask is a chance—"

"She don't want nothin' to do with you. And you can't make her go," Hank interrupted. "And we'll be outta here like a couple of lightning bugs if you don't leave right now . . . *Tiffany*!" he added with contempt.

The quieter tone he'd used with Devon was gone. He glared at Erinn like a wrathful young James Dean, his dark eyes gleaming with an angry derision that shocked her.

"She's going to go to the sheriff, Hank, I know it." Devon's voice shook. "We have to get out of here. I mean it, right *now*. I won't go back, I won't go with her—"

"Devon," Erinn said sharply, "running away won't solve—"

"No? You did it, you ran away. You did just fine. So did I. And now I'm going to run again—you're forcing me to—"

"No!" Erinn blocked her path as she started toward the Blazer, but Hank stepped forward, his jaw set.

"Look, lady, back off. Leave us alone or we'll disappear—for good."

Erinn stared from one to the other, dismay rushing through her. Hank was only a few inches taller than Devon, but he looked almost as formidable as his brother. And Devon's mouth was mutinously set, her eyes as cold and distant as stars in the moonlight.

If Erinn didn't know differently, she'd never believe this girl was the same angelic-looking toddler who'd crept into her room at night whenever she had a nightmare, who'd let Erinn rub her back and brush her hair and tell her stories until she drifted back to sleep.

In that instant, Erinn knew she'd failed. At least for tonight. Short of a knock-down, drag-out brawl with both of them, there was no way she'd get Devon into her car.

"All right, I'm leaving." She had to summon up all of her self-control to speak in an even tone.

"I won't argue with you anymore tonight. And I won't go to the sheriff," she added quickly, as suspicion pinched Devon's face. "But you should get used to having me around," she told the girl softly. "Because I'm not leaving Wolf River without you."

"What—you're going to, like, live at the Watering Hole motel for the rest of your life?" Devon jeered. "Fine. Just stay away from me and Hank."

"I won't leave you behind again, Devon. Think about that." She held the girl's gaze, her tone steady. "No matter what I have to do, I won't leave Montana until you and I get to know each other again."

For an instant, she thought she saw a glimmer of something in her sister's eyes. Something wondering and soft—something like hope. But a moment later it was gone.

"You're a couple of years too late." The girl's voice quavered. Spinning around, she bolted toward the shack. Hank fired one brooding glance at Erinn and followed her.

Erinn flinched as the door slammed shut, locking her out. Sealing them in.

The sound of it reverberated through her heart as she climbed back into the rental Jeep. The night sky seemed to press down upon her as she retraced her route along the crisscrossing country roads.

It was late by the time she slid wearily between the sheets and stared at the motel ceiling. But one thought was firm in her mind, despite her exhaustion.

She was going to prove to her sister that this time she meant what she said.

She wasn't going anywhere until she broke through to Devon—even if it meant paying rent at the Watering Hole motel.

An hour later in the Redrock, Frank Wells waggled his arm in the smoke-filled air, signaling to LeeAnn Culpepper where he was seated as she sauntered in looking mighty fine. Tight-fitting scoop-neck top in canary yellow, big red beaded necklace, jeans tighter than the skin on a sausage.

Mighty fine. But even LeeAnn's generous boobs and hot little butt didn't distract him from the problem weighing on his mind. As she swayed toward him, smiling in her four-inch heels, he was still thinking about solutions to what was fast becoming the "Wheeler problem."

"Sorry I'm late, honey." She sank into the chair beside him and bumped it closer to his. "Angie," she called to a waitress rushing by, "bring me a Bud, will ya?"

The waitress yelled that she would and kept going. Frank leaned over and slipped a hand behind her nape, pulled her toward him until they locked lips.

"I been bored out of my mind, baby doll. Till you got here."

It was a lie, of course. But LeeAnn believed it, because she wanted to. It was like that with most people, Wells had learned. Most people were fools. They only saw, only heard what they wanted to see and hear. Whatever made 'em feel good in the moment.

He was different from most people though. Always had been. He looked at life clearly—not judging things by what was good or bad—but by what was good or bad for *him*.

A whole different ball of wax.

So he was able to easily chat with LeeAnn, savor another beer, even lead her out to the dance floor when her favorite Tim McGraw song came on, while all the while he was reaching the decision that it was getting to be time. Time to bail on the dumb-ass Wheeler boys. On this dumb-ass town.

Mick was pissing him off more every day. All this drinking, fighting—the son-of-a-bitch was out of control. Wells had warned him about drawing too much attention to himself, warned him what their partners had said, but did he listen?

Less and less.

And one of these days Mickey boy might get himself so plastered he blurted out something that could land him *and* Wells in the big house for ten or twenty.

Trouble was, if anyone found out Frank Wells used to be Fred Walters, wanted for the murders four years ago of twenty-year-old Heather Yates and her boyfriend, Lee Bennett, in Tucson, Wells could be looking at a death sentence.

He couldn't afford for that to happen. Not when all he'd been doing was tying up a few loose ends.

Fortunately, Mick Wheeler didn't have a clue about any of that—about Fred Walters, Heather Yates, Lee Bennett. He didn't have a clue about nothing and no one in Wells's past.

He only knew that Wells had the business contacts that were making both of them rich.

For now.

Wells was sorely tempted to close up shop in Wolf River after the very next delivery, to move the operation elsewhere. He always got nervous staying in one place too long, just as he didn't trust sticking to any one identity for long.

If the slightest thing went wrong, and the law found reason to check his fingerprints with the feds' database, he'd be nailed to the wall before he could spit.

And one sure way to get in trouble was by leaving behind loose ends.

Mick Wheeler, his damned kid brother, and that snuffly mouse he'd brought home out of the blue from California were three loose ends he couldn't afford to leave behind.

Damn Wheeler, anyway. He never should have let

those two kids set foot in the place, much less let them find out what was going on.

Wells circled his hand across LeeAnn's buttocks as she rested her head on his shoulder and another country song wailed from the jukebox.

Aside from the small fortune he had tucked away during this operation over the past year, LeeAnn was the best thing in Wolf River right now.

A sweet little distraction made sweeter by the fact that every time Jase Fortune saw them together, it had to stick in his craw like a dead rat.

His former girlfriend was being screwed by the man he'd fired. And there was nothing mister big shot Jase Fortune could do about it.

"LeeAnn, you goin' to the barn dance at the Hanging J?" he asked as the song ended.

"Thought I would, honey."

"Then how about we go together? So long as I don't have to bring you a damned corsage." He chuckled as they returned to their seats and LeeAnn gave a bark of laughter.

"I'm way beyond corsages, Frank. Just bring me what you always do." She took another hit of beer. "Some good lovin' and the pleasure of your company."

Was there a trace of sarcasm in her voice? Or was it sadness?

Wells felt a rush of anger. Sure, she was using him as a weapon against Jase Fortune just like he was using her, he knew that. But there had to be something more. He had to be making her forget about Fortune, at least when they were in the sack, right?

"What do you say we head over to your place right now and practice up on that good lovin' part?"

Her smile came readily enough but it never touched her eyes. "Sure, Frank. Why not?"

But he saw the slight hesitation in her body language, and the way her gaze scanned the bar as they made their way to the door. She looked into every smoky corner, toward the dartboard, and studied the dance floor where couples were prancing around to a Dolly Parton tune.

She was looking for Jase Fortune. She wanted him to see them together.

"He ain't here," Wells muttered, grabbing her hand and jerking her toward the door, then outside into the parking lot. "You want to stay here and watch for him or go home with me and get it on?"

"I don't know what you're talking about, Frank." Her smile was at once sultry and cool. "I came here tonight for you. Only you. You don't believe me?" She pulled her hand free, stopped in the lot, and shrugged. "Then I can just go home all by my lonesome."

She started off walking down Main Street, hips working it, and Wells swore. He went after her, swung her around to face him.

"Okay, baby, you win. You know I can't resist you." He knew how to say what women wanted to hear. He laid it on thick. "If you walk out on me now, I'm just gonna have a real bad night. So let's kiss and make up," he wheedled.

She smiled, her narrow face lighting up as she let him kiss her. "I don't want to have a bad night either, Frank," she sighed, wrapping her arms around him.

Later, after they'd done the deed a few different times, a few different ways, and in a few different places, Wells was satisfied that he'd driven all thoughts of Jase Fortune from LeeAnn Culpepper's mind.

But he lay awake smoking for hours as LeeAnn slept beside him. She'd never know that he hadn't been thinking about her most of the time they were going at it. He'd been pretending he was screwing that sexy new bitch who'd shown up in the Saddleback today, and then at the Redrock.

He'd never had a woman as classy looking as that. Or as flat-out beautiful.

But, he told himself, as he stubbed out the butt of his cigarette in the ashtray beside LeeAnn's bed, *there's a first time for everything, isn't there?*

And maybe, before he pulled up stakes on Wheeler and left this dud town behind, there'd be time for him to get a first taste of that.

Chapter Seven

Erinn was waiting outside the Saddleback Grill when Ginny Duncan arrived to open for business.

"Aren't you the brave one?" The woman grinned at her first customer, fresh as the dew and dressed in low-rise jeans and a white tee. "Can't believe you're not wearing your waterproof pants today."

"I'm willing to risk it for more of your chocolate-chip cookies," Erinn answered with a smile. "But actually," she continued as Ginny unlocked the door, "when you have a second, I'd like to talk to you."

"Sure. Just give me about fifteen minutes to get the show on the road here." Ginny held the door for her and flicked on the lights.

Erinn took a seat in one of the blue upholstered booths, ordered pancakes and coffee, then watched as within minutes a stream of people flowed into the restaurant, filling every booth and table.

When the morning rush subsided, Ginny ambled over and refilled Erinn's coffee cup. She set the pot down and slid into the opposite side of the booth.

"So, now, what can I do for you?"

"I'm guessing you have a pretty good handle on everything worth knowing in Wolf River," Erinn began.

"You could say that."

"I need some advice."

"Well, then. You've come to the right place, Miss...?"

"Erinn. Erinn Winters."

"Pleased to meet you, Erinn." Ginny studied her with eyes that were at once thoughtful and shrewd. "I've been informed I'm pretty good at telling people what they should do. Some call it meddling. I call it straight talk. So tell me what you need."

"I've decided to stay on for a while in Wolf River and I need a place to live. For several weeks, most likely." Erinn sighed, remembering Devon's anger last night. "But possibly for the rest of the summer."

As Ginny's brows rose, Erinn continued quickly. "I'm looking to rent something—a small house or an apartment—even a room, if necessary. I thought you might be able to tell me if there's a real estate office in town or someone you know who rents out property."

"The real estate office is on Market Street." Ginny looked thoughtful. "That's two streets over, near the ice cream parlor. Mostly they handle property sales though. It wouldn't hurt to check there, but..." She tapped a finger on the table. "I do know of one place..."

"Yes?" Erinn leaned forward.

"I'm not sure it would suit you," Ginny said slowly. "Or even if the owner would be willing to rent it out. It's stood empty for some years now—needs some cleaning and fixing up, but you might be able to get it cheap."

"Oh?" Erinn felt a whisper of hope. Cheap sounded good. She'd have to watch her money now, what with her flatlining Devonshire book, and her New York rent and utilities, which she'd be paying while still renting living space in Wolf River.

"How cheap?"

"I'm not sure, but the owner doesn't really need the money." Ginny hesitated. "I don't know if he'd be willing to let you—or anyone—stay there, though . . ."

Her voice trailed off.

"Is it here in town?" Erinn pressed.

"Nope. This little cabin's in a real pretty valley, about fifteen miles west of here. There's a creek running behind the property, lots of trees. Real private."

"It sounds wonderful." Erinn had an image of her and Devon having a picnic beneath one of those trees. And washing dishes together in a cozy kitchen, catching up on the past, reconnecting. "If you'll give me the owner's number, I'll call him," she said eagerly.

"Let me tell you something about the owner first. He hasn't much bothered with the cabin in several years— it's just sitting there. But that doesn't mean he'll rent it to you." Ginny worried her lower lip. "On the other hand, if you head over to the real estate office on Market Street, could be Doug Pryor knows of an apartment in Crystalville. We don't have any apartment buildings in Wolf River," she explained. "This town's just too small."

"Crystalville's too far away, Ginny. I want to be close to Wolf River." *And to Devon, whether she likes it or not.*

"In that case..." Ginny drew a pencil from the pocket of her khakis and scribbled on a page from her order pad. "Here's the cell phone number of the fellow you need to contact. You might as well give it a try. You, um, sort of met him already," she added dryly.

Erinn took one glance at the name on the paper and stared at her in disbelief. "Jase Fortune? *He* owns the cabin?"

"Every square inch *and* the land it's built on. Guess you know he's the one who threw that cold water on you yesterday."

"Oh, yes, I know it, all right," Erinn muttered.

Ginny chuckled at her less-than-pleased expression. "That's not the reaction most women have when Jase's name comes up. You wouldn't *believe* how many single gals in the county have tried to make him forget all about his first wife and her hijinks. But none of 'em have been able to do it, more's the pity."

"First wife?" Erinn's brows arched. "How many times has he been married?"

"Oh, just once. But it was a doozy. And he swears he's never heading down the aisle again." Ginny sighed. All traces of humor had vanished from her eyes.

"That cabin I mentioned—it's where he and his ex-wife lived, before she dragged him off to California. He despises the place."

Erinn stared at her in surprise. She never would have taken Jase Fortune for the sentimental type. Rugged, aloof, sexy, yes. Sensitive? No way.

Before she could think of a response, Ginny bit her lip. "I didn't mean to gossip—not about Jase. He's almost like a son to me—you won't find a better man.

Matter of fact, the only folks who need to watch out for him are those who'd try to hurt anyone in his family, or—" she added with a flicker of regret in her eyes, "a woman naive enough to think she might lasso him to the altar. And," she said suddenly, looking past Erinn, "if you don't believe me, you can ask *him*."

Her glance had lighted on a man sauntering through the diner's door.

"Come on over here, Culp, there's someone I want you to meet."

Erinn studied the tall, thin young cowboy with the reddish hair, sharp brown eyes, and good-natured demeanor as he approached the table.

"Say hello to Erinn Winters. She's new in town. This is Don Culpepper, honey," Ginny told her. "Everyone calls him Culp. He's top ranch hand over at Fortune's Way and he knows Jase Fortune as well as just about anyone."

Before Erinn could reply, Ginny went on. "Erinn's looking to rent Jase and Carly's cabin. What do you think, Culp? Will he go for it?"

"Well, if that was *my* cabin, I'd give you the keys right here and now—and anything else you wanted," he told Erinn enthusiastically. His eyes crinkled as he looked her over, and his smile widened with natural charm. He cupped her hand in his big, gangly one, and held on to her fingers just a moment longer than Erinn thought necessary. But the admiring grin on his good-natured face made her smile right back.

"Down, cowboy." Ginny swatted his arm. "We're not talking about you. We're talking about Jase."

"Well, now. *Jase*. Different story." Culp's lips twisted

as he gazed down at Erinn. "Sorry to have to tell you this, but if I were a betting man, I wouldn't take odds."

"Son, you *are* a betting man," Ginny retorted tartly. She turned to Erinn, shaking her head. "Don't listen to him. Culp here was the hold 'em poker champion of the county last year. He's even better at five-card stud. Tell her how big a pot you won, Culp. Go on, I know you're dying to tell her."

The cowboy shrugged modestly. "One thousand, four hundred and fifty dollars." Then he stuck his thumbs in the pockets of his Levi's. "Course, by the time I finished buying rounds that night, I barely had enough left to buy myself a decent pair of boots. But you know how that goes."

"Aha, sure." First Ginny, and then Erinn, glanced down at the boots on his feet. They were spectacular— deep brown leather cowboy boots, hand-tooled and polished to a high sheen, with fancy stitching and embroidery.

"Nice," Erinn murmured.

"Well, you know what they say," he drawled. "A man's gotta have decent boots. Some things are just *worth* goin' broke for."

She laughed and slid from the booth, stuffing the slip of paper Ginny had given her in her handbag. "Well, I hope your boss is as accommodating about that cabin as you would be."

At that the grin faded from his sun-browned face. "Look, don't get me wrong. Jase is my best buddy—we go way back. And he'd be the first in line to lend a hand to me or anyone in Wolf River who needed it. But that cabin, it's a sore spot."

"What he's trying to say," Ginny sighed, "is that it's worth trying, but best not to count on it."

"Thanks," Erinn said. "I'll remember that."

She paid her bill at the counter as Ginny shooed Culp to a clean table and then seated several other customers, furnishing them with setups and menus.

But Ginny hurried over as she started toward the door. "I hope you can talk Jase into it, honey. If he lets you rent that cabin, you'll have one of the prettiest little places in Wolf River—aside from Fortune's Way, of course." She tilted her head to one side and seemed to be trying to puzzle something out.

"I don't know what brings you here," she said at last, and for one unsettling moment Erinn thought the woman could see the turbulence in her soul. "But I do know that if you spend some time here, you'll like it. Wolf River's a good town. People here work hard and care about their neighbors. Most everyone gets along."

"Does that include Mick Wheeler?" The words popped out before Erinn could stop them.

Ginny stared at her in amazement. "*You* know Mick Wheeler?"

"Better than I want to." Erinn bit her lip, then glanced around the Saddleback. She felt too exposed talking about the Wheelers here. "It's a long story, Ginny. I'll fill you in another time." She straightened her spine and forced a smile.

"Right now I need to see a man about a cabin."

Chapter Eight

Get it over with, Erinn told herself.

She sat hunched in the Jeep, cell in hand, staring at Jase Fortune's number.

What are you waiting for? she asked herself crossly. *So he saw you pass out yesterday. He can't possibly know what it was all about. He thinks you're just some little sissy who fainted right before his eyes. And as for last night in the Redrock, standing up for you with Wells, that has nothing to do with anything. Call him.*

Her finger stabbed the buttons before she could change her mind and she clamped the phone to her ear.

"Jase Fortune." He answered on the third ring. Sounding curt, businesslike, and busy.

Well, she could be businesslike too. "This is Erinn Winters, Mr. Fortune. Lily's friend. We met yesterday—"

"I know who you are."

Not one for small talk, was he? She was tempted to simply end the call, but the thought of Devon at the Wheeler shack made her push on.

"I have a favor to ask."

Silence. She could just picture him, tall and lean and gorgeous, that thick shock of dark blond hair falling over his eyes, his expression one of cool indifference. Did he have any other kind?

"It's actually not so much a favor as a business arrangement. I'd like to . . . hello, are you there?" she said in irritation, when all she heard was continued silence at the other end of the line.

"I'm here. I'm in the middle of a meeting. Why don't you cut to the chase, Ms. Winters, and tell me what I can do for you."

"Fine. You can rent me your cabin for the summer."

This time the silence was deafening. Erinn's heart beat in her ears.

"Why the hell would I want to do that?"

At least he hadn't said no. Erinn forced herself to speak quickly, to get in as much as possible before he could cut her off.

"I need a place to live temporarily and it has to be here in Wolf River—Crystalville is too far away. Ginny told me about your cabin and the creek and how lovely it is and—"

She drew in a quick breath. "And she said you might be willing to rent it to me—inexpensively. I mean, if it's a matter of money, I'll pay whatever you ask," she rushed on, eyes closed, pushing away the image of her waning bank account.

Not to mention how much it was costing her to rent the Jeep.

"The thing is, I *need* a place to stay. And I'd like to move in as soon as possible."

"Sorry, I can't help you." His voice was grim. Firm. "The cabin's not for rent."

"Even for a few weeks? A month?"

"Not even an hour."

Erinn's heart sank. But she couldn't give up. "Please—reconsider. It's very important. I wouldn't ask you otherwise... I'm not in the habit of asking favors..."

Her voice trailed off. What was the point? He wasn't going to go for it. He already thought she was some kind of freak.

"Meet me at two o'clock," he said abruptly.

"I beg your pardon?" Erinn nearly dropped her cell phone.

"We'll discuss it at the cabin. I guess you'll need directions."

Stunned, she scrambled in her bag for a pen and frantically scribbled on the slip of paper Ginny had given her.

"Mr. Fortune... I don't know how to thank you—"

"Don't bother. I haven't agreed to rent it to you yet." He disconnected, leaving Erinn staring blankly out at the pickups and SUVs cruising down Main Street.

All she knew was that she liked the sound of that last word.

Yet.

Chapter Nine

Jase was in a lousy mood.

Not only had there been no news from Guy Farley about the investigation so far, but his meeting with Linc Simmons, the attorney handling the lumberyard purchase, had dragged on for the entire morning. He still had trucking bids to review, feed to order, and a pile of ranch bookwork stacked up to his eyeballs.

He itched for the luxury of spending an entire day outdoors—repairing fences, checking on the cattle and water holes, or just riding up into the foothills alone, headed nowhere in particular.

But he'd have to wait until later in the week for that when he, Colton, Lily, and the hands would be driving the cattle up to their summer pastures.

Lately it seemed he managed to escape his mountain of paperwork less and less. He missed the outdoors, not only the openness and beauty of it, but the rugged physical work that made his muscles burn and ache, that connected him to the toughness of this land. He missed the challenge of riding through frozen winter snow that flowed in gleaming ice-blue drifts, and the warmth of summer sun on his neck and back, and spring mountain breezes slapping at his face, smelling of sage and freedom.

Well, today he was getting a little bit of a break. Even if it was only driving out to the cabin.

The last place he wanted to be.

So why, he wondered darkly, had he told Erinn Winters he'd meet her there?

Because it's as good an excuse as any to get away from the fax and the computer, he told himself as, windows down, he sped past pastures dotted with cattle and freshly branded calves. He turned his silver Explorer toward Black Bear Road and the cabin he had built, with Culp's help, before his marriage to Carly.

His frown deepened as he neared the place.

Erinn Winters had sounded pretty desperate. Still, there was no way he was going to rent the cabin to her. He'd simply found it impossible to turn her down flat over the phone.

Not that it's going to be easier in person, he thought, remembering those dusky green eyes with the gold and black irises, and the full pillowy mouth whose lushness only emphasized her delicate features.

She was beautiful—stunning—no doubt about that. An intriguing combination of aloof femininity—at once both warm and cool, elegant and casual, direct and evasive.

And after the fight had ended last night, and he'd finished making sure Chris and Bonnie were okay, he'd wondered where she'd run off to. He'd guessed she'd been freaked out by the brawl.

That hadn't stopped him from thinking about her continuously on the drive home though. Remembering the sparks in her eyes when she'd ordered Wells to get out of her way. She'd actually sounded like she *could* have handled him herself—though Jase hadn't been about to stand by and let her have to.

Still, beautiful or not, Lily's friend or not, there wasn't an ice cube's chance in hell that she'd talk him into renting her the cabin. Once he let her walk through it and she saw its condition for herself, he had no doubt she'd lose her enthusiasm.

The cabin had been unoccupied for seven years now. *He* wasn't about to invest a dime fixing the place up and *she* didn't exactly look like the handy type. Problem solved.

He took a breath as he drove past the stand of alders and continued toward the end of the narrow blacktop road that led to the cabin. His knuckles tightened on the steering wheel as it came into view.

Set back nicely from the road, it was tucked away like a secret gem nestled amid leafy cottonwoods, wild-flowers, and the banks of Wolf Creek.

She was already here, he realized with a shock. Her Jeep was parked in front and she was standing on the porch, peering through the dust-caked windows, trying to see inside his former home.

She whirled at the sound of the tires crunching down the road and had the grace to look guilty.

"Sorry," she said as he got out of the Explorer and slammed the door. "I was early and I decided to look around. You don't mind, do you?"

"Suit yourself." She looked good, he noted in irritation. Too damned good. Those jeans hugged her curves and the white T-shirt clung to her in all the right places. He forced his gaze upward, focusing on her face. That distractingly alluring, vibrantly beautiful face.

"Let's be clear." Jase's tone was firm to the point of curtness. "I'm here as a courtesy, nothing more. This place isn't right for you. And I've no intention of renting it out."

Her chin jutted. "Then what are we doing here? Why waste my time?"

"It's a waste of my time as well. Take a look inside and you'll see what I mean."

She was angry, he saw, as he brushed past her and fit the key into the lock. He'd tried not to look at her too closely as he'd come up the porch steps, but he'd caught the gleam of silver hoop earrings dangling amid her dark sweep of hair and had noticed that her cheekbones were taut, her jaw clenched.

"Watch your step." Jase shoved the door wide.

Erinn swept past him, skirting the rugs rolled up in the middle of the floor, taking in the gloom and dust, the low-beamed, cobwebbed ceiling. She ignored the man standing in silence in the doorway and turned in a slow circle, studying the faded paint on the walls, the long, shuttered windows, the misshapen shape of sheet-draped furniture throughout the sprawling living room.

A glum and ghostly place, Erinn thought, wrinkling her nose against the smell of mustiness and disuse. There were boxes stacked high against the walls. And the knobby pine floors were so thick with dust she could barely see the grain.

Even the air feels sad, she thought. *Neglected.*

And yet . . .

"Nice place you have here," she murmured.

Jase's lip curled. "Yeah, right."

"I mean it."

She *did* mean it, he realized in surprise, suddenly noticing the intent expression on her face. As she walked forward, studying the wide dimensions of the living room, the generous dining area, and the kitchen with its black-and-cream-veined granite countertops and island, she seemed to be looking beyond the dusty floors and the dimness, the clutter, seeing something he couldn't.

"It's perfect. I'll take it."

Jase stared at her as if she'd just dropped in from Pluto with aluminum foil antennae attached to her ears. "It's filthy. It's a mess. And it's unavailable."

"There's nothing here that a bit of elbow grease won't cure," she argued. "I'll clean it, paint it, make it habitable—and pay you rent by the week. When I leave, it'll be in pristine condition and you'll be able to sell it, or rent it to someone else without having to lift a finger." Her eyes met his, challenging him.

"I'm offering you a great deal," she pointed out as he continued to gaze at her in disbelief. "I wouldn't pass it up if I were you."

"*You're* going to fix it up?"

"That's right. Haven't you ever seen a woman whip a house into shape before?"

"There's probably mouse droppings in the kitchen. There could be a squirrel living in the attic."

Erinn shrugged. "I happen to like mice. And squirrels. I write books about them. And I used to live in Queens, so it wouldn't be the first time I had to deal with mice, rats, or cockroaches. I'm a New Yorker, remember? We're a tough breed."

She didn't look tough, he thought. She looked delicate and beautiful and sexy as hell with the sunlight glinting across her cheeks, her eyes pools of green light. Still . . . her jaw was set, her full lips clamped together with determination.

At that moment, she looked resolute enough to take on a mountain lion with a stick and a chair.

Jase glowered at her—at the world in general. Then he glanced around the cabin, his eyes shuttering, blocking any hint of emotion. He'd built this place with such hope for the future. He'd had dreams back then. Young, stupid dreams.

Now standing here again, he loathed the sight of it. These walls, the dusty floor, the shrouded furniture, brought too much back to him. Here was where he and Carly had been newlyweds. Here was where they'd made love, and fought in the early months of their marriage, where they'd started their life together—and where they'd come apart. Over there in the dining nook, they'd eaten breakfast in stark, cold silence. Shouted at each other over dinner. Through that door to the master bedroom was where they'd tried to pretend everything was all right when they'd gone to bed and turned out the lights.

But after the first six months, nothing had been all right.

To hell with this.

He turned on his heel and stalked outside. Down the steps, toward his Explorer. Erinn followed on his heels and it was her voice at last that made him stop.

"I'm offering you a terrific opportunity—why are you walking away?" she demanded.

When he turned back, her hopes crumpled. If possible, Jase Fortune looked even more closed down, more distant than he had before. His hard, handsome face was devoid of emotion, his mouth a thin slash. If he felt hurt or angry at being here, the only sign he gave was in the coiled tension in his long, muscled body.

"I've got a better question. Why do you want this place so much?"

For a moment, there was silence. Erinn could hear the faint lapping of the creek behind the cabin. A sudden gust of wind whipped down from the mountain and blew her hair around her face.

"I need to stay in Wolf River for a while," she began. "And Ginny told me—"

"I know what Ginny told you. What I don't know is why you're *here*. Why you're staying. Why you can't just go back to where you came from."

In the hard depths of his eyes she saw implacability. He'd made up his mind—his answer was no. Unless she could persuade him otherwise.

"I'm a writer." It was the truth. Just not the whole truth, she reminded herself.

"So Lily said."

"And I have a deadline for completing my next book.

There's an editor breathing down my neck, pressuring me so that I can barely think. This is the worst case of writer's block I've ever had, and I can't write any-more—at least not in my apartment in New York. All that noise, the clamor and soot of the city..." she waved a hand, trying to do as good an impression of an ultra-sensitive artiste as she could muster.

"I thought if I could just spend the summer some-place quiet, someplace close to nature, in a setting that's beautiful and peaceful and pure—exactly like *this*..." Again she waved her hand, indicating the idyl-lic spot where they were standing, with the Beartooth Mountains rising in the distance. "That then I might find my creativity again. My *muse*. I could finish my book and, quite frankly, save myself from financial and professional ruin."

"Didn't you say you write about mice?"

"Mouse," she corrected him. "I write about a mouse. Her name is Devonshire."

"Ahuh." He stuck his thumbs in his pockets and eyed her skeptically, top to bottom.

Erinn stared right back, gazing at him with what she hoped was touching and heartfelt appeal.

"And you can't save yourself from financial and pro-fessional ruin in Crystalville?"

"No. Not after I've seen *this* place. It's perfect. It's exactly what I need. I can write again here, I *feel* it."

I feel it too, Jase thought. *I feel a load of bull tossed at my feet. I'm standing knee deep in it.*

But for some reason, his mood had lightened, and even though he was less than twenty feet from the door of the cabin where he'd gone through hell, he didn't feel the tight anger binding across his chest anymore.

He was studying Erinn Winter's luscious hopeful face, staring into those innocently sexy green eyes and he had to fight to keep from chuckling.

She was good, all right. Sophisticated, outwardly angelic, and smart as a whip.

And he wanted her.

The thought came out of nowhere. Deep and powerful. For an instant he'd almost imagined the taste of her, sweet as a peach. The way she'd feel against him, beneath him, right on this grass. The softness of her skin against his . . .

Jase caught himself, drew in a breath, and banished that train of thought fast. *Get the hell out of here. Steer clear of this woman.*

Frowning, he unclipped the key to the cabin from his key ring. He held it in his fist for a moment, weighing whether he should go to the creek and toss it in. Instead he tossed it to her. She caught it nimbly, with a delighted grin.

"Don't complain to me about leaks, bugs, or broken anything that needs repair," he warned grimly.

"I wouldn't think of it." A smile was washing across her face, and he cursed himself for having agreed to let her stay.

It's done, he told himself. Get out of here. *Now.*

Instead he found himself walking toward her before he even realized it. Wariness entered her eyes at his approach, and he felt a stab of satisfaction. He saw her will herself not to take a step back the closer he advanced.

So he didn't stop until he was close enough to see the quiver of her mouth. To feel the heat of her body. To smell the fresh wildflower scent of her hair as she tipped her head back and met his eyes.

"One more thing," he said coolly, ordering himself not to get lost in the depths of her eyes. To get out before he got sucked in.

"Ye . . . es?"

Jase reached up, tucked a wayward strand of silky dark hair behind her ear. Heard her soft intake of breath at the touch and felt heat jolt through him. He fought the sudden, purely male impulse to pull her into his arms and taste those full pink lips of hers for real, and instead, dropped his hand to his side so he wouldn't give in to temptation.

"I want two hundred dollars a week," he grated out. "Payable on Monday mornings before noon. And a security deposit—one month in advance."

"Of course. Provided I can move in today." She refused to step back. Her gaze locked with his. "I assume that's not a problem."

"As far as I'm concerned, you can move in whenever the hell you want." A muscle clenched in his jaw. "We're done here."

"Oh yes, we're done."

But still, he lingered a moment longer, lost in those calm, steady green eyes, in the rigidity with which she held her shoulders—until he became aware that there was absolutely nothing left to say.

Scowling, Jase wheeled away from her and stalked back to his car.

He didn't allow himself to turn around, to glance back at her standing at the base of the porch.

He knew she was smiling.

And why not? She'd gotten exactly what she wanted. She was going to be living in his cabin. Showering in his glass-enclosed stall. Sleeping in his bed.

Now all he had to do was stop picturing her naked in his and Carly's cabin and get her the hell out of his head.

Chapter Ten

LeeAnn Culpepper sorted through the bottles of nail polish on the shelf of the Glam Gal Beauty Salon searching for the perfect shade of red.

Her outfit for the barn dance at the Hanging J ranch that night was already spread across her bed—the blood-red dress she'd bought in Billings, cut down to *there,* red strappy heels, and the dangling rhinestone and CZ earrings Donnie had given her last Christmas. She was going to knock Jase Fortune's socks off tonight.

And when he saw her dancing real slow with Frank Wells . . .

LeeAnn smiled to herself. Jase was going to realize just how much he'd lost. How much he missed her. He'd be sorry he'd dumped her—damned sorry.

"You decide yet, LeeAnn?" Marge Dale, fifty-two-year-old owner of the Glam Gal, peered over her shoulder. "That one's real nice." She pointed a stubby, unpolished fingernail at the Revlon bottle in LeeAnn's hand. "We'd better get started, honey—I've got two blow-drys and another manicure coming in soon. Everyone's getting prettied up for the dance."

LeeAnn scooped up the crimson-red polish next to the tomato-red one Marge liked. "This goes better with my dress," she said as she sailed toward Marge's station.

Marge's daughter, Betsy, was unrolling curlers from Georgia Weeks's thinning gray hair, and Holt Samson's wife, Carolyn, was getting auburn highlights painted on her brown strands. She was the hostess tonight and therefore the center of attention.

All the women in the salon were chatting with her, excitedly discussing what they were wearing, what dish they were bringing, and whether the rain predicted for later in the day would hold off.

All except for LeeAnn. She was thinking. Thinking about Jase.

She knew she'd played it all wrong with him. Everything had been going great until two months ago when she'd opened her big mouth. They'd been friends—friends who laughed together, drank together, slept together—whenever they both felt like it.

And then she'd blown everything to bits.

She watched Marge layer on the deep red polish, wishing she could go back in time to that last night she and Jase had spent together.

They'd gone to the Redrock for pizza and beer, tossed some darts, hung out with Culp and Stitch and a few of the other Fortune boys. And then the two of them had walked back through town to her place—the small two-bedroom house on River Street she'd bought five years ago with her second ex-husband's money after the jerk left her for a washed-up country singer.

She and Jase had shared a bottle of wine, then gone

at it on the sofa. Eventually they'd made it to the bedroom and finally exhausted, they'd started drifting off around 2 a.m.

LeeAnn had been certain he planned to stay the night.

Which was when she'd made the biggest mistake of her life—next to marrying those two jerks she'd walked down the aisle with.

She'd stroked his muscular arm with her finger, nestled closer against his chest, and told him just as he was falling asleep that they should do this on a more regular basis. That she liked when he stayed with her all night long and that she missed him whenever weeks went by and they didn't see each other.

That's all it took.

Jase had sat up, sexy as all-get-out with his wide bare chest and his hair all rumpled and adorable, and that gorgeous six-pack that always made her want to touch him. He was staring at her, looking all serious and worried, as if she'd just told him she was pregnant or something.

He'd stared her straight in the eye and asked flat-out if she was starting to want more than friendship from him. If she'd changed her mind about that little pact they'd made when they started hanging out together: "just friends and no complications."

She'd denied it, but it was too late. She'd scared him off, just like that. The richest, sexiest, and most decent man she'd ever known, and she'd screwed it all up.

The truth was she *had* started falling for him. He treated her right, and he was hands-down the best lover she'd ever had.

They'd had a damned fine thing going until she started daydreaming, giving herself ideas. And Culp, damn it, had encouraged her.

She'd started spending all her time imagining what it would be like if she became Mrs. Jase Fortune, moving into that enormous ranch house with Jase, being Clay Fortune's daughter-in-law, and most of all, becoming the mother of the next Fortune heir.

"There now, how do they look?" Marge asked, capping the bottle of polish as LeeAnn gazed down at her brilliant red nails.

"Great, Marge. I'll just sit a few minutes until they dry before I go back to work."

She gave it fifteen minutes, then left for Enos's Hardware, where she clerked five days a week and did the books once a month. She heard her name called before she'd gone ten steps.

"LeeAnn, hold on! Where's the fire, sis?"

Culp jogged up beside her, his spurs jangling. LeeAnn loved her brother, but she didn't want to listen to him lecture her about Jase again.

"I gotta get back to work, Donnie. You going to the dance tonight?"

"Course I am." He fell into step beside her as she hurried toward the hardware store. "I'm not on the schedule for patrol tonight so I've got the whole evening free. I think after I've had my fill of dancing I might just head to Butte, play me some cards."

"Back at the Lucky Pony again? You winning or losing these days?"

"Winning." He grinned wide. "And there's some big players comin' in from Reno for a special game. High stakes and all. The thing is, I don't get my pay until next Friday, and I'm a little short. Any chance you can loan me five hundred?"

"Five hundred dollars?" LeeAnn stopped dead and looked at him. "Who the hell are you sitting down with at the table, Donald Trump?"

He threw back his head and laughed. "Come on, LeeAnn, I'm going to win big tonight, I can feel it. Just the same way I felt before I won the hold 'em championship. I'll pay you back tomorrow."

"I don't happen to have a spare five hundred in my wallet, Donnie." She crossed the street toward Enos's. He matched her step for step.

"Two hundred then. You still keep cash in your medicine cabinet, don't you? Come on, LeeAnn, cut me a break here."

"Donnie—"

"I'll pay you back tomorrow, no sweat. And you know, it's all your fault I have to borrow from you. If you'd played *your* cards right with Jase, neither of us would ever have had to worry about money again."

"Damn it, Donnie, I don't need your crap." She whirled to face him, her small pointed face tight with anger.

To her horror, she realized that her voice had quavered over the last word. She could have kicked herself—and then Donnie. She saw him staring at her, his eyes all worried, and she could only hope he couldn't see the unshed tears she felt burning inside her eyelids.

"Damn it, LeeAnn. Jase really hurt you, didn't he?" Donnie muttered in dismay.

"It's just that I thought we were good together," she

said tightly. "And I thought he felt the same. Stupid me, right? Talk about never learning—"

"It's not your fault. Jase doesn't know what he's missing. You'd be perfect for him." Donnie squeezed her shoulder. "You're nothing like Carly, you'd never run off and cheat on him. He'd be damned happy with you if he'd only—"

"Donnie, don't start. I gotta go back to work." LeeAnn paused outside of Enos's Hardware, and drew her small frame up as tall as she could. "It doesn't matter anyway, because I've moved on."

"Yeah, I've noticed. Frank Wells. That your idea of moving on, LeeAnn?"

"Why not? He's working for Holt Samson now. He's as good as anyone else around here."

"That doesn't exactly make him Prince Charming. Or Jase Fortune."

"True, but . . ." She flicked her brother a rueful smile. "He hates Jase's guts and vice versa. I know it's gotta bug Jase that I'm seeing Wells, so . . . it's kinda fun." She gave a mirthless chuckle and a shrug. "For a little while anyway."

"LeeAnn, what about that two hundred? You got it or not?" he asked as she opened the door of the hardware store and Enos glanced at them from behind the counter.

"There's one-hundred fifty in the medicine cabinet—inside the empty Vaseline jar," she said resignedly. "But you'd better only take a hundred. And I want it back tomorrow," she added, as he leaned down, pecked her on the cheek, then grinning, took off back the way they'd come.

"See you tonight!" Donnie yelled over his shoulder right before she closed the door.

LeeAnn walked behind the counter and took over cash register duty so Enos could head to Ginny's for lunch.

She knew it wasn't nice to try to get Jase all riled up by fawning over a loser like Frank Wells, but it was going to feel pretty damned good.

She might not get him between the sheets ever again, but she could sure as hell use Frank Wells to get under his skin.

And at thirty, with two bad marriages under her belt, and now one big fat failed seduction, she'd take whatever small pleasures in life she could get.

Chapter Eleven

Erinn was perched on a ladder sweeping a sunny shade of golden yellow paint down the living room wall when she heard a car approaching the cabin.

She descended quickly, set the brush across the lid of the paint can, and hurried to the window as Lily Fortune ran lightly up the porch steps.

"I wanted to make sure you're all right," she said as Erinn opened the door. "I've been calling and calling and you haven't answered your cell."

"Oh. Sorry, I guess I forgot to charge it." Chagrined, Erinn shook her head. "I've been working nonstop for the past three days, ever since I moved in. And I didn't really expect anyone to call me—"

"Look at this!" Lily exclaimed, gazing with pleasure around the cabin. "I love what you've done. The place looks wonderful."

"It's coming along." Erinn turned and gazed around critically. There was still a great deal to be done, but she had to admit, the cabin's interior looked vastly better than it had when she'd first moved in.

She'd spent two solid days sweeping, scrubbing and

mopping, lifting all the covers off the furniture, dusting the lamps, shaking out the rugs, washing curtains. She still had to paint the bedrooms and the adjoining master bath, but she'd started on the hallway and living room and already the cabin looked transformed.

Its windows glittered spotlessly in the late afternoon sunlight, the walls glowed with warmth and soft color, and the sheer blue curtains that had been thick with gray dust had been shaken outside, then washed and pressed in the small laundry room behind the kitchen. Now they looked fresh as springtime, and so did the living room—at least, the areas she'd worked on.

Next she planned to tackle Devon's room. She intended to paint it a peaceful cerulean blue.

She'd leave the third bedroom for last—she and Devon wouldn't need it. She'd get to it before they went back to New York though, so that she could keep her word to Jase Fortune and leave the cabin ready to be rented or sold. Right now she was focused on making the place not only habitable, but inviting, so Devon would be unable to resist staying once she finally agreed to come here.

"Can I get you something? Iced tea? A Coke?" Erinn asked as Lily plopped down on the cream and rose chintz sofa that had been hidden beneath opaque covers.

"No, thanks—I was just trying to reach you to find out if you'd like to stop by the day-care center next week and read to the kids. Jase told me you were moving into the cabin," Lily explained, "and I figured you'd be busy for at least a week getting settled in, but . . ."

She glanced around again at the gleaming pine floor,

the rugs scattered artfully here and there, the cheerily fresh walls, and the pots and pans Erinn had hung on hooks in the kitchen. "I can see you've made quick work of it. How'd you do it anyway?" the girl asked, leaning back and studying Erinn curiously.

"Do what? The cleaning? There were all kinds of cleansers in the laundry room. I found the ladder in the shed out back, and bought paint at Enos's Hardware—"

"No." Lily grinned. "I meant, how did you talk Jase into renting you his place?"

"Oh. That."

Lily chuckled. "Yes, *that*. My brother's quite the stubborn one."

"You think?"

"I'm serious. It's not easy to get him to change his mind about something once he's made it up. He must like you," she remarked. Suddenly, a speculative gleam flickered in her eyes and she leaned forward.

"Do you like *him*?"

"Lily, I hardly know him."

"He can be a little curt," the girl went on as if she hadn't spoken. "Especially when he has a lot on his mind. But Jase is really kind," she added. "He's a wonderful brother—"

"I'm sure he is." Erinn changed the subject. "How about Tuesday? I could read to the children Tuesday afternoon. Would that work?"

"Perfectly." Lily still had that gleam in her eye. "Are you going to the barn dance tonight?" she asked suddenly.

"What's a barn dance?"

"It's a dance that takes place...in a barn." Lily

giggled. "We have them usually every month over the summer. There's going to be a big one at Fortune's Way on the Fourth of July. Tonight Holt and Carolyn Samson are holding one at their Hanging J ranch. There'll be tons of food, soft drinks, beer, music, dancing, of course..."

She fixed her sparkling blue gaze on Erinn. "You're coming with me tonight!"

"Sorry, I can't." Erinn shook her head. "For one thing, I haven't been invited. And for another—"

"I'm inviting you—as my guest. My dad's going to miss it. He's still at the cattlemen's convention, so you can come in his place." She beamed at Erinn. "Better get going—I'll pick you up in an hour."

"An hour? Lily, I have to finish painting this room and then start on the bedrooms. Don't worry about me—go home and get ready. I'll just zap myself some frozen pizza, and maybe I'll even get some writing done—"

"Oh, come on, think about it," Lily coaxed. "You're going to be in Wolf River awhile, aren't you? Don't you want to meet some people other than Ginny and me and my family?"

"It never even occurred to me." It was Erinn's turn to grin. "I'm a writer, Lily. I'm here to work. Besides, most writers are loners by nature."

"Then why not compromise?" Lily suggested, springing up from the sofa. "Come to the Samsons' for a little while, then you can leave—go home to paint or write, whatever you want. None of us are staying late either," she added. "Tomorrow we have to be up and moving at dawn. We're driving our cattle to higher summer pasture and it's going to be a long day. So you won't be the only one leaving early. And I can guarantee you that Holt Samson's barbecued steak is going to taste a whole lot better than microwave pizza.

"Besides," Lily added, "the Hanging J isn't all that far from here. I'll come by and show you the way and you can follow in your car and leave whenever you're ready. You know, Ginny will be there and Colton and *Jase*—"

But Erinn barely heard this. Lily had just said something that triggered a memory—*the Hanging J ranch.* She'd heard of it before.

Cordovan mentioned it, she realized suddenly. He'd told her that the Wheeler brothers were ranch hands at the Hanging J.

"Do ranch hands usually attend their boss's barn dances?" she asked Lily.

"Sure." Lily looked curious. "Is there a particular ranch hand you're hoping to see?"

No. I'm hoping to see my sister, Erinn thought with a tiny surge of excitement.

But she shook her head and walked Lily to the door. "I don't really know any ranch hands except for Culp," she said truthfully. "But maybe you're right. It would be fun to get out for a little while. What time should I be ready?"

An hour later the ladder was still in the living room, and the wall was still only half-painted, but Erinn had showered, shampooed her hair, and slipped on black linen pants, a silky ice-pink camisole, and wedge sandals. She was swiping on rose-pink lip gloss when she heard a horn toot and hurried outside.

To her surprise, Lily was the driver and sole passenger of the red SUV gleaming in the moonlight.

"Jase had some work to finish up, but he'll get there in time for supper," Lily explained. "Colton drove with some friends. You're welcome to ride along with me unless you still plan to cut out really early."

"I might." Erinn had already decided that if Hank and Mick Wheeler were at the barn dance, but Devon wasn't, she'd leave immediately and seek her sister out at the Wheeler place. It would be the perfect opportunity to see Devon alone, and to let her know that Erinn had found a place to live in Wolf River—that she wasn't leaving, and that Devon was welcome to join her—for a day, a week, or as long as she wanted to stay.

She climbed into the Jeep and began to follow Lily's SUV through the valley. This time she paid attention to the roads and the turns. It took only about ten minutes until they reached the bluff where the Hanging J ranch looked out onto another wide sloping section of the valley. An alpine lake glimmered far in the distance.

The long driveway leading to the ranch was packed with pickups and SUVs. Lanterns with colored lights were strung around the porch, the barn, and the sturdy two-story ranch house.

There were people milling everywhere, chattering and laughing. In the peach-gold haze of gently falling dusk Erinn could smell the smoke of the barbecue pit mixed with the aroma of grilled meat. There were coolers lined up inside the barn, and a boom box perched on a chair right outside it. Country music blared through the night.

Erinn bit her lip. It wouldn't be easy spotting Devon in this throng. But if her sister was here, she'd find her.

Mick Wheeler won't be hard to miss, she thought. Her gaze was already sweeping the crowded grounds as Lily, dressed in a white lace top and denim skirt, hopped down from the SUV and joined her.

Somehow, without even realizing it, she found herself pulled in. The crowd milled and she became one of them. Meeting first Holt Samson and his wife, Carolyn, then their married daughter and son-in-law, then their son, Kevin, the town vet—a chunky, good-natured young man in his late twenties who handed Erinn a beer and offered to introduce her around.

Lily was quickly surrounded by a boisterous group of college-age friends, Erinn noticed, but Kevin Samson gallantly escorted her into the massive barn, where a table had been set up along the walls with bowls of chili, chips and salsa, and a cavernous tray of cut-up veggies and spinach dip. There were plates and flatware, buckets of ice, and at least fifty cans of beer and soda stacked at the ends of the table.

"These here are just the appetizers," Kevin told her as she surveyed the array of food. "My mom's chili is the best in the county, but you might want to save some room for the main course. There's a whole lot more food out back." His eyes twinkled and Erinn did her best to twinkle back.

But her gaze skirted the crowd already dancing to a rollicking Toby Keith tune in the barn. There was no sign of Devon, Hank, or Mick in here—perhaps they were out back.

"Hey, no fair monopolizing the newest pretty lady in

town." Culp clapped Kevin on the shoulder and
grinned down at Erinn. His reddish hair was combed
neatly, his black cotton shirt was freshly pressed, and
his gaze was warm on hers. "How about a dance,
ma'am?" he asked formally.

"How about you butt out, Culpepper," Kevin said
good-naturedly. "You'll have to wait your turn. I already
asked the lady for the first dance, didn't I, Erinn?" An
appealing grin had spread across his face and Erinn
found herself smiling back.

"I believe you did," she agreed, and then Kevin was
tucking her arm into his and leading her out onto the
dance floor.

"Promise me the next one then!" Culp called, un-
daunted.

It wasn't until after she'd sat down to supper in the
lantern-lit backyard, wedged at a long table between
Ginny and Kevin, with Culp and Rawley, the foreman
at Fortune's Way, across from her, that Erinn spotted
Hank.

She froze.

He was moving through the buffet line, heaping
steak, ribs, home fries, and green bean casserole onto
his plate—and then, as she peered behind him, there
was Devon.

Erinn's pulse leaped. Devon hadn't spotted her yet.
She was looking over the array of food, reaching for a
plate. She wore her ripped jeans, Erinn saw, wondering
if they were the only pair of pants she owned, but instead of a faded tee or tank she was wearing a pink shirt
with short sleeves. Her blonde hair had been slicked
into a ponytail high on her head, accentuating her

young face, and for a moment Erinn almost thought she caught a glimmer of the innocent child her sister had once been.

Pain and guilt squeezed through her. She set down her fork, trying to decide what to do. Devon hadn't spotted her yet and Erinn was trying to resist the overpowering urge to go to her immediately.

"Don't tell me you're full already, honey. Hope you saved room for dessert," Ginny said, observing Erinn's barely touched plate. "I brought along two apple pies, a blueberry, and a pecan. You can take your pick."

"That's going to be a tough choice," Erinn said, but she kept glancing over at Devon, watching her move down the line.

Ginny followed her gaze, squinting at the girl and at Hank Wheeler in front of her, then she threw Erinn a thoughtful glance.

"Oh, damn, will you look at that?" Culp muttered in a low tone. Erinn had never heard him sound so disgusted, and she turned to look in the direction he was staring.

The auburn-haired woman she'd seen in the Saddleback had just sauntered to the end of the buffet line with Frank Wells. He had his arm around her waist, holding her close against his side, and the woman's narrow face was tilted up at him. She was laughing at something he'd said.

"What's LeeAnn thinking, spending so much time with Wells?" Rawley asked with a frown between mouthfuls of steak.

"She's *not* thinking," Culp grumbled. "She's looking for trouble."

"Well, I'd steer her away from Wells if I were you, Culp." Kevin Samson lifted a forkful of green beans to his mouth. "The man has a mean streak a mile wide. My dad's reprimanded him a dozen times about the rough way he handles the horses. And he's got a bad attitude about showing up every day for work. If he doesn't straighten up real quick, my old man's going to fire him just like Jase did."

Culp watched darkly as LeeAnn slanted an openly provocative smile up at Wells. "Don't you think I've been *trying* to warn her away from him? Lord knows, she's not a woman who takes kindly to advice."

"My guess is she's just on the rebound from Jase and bein' reckless," Ginny put in comfortingly. "I'd guess LeeAnn is smart enough not to get in too deep with Wells. At least I hope she is."

"Jase Fortune and...your sister...were a couple?" Erinn asked Culp before she could stop herself. When he nodded, she found herself studying the red-haired woman, trying to imagine her with Jase Fortune. And doing her best to ignore the sudden uncomfortable knot tightening in her stomach.

"For a while they were seeing each other." Culp chugged his beer. "Jase broke it off a few months back. It hurt LeeAnn pretty bad."

He scowled as Wells pulled out a chair for his sister, then leered down the front of her low-cut red dress as she took a seat.

"If that bastard doesn't quit looking at her like that—" Culp threw down his napkin and stood up.

"Culp, no!" Ginny grabbed his arm across the table

and held on. "LeeAnn's a grown woman and she won't appreciate you butting into her business."

"She's right, Culp." Kevin regarded the ranch hand sympathetically. "LeeAnn's smart. She'll see Wells for what he is sooner or later."

But Erinn was alarmed by the anger still suffusing Culp's face. And remembering Frank Wells's obnoxious behavior at the Redrock the other night, she couldn't blame him for his concern.

"How about that dance?" she suggested quickly, hoping to defuse the situation. "Are you ready to make good on your offer?"

As he glanced at her, the rigid line of his jaw slowly relaxed. He managed a smile. "Ready, able, and willing. Let's do it, lady."

As they made their way toward the space cleared for dancing, Erinn saw Jase Fortune. He had just reached the yard and stopped in the shadows, beyond the colored lights, his gaze fixed on her as she walked beside Culp. He looked more handsome, lean, and dangerous than ever in the faint light that touched him.

Erinn felt her heartbeat quicken and swiftly looked away. She tried to concentrate on the music booming from the CD player as Culp's arm draped around her waist. But she'd seen in that brief instant the tautness in Jase's face, the hard gleam in his eyes.

She forced herself to concentrate on the dance, on making light conversation with Culp, and refused to let herself look back in Jase's direction.

By the time the dance ended, there was no sign of him.

Which suits me just fine, she told herself as Culp

headed to the cooler for another beer. *How could I possibly enjoy myself with my landlord looking on?*

Then she spotted him, deep in conversation with two young women, neither of whom could be a minute over twenty-two. One was slim and brunette, dressed in a black miniskirt with a low-cut green top, the other wore jeans and a silver-gray sweater that glinted in the lights. Whatever she'd said to Jase had just caused him to throw back his head and roar with laughter.

Erinn spun away. She strode across the backyard, searching for Devon, pushing away the image of Jase with those other women. Her chest felt tight. With anger? Jealousy?

She gritted her teeth, annoyed with herself and her reaction. *Find Devon,* she thought irritably. Her gaze skimmed across everyone seated at the various long tables, and there was her sister, seated beside Hank at the end of a table farthest from the barn. Mick Wheeler was nowhere in sight.

Hope flickered inside her as she saw that Devon was staring right at her. The girl's expression was akin to a startled deer watching a wolf from across a stream. Erinn didn't know how long Devon had been peering at her, but she was suddenly encouraged by that riveted gaze and moved quickly toward her.

Hank didn't notice her until she paused beside Devon's chair.

But Erinn wasn't even looking at him. She was wondering why Devon suddenly looked deathly pale.

"Why are you still here?" her sister gasped. "I thought you left days ago."

"I told you, Devon, I'm not leaving you again. You can't get rid of me."

"You've been staying at the Watering Hole all this time?" Devon's voice was so low Erinn had to strain to hear it.

"Actually, I've rented a cabin for the summer. It's quite nice and I think you'd like it." Erinn smiled. "You're welcome to come see it anytime you want. And we can talk—as much or as little as you prefer."

To Erinn's dismay, Devon didn't look the least bit happy—she looked scared. She was staring at Erinn incredulously, as if she couldn't believe what she'd heard.

Hank believed it though. He shoved back his chair and surged to his feet, advancing on Erinn. "How many times do I have to tell you—stay away from us!"

"Wait a minute, Hank. Don't . . . yell at her—"

"Shut up, Dev—Mick's looking this way," the boy bit out. "Damn it, he's coming over here. *Get rid of her.*"

Erinn saw the fear in Devon's eyes as she turned her head and saw Mick Wheeler bearing down on them, a beer can clenched in his fist.

"You'd . . . better go, Tiffany," the girl said shakily. *"Now—"*

Before Erinn could tell Devon that Mick Wheeler wasn't about to scare her off, he barreled up to them, his mean small eyes fixing on her with unmistakable menace.

"Didn't I tell you to stay away from us?"

"I don't need your permission to talk to my sister."

"She doesn't want nothin' to do with you—why don't you get that?" Wheeler took a step closer. "Get outta here. Right now."

"Mick, it's all right," Devon said quickly. "She just said hi. You don't have to yell—"

"Now you're telling me what to do?" He turned on her, his scowl spreading across his heavy face, then he wheeled toward his brother. "What'd I tell you? I knew she was trouble!"

"Shut up, Mick, just shut up," Hank said furiously. People were starting to glance their way. He grabbed Devon's hand and pulled her from the chair. "Come on, Dev, let's see what's for dessert," he muttered.

She let him pull her away, glancing back once at Erinn before Hank dragged her around the side of the house.

Erinn struggled to control her frustration. It had almost seemed as if Devon *wanted* to talk to her until Mick Wheeler interfered. *Screw him.* She started after them, but Mick shot out one beefy arm and snagged her wrist in an iron grip.

"Listen, lady, I'm warning you for the last time."

Erinn tried to wrench free, but his fingers only dug in harder. Pain shot through her arm.

"Let me *go*!" she gasped. His grip tightened and she winced, biting her lip to keep from crying out.

"You stay away from us, you got that? You come around to my place and hassle us again and you're gonna be real sorry."

Erinn suddenly stepped closer and stomped down on his foot. Mick groaned in pain and staggered back a step, releasing her. Rage and pain lit like dynamite in his eyes.

"You bitch," he rasped. He lunged toward her, but

even as he did so, a man's fist shot out, connecting with Mick's jaw.

Wheeler crashed into a table.

Erinn whirled to see Jase standing beside her, those dangerous blue eyes of his burning cold with fury.

She rubbed the raw skin where Wheeler's fingers had clamped, aware that everyone in the Samson backyard was now staring at the three of them. And that Jase Fortune had once again jumped to her aid.

"It's all right." She swallowed, her heart still racing, as Mick pushed away from the table and eyed Jase. "Really," she told Jase quickly. "Let's just—"

"I've a question for you, Wheeler."

Jase was ignoring her. And somehow he had positioned himself so that he stood between her and Mick. All his attention was focused on the other man, who was his equal in height. But Mick was heavier, built like a thick-jawed bull, while Jase had a whipcord toughness in his broad-shouldered physique.

"Tell me something, Wheeler—have you been hunting on my land?"

"What the hell are you talking about?" Mick's hands were clenched into fists as he moved toward Jase.

"I'm asking you if you've been picking off my cattle."

"You must be hittin' the bottle, Fortune. What would I want to shoot your cattle for?"

"Why don't you tell me?"

An odd hush had spread over the crowd. Every person in the backyard was watching, listening.

LeeAnn was staring at Jase, and Frank Wells had leaned forward in his chair as if trying to hear every word. But while she looked uneasy, anger tightened Wells's features.

Suddenly a man in his fifties strode forward with an air of authority. He wore a badge and a gray sheriff's uniform.

At the same time Colton and Culp rushed forward from opposite sides of the yard, lining up on either side of Jase.

"Let's cool this down a mite, boys," the man with the badge suggested.

Jase didn't even glance at him. At any of them. His gaze was locked on Wheeler's flushed face.

"I'm just waiting for an answer, Sheriff. I asked Wheeler if he shot my cattle and so far, he hasn't said no."

"To hell with you!" Wheeler exploded. "Damn it, I didn't shoot nobody's cattle, not even yours. And if I did, so what? You've got plenty more, don't you, Fortune? What's a half dozen head or even a *hundred* head to a bigshot cattleman like you?"

Without warning, Mick swung a fist at Jase's face. Erinn gasped, but somehow Jase moved like lightning, blocking the punch, then delivering a sickening thwack straight into the other man's gut. Mick doubled over, fighting for breath as the air was knocked from his lungs.

Erinn was suddenly shoved aside by Hank Wheeler diving into the fray. But before he could reach Jase, Culp grabbed the boy by the shoulder, spun him around, and knocked him into a table with a right hook that caught him in the jaw.

"Stay out of it!" Colton warned Hank as the boy

pushed himself away from the table, one hand to his jaw. But Hank swore and tried to lunge past him. This time it was Colton who blocked his path and shoved the boy to the ground.

Erinn stood frozen, her heart thundering with fear as Mick Wheeler charged at Jase full force. To her astonishment, Jase merely stood his ground, then at the last second, punched the big man square in the nose. Blood spurted and Wheeler grunted in pain, but before he could react, Jase landed another blow to his midsection. Wheeler crashed to the grass, knocking over a chair and sprawling on his side as the onlookers gasped.

Before he could get up, the sheriff jumped between the two men.

"That's enough," he shouted, then glanced down at Wheeler. "Let it go, Wheeler, or I'll haul your butt into jail for assault."

Mick grunted. But rage spewed from his eyes as he pushed himself to his knees and glared up at Jase.

He staggered to his feet, scowling around the Samson yard at all the citizens of Wolf River eyeing him. At last his gaze shifted to Erinn, standing still as a sculpture only a few feet away.

"*You*. Stay away from my place, you hear?" he muttered.

Pressing a hand against his bloodied nose, he stomped away, Hank following, and Devon, paler than the moonlight, scurried alongside.

"It's all over, folks. Let's not let a little fisticuffs interfere with this nice dance," Sheriff Farley told the throng in his gravelly tone.

Holt Samson strode forward on the words. "Carolyn's got dessert waiting in the barn. Dig in, and let's get on with the dancing!"

Erinn realized she was trembling. She turned away, needing to escape for a moment, to compose herself, but instead she found Jase Fortune blocking her path.

He took one look at her face and took her arm with surprising gentleness. "Come on."

He led her to one of the farther corrals. The horses had been stabled for the night, and the rowdy sounds of the barn dance had receded. They were alone in the cool black darkness, a short distance from the sparkle of the lanterns. Only starlight lit her face as she leaned against the corral fence, and drew a deep calming breath.

"Are you all right?" Jase asked.

She nodded.

"Care to tell me what that was all about?"

Erinn forced herself to reply nonchalantly. "What are you referring to?"

"Mick Wheeler going after you, that's what I'm referring to." Jase looked formidable in the moonlight, his powerful arms folded across his chest. "Everyone heard him order you to stay away from that hovel of his he calls home. What I want to know is why he thinks you'd set foot there in the first place. It sounded to me like you'd been there before."

Chapter Twelve

The plaintive sounds of a country song filtered through the night as Erinn met Jase's eyes.

"It's a long story."

"I'm not going anywhere."

She looked away, studying the empty corral. "It's private."

"Then it stays just between us."

Her gaze swung back, searching his face. Was that concern she saw?

"Spill." His tone was firm—and also tinged with amusement. "Better do it quick or folks will think we're hooking up out here."

"And we wouldn't want that," Erinn muttered.

His eyes gleamed at her. But he said nothing, waiting for an answer. She took a breath and made her decision.

"I lied to you the other day about why I'm staying in Wolf River. About why I needed to rent your cabin. Don't get me wrong—I *do* need to finish writing my book—and it's true I hope to be able to concentrate better here. But that's not the real reason I'm staying."

"Now tell me something I don't already know."

"That girl who was with Mick and Hank Wheeler. Do you know who she is?"

Jase looked surprised. "Their cousin from Nevada, that's what Ginny told me. Devon something... Devon White, I think. She came to town with Hank awhile back after he'd visited relatives in Reno. Word was that his aunt and uncle kicked her out the day she turned eighteen. Now she cooks and cleans for Mick and Hank."

He frowned, not sure he liked where this was going. "What does she have to do with you renting my cabin?"

"She isn't their cousin." Her voice shook ever so slightly. "She's my sister. And I came to Wolf River to take her away from the Wheelers."

Erinn Winters was shivering in the nippy night air and there was no mistaking the pain shadowing her eyes. Jase fought the sudden impulse to wrap her in his arms, to hold her close—for warmth, for comfort, for... whatever she needed. He pushed the urge away.

"I think you'd better start from the beginning. How did your sister get mixed up with the—"

"There you two are!" Lily was hurrying toward them. "Taking a break from all the drama, I see." She hugged her brother, then turned to Erinn.

"Now the truth comes out. It wouldn't be a barn dance in Wolf River without some kind of a dustup. Last month a couple of liquored-up hands fought over who was going to get the last slice of Ginny's apple pie. It never takes much to set *some* people off. Especially Mick Wheeler—"

"Lily," Jase interrupted. "Not now. We're talking."

"I know, but—" Lily broke off. She glanced quickly back and forth between Erinn and Jase, and her eyes rounded.

"I *see*. Sorry. I didn't realize I was interrupt—"

"Lily," Jase said warningly, as she backed away, but his tone only caused her to burst into a wide grin.

"As you were, cowboy. Far be it from me to intrude." She winked at Erinn, then whirled and ran lightly back toward the lights and the music wafting from the barn.

Suddenly Erinn realized something. The dented blue pickup was nowhere in the Samson drive.

"They're gone," she gasped, fear jerking through her body. *Oh, God.* Once more Mick Wheeler was in a rage, furious that she'd spoken to Devon, that Jase had hit him—was he angry with Devon too?

She took off at a run for her Jeep, but Jase sprinted after her and headed her off. "Wait, Erinn, where are you going? If you're thinking of going back to the Wheeler place alone—"

"It's none of your business!" She darted around him. "Don't you understand? I have to get to her. He might hurt her—"

"That's not going to happen," Jase said sharply. "Come on, we'll take my rig. Yours is blocked in."

He was right. There was a line of cars parked in front of and behind the Jeep. Jase had come late and his Explorer was near the top of the long drive.

She raced beside him and slammed the passenger door shut as he started the engine.

Then they were roaring through the darkness, Erinn's fingernails digging into her palms as she silently prayed they wouldn't be too late.

Chapter Thirteen

Erinn clutched at the dashboard as the Explorer jolted down the backwoods roads.

"How did your sister end up living with the Wheelers?" Jase sounded ruthlessly calm despite the alarming speed with which they were taking one sharp turn after the other.

"I still don't know the answer to that myself." Erinn drew a ragged breath. "She ran away from home when she was fourteen. I didn't even know until recently. A private detective I hired found her last week—he showed me photos of her at the Wheeler cabin."

She gasped as a fox slunk across the road, caught in Jase's headlights, barely making it to the safety of the trees. "That's why I came to Wolf River—I drove out to the Wheeler place the same day you and I met in the Saddleback. But . . ."

She grimaced, and bit out the words. "She wouldn't talk to me, much less come with me. She . . . hates me. And I can't really blame her."

He glanced at her. "I doubt that. Don't you think it's

more likely she's just mad at you—mad at the world? Any idea why?"

"Oh, yes, lots of ideas. I deserted her when I was eighteen. I left her living in that house. With our father."

"What was so bad about that?" he asked with a frown.

"Everything." As Jase swung a quick concerned glance at her, she shook her head, bitterness in her tone. "He was a monster—but not in the way you might think."

"Enlighten me."

"He never laid a hand on us. Not with anger—and not with love." She gazed unseeingly ahead as the black trees whipped by and the Explorer jostled over a particularly rough patch of road. In her mind's eye, she saw Dane Stanton, dressed for tennis, telling her she couldn't attend her best friend's sweet-sixteen party that afternoon because she'd refused a date with the son of a business associate he wished to cultivate.

He'd then grounded her for the next two months.

"He was a cold, critical man," she said in a low tone. "And he always had to be in control—of everything. His business, his home, his family. My mother escaped..." She paused, closed her eyes, then opened them and forced herself to go on. "And so did I—eventually." She knew she sounded bitter, but she couldn't help it.

"I told Devon I'd come back for her, but I didn't. I mean, I did, but..." She swallowed hard. "It's my fault she ran away, my fault she's living with the Wheelers. And if anything happens to her—"

Erinn broke off, pressing her knuckles together. She'd already told him too much. Far too much. She, who was so private, so proud of her independence and her self-control, had just told Jase Fortune more than she'd ever told anyone about her past. But the guilt rushing through her was nearly overwhelming, especially as she remembered the threatening expression on Mick Wheeler's face when he'd turned on Devon at the barn dance.

"How much farther?" she asked, hugging her arms around herself as the knot of fear inside her tightened.

"Two miles," he said grimly.

They rounded a curve and accelerated—then suddenly Jase slammed on the brakes.

They both saw the carnage at the same time.

Erinn's breath whooshed out of her and cold terror slid through her veins. Fifty feet ahead, the blue pickup had smashed into a tree. Broken glass was everywhere, the front doors were open, and, in the headlights, as the Explorer shuddered to a stop, Erinn saw two bodies sprawled on the ground.

"Oh my God," she cried.

Wrenching open the door, she hurtled toward the wreck. Mick Wheeler was on the ground, blood pouring from a gash on his head, his eyes open and his breathing harsh. On the other side of the pickup, Hank lay facedown in the brush.

He wasn't moving.

Where's Devon? she thought frantically.

Then Erinn spotted her. She was still inside, in the back passenger seat, slumped forward. Erinn yanked open the door and panic filled her as she saw the blood, heard her sister's almost imperceptible moan.

"Devon!"

"Don't move her!" Jase ordered behind her as she reached toward her sister. She froze. Jase strode to her side, pocketing his cell phone.

"There's an ambulance on the way. Is she conscious?"

"I don't know." Erinn's voice cracked. She struggled for calm. She didn't know much about first aid, but she remembered hearing that you shouldn't move people who've been injured in an accident unless you knew what you were doing. Fortunately, Jase had remembered that before she did.

"Devon . . . honey, can you hear me? Are you okay?" Erinn had to struggle not to reach for her, to ease her back in the seat. She heard a low sound. Sobbing.

"Devon, hold on," she cried. "Help's coming. You're going to be all right. I'm here."

"Tiffany . . ."

Her heart leapt. "Yes, honey, what is it?"

"My head . . . hurts . . ."

"I know, baby, I know." Worry knifed through her but she kept her tone calm. "Hang on, sweetie. The ambulance will be here soon, and we'll get you to a doctor—"

"Hank. Is he . . ."

"He's right here. Don't you worry," Erinn said quickly.

Jase was kneeling beside the boy, checking his pulse. He looked grim as his eyes met Erinn's. "Out cold," he muttered. The wait was excruciating until they heard the scream of the ambulance in the night.

"There's the siren now, Devon. Can you hear it?" Erinn gently touched her sister's arm. "They'll be here any minute. Hang on, baby, just hang on."

It seemed forever before the ambulance screeched to a stop, lights whirling—before the EMS personnel had strapped Devon and Hank and Mick Wheeler into two separate vehicles—before they roared off, sirens screaming, toward the Wolf River Community Hospital.

Erinn and Jase followed in the Explorer, a heavy somber silence filling the space between them.

Jase let her off at the hospital entrance and went to park the car.

Erinn bolted inside, but was forced to wait, pacing, in the visitors' lounge as the doctors examined Devon.

When Jase came in, he took one look at her haunted face and steered her to a chair. "Come on, sit down before you pass out. How about some coffee?"

She shook her head. The lump in her throat was too thick and painful to allow her to swallow anything. This was her fault. Just like Devon running away from home. If she'd gone back after that last disastrous day, if she'd kept in touch with Devon as she'd promised, everything might have been different.

Maybe Devon wouldn't have been hurt, she wouldn't have been in a car wreck, she wouldn't have been living in a shack with the Wheelers ...

The ER doors swung open and a young black doctor with a weary face and five o'clock shadow walked out into the waiting room. He and Jase apparently knew each other and shook hands, then he introduced himself to Erinn as Dr. Coates.

"Your sister is in stable condition at the moment. She hit her head pretty hard against the back of the seat and she has a concussion."

As Erinn swallowed hard, he offered a reassuring smile. "None of her injuries are life-threatening. She has some contusions and bruises, and a sprained ankle. She'll probably be rather sore for several days. I'm going to keep her overnight and see about releasing her tomorrow."

"What about the Wheeler brothers, Marty? Mick didn't look so good."

"Yeah, he's in shock, but the guy's head is harder than a bowling ball," the doctor said drily. Then he caught himself, and flicked Erinn a half-smile. "That didn't sound very professional, did it? What I mean is, he's conscious, has no broken bones, no sign of concussion or cerebral contusion."

"Lucky bastard," Jase said under his breath.

Dr. Coates nodded. "He has a cut lip, a gash on his head, and a sore shoulder, that's it. Hank, though, that's a different story. The boy has two cracked ribs, some bad bruising, and a serious concussion. Do you know how long he was unconscious?"

As Jase and Erinn shook their heads, the doctor continued soberly. "He was incoherent when he woke up. We'll do a CT scan in the morning and keep him several days for observation. Do either of you know of any family members we should contact?"

"I'm not exactly on close terms with the Wheelers," Jase replied. "But Ginny would know if anyone does.

She knows pretty much everything about everyone in Wolf River."

"I'll give her a call in the morning." Marty Coates made a notation on a pad of paper, then turned back toward the ER.

"Doctor, can I see my sister now?" Erinn asked.

He turned back. "They're setting her up in a room as we speak—I'll have the nurse let you know when you can go in."

She waited until he'd returned to the ER before she shoved a hand through her hair. "You don't need to wait with me. I'm staying overnight, even if it's just catching a catnap down here. You've done enough—"

"Hold on a minute. They're going to give Devon something to help her sleep, so what's the point in your staying here? Tomorrow she'll probably be released and she'll need you then. Erinn, don't you think you should get some rest so you can take care of her when she goes home?"

It made sense. Erinn realized she wasn't thinking clearly. His last words in particular repeated themselves in her head.

When she goes home.

Devon would go home tomorrow . . . and not to the Wheeler shack. *She'll go to the cabin, with me.*

Hank would be in the hospital for the foreseeable future and there was no way Erinn was letting Devon go anywhere with Mick Wheeler ever again.

"You're right," she said slowly. "But you should still go ahead. Lily told me you're all going to be up at dawn, moving your cattle to a pasture tomorrow. I can just catch a few winks in one of these chairs . . ."

Her voice trailed off doubtfully as she stared at the two rows of padded folding chairs arranged in a circular arc around the small waiting area.

Jase shoved back his hat and his eyes bored directly into hers. "My father taught me never to leave a woman alone in a tenuous situation. So don't waste your breath arguing. Go check on your sister, and then I'll take you home."

She wanted to argue anyway, but she didn't have the strength at that moment. Besides, he was right. She'd need to be rested for Devon tomorrow.

"All right, you win. But . . . I owe you one."

She said the words as if the very notion of owing someone something, anything, was anathema to her.

A ghost of a smile touched his lips. "Damn straight. And don't think I'll let you forget it."

Suddenly, Erinn had the oddest urge to lean against him for a moment, to try to soak up some of that easy casual strength he seemed to exude so effortlessly. But of course she'd do no such thing.

She stiffened her back, and took a slight, deliberate step backward, then she heard someone speak her name.

"Ms. Winters? I'll take you to your sister now." A wide-hipped young nurse wearing white-soled shoes and a sympathetic smile beckoned her toward the elevator.

Jase watched her walk away, watched until the elevator doors closed, then folded his arms across his chest and leaned against the wall to wait.

———

A short time later—after Erinn had seen her sister, studied her asleep in a hospital bed, smoothed the hair back from her face, and left with Jase—a man got out of a Chevy truck parked in the far side of the hospital's parking lot and strolled inside.

He skirted the receptionist's desk, which was empty at the moment, and moved swiftly toward the elevator.

It didn't take him long to find the room he was looking for.

Slipping inside, he studied the burly bear of a man lying on his back, his eyes closed, his jaw swollen.

"You're damned lucky I don't shoot you right here and now," Frank Wells said softly.

Mick Wheeler's eyes flew open. As Wells moved to the side of the bed, a myriad of emotions crossed Wheeler's face. He couldn't tear his gaze from the gun Frank Wells was pointing straight at his chest.

"You have ten goddamned seconds to tell me the truth. I warned you about letting that little slut in your door, letting her find out *anything* about what we do," Wells hissed in a soft, feral tone.

The safety clicked off the gun.

"Now I need to know and you'd better tell me fast. What the hell does she have to do with that bitch who left here with Jase Fortune?"

Chapter Fourteen

Erinn awoke at dawn, all vestiges of sleep fleeing as she remembered the events of the previous night.

Devon was in the hospital—hurt, alone. And she had a million things to do before she brought her sister home.

Throwing aside the faded rose-and-blue quilt she'd found tucked inside an old hope chest in the spare bedroom, she sprang from the king-size bed. In the prelight of dawn she sprinted toward the bathroom and half an hour later, dressed in gray sweats and Reeboks, she gulped down coffee and popped a frozen bagel in the microwave, all the while mentally listing everything she needed to do.

First off was to call the hospital, see how Devon was doing. If all was well, she'd take the time to shop for groceries before picking Devon up. She needed to stock up on food—there was no way she'd go out and leave Devon alone to shop until the concussion was gone and her ankle was better. She'd go straight to the hospital from May's Grocery and bring both Devon and the groceries home.

Suddenly, she stopped short, setting her coffee cup down so hard it clanked against the maple table.

The *Jeep*. It was still at the Samson ranch.

Erinn shoved back her chair and reached for her cell phone on the counter. She wasn't going anywhere until she got her wheels back. Maybe Lily would give her a lift to the Hanging J.

No, she realized suddenly, dismay flooding her. Lily—and the rest of the Fortunes, except for Clay—were trailing cattle today to their summer pasture—whatever that meant.

She was stuck. And Devon was waiting—

Suddenly she heard a car rumbling down the drive. To her amazement, it was her Jeep fast approaching the cabin.

And Jase Fortune was behind the wheel, braking smoothly less than twenty feet from her door.

She seized her purse and tore through it frantically. Her keys were still inside. *How the hell?* . . .

"Don't think I'm not appreciative that you returned it to me, but how did you manage to start it?" she burst out, hurrying down the porch steps as faint opal light broke over the horizon. "The keys are still in my purse."

"Who needs keys when you have imagination?" Beneath his hat, she thought she saw amusement glimmering in his eyes.

"Imagination?"

"Not to mention technique." Jase shrugged. "I learned how to hot-wire any vehicle bigger than a tricycle when I was sixteen. It takes all of five seconds. Now you owe me three."

"Three what?"

"Three favors. You said last night you owed me one. I'm counting letting you have this cabin as two. How quickly we forget."

"It seems *you* haven't forgotten anything."

He eyed her speculatively. "Tell you what. I'll let you repay one of those debts with a cup of coffee. And a few more answers."

"It depends what the questions are," she said warily. "But if a cup of coffee will wipe away some of my debt, then fine. You know the way in."

She turned and went up the porch steps, feeling like a mess in her sweats and sneakers. Not that it mattered what she looked like, she told herself. Just because he was drop-dead handsome, and she'd seen the way all the women at the barn dance looked at him last night, didn't mean she had to try to impress him.

Her appearance had nothing to do with anything. *Nothing.* She could be wearing the ratty torn T-shirt she'd painted in yesterday and . . . and her old running shorts that had a mustard stain on them, and it wouldn't matter. She couldn't care less what Jase Fortune thought.

He had helped her last night, of course, and she appreciated that. But she certainly didn't need to dress up for the man.

"How do you like your coffee?" she asked, not looking back as she headed into the kitchen. "I have milk and sugar, but no cream, so if you—"

She broke off at the silence behind her, and turned. Jase was no longer following her. Or listening to her, she realized.

He was staring around the living room in astonishment, first at the still-unfinished wall that was three quarters painted. Then at the furniture she had rearranged, the windows shining like crystal in the light of the rising sun. He seemed to be eyeing the needlepoint pillows she'd found in the hope chest beneath the quilt she'd draped across the four-poster bed.

"I . . . I made some changes. You said it was all right to paint and everything," she reminded him quickly. For some reason, she felt defensive. "Those pillows . . . they were so pretty I thought they'd warm up the sofa, make the cabin look more homey . . ."

Her voice trailed off. "I hope you don't mind that I took some things out of the hope chest," she finished, dismayed as he continued to study the cabin in silence.

"The place looks great," Jase said slowly.

"Really?" Erinn was startled. His gaze met hers and settled there, his eyes more blue than ever in the natural sunlight.

"I haven't seen those pillows in a long time. My grandmother did the needlepoint. She made two pillows for each of us kids, and sewed a big quilt for us to use when we were ready to start our own families. But my ex-wife didn't like them—she thought they were too old-fashioned."

"I had no idea they were your grandmother's work. I just thought they were beautiful, and since they were in the hope chest—"

Jase interrupted her. "I like what you've done with the place," he said curtly. "Don't worry about it."

He saw her slim eyebrows lift at the curtness of his tone and was sorry for it. He wasn't angry, not in the least. He was actually relieved. The ghost of Carly, of their ruined marriage, no longer lived here . . . at least not in the living room or kitchen.

The bedroom might be a different story.

But this space not only looked different, it felt different too. More airy, open. It was a room he could breathe in.

His eyes lasered in on the woman who was watching him warily, wondering bitterly how she managed to look as sensuous in nondescript sweats as she did in tight jeans and a revealing tank top.

Damned distracting of her.

"How's your sister today?" he asked, trying not to think about how he'd felt last night, when he'd seen her dancing with Culp and with Kevin, smiling easily at them and laughing, not at all cool and wary, the way she was with him.

"I don't know yet. I was about to call the hospital when I realized I had no means of picking her up. You know, you could have dropped me off back at the Hanging J last night," she pointed out as she set a mug of black coffee on the table near him. "I was too freaked out to think of it, but you—I get the feeling not too much freaks you out, does it?"

He lifted the coffee cup and took a gulp, taking it black, as she'd somehow expected. She stuck the milk back in the fridge.

"It's happened on occasion." One corner of his mouth quirked upward. "But it was pretty late last night when we left the hospital and I figured you were tired enough without having to find your way home alone in the dark . . . I mean, back *here*."

This wasn't her home. It wasn't his anymore either, Jase thought, leaning back in his chair.

"Colton drove me to the Hanging J today to pick up the Jeep, so it was no big deal. Now if you don't mind dropping me back at Fortune's Way, I can catch up with the trail drive. Then I reckon we'll be even."

"Really? I thought I needed to answer some questions to even things up." She sat down opposite him and folded her hands atop the table. "Let's get it over with, shall we?"

Jase drained the last of his coffee. "The sooner, the better . . . Tiffany."

Erinn stiffened. She felt a flush of color burning into her cheeks as she suddenly remembered that Devon had called her Tiffany yesterday. She'd been so upset at the time that her sister's words hadn't even registered. But Jase Fortune had noticed.

Of course he had.

"It's a long story," she began, but he cut her off.

"I've heard that one before."

She stood up and began to pace around the kitchen in frustration. She could feel his gaze on her, and she whirled back toward him.

"Devon isn't the only one who ran away from home. I did too, when I was eighteen. I waited until then so I could legally change my name to Erinn Winters."

"So neither of your names are real? Not Erinn, not Winters?"

"They are now." Her full sexy mouth was set with a firmness he was beginning to recognize, the sensuous lower lip pushed out in a slight, adorable pout. "I've been Erinn Winters for the past eleven years. I'm not Tiffany Erinn *whatever* anymore."

"Why'd you run away?"

None of your business, she thought, then she saw the way he was looking at her. Not with pity or with disapproval or anything else she might have expected. He was leaning back in his chair, studying her with calm acceptance—not judging, she saw. Not demanding. Just asking.

She went to the window, stared out at the mountains lit by glorious dawn, and at a rabbit hopping toward the trees that ran alongside the road.

She didn't have to answer him. She didn't have to tell him a thing. But she heard herself speaking in a low, unemotional tone as her gaze followed a pair of squirrels scampering up a tree.

"I told you that my father was a powerful man," she said at last. "And a difficult one. He controlled not only his very successful business, but his family. He was what people now call a control freak. In every sense of the word."

She turned from the window, met his gaze. "He criticized, demeaned, and controlled my mother every day of her life. Finally, she couldn't take it anymore. She couldn't go on the way things were. I told you she escaped." Erinn swallowed. "But I . . . I didn't tell you how. She killed herself."

Silence filled the room until at last Jase broke it.

"My God." His voice was low with shock. "I'm sorry. How old were you?"

"Eleven." Erinn hugged her arms around herself, leaning back against the counter. "Even as a child, I saw the way he treated her, the way he talked to her. And then . . . I saw her shoot herself."

"Erinn—" He was halfway out of his chair but she raised her hands, gestured him back.

"Don't feel sorry for me—that's the last thing I want."

She thrust a hand through her hair, shoving it away from her face as if she could shove the past away too. Her tone was brittle. "When my mother was gone, my father tried his best to control *me*. But I fought him every step of the way. My mother was always fragile, but I wasn't. I'm *not*."

Her eyes darkened. "Of course, there was no way to win that battle, not while I lived under his roof. There was always tension, always silence in that house. Whenever I resisted his control, he withdrew—he wouldn't speak to me for long periods, wouldn't even look at me. It was as if I didn't exist for months at a time."

"Bastard," Jase said quietly.

Erinn nodded. "I knew I had to get away. And I lived for that day, when I would turn eighteen, when I could legally run, and there wasn't a damned thing he could do about it. It was the only thing that kept me sane."

Jase couldn't help it. He went to her, gently cupped her chin. "It sounds like a helluva way to grow up. I'm sorry, Erinn."

She was caught off-guard by the gentleness of his voice.

His nearness, his understanding, and the raw physical magnetism of him were having a strong effect on her. And she didn't want it to—she didn't want to feel anything...not for him.

Yet his touch was so gentle. And the firmness of his strong fingers made her feel cared for and...and alive in a way that was entirely new. His eyes were locked on hers with an expression of compassion that was knocking down her defenses.

She drew a breath and moved deliberately away, using the distance to try to shore them back up.

"So now you know. I ran away. And I left my half-sister to suffer. I left her in that house and started a new life and never even knew when her mother moved out and left her to be raised by that man. Devon didn't wait until she was eighteen to run off—she cut and ran when she was only fourteen, a child, and now..."

Erinn straightened her shoulders. "Now she's in a hospital and I need to call and see how she is. I need to bring her home and try to win her trust. Though only God knows what damage has been done to her—between Dane Stanton and the Wheelers—"

"Dane Stanton?" Jase thought for a moment he must have heard wrong, then he saw the dismay on her face. "You're Dane Stanton's daughter?"

Oh, damn.

"I *was*." Her chin lifted. She was angry with herself for having let the name slip, but there was nothing to be done. "He's dead now and so is Tiffany Erinn. I'd like it to stay that way."

Dane Stanton. Chicago banking tycoon. Billionaire ski enthusiast. Friend of three presidents and numerous foreign heads of state and founder of several global charities.

Jase's mind reeled. Until Stanton died a few months

ago, his name had been a daily staple in most major newspapers, including the *Wall Street Journal*. He'd been mentioned almost weekly in *Time* or *Newsweek*.

Jase had seen a newscast after Stanton's death, where the anchor had mentioned his two daughters, both of whom had run away from home. No one knew where the missing heiresses were, but for a while, the papers, the broadcasters, the tabloids, and all the entertainment shows had a field day speculating on how long it would take them to surface, if they would attend their father's funeral, alongside the vice-president, several U.S. senators, and Fortune 500 CEOs by the dozen.

Mostly, everyone wanted to know *when,* not *if,* they would come forward to claim their fortunes.

They never had.

"Your secret's safe with me," he said.

Erinn studied him, her hands on her hips, weighing whether she could believe him as Jase gazed silently back.

It was dangerous, looking at him so intently. He was too wildly sexy with that tumbled dark blond hair and eyes like blue smoke. *And too delicious.*

He'd somehow seduced her into telling him her secrets. Now was he trying to seduce her into thinking he could be trusted to keep them?

Last night and this morning she'd told him more than she'd ever told anyone about her past, her secrets.

But not all of them. He still doesn't know everything about me. And he isn't going to.

She broke away from those mesmerizing eyes, from the heat radiating off that superbly muscled body, and hurried to the counter where she'd left her cell phone. Scooping it up, she stuffed it into her purse.

"We need to get going. You're late enough as it is. I'll call the hospital from the Jeep while I'm taking you back to Fortune's Way. But—" She shot him a cool glance. "If I find out you've told anyone who I am . . . who Devon is . . ."

"Yeah?" Jase set his coffee cup in the sink beside hers. He stalked to the door and held it wide. "What dire torture do you have in store for me if I squeal?" he asked with an interested grin.

Erinn sailed past him into the sunlight, annoyed that her heart was beating a little too fast. "Trust me," she said, scowling at the beautiful morning, "you don't want to know."

Chapter Fifteen

Devon stared at the ceiling as the middle-aged nurse with the freckled arms checked her blood pressure.

"I need to go see my boyfriend."

"Hmmm, blood pressure's a little high," the nurse mused as she peered at the readout. She began unwrapping the monitor from Devon's arm with a cheerful smile. "But not too bad."

Immediately Devon swung her legs over the side of the hospital bed and started to get up, but the nurse grabbed her by the shoulders. "Hold on there, young lady. You can't go anywhere right now."

"Please, just tell me what room my boyfriend is in— I have to see him!"

The nurse eased her back into the bed. "First of all, you need to stay off that ankle. Second, it's time for your pain meds. First things first, that's how it works around here." The nurse regarded her sympathetically as Devon squeezed her eyes shut tight.

"I expect your sister will be along anytime now to take you home. I'm sure she'll let you stop by your boyfriend's room on the way out," the woman said cheerily.

Devon's eyes flew open. "What did you say? About my sister?"

"She called the desk an hour or so ago to see how you were doing today and the doctor told her he's discharging you. She said she was on her way. So you just need to be a little patient, hold on tight, take these..."

The nurse shook out two Tylenols into a small paper cup and handed them to the pale-haired teenager, along with a larger plastic cup of water. "And then before you know it—"

"Good morning, Devon."

Devon jumped, her gaze swiveling to the doorway where Tiffany stood, casual and pretty in a cute sweatsuit and sneakers, her curly dark hair twisted into a thick ponytail.

"I...don't want to go with you." Devon's voice quavered as she turned her head away, staring sightlessly out the window.

Erinn's heart fell. The nurse glanced back and forth in concern between the sisters, then she offered Erinn a sympathetic smile before whisking from the room.

"How are you feeling?" Erinn approached the bed. Devon looked so small and sad in the shapeless hospital-issue gown, her uncombed hair hanging in her face. There was a bruise on her arm, and her skin was almost as pale as the sheets as a huge tear slid down her cheek. But her sobs were silent ones.

Erinn realized she was too proud, too dignified to wail.

"Honey," she said softly, her heart aching. "It's all

right. Don't cry. I know everything must hurt, but it'll get better. I'll take care of you—"

"I want Hank! I . . . I won't go with you!"

"Hank needs to stay in the hospital for a while, Devon. You don't have to. You can come home with me—"

"No!" Panic shone in the girl's eyes.

"There's no way I'm letting you go back to live with Mick Wheeler," Erinn said sharply. "That's out of the question."

"But . . . I have to . . . I . . . I w-want to!"

Erinn stared at her. That was fear in her sister's eyes. Not anger, not defiance. *Fear*.

Why? Her pulse quickened. "What is it, Devon? What's wrong?"

"Nothing's wrong." Devon threw herself back against the pillows as tears slid down her cheeks. "Please, just let me go back and stay with Mick," she bit out desperately. "He won't like it if I don't!"

She's afraid of him. He has some kind of hold on her, Erinn realized in shock as a chill scraped down her spine like a blade of mountain ice.

"Why won't he like it, Devon?" Erinn reached for her hand, trying to keep her tone calm. "What are you afraid of?"

"I'm not afraid!" Devon jerked her hand away. "I just . . . like it there!" She wiped wildly at the tears streaming down her face. "I want to go back!"

"That's impossible. You belong with me." As the girl flashed her a despairing glance, Erinn used her ace.

"If you don't want me to go to the authorities and tell them you're underage and have been living with two men—which could get both Hank and Mick into a great deal of trouble—you need to accept that I'm bringing you back to my cabin. From now on I'm going to take care of you. We don't have to talk about anything else until you're ready," she continued quickly, "but you *are* coming home with me. Today."

"You don't understand..." Devon broke off, swallowing hard. Pleadingly, she stared into Erinn's face.

"Mick will...he'll be..." She sucked in her breath and closed her eyes. No, no, she couldn't say that Mick would be furious. Tiffany would ask questions. And she couldn't tell Tiffany anything—not about Mick or Frank Wells, or what they were doing in the back room of the cabin...*anything*.

She was still shaken from what had happened last night, long after the accident. She'd been sound asleep when Mick had appeared in her hospital room, standing over her bed.

She'd woken up with his icky breath all over her face.

A shudder went through her as she remembered how she'd stared at him as if he was part of a nightmare, her heart jumping like a rabbit inside her chest.

He'd warned her again what would happen to her if he found out she told Tiffany one *word* about what he and Wells were doing. He'd squeezed her arm while he was talking to her, squeezed it so hard it felt like her veins would burst, but she couldn't scream or make any noise, because someone would hear and come in, and Mick said if anyone ever found out about this or anything else she knew about him, she'd be real sorry.

And he'd said Tiffany would be sorry too.

He'd ordered Devon to stay away from Tiffany from now on and to keep her mouth shut. He'd sworn that if she didn't, he'd rearrange Tiffany's face and she wouldn't look so pretty anymore.

And then he'd given her arm one last terrible squeeze and left the room.

If he heard she was going to start living with Tiffany now, he'd come after her.

"But I . . . I like living there." She had to try one last time. "You have to let me go back—"

But Erinn was already opening up the plastic bag containing the clothes Devon had worn last night. She removed the pink blouse that was wrinkled, spattered with blood.

"I guess for now you'll have to wear these clothes, until we get home. I'm sorry, I didn't think to bring clean ones for you." She offered Devon an encouraging smile. "As soon as you're up to it, we'll go in to town and buy you all new clothes."

Devon stared numbly at the blood-stained blouse. Without another word, she took it and clutched it in her hands.

"Do you need some help or should I wait outside?"

"I don't need help."

Devon's mind raced as she struggled into her clothes. By the time she zipped up her jeans, she knew what she was going to do.

She just wouldn't tell Tiffany anything, and maybe Mick would leave them alone. She'd stay with her sister until the minute Hank got out of the hospital, and then the two of them would run away, far away, someplace where nobody could find them.

And she'd never have to worry about Mick again.

Her body ached everywhere. She had to fight back a moan when the nurse returned with Tiffany and started helping her into the wheelchair.

"Can I at least see Hank before I leave?" she asked as she was wheeled out into the hall.

"I'm afraid that isn't possible right now." The nurse's tone was brisk, but kind. "I just came from his room and the doctor is examining him now. We can't interrupt. Why don't you come back tomorrow—I'm sure by then he'll feel better and you two can have a nice visit."

Devon sank back in the wheelchair. What if they were lying to her? What if Hank wasn't all right?

But the nurse was already wheeling her into the elevator, and Tiffany was walking alongside, asking questions about Devon's ankle and the pain medications she was supposed to take, and carrying a cane that one of the other nurses had given her.

As if I'm going to walk with that, Devon thought.

Her life was all turned upside down now that Tiffany had found her. It hadn't been so great ever since she and Hank had come here to live with Mick, but now . . . now everything was even worse. Hank was hurt and Mick . . .

Mick was scarier than ever.

She glanced around the hospital parking lot as Tiffany went to get her car and the nurse waited with her. There was no sign of Mick, which was good.

But she had a creepy feeling—like someone was watching her.

Devon tried to shake it off. She told herself to forget about Mick and Frank Wells. They wouldn't hurt her or Hank or Tiffany if she only kept her mouth shut.

So everything would be okay. Because that's exactly what she was going to do.

Chapter Sixteen

Jase spurred Dakota forward as some strays tried to break free of the herd, but the bay horse he'd personally trained needed little instruction. Expertly the gelding drove them back in line with the cattle being moved in a streaming mass toward their summer pasture.

With the sun beating down on his shoulders, he ran a hand along Dakota's neck. They made a good team, always had. The horse was so expert at his job, Jase barely had to think as he rode along beside Rawley into the foothills. Up ahead, Culp and Lily had the lead, while behind him, Colton and Stitch brought up the rear of the cattle being systemetically moved—part of Fortune's grazing management system, where rotating pastures in the summer helped sustain both the cattle and the ecosystem.

He'd deliberately scheduled this drive while his father was still away. Otherwise, Clay would've been at the head of the herd, riding, working, supervising everything and everyone from dawn until dusk.

This way he could avoid fighting Clay tooth and nail

while his father tried to ride and work like he was a twenty-year-old with an undamaged heart.

Jase had always enjoyed trailing the cattle in the summer, being one not only with his horse, but with the land, the air, the rhythm of the range. But today his mind just couldn't stay focused on the task.

His thoughts kept drifting back to what Erinn had told him this morning about her father, and about witnessing her mother's suicide. He couldn't forget her fierce expression when she ordered him not to feel sorry for her.

There was still a whole lot he didn't know about Erinn Winters, but he sure knew one thing—she was very careful about letting anyone get too close. It was almost instinctive with her to keep her distance, to lock everything up inside.

And after being raised by a bastard like Dane Stanton, who could blame her? he thought, slapping his rope to keep another would-be stray in line.

Suddenly a gunshot cracked above the sound of cattle and horses, and Rawley tumbled from his saddle.

"Rawley's down!" Jase yelled, reining Dakota in. His gaze whipped toward the trail above, across the hills, into the gully. He saw no one, nothing moving, not in the shadow of the trees, not in the approach to the pass.

Only one gunshot, he thought even as he vaulted from his saddle and knelt beside Rawley. Ahead of him and behind him, all hell was breaking loose. Culp was yelling and he and Lily were galloping back, while behind him the sound of hooves pounded closer.

"How bad is it?" he asked Rawley, stripping off the foreman's plaid shirt to uncover the bullet wound.

"You tell me, boss," Rawley grunted, his leathery face gray with pain as he struggled to sit up.

"Hold still, let me have a look." To Jase's relief, the wound appeared clean. The shot had missed all the vital organs.

"He winged you, that's it. We got lucky. Just sit there a minute, take it easy."

Culp reached them first, Lily right behind him.

"Rawley, you okay?" The ranch hand's good-natured face had gone ashen beneath his tan. He leaped off his horse, sweat dampening his armpits as he stared at the man on the ground. "Where'd it come from? I didn't see a thing, no one moved out there!"

"Rawley, hold still," Lily ordered, dropping to her knees beside the foreman. She whipped off the bandana knotted around her throat, pressed it against his wound. "Where do you think you're going? You're *not* going to ride back."

"Why not? I came on my horse, I can damned well go back on my horse," Rawley bit out aggrievedly. "It's . . . nothin' but a scratch."

"It's bleeding pretty good," Jase told him as Colton thundered up. "I'm going to call Murdock and have him bring the rig for you. He'll drive you to the hospital. No arguments."

"Aw, Jase, there's no need to . . . make such a fuss," the foreman muttered. "Though I'd like to know who's the son-of-a-bitch that did it."

Jase and Culp exchanged glances, as Lily bit her lip and clasped Rawley's hand.

"So would I, Rawley." Jase's mouth was a thin, hard line as he tore off his own bandana and bound it tightly around the foreman's upper right arm. Blood continued to ooze from the hole the bullet had torn in his flesh as Colton turned and scanned the countryside, hunting for the slightest human movement.

"You done now?" Rawley rasped. "Then help me up. You got cattle to tend to, and I'm telling you I can ride back to the ranch—"

"No, Rawley, you can't. And you won't." Lily's fingers squeezed his hand. "Please stop arguing. When I think what almost happened to you—" She broke off, blinking back sudden tears.

"Aw, Lily…" He frowned into her anxious face. "Don't you start mothering me now—"

"I can't help it," she said with a watery smile. "So Murdock will bring the truck and you'll go straight to the hospital. Promise me."

"Fine." Rawley fought back a grimace. "I promise."

Jase stood up and glanced at Colton, suddenly punching buttons on his phone.

"Calling Farley?"

"Yep." Colton's eyes were grim.

Jase's chest was tight as he again scanned the surrounding area, peaceful and still but for the cattle still rumbling along the trail. Stitch had stayed on horseback, continuing to guide them, though Jase knew he must be wondering along with everyone else what was going on, who had taken a shot at Rawley in broad daylight.

"Anyone see anything?" he asked, still searching the

crests of the hills, then the valley far below, brimming with thick grass and wildflowers.

There was no movement anywhere, except for a lone hawk circling overhead.

"Not a damned thing." Culp joined him as Lily continued to sit beside Rawley. "Damn it, Jase, who the hell is out there? And where'd they go?"

"Good question, Culp. I don't have the answer yet. I wish I did."

Jase's eyes continued to sweep the open countryside, trying to penetrate the rich high country, the pine- and fir-lined ridges, the slate-gray rock walls that dropped sheer to the distant plains.

There were too many places out here where a man could hide. He turned back grimly and looked at his sister.

Lily was biting on her lower lip, a sure sign that she was a lot more upset than she was letting on. She stayed where she was, continuing to hold Rawley's hand—more for herself, Jase guessed, than for him.

He suddenly wanted to get her out of here. Out of the open, where another gunshot could come without warning.

"Lily, you go with Rawley to the hospital. I expect he'll listen to you better than anyone else—"

"No need to talk about me like I'm not here, boss," the foreman interrupted. "I been shot, I'm not dead."

That made Lily smile a little, though her eyes were still dark with concern.

"Jase?" She stood up, drew him aside from the others. Her somber expression heightened Jase's anger. For a young woman who was so carefree, so high-spirited, who gave off light and laughter in every gesture and expression, Lily now looked as shaken as she had the night their mother died, and the day Ginny had told them she was quitting—and the day Clay had suffered his heart attack.

"Who . . . who do you think did this?" she asked in a low tone. "Who in Wolf River would *do* such a thing?"

Jase knew in that instant that she and all the others were thinking the same thing he was. That whoever had been killing their cattle had just upped the stakes bigtime—shooting at Fortune ranch's foreman.

Or maybe they'd been shooting at him. And missed.

Anyone else on the ranch could be next.

"I think that finding whoever's behind all this is now at the top of my priority list, Lily. Guy Farley hasn't seemed to make any progress, but don't worry." His gaze rested grimly on his sister's taut face. "I will."

Chapter Seventeen

Devon was silent during the drive to the cabin. After two unsuccessful attempts at casual conversation, Erinn ceased trying to exchange even the most perfunctory of sentences.

Instead, she did her best to relax as she drove, allowing the silence to hang benignly between them.

As the cabin came into view though, she watched Devon's gaze flit over the lovely, leafy setting, the solid timbers and wide windows of the home, the generous porch—and the glow of silver-capped mountains in the distance. Devon took it all in, but remained expressionless.

Erinn sensed her isolation with a heavy heart—even though she knew it was largely self-imposed. *Devon's learned, as I did, to keep everything locked inside. That's how you survive in the house of the Great Dane. Outbursts weren't tolerated, rebellion was squashed. Imperfection punished.*

The effects of that sort of upbringing didn't fade away quickly, if ever. From her own experience, Erinn knew it took a lot of time, growing up, and self-acceptance.

"Can you make it all right with the cane?" she asked as Devon refused her outstretched hand while clambering awkwardly out of the Jeep.

"I'm fine." Devon limped toward the porch, looking straight ahead. "Just don't worry about me."

It's about time I did, Erinn thought ruefully.

"I'm still in the process of painting and fixing the place up," she explained as she unlocked the front door and pushed it open. "So for now, you're welcome to sleep in the master bedroom—it's freshly painted and quite pretty. In a week or so, when I've painted the larger of the other two bedrooms, you can move in there if you'd like . . . there's a double bed, a nice brass headboard, and I can paint the walls any color you want. I brought home some paint samples from the hardware store. We can look them over together—"

"Do what you want, I don't care." Devon limped across the floor and sank down on the sofa. "I don't want the master bedroom. I'll take the other one."

"But—"

"I'm only staying here until Hank gets out of the hospital, so don't make a big deal out of it," Devon muttered.

That's what you think. But Erinn regarded the girl more with sympathy than with annoyance. Somehow she understood Devon's need to act tough. She'd no doubt been bullied and dominated all of her young life right up until the day she ran away—and who knew what had happened after that, what sort of relationship she'd had with the Wheeler brothers. Her sister needed to assert some control over her own life, and if it made her feel better right now, stronger, more in charge, then Erinn wasn't going to quarrel with her.

"All right," she said calmly and saw surprise cross the girl's face. "I'll make up the bed in there and you'll be all set. Do you want to watch some TV while I make lunch?"

"No."

"Me either. It's nice sometimes just to enjoy the quiet out here. It's so peaceful. Very different from New York, where I live." Erinn breezed into the kitchen.

"I thought I'd fix us some tuna salad sandwiches and chips for lunch. There's also a cherry pie I picked up at the Saddleback Grill this morning. Ginny remembered that it's your favorite."

"Have you been talking about me to everyone in town?" Devon asked, anger flushing her face.

"No. I've only been talking to Ginny—and to Jase Fortune," she added truthfully.

"What did you tell them?"

"That we're sisters, that I broke a promise to you, and that now I'm going to do my best to make up for that."

"Yeah, good luck," the girl muttered, her voice so low Erinn could barely hear it.

"I guess I'm going to need it. Deservedly so." Erinn studied her quietly, until at last Devon shifted uncomfortably on the sofa, stretching her hurt leg across it, then met Erinn's gaze.

"Maybe I don't deserve it, Devon, but think about giving me a chance. That's all I'm asking. A chance."

Devon leaned back against the cushions as if exhausted and closed her eyes.

She looks utterly miserable, Erinn reflected in dismay. Frustration twisted through her. Connecting to Devon might take longer than she'd thought. For the first time it occurred to her that she really *might* have to stay in Wolf River the entire summer.

Surprisingly, the idea didn't displease her as much as it might have a week ago. She'd begun to enjoy waking up out here in the open, amid aspens and wildflowers.

Staying in Wolf River was costing her a great deal of money, between the rental car and the cabin, and all of her expenses ongoing in New York, but she couldn't afford not to do it. She couldn't risk Devon running away again, not until the girl began to accept her. If she took Devon to New York before Devon trusted her and truly wanted to stay with her, Devon could easily slip away and disappear in the tumult of the city.

And I might never find her again.

She prepared the tuna salad, trying not to think about the possibility of losing Devon again . . . trying not to think about anything but the peaceful calm of this cabin, the friendliness of Ginny and Lily and Culp, of Kevin Samson and everyone she'd met at the barn dance last night . . .

And found herself thinking instead about Jase Fortune. And how, in so many ways, he'd come through for her.

She couldn't deny it. He'd been a rock for her last night. Not only defending her against Mick Wheeler at the barn dance, but going after Devon with her, calling the ambulance after they discovered the wreck, staying with her at the hospital—bringing her car back to her this morning.

She owed him. But that was scant reason for his image to keep popping into her mind. She tried to stop thinking about him, but even after lunch, when the dishes were washed and put away, when Devon fell asleep in the smaller bedroom and she'd tried writing for several hours with her laptop at the kitchen table, Jase Fortune's tall frame and thick dark blond hair kept distracting her from Devonshire and the Emerald Forest.

In the end, she gave up on extricating Devonshire from her predicament. Restless, she wandered outside to attack some of the weeds sprouting around the edges of the porch and steps.

She'd been so worried about spiffing up the inside of the cabin that she hadn't done justice to the outside yet. She knelt in the grass, methodically yanking the stubborn stems from the ground, trying to concentrate only on clearing them all—but still she kept seeing Jase's face this morning as he'd heard her out, remembering the gentle calm he'd exuded, the sure, steady timbre of his voice.

Forget about him, she told herself, struggling with a particularly unyielding weed. *Don't build him up to be Mr. Wonderful. You don't have time to get involved with a man right now, any man, especially a heartbreaker like Jase Fortune. Not when you finally have a chance to help Devon. Letting him into your life would be a mistake. A distraction. And you can't afford any distractions.*

But as she sat in the weeds beside Jase Fortune's cabin, his image stayed in her mind, fixed and steady.

That slow, heart-churning smile. Those hot, incisive blue eyes. Even the thrust of his lean jaw when he'd set his mind to something, like when he'd refused to leave her alone at the hospital.

Resolutely, she pushed his image away and grabbed another fistful of weeds—but suddenly an odd feeling came over her. She glanced up quickly and from the corner of her eye, she saw something.

A swift movement. Furtive as a shadow.

Erinn was on her feet in an instant, her heart hammering loudly in her own ears. Someone—a man—had been near the top of the road, then slipped away into the cover of the trees.

Had he been watching her?

She moved forward, uneasiness rushing through her. Who was it? She had to see.

This cabin is supposed to be a safe place, a second-chance place, for me and for Devon, she thought angrily. She wouldn't have anyone intruding on the peace she was trying to build here.

Had it been Mick Wheeler? She'd had an impression of bulk and brawn, but she couldn't be sure. She broke into a run, straight up the road, needing to know who had been there, who was spying on her.

And needing to know why.

Chapter Eighteen

The sun shifted behind the clouds as she plunged into the thicket of trees. Twigs and brush crunched underfoot. She ran faster, peering through the maze of branches and huckleberry and scrub.

But she saw only a squirrel skittering across a log, a pair of rabbits darting for cover—then suddenly caught a glimpse of what she was looking for.

A man—a big bruiser of a man—bolting through the woods up ahead.

Mick Wheeler.

She couldn't see his face, but she was almost certain it was him.

Erinn jerked to a halt, her breath coming in short ragged gasps as he leapt over a fallen tree trunk, and suddenly hurtled down a steep incline leading to another road.

She stood rooted to the spot. Trembling, she wondered what she'd have done if she'd caught him.

Moments later she heard an engine come to life from the direction in which he'd run. He'd parked on that other road. Hidden his car out of sight. Had he been *spying* on her? Or perhaps, she thought with a chill, he'd been sneaking up to the cabin?

Why?

Uneasy, she hurried back, leaving the woods, racing down Black Bear Road. Clouds were moving in, scudding across the sun, and a shiver tingled across her shoulders, down her back.

The air smelled of rain now. Stepping inside the cabin, she closed and locked the front door, then checked on Devon, still dozing on the freshly made-up bed in the second bedroom.

Moving quickly, but quietly, Erinn went around to the back door and locked it as well.

She went to the front window and stared out at the road as the wind picked up, howling down from the mountains.

There was no sign of anyone. Nothing moved but the tree branches swaying in the wind, which scuttled and swirled the dead weeds she'd plucked from the garden only a short while ago.

But apprehension tingled through her. If she hadn't looked up when she had, she never would've seen Wheeler, might never have known he was there.

And there was only one reason she could think of why he might have come here today.

She thought of her sister, whose eyes were still closed, whose breathing sounded light and peaceful in the small second bedroom.

Devon.

Chapter Nineteen

Mick caught up with Red Drummond repairing fence along the northern edge of the Samson ranch.

"How's Hank feeling?" Red asked, wiping sweat from his face with his sleeve as the wind blew through the tall grasses.

"Not too good. The doc wants to keep him another day or two at least."

"That's a real shame. Guess it could'a been worse though." Red glanced over at Hank's Blazer, parked twenty yards back. "Your rig get totaled?"

"Don't know yet. They towed it last night and I didn't have a chance to stop by the shop." Wheeler shrugged his shoulders, then shot the other ranch hand a piercing glance. "Listen, Red, don't forget—in case anyone asks, I've been repairing fence with you all day."

"Yeah, yeah, I know."

"It's important." He stuck a wad of tobacco in the side of his mouth. "If Samson finds out I got released from the hospital and still missed work, he'll fire my ass for sure. I been drinkin' too much, missed too many days, but now I gotta buckle down. I got all Hank's damned hospital bills to pay for."

"Yeah, that's tough. Don't worry, I'm not plannin' to rat on you just because you took off a few hours to visit your brother."

"Damn straight. 'Preciate it." Mick picked up the splice crimper and turned toward the broken fence, barely containing a smirk.

There it was. His alibi for the entire afternoon.

No one needed to know he'd only looked in on Hank for a minute—since no one at the hospital had seen him slip out. He'd made sure of that.

They could never tie him now to Rawley Cooper's shooting. And he didn't think that uppity bitch sister of Devon's had seen his face before he ducked back into the woods. She couldn't identify him for sure, and besides, he hadn't done anything.

Not even what he'd gone there to do.

That was the only thing that bothered him as he worked on the fence alongside Red. He'd hoped the sister would be gone, running errands in town or some such thing—and that he'd have a chance to catch blondie alone at that cabin.

He needed to show her that he could get to her anytime he wanted—to her *and* her sister.

Wells was pissed as hell, convinced that the stupid girl was now a threat to the entire operation. He claimed she knew too much—and was no longer just Hank's mousy little girlfriend, a nobody, with only the Wheelers to rely on.

Now she had a damned sister, one with a big mouth

on her. And the sister had been backed up last night by none other than Jase Fortune.

Hell, Mick thought, *Wells hates the Fortunes almost as much as I do. All of 'em. And he does have a point. If little blondie decides to blab to her sister about what she knows, it'll all be over.*

Fortune would have Farley and his Keystone Kop deputies out there swarming the hills before Mick and Wells could get within a mile of their stash. They'd end up staring at prison walls most of the rest of their lives while the half million in cash would be as out of reach as the Great Wall of China.

Already Wells was worried enough that he was ready to either kill the girl or shut down the operation—cut and run. *Damned coward,* Mick thought contemptuously. Wells was getting to be a real pain in the ass—always riding him about his drinking, about the fighting. *I'm damned sick of him nagging me to quit the liquor and keep a low profile.*

He didn't appreciate Wells sticking that gun in his face last night either. He ought to whip his ass for that. Except not yet.

Wells had all the connections, he was the only one who knew how and when to get in touch with the boys who paid the big bucks.

Otherwise, Mick could think of a few interesting ways he'd like to pay Wells back. And keep the stash for himself.

As it was, Wells had come damn close to killing the girl right in the hospital last night, just to make sure she never had a chance to spill the beans to her sister. But Mick had known Hank wouldn't like that. Hank might just go to the cops if his little girlfriend wound up dead—but Mick couldn't tell Wells that. He didn't want Wells getting any ideas about knocking Hank off too.

So now it was up to him to protect his brother *and* the operation. He'd managed to do both by convincing Wells there was no need to kill anyone—yet.

Keeping a scared little chipmunk like blondie in line would be a hell of a lot easier than getting away with murder, Mick had told him. Nobody had to die. At least not yet.

The good thing was, the little punk had looked like she was going to die from fright when Mick had popped into her room early this morning.

He'd scared her but good. No way she was going to talk.

And if he had to pay her another call or two to make sure she didn't forget what he'd told her, so be it.

Mick considered it all a good day's work. No one was talking, the operation wasn't in danger. And the money was piling up, more every week. The line of customers was endless.

Life was sweet.

Except for last night—when Jase Fortune had humiliated him in front of half the town, landing him and Hank in the hospital. Not to mention forcing him to wreck his pickup.

It was all Jase Fortune's fault. His kid brother's too. They both had some payback coming. One of these days it'd be a helluva lot more than just taking a potshot at their foreman.

Mick imagined the fun it would be to use this little

splicer on those two Fortune boys. Maybe even on their snotty little sister. Those rich folks had no idea how mean and dirty he could get if he had to.

No idea at all.

Mick smiled to himself as he strung the new wire, working beneath a sky growing dark and bloated with rain.

And if blondie's big sister doesn't keep her turned-up nose out of it, I might just have to get mean and dirty with her too.

Chapter Twenty

Rain fell in bucketfuls as Jase drove through the darkness.

He barely noticed the downpour though. Or where he was headed. He was lost in his own thoughts.

It had been a long, hellish day.

And he was willing to bet that Mick Wheeler was responsible for that.

Eventually Guy Farley and his deputies had reached the crime scene, taken a report, then searched the site for hours with no success finding the slug that had torn a hole through Rawley's arm. Eventually more ranch hands had ridden up to help finish trailing the cattle, and finally, right around suppertime, Rawley had been released from the hospital with his arm in a sling and a bottle of pain pills, another of antibiotics.

Jase was hungry, covered with trail dust, and frustrated. He'd followed Farley back to his office in town to finish going over every detail of the shooting with the sheriff, demanding that Mick Wheeler be questioned—especially in light of the preceding night's events. Then he'd driven straight to the hospital, only to discover that Lily, Murdock, and Rawley had already left for home.

He'd then intended to follow them back to Fortune's Way, until with the rain pelting his windshield like bullets, he abruptly realized he was on the wrong road.

He was headed toward Black Bear Road—the cabin.

Yet he didn't stop. Didn't even slow. He gripped the wheel tighter, scowled through the streaming torrent of water, and turned when he reached Black Bear Road, heading toward the cabin.

Toward Erinn.

By the time he got out of the car and stamped up the porch steps, the downpour had lessened to a drizzle, but water dripped off his hat as he rapped on the door.

When she opened it, staring at him in surprise, he didn't know what he wanted to say, but after that first instant of stunned silence, she'd been the one to speak.

"Come in. You're soaked."

She held the door wide and light spilled out, warm and welcoming. So did the delicious aroma of roasted chicken. Jase stepped inside and closed the door behind him.

She was still wearing sweats and sneakers, and she still looked prettier than any woman had a right to.

Her hair was loose and untamed, the dark curls cascading past her shoulders. He suddenly found himself wondering what it would feel like to plunge his fingers through that cloud of hair, to place his hand at her nape and slowly, gently pull her closer . . .

With an effort he blocked the scenario from his mind and shifted his gaze to the slip of a teenage girl lying on the sofa, legs propped up, and a light blanket draped across her lap.

"Sorry to interrupt," Jase said. "But I wanted to see how Devon was doing." His gaze shifted to Erinn. "And I need a few words with you. Alone."

She looked startled. "I'm . . . in the middle of making dinner."

"All I'm asking is five minutes. Outside." Taking her arm, he steered her to the front door before she could protest.

"We'll be right back," he told Devon over his shoulder.

Erinn gasped as he pulled her out into the wet, chilly night. The drizzle was misty and soft now, blowing in damp gusts through the trees. "What are you doing? Are you crazy?"

"I don't want your sister to overhear."

"Obviously." Erinn blinked against the cold kiss of the wind. "What in the world is this all about?"

"Bad news. Someone shot my foreman today."

Shock widened her eyes. She went still as a gravestone. "I'm . . . sorry. Is he . . ." Erinn couldn't bring herself to say the word.

"He's alive. He got hit in the arm, no serious damage. But it could've been a lot worse—and I think Wheeler was the shooter."

She felt the color draining from her face. Her earlier apprehension took on a whole new dimension. "He came here today," she whispered.

Jase's eyes were grim. His insides tightened. "What happened? Did he hurt you? Threaten you?"

"No, nothing like that. I didn't actually speak to him. I only caught a glimpse of him on the road. As soon as I turned toward him he ran into the woods and disappeared. But I followed him—I can almost swear it was Wheeler."

Jase didn't like the sound of this. Not one damned bit. Unconsciously he shifted his body so he was shielding her more from the damp and the wind. "Any idea what he was up to?"

"Devon." She swallowed. "I have this terrible feeling he wants to get her away from me. And not just because Devon originally said she didn't want to see me. Something is very off."

Erinn looked directly into those searing blue eyes. "Last night at the barn dance he went ballistic just because he saw me talking to her. She was *telling* him to let me go, that all I'd done was to say hello, and Wheeler didn't care. He was furious, out of control—he just wanted me to stay away from her. Not for her sake, but for some reason of his own. And this morning, at the hospital, Devon seemed frightened of coming home with me—she kept saying that Mick wouldn't like it."

"I bet I can guess why."

She bit her lip and met his gaze, waiting for him to explain.

"Devon might know more than she should about Wheeler, about what he's been up to." Jase frowned. "Things like shooting Fortune cattle."

"Jase, what are you talking about?"

"Someone's been picking off our cattle—we've found about a half dozen so far. There've been three incidents over the past two months. Now, today, someone took a shot at Rawley."

His eyes narrowed in the damp, misty darkness.

"The sheriff hasn't found the slug yet, so he can't prove it was the same make of firearm, but I have a pretty good idea it would be a match."

"But . . . why? Why would Wheeler do any of that?"

"The same reason Wheeler does anything," he said in a hard tone. "He's a low-down son-of-a-bitch—with a mean temper. And he carries a grudge. As far as I know, there's only two men in town who have grudges against me and my family: Mick Wheeler and Frank Wells. I fired Wells for his drinking when he was supposed to be at work, and Wheeler picked a fight with Colton awhile ago. Colton roughed him up a little, more or less like what I did last night." Jase's mouth thinned.

"The bastard even had words with Lily after Colton decked him, waiting for her when she left Ginny's place."

"Does the sheriff know all this?"

"Yeah, but there's nothing to link Wheeler to any of the shootings. No proof. Not yet."

Erinn's thoughts were whirling. It all made sense. Devon had been living with the Wheelers for months. She knew more about Hank and Mick than anyone. And if she knew something that Mick Wheeler didn't want anyone else to know . . .

"I need to get her to tell me the truth." Her nails dug into her palms as she stared at Jase. "Before Mick Wheeler comes back here and threatens her—or worse."

"That's why I want to talk to her." Jase tipped his hat farther back on his head. "Right now."

"No—I'll do it. After you leave."

"Sorry. I'm not leaving so fast." His tone matched the determination glinting in his eyes. "I need answers and I need them tonight."

Erinn stiffened. "Don't think I don't appreciate your warning about Wheeler, but I'll handle this myself. Devon is *my* sister. It's none of your—"

"The hell it isn't." Jase gripped her arms. His strong hands clamped only lightly around her flesh, careful not to hurt her, but she felt a circle of electricity spiral through her where his fingers touched.

"Someone's been shooting at my cattle for months," he said roughly. "Today my foreman was nearly killed. And Wheeler showed up *here*—and *not* to bring you a housewarming gift. I need to find out what Devon knows."

"I'll find out for you."

"Not good enough."

Erinn was caught between the hard determination in his eyes, the warmth of his touch, and the turmoil roiling inside her.

She hated that on Devon's first night at the cabin, Jase Fortune wanted to grill her. But the truth needed to come out—for Devon's safety as well as for everyone else's.

"Fine," she said at last. "You can stay. But I'll ask the questions. Deal?"

He frowned, and for a moment she thought he was going to argue about this too. Instead he nodded. "Deal. But if you don't get anywhere, I'm going to take over."

"Jase, I don't want her upset."

"She's going to be—no matter what. But I'll try not

to make things worse." Jase felt a stab of sympathy at the anxiety in her eyes. He struggled against the protective urge rolling through him.

"There's one more thing." Her chin inched up. "We're going to eat dinner first. You're welcome to stay if you like, but I'm not letting a perfectly good roast chicken go to waste. By the time this is over, none of us will feel like eating, so we may as well do it before the fireworks start."

A glint of humor flickered in his eyes. "I hadn't figured you for such a practical woman."

"I'm not. You wouldn't say that if you knew me better."

"Is that so?"

She nodded, suddenly keenly aware that he still held her, gently, his hands warm and strong against her skin.

"Sometimes," she said, trying not to be distracted by his nearness, or by the intent way he was gazing at her, "when I'm really into my writing I work until ten o'clock at night without eating anything all day except Milky Ways—"

"I'd like to," he interrupted. She stared up at him, confused.

"Like to what?"

"Know you better." The words came out softly, before Jase quite realized he was saying them aloud. And without pausing for once to consider his actions, he pulled her closer in the darkness, wrapped his arms around her waist, and lowered his head to kiss her.

Chapter Twenty-one

It was a simple kiss. Warm, gentle.

But as his mouth brushed against hers, everything changed. Heat. Fire. Lust. All three rocked him.

Her mouth was sleek, and soft as dawn. It parted in surprise even as his lips slanted against hers, and he heard her mewing gasp of surprise even as his muscles tightened.

From the first second of contact she was swaying into him, pliant and willing as if she'd wanted this every bit as much as he had.

Raw lust pounded through him like a double shot of Jim Beam, obliterating caution in the blink of an eye. He tangled his hands in the lush thickness of her hair and dragged her roughly closer, eliminating every millimeter of space between them.

When he heard her tiny moan of pleasure, felt her sway in his arms, his mouth turned demanding, taking the kiss to a whole new level.

This time it was long, deep, and scorching. Jase dragged her against him, plunging his tongue toward hers, sliding his hands down that slim, curvy body, exploring her hips, cupping her bottom.

Her arms had closed tight around his neck and her mouth clung to his as if they'd been melded. Together they kissed and touched and breathed as one.

He forgot all about the lost teenage girl waiting inside, he forgot the terrible events of the day, he forgot everything but the woman in his arms, the beautiful woman whose breasts were pressed against his chest, whose lips were giving and demanding all at once, the woman he couldn't tear himself away from.

"Tiffany!"

Devon's voice shattered the darkness. Erinn was yanked from the warm bubble of pleasure that enveloped her. She jerked back.

Jase was smiling at her.

"Erinn, wait a minute . . ." he began softly, but she shook her head.

Without a word, she turned and opened the door, rushing back into the cabin. Devon was limping toward the front door, using the cane Erinn had left beside the sofa. For once she appeared more annoyed than angry.

"I'm starving. Isn't dinner burned to a crisp by now?"

As Jase entered the cabin, the girl flicked each of them a suspicious glance. "What were you two doing out there?"

"Talking." Erinn hoped her voice didn't sound as breathless as she felt. She had to pull herself together. "Come sit down," she said quickly. "I'm sure it's ready now."

Hurrying over to the oven, her mind whirling, she grabbed a potholder and yanked the roasting pan out.

She wanted to analyze and dissect what had just happened between her and Jase, but there was no time.

"Perfect timing, it's ready," she announced in a breezy tone.

"Smells delicious," Jase said.

He sounds much too calm, she thought, glancing at him suspiciously. He was now holding his hat in his hands, but he looked anything but humble.

He looked assured, amused, and quite pleased with himself as he strode to the table. "Your sister invited me to stick around for dinner. I'm starving too," he told Devon.

Erinn suddenly wasn't sure if Jase was staying only to question Devon, or because he was hungry, or because he hoped to pick up where the two of them had left off. From the gleam in his eyes as he approached her, she suspected all three.

Her heart skipped a beat and she told herself to be careful. She eyed him warily as he came right up to her and grinned.

"How about putting me to work? Letting me carve for my supper?"

"You might as well do *something* useful." She ignored his grin and opened the drawer with the carving knives. "These are yours anyway, I believe."

"What do you mean, they're his?" Devon piped up from the table.

"This cabin belongs to Mr. Fortune," Erinn told her as Jase expertly transferred the roast chicken to a carving board. "He's letting us rent it from him."

"Why?"

Jase answered before Erinn could reply. "Because I'm such a nice guy. And because your sister asked me to."

Devon was silent as Erinn spooned mashed potatoes into a serving bowl.

As all three of them took their seats, Erinn passed her sister the platter of chicken. Jase's eyes met hers across the table. Her heart lurched at the way he was looking at her. As if they were alone still on the back porch, in the rain, kissing.

She reminded herself that she was going to be questioning Devon after dinner, that Jase would take his turn if she didn't get the answers he sought. She tried to turn off the attraction she felt for him, to concentrate on Devon and Wheeler and what her sister might know, but all the time she was thinking of how it had felt to be held in those strong arms, of how his mouth had electrified hers.

And of how, despite everything, she wanted him to do it again.

Chapter Twenty-two

It seemed to Erinn that dinner would never end. She was amazed and annoyed that Jase could compliment her cooking and engage her and Devon in small talk as casually as if they were merely polite acquaintances—and not at all as if he'd just kissed her breathless in the cool, rainy night.

But then she'd find his gaze on her, and he seemed anything but casual. Her blood heated at the way his eyes seemed to linger on her mouth.

Stop it, she told herself as she passed him the mashed potatoes for the second time. He'd already demolished a quarter of the chicken and had enjoyed a sizable helping of green beans.

You're way out of your league. He's handsome as sin, divorced, and not into commitment, remember? Landlord and tenant—that's the closest you and Jase Fortune should get to any sort of relationship.

But something inside of her wanted to get a whole lot closer and it took all of her willpower to block the memory of those hot, overwhelming kisses from her mind, of his strong hands gliding down her body, creating tingles everywhere they touched.

Then Devon knocked over her glass of Coke. The girl froze, terror flashing across her face.

She couldn't move, not even to get out of the way of the spill, or to right the glass.

Jase reacted quickly though, tossing his napkin over the flowing soda, righting the glass with one hand and pulling Devon's chair from the path of the streaming Coke with the other.

"You okay?" he asked her as Erinn rushed for the paper towels.

No answer.

"Just be glad you didn't spill hot coffee on yourself." Erinn filled the gap quickly, with a reassuring smile as she dabbed at her sister's lap. "He'd have poured ice water all over you."

"He...what?" The terror had faded, now Devon just looked confused. Cornered, almost.

Jase dropped a light hand on her shoulder, and proceeded to describe what had happened in the Saddleback, making his actions out to be those of a hero.

"And what thanks did I get?" he asked Devon as Erinn finished blotting up the spilled Coke. He slid Devon's chair back into place. "She hated my guts, all because I tried to help her."

"Don't flatter yourself," Erinn retorted. "I barely knew you—I didn't feel much of anything for you. Still don't!" she added, but she couldn't suppress a smile.

To her relief, Devon giggled. Erinn's heart squeezed tight in her chest. It was the first time since Devon was a toddler that Erinn had heard her laugh. It transformed her face for a single moment, then, quickly, she picked up her fork and started eating again.

"When my sister, Lily, was younger, she'd spill something just about anytime she went into the kitchen," Jase went on easily, taking his seat once more. "It was the family joke. Ginny was our cook then, and the instant she saw Lily come in for a glass of milk, she grabbed the mop."

He winked at Devon, and Erinn was pleased to see her sister's lips curve upward again.

"I spilled things too, when I lived at home," Devon said. "My father hated that." She looked at Jase with tentative curiosity. "What did your father do when your sister spilled?"

"That's the funny thing. He was the only one of us who didn't seem to notice. As I recall, he just went on talking. But then, Lily's always been the apple of his eye. She could've hit a baseball through the living room window and he'd have told her she should try out for the majors." He grinned. "If Colton or I did something like that we'd have had to sit through a lecture, and he'd have docked our allowances and given us extra chores for a week."

"That's not so bad." Devon looked down, staring at her plate. "One night I spilled my milk when we were having dessert. We had guests ... my father's business friends ... and some milk splashed on a man's sleeve."

Erinn felt a knot in her stomach. The Great Dane didn't like mistakes. He took them personally. Apprehension surged through her as Devon's voice dipped lower, and she had to lean forward, straining to hear the words.

"He made me leave the table. And write the man a note of apology." She spoke in a monotone, her eyes glued to her plate.

"Then the next day . . ."

She broke off, and Erinn saw her hand, still holding the fork, begin to tremble. Slowly, Devon set the fork down. She just stared at her plate, but Erinn could see the muscles working in her throat as she fought back a sob.

"Devon," Erinn said softly, her stomach clenching. She could just imagine her father, and his fury—his quiet, cutting tone and glacial eyes. "Can you tell me what happened the next day?"

Silence. Tears filled the girl's eyes.

"Devon . . ."

"He sold my horse," Devon whispered.

Tears were streaming down her cheeks. Erinn reached her side in an instant and wrapped her arms around the girl.

"I'm sorry, honey, I'm so sorry," she soothed as Devon sagged against her, the sobs bursting from her like small grenades.

"That was cruel, Devon. *He* was cruel. Try not to think about it—"

"Her name was Genevieve," Devon gasped. Her tear-filled eyes lifted to Erinn's. "I l-loved her so much. I used to go to the stable four times a week. She was my . . . best f-friend. My only . . . real . . . friend."

Erinn's throat constricted. She understood all too well. It was hard to make friends with Dane Stanton for a father. He didn't allow sleepovers or long phone conversations; he had to approve not only the friend, but the parents. And the Great Dane had exacting standards. And expectations. And rules.

Control was a religion to him and he wielded it like a holy sword.

She held Devon tighter, speaking against her pale, wispy hair. "He was sick, Devon. Sick and wrong. The Great Dane isn't worth your tears, he never was."

"He t-told me I was wasting too much time on Genevieve—that I needed to learn how to be graceful." Devon couldn't seem to stop, couldn't seem to hear Erinn's words. She was lost in her anguish. She pulled away, her eyes red and swollen as the tears continued to fall.

"He said I couldn't ride anymore until I im-improved myself. For the next two years, he made me go to ballet class instead of riding. I was terrible at ballet—the teacher yelled at me and the other girls l-laughed. But he wouldn't let me quit." The words poured out in a rush of pain. "He said I had to go until I was g-graceful. Until I could walk into a room without tripping over my feet, or until I stopped spilling things . . . embarrassing him."

Tears stung Erinn's eyes too. It was all too familiar. The criticism, the cold silences, the condemnation offered in place of love. All the things that had destroyed her mother.

"T-Tiffany," her sister gasped, shoulders shaking as her sobs rose. "He just took Genevieve away. Sold her to s-strangers. I never saw her again. I never had a chance to say g-good-bye."

Erinn held her, her arms clamped tight around the girl as the tears and loneliness and grief poured out of her, as Devon's thin shoulders shuddered and her sobs filled the cabin.

Jase stood silent and apart, watching the two of them, fury coiling in his gut.

He'd thought Clay was strict. Tough, often grouchy, sometimes curt. But he'd never been cruel. He'd never withheld love or piled on criticism or tried to stifle his children from friends or hobbies they loved. He had a fierce bark, but he never bit. Not hard, anyway.

The father of these two young women had been a bully, not a man. A bully who used rules and words instead of fists, but a bully all the same.

"He's gone now," Erinn was whispering. "Devon, you don't ever have to see him again or talk to him. Never again."

"I know." Devon lifted her head, swiped the back of her hand across her eyes. "I heard . . . when he died. It was on the n-news. In the papers . . . everyone was talking about it. I'm glad he's dead!" Devon said suddenly, staring at Erinn.

"I don't care if I'm horrible, Tiffany. I can't help it— I'm *glad*! And I wouldn't go back to that house or . . . or . . . touch a penny of his money for anything—anything in the world!"

Erinn nodded, took her sister's hands in her own. "I'm with you, Devon. And if you're horrible, I am too. I felt the same way when I found out. But *he* was the one who was horrible," she murmured. "Not you, Devon. Never you."

And as Devon's sobs filled the kitchen once more

and Erinn stroked the girl's hair and held her close, Jase slipped outside onto the porch once again and stared out into the misty starless night.

He thought of all the dinners at Fortune's Way. Sure there had been some arguments, some butting of heads—especially between Jase and Colton and Clay. But Clay had never taken away anything that mattered to them, never torn them down, tried to control every movement, every mistake, every corner of their lives.

There had mostly been laughter, and banter, and warmth. Clay might be guilty of wanting to take everything on his own shoulders—the running of the ranch, the running of the family—but he'd never diminished the goals or passions or competence of his children.

Of anyone he loved.

By the time Jase went inside again, Erinn was settling her sister on the sofa, tucking a blanket around her.

When she saw Jase, she bit her lip.

"I'll be right back," she told Devon, and walked to the door.

Jase followed her once more onto the porch.

"Are you okay?" he asked in concern.

She leaned against the porch rail and took a deep breath. "I will be."

But she looked shaken and anguished and weary beyond words.

"It's probably a good thing that she let all that out in there. She'll be the better for it."

"I hope so. But I'm sure there's lots more where that came from." Bitterness tinged her words. "I ran away to save myself from him—and I didn't save Devon. That's why she had to live with him for fourteen years in that house—that's why she was forced to run away, and ended up in shelters and that shack with the Wheelers. Because of me."

"Hold on," Jase said sharply. "You were only eighteen. She wasn't your responsibility. What about her mother?"

"She left, of course. She gave the Great Dane full custody of Devon in exchange for a juicy divorce settlement and the house in Palm Beach."

"Devon was her responsibility to care for and protect, Erinn, not yours."

"That doesn't make me sleep better at night, but thanks for trying," she muttered.

He moved closer. "Are you always so hard on yourself?"

"I should have gone back for her again. You don't understand," she said, her eyes grim. "Devon doesn't know, but I *did* go back—once. Only once. But I didn't get to see her—I only saw *him*. And I was a coward. I ran. I let him scare me away—from Devon."

"How?" Jase's eyes searched hers on the porch. "What did he do to you?"

"It was what he said, not what he did. Always what he said." The memory of that terrible afternoon was still vivid in her mind, even after all this time. "It was a year after I ran away, after I'd made a life for myself in New York. With school, work, and the idea of becoming a writer . . ."

Erinn's voice trailed off and her shoulders drooped. "I'd tried to call Devon numerous times, I'd written to her, but never reached her or heard a word. So I went back to see her, to check on her. It was during the day, a hot day in July, and I thought my father would be at work—but he was at home. Almost as if he sensed I was coming," she added in a low tone.

Jase waited, as if sensing that she needed to do this in her own time, her own way. He was silent as she hugged herself in the dimness of the porch.

"A new maid answered the door. He came out of his office suddenly while I was trying to talk my way in to see Devon, and he ordered me to come into the house. I . . . I wanted to see her, so I did, even though the sight of him made me want to tear out of there like a squirrel running from a dog. But Devon wasn't there," Erinn said softly. "Only he was there and he looked me up and down, this sneer on his face, and he told me that I'd turned out as disappointingly ordinary as he'd always feared."

Jase stiffened. "What the hell," he began, but Erinn shook her head wearily.

"That was only the beginning. I tried to ask about Devon, but he told me he'd never allow me to see her again. That he still had hopes she'd become worthy of the Stanton name, and he'd be damned if he'd let me ruin her. He spoke of my mother." She swallowed. "Of how I was just like her, weak and spineless, and that my running away had proved that I was doomed to be a coward and a failure just as she had been."

"Erinn. My God." Jase moved closer, his arms going around her. "Don't do this. Don't think about it. He was a sick bastard and—"

"I know that, Jase. I know that." She rested her head for a moment on that strong shoulder, as her heart quivered with remembered pain. Then she drew back. Stepped back, determined to finish it.

"He said other things while I stood transfixed, rooted to the spot, too numb to run away. I listened to him tell me how the night I was conceived, he'd had sex with the woman he loved before he went home to my mother, that she was his mistress for years before and after I was born—and that he wished to hell she was the one who'd borne him a child. Because then that child might not have turned out to be as disappointing to him as I was, as my mother was. He should have bred with stronger stock. Because look what Evangeline, his weak, clinging Evangeline had produced. A daughter every bit as pathetic as she had been."

Her voice trembled. "I was stunned. I felt as if he'd slammed me in the knees with an iron bar. I could barely stand. And as I started to cry, he laughed. He pointed at me and said, 'See. You can't take it. I knew you'd crumble. You're just like her. Should I get my gun and you can kill yourself right here?' "

There was an instant's shocked silence during which she heard Jase's indrawn breath, then, the far-off, lonely wail of a coyote.

"It's a good thing that bastard's dead or I'd be tempted to go back there and rid the world of him myself," Jase said darkly. "Erinn—"

"No. It's all right. I'm fine." She stiffened, unable to bear the way the hard contours of his face had softened, unable to endure his sympathy.

"Look," she said desperately, needing to change the subject, needing to think about Devon, not herself, as she should have long before now. "I have to go back inside, I need to stay with her."

"I get that." The wall had gone up. She was shutting him out, retreating back into the private world of a woman who insisted on taking everything on her own shoulders. Who didn't like asking favors. Or relying on anyone but herself.

He had to respect it, but at this moment, he didn't like it much. Hell, he didn't like it at all.

"We still need to talk to her about Wheeler," he reminded her, but she shook her head.

"Not tonight, Jase—I can't do that to her. She's been through enough. The past twenty-four hours have been hell."

For you too, Jase thought. But it was clear from the determination in her eyes that she wasn't going to change her mind, and he couldn't really blame her, considering the shape Devon was in right now.

The questioning would have to wait, but he didn't like leaving the two of them alone out here. On this black, wet night the cabin seemed more isolated than he'd realized.

"Maybe you and Devon should come stay at Fortune's Way until we get this Wheeler business all figured out."

She stared at him in astonishment, then shook her head. "No. Absolutely not."

"I'm worried, Erinn. You must be too, you're just too stubborn to admit it. Wheeler was here today, that's what you said. What if he comes back?"

"All the locks and windows and doors on the cabin are in good working order." She met his gaze. "I've checked them all. They're secure. And I'll speak to

Devon tomorrow, as soon as I find the right moment. Then I'll let you know what I find out. In the meantime..."

She glanced around in the darkness, before straightening her spine. If she felt uncertainty, Jase thought, she damned well wasn't going to show it.

"In the meantime, I'll be careful and I won't let Wheeler get anywhere near Devon."

I don't want him anywhere near you either, Jase thought.

"Look, I get the point. You're good at taking care of yourself. But for once, can't you accept some help?"

She managed a smile. "We'll be fine."

"Do you know how to use a gun?"

The question startled her and she nearly jumped. "No," she said firmly. "And I don't have one, anyway, so..."

He moved closer, his voice barely above a whisper, so quiet she could scarcely hear it. "There's a trap door in the kitchen floor. Four feet to the right of the table. It looks like a knothole in the pine, but there really is a hole there. Lift it up, and there's a place to hide underneath, big enough for two adults. There's also a gun down there. A .45. Loaded. Click off the safety and you're good to go."

Her eyes widened, fury swirling in their depths. "There's a loaded gun in this house and you never told me?" she whispered back.

"I'm telling you now. It's not all that unusual. My father always told us that several generations of Fortunes out west had built in secret cellars or hiding places. Sometimes they've come in handy. A hundred and ten years ago my great-grandmother in North Dakota saw two strange men approaching the house. She didn't like the look of them and my great-grandfather was away in Sioux Falls on business. So she and my grandfather— who was only ten at the time—hid under the floorboards beneath the trap door in the bedroom."

He eased closer to Erinn, gazing down into those still angry eyes. "Good thing too—the varmints broke in and tore the place apart, looking for whoever lived there. Turned out they were bank robbers, searching for a place to hide out. When they thought no one was home, they bunked down on the floor in front of the fire."

Erinn was intensely aware of how close he had moved to her. She could feel the heat pulsing off that hard, toned body. She could smell the clean scent of soap and leather that seemed as much a part of him as those piercing eyes or the long, swift strides with which he walked.

Then she felt her heartbeat quickening as Jase Fortune cupped her chin in his hand and tilted her head up to meet his gaze.

"Don't you want to know what happened?"

"I suppose you're going to tell me whether I want to know or not." She tried to appear offhand, but her voice was breathless, even to her own ears.

He smiled. "She and her son stole out of their hiding place in the middle of the night. She hit one of the robbers over the head with a poker while he slept, and when the other one woke up, she held a gun on him, while my ten-year-old grandfather rode to town and brought back the sheriff."

"That's . . . remarkable."

"Sometimes hiding places—and guns—can come in handy."

"I'm counting on it not coming to that," she assured him.

His finger slowly shifted to trace the contours of her mouth. Her heart stopped beating for a moment as he brushed her lips with a feather touch that made her insides tremble. A languid heat half closed her eyes.

"Then again," he said quietly, studying her, "I could always bunk down on the porch."

Erinn's lips were tingling from his touch and an ache was building inside her. His eyes seared hers, hot and intense, drawing her in. "That . . . won't be necessar—"

That was as far as she got. He stopped her words with a kiss. A long, searching kiss that made her forget everything else. She kissed him back, dizzy and warm, just holding onto him, not ever wanting to let him go.

She felt something slipping from her—all her reasons not to let him get too close. Her hesitation, her wariness, her calm, sensible good judgment. His slow deep kisses set her on fire. He edged her back against the outside cabin wall, his warm hand sliding beneath her sweatshirt. He reached the wispy lace bra beneath, and his fingers slipped inside, his thumb circling her nipple with rough strokes even as his mouth caressed hers with such tenderness her knees trembled.

She hadn't felt anything like this in a long time . . . the ache of need, of pleasure, of *wanting*. But Jase had only to touch her and she wanted *more*. He nibbled at her lips and she drank in the taste of him, moaning against his mouth, arching her back with pleasure as her tongue sought and tangled with his.

Suddenly, something rustled in the brush, and Jase let her go with the abruptness of a free fall. He spun around, eyes boring into the darkness.

Erinn stared where he was looking, her heart pounding. But a moment later she caught sight of glinting eyes close to the ground, then a fox showed itself briefly before gliding through the tall grass toward the creek.

Jase sprinted down the steps, moved toward the brush, scanning it for another full minute before returning to the porch.

"Sure you don't want me to stay?" he asked.

I'm not sure of anything right now. Not sure if I'm more afraid of Wheeler or of you. Or of myself. A thousand emotions churned through her. But she shrugged and tried to sound confident. "It was only a fox. I . . . should get back inside."

He nodded, studying her, his eyes unreadable. "You'll let me know what you find out?"

"Yes. Tomorrow."

Her heart fluttered as he seemed about to say something more. Instead, he nodded again and strode to his Explorer with long, sure strides.

A sense of loss swept over her, but she quickly dismissed it. Without glancing at Jase Fortune again, even as the SUV's engine and headlights sprang to life, she hurried back inside and locked the door.

Devon was asleep on the sofa, her breathing even.

Erinn had dishes to do. And painting to finish. And a book to write.

But all she could think about, as she turned on the faucet and soaped up a sponge, was Jase Fortune.

He had only just left, but a part of her hadn't wanted him to go. A part of her had wanted to call him back.

And that worried her almost as much as the specter of Mick Wheeler did.

Maybe more.

Chapter Twenty-three

"Can I visit Hank today?"

Devon was already seated at the kitchen table, wide awake, munching Oreos from the box when Erinn emerged from her bedroom the next morning.

There was a touch of color in her cheeks and she looked much better than she had the previous evening.

Erinn went to the refrigerator and took out the carton of orange juice. "I know you're worried about Hank. We can stop by the hospital after breakfast."

Devon let out a deep sigh of relief.

"Then," Erinn continued, pouring two glasses of juice and passing one to her sister, "I thought we'd take a drive into town and buy you some new clothes. Unless you'd prefer to go to the Wheeler cabin and get some of your old things from there," she said casually.

"N-no. That's okay. I don't want to bother Mick," Devon said quickly.

Because you're afraid of him, Erinn thought, Devon's reaction confirming her fears. *And maybe you don't want me to see any more of what's in that cabin . . .*

"Well, if you have a key we could go while he's at

work." Erinn took out a skillet, then a carton of eggs from the fridge, and cracked four of them into a bowl as Devon eyed her uneasily.

"I don't have a key. I don't want to go back there . . . not until Hank comes home. I can just wear this, with my jeans." She glanced down at the pale green cotton T-shirt Erinn had given her to sleep in the night before.

"Most girls would jump at the chance to buy some new clothes," Erinn pointed out. She beat the eggs lightly with a fork, then heated the skillet. "Let me treat you. It's the least I can do."

Devon pushed the box of cookies away. "Okay . . . just don't get the idea I'm going to stay here because you're buying me some clothes," she mumbled. "I want to go back as soon as Hank comes home."

"I don't expect you to stay here because I'm buying you some new clothes," Erinn said quietly. "I hope you'll stay because I'm your sister and it would be nice to get to know each other better."

She poured the beaten eggs into the skillet and they made a soothing crackling sound that triggered every hunger pang in her stomach. "That's all I want, Devon. For us to be sisters again—a family. I know I screwed it up before, but I think we both deserve a second chance."

Devon didn't look exactly happy, but at least she wasn't shouting *Get out of here—leave me alone!* at the top of her lungs, Erinn thought.

She waited until Devon had gobbled the last bits of scrambled eggs from her plate and finished two slices of toast with jam before she took the plunge.

"There's something we need to talk about before you get dressed."

That set off an alarm. As Devon's head flew up and she regarded Erinn warily, Erinn took a calming sip of coffee.

"It's Mick Wheeler."

Devon's gaze slid away. "I don't want to talk about Mick."

"Why not?"

"I just . . . don't." She began tracing circles on the table with her finger, not looking at Erinn. "I know he yelled at you the other night, but he's not always like that. He just—gets mad at people sometimes."

"I think you're afraid of him. And I'd like you to tell me why."

"That's crazy!" Devon's voice rose shrilly. "No way I'm afraid of him. Why would I be?"

"For starters, he doesn't have a very good reputation in this town. He has a temper, he picks fights with people. He's been in prison before. Did you know that?"

"Yeah. So what?" Devon mumbled. "That was before I even knew him."

"Maybe he's doing something illegal again. You lived with him, you would know about it if he did, wouldn't you? You might know things he's done, things that scare you—"

"That's the dumbest thing I ever heard!" Devon pushed herself to her feet, holding onto the edge of the table, wincing as she put weight on her injured ankle. Despite Devon's protestation, Erinn saw panic shimmering in her eyes. "I don't know *anything*. I mean, he hasn't *done* anything! I don't even pay attention to Mick—I hardly talk to him—"

"Jase Fortune thinks he's been killing some of the Fortune ranch's cattle," Erinn interrupted. "If you know anything about that, Devon, you have to tell me. Don't be afraid, I won't let anyone hurt you and Jase Fortune won't either. But you need to tell me the truth."

"That's so lame! Why would he kill a bunch of cattle? I don't know *anything* about that."

"Are you sure? Devon, this is important." Erinn came around the table, put a hand on her arm. "Please, think about this carefully . . . tell me the truth."

"I am!" Jerking away, Devon limped toward the bathroom adjoining her room. "I already told you— it's not my fault if you don't believe me. I'm taking a bath now."

"Devon, wait—"

But her sister didn't look back. The bathroom door slammed behind her and a moment later, Erinn heard water rushing into the tub.

That went well. Not.

Erinn sighed as she cleared the table and loaded the dishwasher. She'd have to tell Jase she'd failed to learn anything from Devon—and she knew just where that would lead. He'd insist on questioning her himself.

And though the last thing she wanted was for Jase to upset Devon, she doubted he could do much worse than she had herself.

Jase.

She had half expected the phone to ring during

breakfast. Jase wanted answers as soon as possible. And he wasn't going to ease off until he got them.

Talk about a man who goes after what he wants, she thought.

Then she went still, plate in hand.

Last night, he wanted you, a voice inside her whispered. *And you wanted him back.*

She paused at the sink, her skin growing warm as she remembered those two encounters on the porch.

Scorching kisses. Intimate touches. It had been all that. And more.

It had been a long while since she'd felt anything deeply—except loneliness.

Oh, she'd gone on plenty of dates, but none of the men she'd been with had ever intrigued her the way Jase Fortune did.

And last night . . .

What was she thinking? Of going on a *date* with Jase Fortune? Because he was devastatingly handsome and sexy enough to light a fire in an anemic nun? Because his eyes fascinated her and drew her in, and she wanted to stroke her hands through that thick dark blond hair of his . . . to touch that strong jaw . . . and maybe a few other places as well . . .

It was perfectly ridiculous. He'd never even asked her for a date. Not that she would go.

But last night, she'd let him kiss her. Touch her. And worse, she'd *liked* it. She'd liked it altogether too much.

What was wrong with her? Didn't she have enough to deal with right now? The answer was clear, especially in the merciless bright light of day. The earth was damp and clean and washed, the sky was clear crystalline blue, and she had a lot more important things to worry about than what Jase Fortune had been thinking when he'd kissed her like he couldn't get enough of her on the porch.

Not least of which was what *she'd* been thinking when she'd kissed him back.

You need to think about Devon, she told herself. *And Mick Wheeler. And getting Devonshire out of that spider web...*

Think about your visions...who it is in that cave, or in that coffin. And where it's happening—or going to happen—or did it happen yesterday, last month, or long ago?

She sighed. The visions were so random, so unpredictable. And she had as little control over *when* the tunnel would sweep open before her as she did over *what* she'd see when it did.

The only thing she could control right now was this chance to make things right with her sister. And to keep Devon safe.

There was no room in her life for a casual affair with Jase Fortune or anyone else, so what she needed to do was get him out of her thoughts.

And keep him out.

Be a grown-up about what happened last night, and don't let it happen again, she told herself. *It's easy. Simple.*

Done, she thought, and then her cell phone rang.

Devon soaked in the flower-scented bath water, feeling like she could drown of despair. If only she could stay here all day. Not have to face Tiffany again and all the questions.

She couldn't tell her anything about Mick, no matter how much Tiffany yelled at her or begged her to open up. Tiffany would only get hurt, and so would she. Mick would find out and he'd make her pay. He'd make both of them pay.

He'd almost hit her once before, when she left his steak under the broiler too long. But Hank had stopped him. For a moment she'd been more afraid than ever before in her life because of the expression on Mick's face. Pure fury like she'd never seen. Added to the fact that he was so frighteningly strong.

She closed her eyes, settling her shoulders down into the bubbles, trying to relax as the hot scented water enveloped her.

Tiffany had put these pretty bath beads on the shelf, along with matching body wash. They smelled like a combination of lavender and rose. Delicious. Relaxing.

It's supposed to make you feel calm and beautiful, she thought, thinking of all the ads on TV and in magazines.

But she felt nervous and scared.

Sometimes she wished she'd never met Hank at the shelter. She'd had such a crush on him at first, but now . . . well, things weren't as good between them anymore. They still messed around, but it wasn't the same. She'd seen him in town once or twice talking to other girls. And that scared her. What if he dumped her?

If that happened, Mick might figure he could do anything he wanted to keep her quiet. Even kill her.

And even though Hank insisted he wouldn't let

anything happen to her, no matter what—maybe he'd get tired of stepping in and would just let Mick do it.

Her throat closed up as she thought of how different things might have been if she hadn't met Hank. Hadn't come here with him to live with his brother.

She should have stayed on her own. Then she wouldn't have ever met Mick Wheeler—or Frank Wells. She wouldn't know anything that could land her in jail. Or get her killed.

A sob choked in her throat, and she struggled to swallow it.

There was no way out. She couldn't tell Tiffany anything or Mick would hurt them, kill them both, without blinking.

Her hand shook as she reached for the shampoo. It wasn't the cheap kind she used at the Wheeler cabin, but this thick, foamy one in the pearly rose bottle. *Maybe,* she thought wistfully as she lathered her hair, *when I talk Tiffany into letting me go back to live with Hank at the shack, I could take some of this nice shampoo with me. Some of these bath beads too.*

By the time she'd rinsed her hair and wrapped herself in a towel, she felt cleaner and more refreshed than she had in a long time, even with all the bruises.

Being here with Tiffany wasn't so bad, actually. If only Hank wasn't hurt, and Mick wasn't threatening her. If only she didn't know things that could get everyone in trouble.

But she did. And the sooner she was able to get away from Tiffany and go back to the Wheeler cabin, the better off everyone, including Tiffany, would be.

"Hope I'm not calling too early."

The sound of Jase's voice was oddly reassuring. Low, deep, even. But there was tension in it too, Erinn noticed. It was subtle, but it was there.

"Not at all." Erinn glanced at the bathroom door and lowered her tone. "I struck out this morning," she said softly. "Devon just closed up on me. She wouldn't tell me anything about Wheeler. I tried, believe me."

"I do. But there's another problem." Jase sighed. "I spoke with Sheriff Farley this morning. Wheeler has an alibi for yesterday. According to his account, he couldn't have shot Rawley. He claims he was at work at the Hanging J, repairing fence with another hand, Red Drummond. And Red vouched for him being there all afternoon."

Erinn closed her eyes, remembering the fleeting glimpse of the man she'd seen yesterday on the road and in the woods. "That's not possible. I could swear I saw him on our property—er, *your* property. How far away from here was your foreman shot?" she asked suddenly.

"A good thirty miles. He could easily have shot Rawley, then hightailed it to your place—but *not* if he was really repairing fence all afternoon."

"Why would that other ranch hand lie for him? Unless he's in on this too—whatever this is."

"I'm planning to have a few words with Red and see if I can get at the truth. Right now, Farley's inclined to look elsewhere for the shooter. But he doesn't have a damn thing to go on. His men haven't even been able to locate the slug."

"I'll try again with Devon later," Erinn promised, but her heart felt heavy as Jase told her he'd be in touch.

Closing her phone and dropping it into her purse, she took a deep breath. Part of her wished she could just whisk Devon back to New York today, away from whatever ugliness Wheeler was involved in. She didn't like how any of this business felt. Not at all.

But another part of her didn't want to run. She and Devon had both run away in the past. In some ways, they were still running.

Perhaps it was time to hold their ground.

Besides, it would be hell getting Devon to leave Hank right now. *And if I did manage to get her to New York, who's to say she wouldn't run off and disappear all over again?*

At least here, Devon felt a bond to Hank. A strong one. There was no chance she'd run away without him.

There was another reason Erinn didn't want to leave Wolf River yet. A reason she knew she'd have to face. It wasn't only all the work she'd put into the cabin, how the place was growing on her, how much she enjoyed looking out at cottonwoods and wildflowers and snow-crowned mountains in the distance.

It was the man who owned this cabin. The man who'd kissed her on the porch in the darkness last night, who'd called her first thing this morning.

Maybe she should run away from him—but she didn't want to. Not yet.

She wanted to see if she could hold her ground.

Chapter Twenty-four

It was almost midafternoon but the Saddleback Grill was still fairly bustling when Erinn shifted the large shopping bag to her other hand and opened the door for her sister.

But Devon hung back. "Can't we just go to the cabin? I want to try everything on."

By "everything" she meant the two pairs each of jeans and khakis, three pairs of shorts, and assorted T-shirts and tank tops Erinn had bought her in a multitude of colors, along with a new pair of sneakers and pretty open-toed pale green sandals.

"We won't stay long," Erinn promised, "but I'm famished for some lunch after all that shopping. Besides, there's someone here I want to talk to."

"Who?" Reluctantly Devon limped into the restaurant, and Erinn followed her.

"Straight ahead. Lily Fortune."

She'd spotted Lily as they passed the window, seated in the back at a large round table with Ginny, Colton, and Culp.

But as they made their way through the restaurant,

she could sense Devon's tension. The girl seemed to
withdraw even more within herself when there were
other people around. Erinn had noticed it when they
shopped, and even now, as Amanda, the pretty teenage
waitress who'd spilled coffee on Erinn last week,
rushed past them, murmuring, "There's a table in the
corner—I'll be with you soon as I can," Devon kept her
gaze downcast, seemingly unwilling to engage with
anyone else unless absolutely necessary.

She'd been different with Hank this morning though.
She'd hurried to his hospital bed, and immediately
burst into tears when she saw him with an IV in his tat-
tooed arm and bruises covering his face.

"It doesn't hurt hardly at all," the boy told her as
Devon clutched his hand and Erinn watched quietly
from just inside the doorway. "I'll be okay, Dev."

"When can you go home?" Devon had whispered,
but Erinn had managed to hear the softly spoken
words.

"The doc thinks maybe in a few days. You just gotta
hold on, Dev. Okay?"

He'd glanced, frowning then, at Erinn.

"I'm trying, but—" There'd been no mistaking the
urgency in Devon's tone. "It's just that . . . oh, never
mind. Don't worry, I'll be okay. As long as I know
you're coming home."

She still thinks she's going back to that shack, Erinn
had realized. That was never going to happen.

But she'd decided not to worry about that next battle yet, especially since she had no doubt who was going to win it.

"Well, look who's here," Ginny exclaimed as she and

Devon approached the table and Erinn performed the introductions. "We were talking about you two earlier."

"Jase told us the news," Lily added as Culp and Colton both came to their feet and pulled two extra chairs over to the table. "He told us the two of you are sisters, and that you've only just been reunited. He was a little vague about the details," she said with a smile that looked strained as both Devon and Erinn took their seats. "But I haven't had much time to question him yet—what with everything else that's going on."

"You're talking about Rawley." Erinn had already picked up on the grim mood of the group. "How is he today? He's going to be all right, isn't he?"

"Yes, thank God." Lily's blue eyes flashed with anger. "No thanks to whoever ambushed him."

"Jase is meeting with Farley over at the sheriff's office right now," Colton told Erinn. "We're just hoping Farley has some kind of lead. It's getting old—being someone's punching bag. I've just about had enough."

"What happened to Rawley yesterday is the last straw." Culp downed the remains of his coffee and set his mug down with a thump.

"I'm on patrol the next two nights," he added, turning to Colton. For once his good-natured face was somber, bereft of all humor. "And man, would I love to get lucky—catch someone out there who's got no business being on Fortune land. I'd give my hat, my boots, and my teeth to get my hands on the son-of-a-bitch who plugged Rawley," he added with a scowl.

Erinn saw Devon trying to follow the conversation and explained. "Someone shot the Fortune ranch's foreman yesterday—he wasn't badly hurt, but no one knows who was behind it."

"But everyone in town's talking about it," Ginny put in, her lips pursed. She pushed back her chair and started gathering up plates. "Every single person who's walked in my door today has been flapping their jaws about Rawley. Everyone's worried."

"Wolf River is usually such a quiet town." Lily sighed. "Now, within two days, we've had a car wreck and a shooting. Normally the biggest happening around here is someone's dog having puppies."

"Or Mick Wheeler getting in another barfight at the Redrock," Colton snorted.

Devon stared at him, then dropped her gaze, flushing.

Lily elbowed her brother in the ribs.

"Hey!" He looked at her blankly for a moment, then suddenly his lean, tanned cheeks turned pink. "Sorry. I didn't mean anything, Devon—you're well away from those Wheeler boys. You've got nothing to be embarrassed about—"

"Colton," Lily broke in, this time glaring at him.

But it was Ginny who managed to change the subject. "What can I get you two?" she asked Erinn and Devon, her arms loaded with plates. "I have to get back to work anyways."

They both ordered burgers and Cokes, and as Ginny sauntered toward the kitchen, the bell over the diner's door tinkled and two men entered the restaurant.

One was tall and broad-shouldered, with thin red hair and a matching mustache. The second man's mop of brown hair nearly touched his shoulders—he was younger, maybe early twenties, with the whipcord physique of a rodeo rider. Erinn recognized them from the barn dance. The younger one had danced with Lily several times.

"Sit wherever you want, boys," Ginny called, poking her head out from the kitchen.

As they headed toward a booth near the front of the restaurant, Culp and Colton both immediately turned to check out the newcomers, as if half expecting some suspicious-looking stranger to amble in, someone who might have shot up Rawley and the Fortune cattle— someone who didn't live in or near this small, usually peaceful town.

"Hey, Brock, Dusty." Colton nodded at the two, re- laxing, then turned back to the table.

"Well, I'd better head out." Culp thrust some bills down next to his coffee cup and shoved back his chair. "Need to catch a few z's before I go on patrol." The ten- sion had returned to his face.

If anything, Erinn thought, he looked even more grim than before. "Sorry I'll have to miss Clay's welcome-home shindig, but with any luck, maybe I'll be throwing a little party myself."

With a quick nod at Lily and Erinn, he headed toward the door.

"Culp, please—be careful tonight," Lily called after him just before the door banged shut.

The two men at the other booth, who'd looked up briefly when Culp passed their table, returned to their perusal of the menu, and Erinn glanced at Lily.

"Your father's coming home tonight?"

"Yes, a day early. He called this morning to check on

things and Colton just *had* to tell him what happened to Rawley."

"He knew something was wrong before I said a word, I swear it," Colton exclaimed. "That man has a sixth sense about this kind of thing and you know it, Lily."

"All I know is that he booked the first flight he could get out of Houston, and he'll be breathing fire until whoever shot Rawley is caught." She blew out her breath. "Which is why I'm organizing this little welcome-home dinner party for him. Rawley's the other guest of honor, so Dad can't refuse to come. He'll see Rawley's all in one piece, even if a little worse for wear. And maybe having a little welcome celebration will distract him from wanting to go gunning at midnight all over the range for anyone within a hundred yards of Fortune land. So," she said suddenly, her face lighting as she looked from Erinn to Devon. "Why don't you both join us?"

"Now there'a a good idea," Ginny said, reappearing with their food before Erinn could demur. She set plates heaped with hamburgers, french fries, lettuce, and sliced tomatoes before Erinn and Devon, as Amanda set down their Cokes.

"I'll be closing up early and coming over to fry up some chicken—Clay's favorite dish," Ginny said. "Especially with mashed potatoes, so we'll be having that too."

"And remember you promied me a rain check," Lily reminded Erinn. "We owe you some Western hospitality, remember?"

Clay Fortune's welcome-home party? I don't think so,

Erinn thought. Aloud she said, "I'm not sure Devon's up to it—"

"How about it, Devon?" Colton cut her off, suddenly flashing his devastating smile at the girl. "You like fried chicken, don't you?"

Devon took a peep at him and a slow blush bloomed in her cheeks. "Y-yeah," she mumbled. She glanced at Erinn's astonished face, and her chin tilted up defiantly. "Sure."

Colton's smile widened. "Then you're in for a treat. Ginny's is the best in the county. You ever had her chicken before?"

Devon shook her head.

"Well, then, it's settled." He winked at Devon, grinned at Erinn, and peeled a handful of bills from his wallet.

"Don't eat too much, ladies," he advised them. "We'll see you at six. Lily and I have to get a move on— we're picking up the old man at the airport."

"I almost forgot!" Lily pushed back her chair abruptly. "Pop will blow a gasket if we're late," she explained with a chuckle. "See you both tonight."

Devon munched her fries after they left, absorbed in her own thoughts, but Erinn found her appetite was gone.

Dinner at Fortune's Way. With Clay Fortune.

She wasn't looking forward to it. One encounter with the Fortune patriarch had been quite enough. On the other hand, the invitation also meant she'd be having dinner with Jase.

But she knew she should be staying away from him. Weren't there enough complications in her life at the moment without getting involved with a sexy alpha male who'd offer her nothing beyond a one—or maybe two—night stand?

But what nights they would be, she thought wistfully, remembering the hard strength of his body pressed against her, the sparks that had ignited all through her when his warm mouth crushed against hers.

Big mistake, she told herself, yanking her mind free of the memories. *You need to concentrate on Devon. On getting her back to New York, away from the Wheeler brothers. On finishing your book . . .*

Her book. Speaking of which . . .

She'd completely forgotten the reason she'd come in to the Saddleback today in the first place. *The day-care center.* She'd meant to ask Lily what day it would be convenient for her to come in and read to the children. But with all the talk about Rawley, and the welcome-home party, she'd forgotten all about it.

I'll ask her tonight, she thought with a grimace. *Since it looks like there's no way of getting out of it now.*

"Can I wear my new khakis with the dark green shirt tonight?" Devon asked suddenly, breaking into her thoughts.

To Erinn's surprise, her sister's gaze was fixed avidly on hers, and there was a gleam of what could only be hopefulness in her eyes.

"Yes. Of course . . . whatever you want."

"And the sandals?"

"Yes."

"What are *you* going to wear?"

Erinn stared at her, baffled. Until this very moment

Devon hadn't initiated any conversation with her that didn't center around visiting Hank Wheeler, but now her sister was eyeing her with great interest—as if what they were going to wear to Fortune's Way was the most important topic in the world.

"I . . . I don't know yet," she hedged. "Why?"

"Jase Fortune likes you. And you like him, I can tell." Devon shrugged. "So you'll wear something pretty, won't you? I know he kissed you last night. I saw you two through the window."

"Devon!" Embarrassment surged through her.

"It's no big deal, I've seen people kiss before." Devon threw her napkin down on the table and took one last hurried sip of her Coke. She suddenly seemed very much in a hurry.

"Can we go home now? I have to try on my new clothes."

Home? Devon called the cabin home?

Don't make too much of it, she warned herself, even as her spirits lifted. *She's just excited about tonight. Because of Colton.*

The Fortune men possessed a dangerously magnetic charm, she thought ruefully. And both of the Stanton sisters were proving all too susceptible. Which was all the more reason to beware.

"Yes," she told her sister, as she inwardly vowed not to let Devon's heart get broken—or her own. "Let's go home."

Chapter Twenty-five

Delicate ribbons of lavender and crimson swept across the sunset sky as Erinn parked on Fortune's Way's long paved drive.

The house, outbuildings, and pastures burnished in rich gold light glowed serene and magnificent. Adding to the scene of peaceful grandeur were the two horses grazing beyond a pasture fence near the barn. Devon was watching them, a wistful expression on her face as she climbed awkwardly down from the Jeep.

She'd been even more quiet than usual during the drive to Fortune's Way, barely speaking a word. Erinn had wondered what was going on in her mind—if it had to do with Mick Wheeler and the questions Erinn had asked her, or if something else was troubling her.

But she'd been unable to draw Devon out.

"I want to go see them," she murmured, never taking her eyes from the horses.

"I'm sure you can, but after dinner. They're probably waiting for us already."

Erinn's stomach clenched as she lifted the brass

door knocker in the shape of a running stallion and let it rap against the solid wood door.

Lily opened it almost at once and welcomed them into the ranch house.

Clay Fortune was nowhere to be seen, Erinn noted with relief. But then, neither was anyone else, she realized, scanning the long hallway and the vast dining room visible ahead to her right.

She told herself she really didn't mind that it was Lily who had answered the door, eager for their arrival, and not Jase.

But a faint wave of disappointment filled her as she and Devon followed Lily through the sunlit foyer and into the living room and there was no sign of him.

"You're the only ones with the good manners to show up right on time." Lily grinned over her shoulder. "My father's on the phone, ripping into Sheriff Farley for not having caught whoever shot Rawley yet, Jase is finishing up a meeting in town with our attorney, Colton should be back any minute, and I'm not sure what's keeping Rawley. But Ginny's in the kitchen helping me pull everything together."

Erinn hadn't noticed much on her previous visit to the ranch—she'd been too busy trying to escape to pay attention—but as Lily ushered them into the spacious living room she had a swift impression of wood-beamed Western grandeur intermixed with fine antiques and paintings, creating a space that was pleasantly homey and colorfully elegant all at once.

Sprawling hardwood floors, high-beamed ceilings, and ornate black iron chandeliers blended comfortably with subdued Oriental rugs and olive green leather

sofas facing one another, clustered with several upholstered chairs in a cream-and-green and gold-vine pattern that gracefully balanced the rough manliness of
the leather. A granite fireplace dominated one entire
wall, its massive mantel lined with family photos, a col-
lection of candlesticks, and several Remington sculp-
tures.

Above the mantel was a gold-framed painting of a
woman in her thirties. She was slim and blonde and elegant, seated in one of the chairs that graced the living
room, wearing a knee-length black silk evening sheath
with a strand of pearls lustrous at her throat.

Her eyes were a sparkling blue, the color of a mountain lake, and an impish smile lit the woman's face, a
smile so mischievous and full of spirit it made an amus-
ing contrast to the sophisticated dress and the neat, la-
dylike way her hands were folded in her lap.

"That's our mother—Anne Fortune," Lily said, seeing Erinn studying the painting. "She was every bit as
strong-willed as our father, but much more subtle
about it," she added with a laugh.

"You'd never know she was determined to have her
way, until she'd gotten it. She was actually engaged to
marry another man when she met Dad, back when she
was only twenty-two years old—but the very next day
after she clapped eyes on him, she called off her en-
gagement."

"Had she been having doubts?" Erinn asked, still
studying the woman's image. The portrait artist had
captured steel in Anne Fortune's proper bearing, in the
way she held her head—but it was matched by the humor and warmth that shone through those vivid eyes.

"She claimed that she hadn't had a one—not until she set eyes on Dad. It was love at first sight—for both of them." Lily shook her head. "She knew it from the first moment, and she told me once that it made what she felt for her fiancé, what she thought was love, pale like a bleached sheet, with all the color faded from it."

Lily turned from the painting, a hint of sadness in her voice. "She died of a brain aneurysm when she was forty-six. It was a sudden loss, a huge one. We miss her. All of us—but no one more than my father. She would have wanted him to remarry, but..." Lily shrugged. "He never will. He's too stubborn. About that, as well as so many other things," she added with a grin.

"I don't believe I've met these pretty ladies," a rough voice scratched out behind them.

Lily introduced them to Rawley. The ranch foreman's knees seemed permanently bent, and his left arm was in a sling, but his deep-set eyes were as acute as any man's twenty years his junior.

"Pleasure, ma'am. And *miss,*" he added, those observant eyes fixing on Devon, standing slightly behind Erinn, silent and pretty and withdrawn in her dark green shirt and khakis.

"I hope you're not in too much pain," Erinn said.

"No, ma'am. Not a mite. It takes more than a measly little flesh wound to bother old Rawley. If you ask me, everyone made a bigger fuss over it than need be."

"Is this a private party or can anyone come?"

Colton sauntered in, his arm around the waist of a tall striking young woman in snug-fitting white jeans and a yellow cotton sweater.

Devon's face fell.

"I'd like you to meet my girlfriend, Sue Lynn Platt," he said, taking the brunette's hand as he introduced her to Devon and Erinn. "Sue Lynn lives in Crystalville," Colton explained, oblivious to Devon's barely mumbled greeting. "She and her mom own a camping outfitter there. They're thinking of franchising it out across Montana, Wyoming, and—"

Erinn heard Devon mumble something else and turned toward her. "I'm sorry, what did you say?"

The girl's entire body had gone stiff as a board. "I'm going outside to see the horses," she muttered in a strained tone.

"Sure." Lily smiled at once. "Go right ahead. We'll come find you when dinner's ready."

But Erinn's heart sank as she watched her sister limp from the room as quickly as she could manage. The fact that Devon had a crush on Colton Fortune reassured her in one sense—that the girl's attachment for Hank Wheeler might not be as serious as she'd feared, and that perhaps it was based more on need and dependence than anything deeper. But now Devon was hurting because she'd made too much of Colton encouraging her to come to dinner.

Being a teenager sucks, she thought, as she chatted with Colton and Sue Lynn about camping equipment and the tourists who passed through Crystalville on their way to the national forests and parks.

But she was fully aware that she wasn't much better. She found herself glancing every few moments at the door, wondering when Jase would put in an appearance.

Even as she tried to tell herself it didn't matter to her if he did or not.

Yet when he finally walked into the kitchen a short time later as she was tossing the salad for Ginny and Lily was carrying out platters of fresh grilled corn on the cob, her heart leaped with so much pleasure it shocked her.

Just the sight of his tall, powerful frame, the calm expression in his eyes, the way they seemed to light up as his gaze met hers, made her heartbeat quicken as if she was still a hormonally charged teenager of fifteen herself.

"Glad you could make it," he said casually as Ginny looked up from arranging golden fried chicken on a platter and Lily stopped in her tracks, the platters of corn in her hands as she studied her brother and Erinn with unabashed interest.

"I'm glad you could too."

Everyone laughed, Jase included. "Blame our attorney. He needed me to help him solve a business problem right now. But where's Devon?"

"Checking out your horses. Lily said it was all right."

Jase nodded, his gaze meeting hers. Erinn knew he was remembering what Devon had told them last night about Genevieve.

"She's welcome to come over and ride whenever she'd like to—as soon as her ankle's better," he said thoughtfully. Then he noticed his sister was still standing there, watching them converse with a rapt expression.

"Don't you need to set those on the table?" he asked. "And where's Pop?"

"Haven't seen him. He must still be on the phone bawling Farley out. Can you grab the coleslaw, Jase?" Lily hurried to the dining room and Ginny followed.

"Any luck with Devon today?" he asked Erinn as they found themselves alone in the kitchen.

"None. She hasn't told me anything more since I struck out this morning. What about you? That ranch hand from the Hanging J you were going to speak with?"

"Red stuck to his story. But he's lying."

As she stared at him in surprise, he rubbed his jaw, his gaze narrowing. "He looked shocked when I told him about Rawley getting shot. Then he hesitated just a second before he reiterated his story that Wheeler was with him, working all afternoon. But he didn't sound quite as sure of himself. He's covering for him—I'd stake my life on that. But he won't admit it, at least not yet."

"So that does you no good with the sheriff."

"For the time being." Jase's eyes narrowed. "Farley's been busy working with the county cops busting meth labs—the latest one was outside of Bridger. It makes good newspaper copy if he gets his name linked to those busts. And election year is coming up before you know it, so he figures he has bigger fish to fry than Wheeler right now. Of course, if the bastard had actually killed Rawley it would've been a different story."

His lips twisted. "Anyway, Rawley getting shot at isn't his main priority right now—but it is mine," he said grimly. "I'm not willing to let it get to the point of someone getting killed before I put away whoever did it."

"Jase! Erinn! What's going on in there?" Lily called teasingly from the dining room. "Where's the salad and the coleslaw? Colton went upstairs to drag Dad down here and the rest of us are already seated."

"Oh—" Erinn looked startled. "I have to go find Devon," she recalled with a start.

"Here, let me take that in for you." Jase reached for the brimming salad bowl. "You go ahead and find her." He scooped up the bowl of coleslaw as well and headed out to the dining room.

It was unfair the way the man could look so comfortably domestic and still rugged and sexy as hell, she mused as she slipped out the kitchen door.

Dusk was settling over the mountains, shadowing the rich rolling foothills beyond the ranch house. With it came a deep peaceful quiet that would have transfixed her if she'd had time to pause and contemplate it. But since there was no longer any sign of the horses in the pasture and Devon was nowhere to be seen, she hurried toward the barn. As she reached it, she heard a sound from inside that made her freeze.

Laughter. High-pitched, girlish laughter.

Devon's laughter.

And the low rumble of a man's voice.

Erinn grabbed the door and yanked it open.

For a moment, she could only stare in blank amazement at the unlikely scene that met her eyes.

Devon stood on a box in the first of the stalls, brushing one of the buckskin horses with smooth, even strokes. She was smiling, her face lit up, her expression calm, happy, and totally relaxed.

That was only one of the surprising things that made Erinn stare in mute amazement. The second was Clay Fortune.

Jase's father was sitting on a bench, his back to the barn wall. He was stitching a saddle, wearing jeans and a black shirt, looking every bit as content and relaxed as her sister. Both of them had turned toward the door as Erinn entered, and they were looking at her as if she'd intruded upon some private club among old dear friends.

For a moment, she didn't know what to say.

"I . . . dinner . . . it's ready. I didn't know where you were," she blurted.

"Guess what, Tiffany!" Devon appeared not to have heard what she'd said. "Mr. Fortune told me I can ride any of his horses—anytime I want to. Including Peaches, this one—isn't she pretty? And there's a gelding named Diego, that was the other one we saw in the corral. There's even a mare that's in foal! They're quarter horses—they breed them and raise them at Fortune's Way. He said anytime I want, I can help groom them or ride them or—what's wrong?" the girl broke off at last as the frozen astonishment on Erinn's face finally sank in.

"Nothing's wrong. I'm glad you'll have a chance to ride. It's . . . very kind of you, Mr. Fortune." Erinn flashed a glance at the older man, who was regarding her from beneath fierce brows, his blue eyes almost as unreadable as his eldest son's.

"Not kind at all," he grunted. "This young woman

has a genuine way with horses. I've got some, she loves them, why shouldn't she spend as much time with them as she wants?"

Devon's face shone in the dim light. "He thinks the horses like me better than anyone else. I guess Peaches is particular about who grooms her . . . but she took to me right away. She hasn't moved at all since I started, except to nuzzle me now and again." She giggled. "It tickles. Just like when Genevieve . . ." Her face sobered.

"She even looks a little like Genevieve," she said in a softer tone.

A lump rose in Erinn's throat. "I'm glad, Devon. But you may have to check with the doctor before you start riding—"

"Will you call tomorrow and ask if I can? Because Mr. Fortune—"

"Clay," he interrupted her sternly.

"Right, *Clay*," Devon corrected. "He says riding's good for the soul and the body. He might even teach me how to train horses. The mare will be foaling soon and I could even help out when the foals are big enough—" She broke off breathlessly, running a hand along Peaches's mane. The horse dropped her head, raised it again, and shook it with apparent pleasure.

"You said something about supper being ready." Clay Fortune set down the saddle and got to his feet. "I guess Ginny and Lily will tan my hide if I don't show up. Considering I'm supposed to be the guest of honor. Damn foolish idea, if I ever heard one. All I did was come home. Anyway, little lady—" he gazed at Devon, his brows lifting.

"If you're about done, we ought to wash up before

they send a search party for us. A bigger search party, I mean," he added with a brief glance at Erinn. To her astonishment, she saw a twinkle in those shrewd blue eyes.

"Okay." Devon planted a kiss on Peaches's nose and reluctantly slipped from the stall. She set the brush down on a shelf and sighed. "I guess we can eat now, but I'd like to come back and get to know some of the other horses after dinner—if that's all right?" she asked, peeping up at him.

"Can't think why not." He held the barn door open for the two of them. "I'd rather spend a few hours with a horse than most people I know. Though I'd make an exception for my own family and my ranch hands. Course, that includes Ginny too, since she *is* family. Has been for years. You coming—*Tiffany*?"

Chapter Twenty-six

Usually family dinners relaxed Jase—but not tonight. Tonight he was still on edge over the brutal reality of Rawley's getting shot. Proof that someone—either Wheeler, or Wells, or whoever had a grudge against the Fortunes—was getting bolder, and far more dangerous.

But that wasn't the only thing that preoccupied him and kept him from joining in the dinner table conversation. Something was troubling Erinn. And it wasn't her sister. Devon seemed to be enjoying the meal—she'd devoured two helpings of fried chicken and corn on the cob, and had hung on Clay's every word.

Especially when he began talking about the wild mustangs in Montana, offering to take the girl up to Red Horse Canyon to see them sometime. She'd looked like she was ready to leave at that very moment.

Erinn, though, had seemed distant, somewhat distracted.

It wasn't until the table was cleared that he found a moment to get her alone.

"Is something wrong?" he asked quietly.

They were alone in the dining room. Everyone else

was in the kitchen with Lily as she put up coffee, gathered around the huge granite island, swiping tastes of the brownies and blueberry pie Ginny had brought for dessert.

Erinn shook her head with a slight, forced smile. "Nothing, just a little headache." It had started right after she'd returned from the barn. "I can't seem to shake it."

"Some fresh air might help."

"Is this your way of luring me out onto the porch again?"

He grinned. "Actually, I've got an even better idea. This way."

Taking her arm, he drew her down the hallway to a side door opening off the library.

Erinn felt her headache recede as she stepped outside into a breezy, beautiful night. A full pearly moon and thousands of stars dazzled against the inky sky.

"I promised you fresh air, didn't I? The breeze coming down from the mountains is about as fresh as you'll ever get."

Closing the door, he caught her hand, his fingers closing around hers as he drew her down some steps.

"Where are we going? Anyplace in particular?" Erinn asked, intrigued, as they set off across thick grass in the moonlight.

"It's a surprise."

"You've got the wrong woman. I'm not fond of surprises."

He chuckled in the darkness. "Trust me."

Oddly enough, she did. *When did that happen?* she

wondered as they strolled through the night, her hand warm in his.

She shivered as a sudden sharper gust swept across the grass.

"How much farther is this surprise?" The grass had given way to a dirt track, and they were now following it, passing willows and cottonwoods whose summer leaves swayed in the breeze.

"You're cold." He glanced at her. "Sorry, I should have thought to give you a jacket. Come on, let's run. That's one way to warm you up."

She could think of a few other ways it could be done, but she was trying hard not to as they ran down the track, veering slightly downhill from the ranch house.

"Okay, watch your step here," Jase warned when they reached a small clearing, and up ahead she saw a barn.

The ranch house was no longer in sight behind them and Erinn realized they must be a good quarter of a mile away now.

"What is this place?" To her surprise, Jase produced a key and fit it into a lock on the barn door.

"It's my home."

"You live in a barn?"

He opened the door and switched on a light, then touched a hand to the small of her back, guiding her inside.

He *did* live in a barn. But a barn like none she'd ever seen. Tall beams crisscrossed beneath the roof, the walls were painted a rich dark blue. There were no horse stalls or harnesses or benches. The place was open, clean, mostly barren, except for the king-size bed in one corner, with a black quilt across it, a galley kitchen set in where the stalls might have once been, a bathroom, and a maroon leather sofa and brass trunk coffee table facing a stone fireplace.

It was spartan, rustic—and oddly attractive in its rugged simplicity.

"Why?" she asked, turning to face him as he pushed the door closed. He grinned at her, a slow, sexy grin that made her heart gallop.

"Because I'm too old to live at home?" He led her to the fireplace. "It's warmer over here. I'll get a fire going. I don't use the central heat in the summer, but the nights get cool."

Erinn sank down on the sofa and watched him light the logs in the hearth, stirring them with the poker until a blaze crackled.

Warmth crept over her as Jase sat beside her on the sofa.

"After my divorce, I came back to Fortune's Way to help run the ranch. My father had suffered a heart attack and I basically had to force him to let me take over the day-to-day operation. But once I had things under control, I moved out. I needed my space," he said, "and my privacy. This old abandoned barn happened to adjoin our property. I restored it."

"So now you have the best of both worlds."

He nodded. "I can work at the big house, have meals with my family when I choose, and have this place to come home to. I like the peace here. The quiet."

"It must have been a lot of work to renovate this. But . . . I guess moving back to the cabin you built when you got married wasn't an option."

The yellow-orange licks of firelight seemed to accentuate the hard planes of his face, the stubble on his jaw. "No. It wasn't. Too many memories there. Some good ones, but mostly bad."

He sighed and glanced over at her wryly. "My marriage was a mistake from the beginning. We were both too young, we wanted different things. I should have thought it through, waited, given us time to figure out who we were, where we were headed. I know that now—I didn't then."

"It sounds like you're blaming yourself."

"It was both of our faults. I was in too much of a hurry. And it cost me." His gaze pierced hers. "I was in a fever to tie the knot, to rush into my future and bring it to its knees, like a cow I was lassoing. But when the rope snaked around its neck, I was the one who went crashing down."

Her chest tightened at the regret in his face. Without thinking, Erinn placed her hand gently over his.

"The truth is," Jase said slowly, "I loved Carly. At least, I thought I did."

"Then . . . what went wrong?"

"Reality." Jase turned to her, his gaze steady on her face. "We wanted different things. Always did. My roots were firmly planted at Fortune's Way—in the ranch, in my family. Carly itched to escape. To her Wolf River was Hick Hell. But after college, she was all for building our own home, a nice cozy cabin, and I thought that meant she was ready to settle down." He grimaced. "On our six-month anniversary, I found out different. She sprang the news that she wanted to move. To California."

Erinn shook her head. "Why?"

"She said she had a plan, a plan for both of us. We'd move to California, she was going to become an actress, and the cabin would become our *vacation* home. It was the first I'd heard of it. I thought she was kidding at first, but she was dead serious. Was I going to give her a shot at her dream, so she could pursue an acting career, or be selfish and insist she stay in Wolf River? We argued about it for months, then things got really rocky. I wanted the marriage to work, so I agreed to move."

Sympathy seeped through her. She'd already concluded that Jase wasn't the type of man who gave up on anything easily. Especially something as important as marriage.

"What happened in California?" she asked as he leaned back on the sofa and rubbed his jaw.

"I bought a small ranch and horse-breeding operation outside of Santa Barbara—a little over an hour from L.A. Carly spent several months driving back and forth constantly to L.A., auditioning, trying to get herself an agent. Finally she landed a walk-on in a soap opera, a few bit parts in some studio movies. She got to play a doped-up hooker in a Bruce Willis thriller— three seconds of screen time. It only made her hungry for more."

He stood up abruptly and paced to the window, then back, shoving his hands in his pockets.

"I didn't blame her for wanting it. I'd always known she'd dreamed about fame, celebrity, sophistication. She wanted to walk down the red carpet, see her face splashed across *Entertainment Tonight*. I guess I thought she'd outgrow it after we were married and settled down, but that wasn't what happened."

The frown lines between Jase's eyes had deepened as he talked, and she sensed the bitterness in him.

"What did happen?" she asked quietly.

"She started spending more and more time away from home. In L.A. Eventually I found out why. She was screwing her agent. They'd been having an affair for a month before I caught on."

Erinn went still.

"It turned out she was also sleeping with the fifty-two-year-old director of an upcoming film, lobbying for a part. It didn't mean anything to her, that's what she told me. It was just what she had to do to get ahead. To get *noticed*."

Shock, sympathy stabbed through her. "I'm sorry, Jase. So very sorry."

He returned to sit beside her, his expression hard. "It got pretty ugly after that. I moved out, said I wanted a divorce. Turned out she did too. Our marriage was holding her back. She needed to be in L.A. full time. She followed me back to Fortune's Way, though," he added, his voice coolly controlled.

"She told me she wanted to work things out. But it wasn't the marriage she wanted to work out—it was the divorce. She had a list of demands, and when I told her we would do it through our lawyers, she went ballistic. She left, but not before she snuck into my office and cleaned out ten thousand dollars from the safe—and then snatched my mother's pearls from Lily's jewelry box."

Erinn gasped. "What? Not the pearls your mother was wearing in the painting?"

"The same ones." His lip curled. "Don't worry. I got

them back. I went to L.A. one more time, got the pearls, told Carly I'd give her whatever she wanted, a more than generous settlement, if she stayed out of my life for good, never came near Fortune's Way or anyone in my family again. And that," he said evenly, "was that."

For a moment there was silence. The only sounds were the wind whooshing outside through the trees and the hiss and crackle of the fire.

"But it's not really over, is it?" she asked quietly. "Carly . . . she's still there, hurting you. Every day. Isn't she?"

"That's the funny part. She was—for a long time." Jase held her gaze. "Lately," he said, a note of surprise in his tone, "she's gone. Just gone. And so, strangely, is the pain." His eyes gleamed in the firelight, and Erinn felt a warm tingle clear down to her toes.

"I actually think it helped being forced to see the cabin again. To take stock of it. Even," he added, "to see how you changed it. It's different now. Because of you. So am I."

Her breathing quickened. His eyes were locked on hers. "As a matter of fact, Carly . . . our marriage . . . the divorce too . . . seem a lot more distant than they ever did before. Right now—"

He broke off. Erinn held her breath.

"Right now what?" she whispered.

"Right now I can't even picture her in my mind. Not her face, not her hair, or her smile. Dammit, Erinn, all I can see is—you."

She didn't know how it happened, but she edged closer, he drew her in, and suddenly she was in his arms, being held close and powerfully, his eyes glinting into hers.

"And that's . . . a good thing?" she murmured. Heat fired through her like an electrical jolt as she fitted herself against hard sinew and rock-solid muscle.

His smile was slow, intensifying as he took in the soft light glowing in her eyes. He lowered her beneath him on the sofa, reached down, and slid a gentle hand through her hair.

"Why don't we find out?"

He kissed her then and she forgot the question. She forgot everything as his hard body pressed against hers, as he explored her mouth and she savored the taste of him, the sensuous thrusting of his tongue against hers. Her heart pounded against her ribs as the kiss deepened, turned demanding, raw with need.

Erinn clutched at his shoulders, feeling alive, so very alive even as she felt herself slipping into a netherworld of heat and swirling madness. Jase's smooth, hot mouth was stirring a desire in her, a desire so elemental it was like molten lava shooting through her bloodstream.

Touching his skin, she knew she wasn't alone. Heat and fire radiated from his powerful body. He groaned deep in his throat and plunged his hands into her hair.

Slow down, a voice told him, but he ignored it. He didn't want to slow down. Or to think. Or to be cautious. Not tonight, not with her. Erinn was so beautiful, so incredibly sexy and vibrant, he was ready to explode from the wanting of her.

Even the scent of her, reminiscent of the most delicate of flowers, filled him, wrapping him in the beauty of her as he kissed her the way he'd wanted to from the first time they met.

Everything else was swept from his mind—there was only Erinn, so soft, so sensuous, so right in his arms.

Her hands tore at the buttons of his shirt, pushed it aside. Eagerly her fingers danced across the mass of crisp golden brown chest hair, caressing him as raw need squeezed him hard, tightening his entire body.

When her hands rubbed across his nipples he drew in his breath. Her fingers were magical and light, skimming downward, over his flat belly, then lower, lower still, brushing across the whorl of hair that disappeared inside his jeans until he growled with pleasure and crushed his mouth to hers.

"Erinn." His breath was warm against her lips. "God, I want you."

"Then take me," she whispered, her eyes burning into his, her hands snug around his neck now, pulling him closer. "Please, Jase, take me."

"You got it, babe." His lips captured hers, and her senses swam. "But it's not going to be fast and it's not going to be easy. Are you ready for a hell of a ride?" he asked hoarsely. Before she could answer, he reached for her peach silk tank top and yanked it in one smooth movement over her head.

Erinn gasped with laughter and tugged frantically at his belt buckle. *Two can play this game,* she thought, heady warmth flowing through her as she unsnapped his jeans, dragging the zipper down.

"Are *you*?" she challenged, then trembled beneath an onslaught of dizzying kisses.

What happened next was a blur of frantic move-ment—clothes stripped off and flung aside, wild kisses, twisting bodies, sofa cushions tumbling to the floor.

"So beautiful," Jase murmured as he kissed and ca-ressed her breasts. She was naked and trembling be-neath him, her skin golden, silky—exquisite. Her lips were red and swollen, yet still begging for more.

Tension coiled within him as he cupped her breast, caressed its smooth lush softness and felt her quiver. When he took her nipple in his mouth, she moaned and his groin ached with the urge to take her now, all of her, to bury himself in her hard and quickly. But he held back, taking his time as he pleasured her, savoring the way her body clenched with exquisite tension as he circled his tongue around the taut peak with lan-guorous, teasing strokes.

"Stop...no, don't stop..." she breathed, and he grinned, then kissed her neck, his mouth pressing against the soft flesh.

She tasted delicious, felt delicious. He'd never wanted any woman so much. Never felt anything like what he felt for her.

"We're only just beginning," he whispered in her ear.

"Oh, God, Jase." She kissed him fiercely, twining her legs about him.

He loved each breast in turn, tormenting her nipples with his mouth and his thumbs, arousing her until she couldn't even whisper, but just gasped and arced help-lessly against him, her hands scraping down his back.

Only then did he slide his hand lower, stroking her

hot lithe body as his blood coursed through him, raging like a fire.

His muscles were rigid with self-control as at last he brushed his fingers against the tangle of dark curls between her thighs and felt a shudder of anticipation run through her.

She felt like damp velvet beneath his fingertips. Slowly, watching her eyes, he slid his finger inside her. She was slick and ready, her breath coming now in gasps.

Instantly she opened her legs, her eyes shimmering like green crystals into his, nails digging into his shoulder. She wrapped her legs around him, her body straining toward his.

"Jase, now." Her hand teased his erection, moving with firm, rhythmic pressure. His throat thickened. "Please . . . now . . . you're driving me crazy . . ."

"Hell, sweetheart, that's nothing compared to what you're doing to me." His voice was raw, his lust roaring as at last he moved inside her.

He filled her gently at first, then urgency swamped him. He plunged more deeply. She took him in, welcoming him with frenzied thrusts and soft cries, her body arching fiercely in rhythm as he thrust deeper and harder, faster and faster.

Their bodies fused in a mad ecstasy as sanity fled, the earth spun away, and neither knew where one ended and the other began.

Erinn only knew that Jase filled her senses, her body, her world and she would be empty without him.

Together they twisted and rocked upon the sofa, as

sweat slicked their skin, and pleasure exploded again and again within them. The world outside was forgotten. Fortune's Way, the Wheeler brothers, even Devon, were no more.

There was only the two of them in this big drafty barn, the roaring fire, and the need that sent them soaring, flying, spiraling to the clouds, racing to the moon, beyond the stars, until a splintering climax shook them to their cores and they free-fell back to earth. Floated at last *down* and *down* and *down* onto the cushions of the sofa, locked and sated in each other's arms.

Dazed, Erinn lay with her head nestled upon Jase's chest. Her breathing had slowed, and sanity was returning in small, rational trickles. Yet she didn't want to move. The moment was perfect.

Firelight flickered gently through the barn, across the sofa. Jase's body was warm and solid against hers. She closed her eyes and sighed with pleasure as his breath ruffled her hair and his arms tightened around her.

The peace of that drifted away suddenly as she remembered. *Devon*. Back at the house . . . the Fortunes, Ginny . . .

"What time is it?" she shot up to a sitting position, her throat dry.

"Time to start all over again?" Jase murmured. He tugged her back down, but she shot up again, shoving her curls from her eyes, staring at him. "How long have we been gone from the house?"

He grinned then, consulted his watch, the only thing he was still wearing. "About an hour."

An hour. She closed her eyes, opened them quick. "They're all...looking for us. Wondering where we are—"

He chuckled, and reached for her, pulling her back down atop him. "Should we hightail it back there naked or take a minute to put on our clothes?"

"You—" She broke off, laughing, almost seduced anew by the gleam in his eyes, the lazy, wicked smile that made her blood race.

Somehow she found her lips exploring his one more time, lingering, nipping, before she pulled away abruptly. If she didn't, it would soon be another hour...or longer, before either of them remembered the outside world again.

What was she doing?

More to the point, what had she done?

"We have to go back," she muttered, pulling away. "Right now."

Jase sighed and sat up, letting her go, watching as she raced around, gathering up her clothes, tossing his shirt and jeans at him.

She was more beautiful than ever at this moment and he wanted her again. Hell, he wanted her all night.

He drank in the sight of her breasts before she snapped on that wispy pink bra and pulled her silk top over her head. Her bottom curved enticingly both with and without the pink lace thong she pulled on, and as she yanked on her pants, he figured he'd better stop looking or they'd never get out of here before dawn.

"Okay, so you're eager to go back. I'm not insulted, not at all," he said, tugging on his jeans. "It's Ginny's brownies, I figure. They're almost as good as her pies, but—"

"What are we going to tell them? That we got lost?"

He laughed. The sound made her smile, in spite of the panic that had begun building in her chest.

"That's as good an excuse as any, isn't it?" Jase started buttoning his shirt. "Of course no one in my family's going to buy it, and neither will Ginny, but maybe—" He broke off frowning.

"Erinn?"

She stood frozen, barefoot in her pants and silk top, a frozen expression in her eyes.

"Baby, what is it? Are you all right?" He reached her in a split second, but even then, her eyes were glazed and she was shivering as if she were outside coatless in a snowstorm.

"Erinn!"

Suddenly she teetered forward and he caught her up, sweeping her into his arms.

In two swift strides he reached his bed and set her down gently. Her eyes were open wide, staring, but she wasn't seeing him. Because whatever she was seeing was terrifying.

She was trembling all over, her lips quivered, she was trying to form words.

"Erinn, can you hear me?" He bent over her, touching her face, but he already knew the answer. She couldn't see him, or hear him. She was gone.

————

The darkness was terrifying. She flew down the black tunnel like a rocket, all the breath sucked out of her, and she was hollow but for the terror.

The coffin lay ahead in the darkness and the mist... everything was murky. Where was she... a cave? No... underground? She was cold, so cold. Through the wooden boards like walls enclosing her she saw the figure... still, so still...

Dead, she thought, horror filling her throat like sand crawling with bugs.

No... alive... there was still life... still beating of the heart... beat... beat... beat...

It grew fainter, weaker. Beat... beat...

"She's going to die!"

The words echoed through her head, spinning around and around before they faded to nothingness and she was left with only the clutching horror, the fear, and the cold.

The coffin was gone, the air sucked from Erinn's lungs. Light burned against her eyes, cutting like glass. She was blind, gasping, freezing.

Alone...

Not alone. She tore her eyes open, squinted against the light. Jase's face slowly took form. He was bending over her, speaking.

She couldn't hear the words.

Jase's stomach plummeted. This had happened before, the first day he met her, when she'd collapsed beside her Jeep. But this time, the words she'd screamed were different. And she wasn't waking up as quickly.

Fear had him pounding the keys of his cell phone for

an ambulance, but at that moment she opened her eyes. Thank God. But just like the last time, he could tell she wasn't really there with him . . . not yet.

"Hold on, Erinn," he told her, tossing the phone onto the bed. "I'll be right back."

He grabbed a bottle of wine from the counter, sloshed some into a glass, and strode back to the bed.

Color was beginning to seep back into her ashen cheeks and as he reached her she was struggling to sit up.

"It's okay, baby," he said gently. Her eyes still had that glazed look, her hair was tumbled anyhow about her shoulders. She looked shaken, fragile, lost.

"Let me help you." He propped up the pillows and eased her back against them.

"Sip this," he told her, placing the wineglass in her trembling hands, his own closing around her fingers, steadying her grip.

Erinn's skin felt clammy all over as she sipped greedily at the wine. It burned, comforting in its warmth and tartness as it slid down her throat. Her head ached, pounded, as slowly, the final numbing effects of the vision faded.

Another journey down the tunnel. The third in a week. Something about these was different though. The effects were even more intense, each one lasting longer. Usually they were gone in an instant; usually they came when she was asleep. Now they were closer together, and each time she was being dragged deeper. Each time it was becoming harder to wake up, to shake off the mist and the cold and the darkness.

And the fear.

"Better?"

Jase's voice called to her again, summoning her out of the fog, and she focused on his face, clinging to the solid strength of him, to the here and now.

"Y-yes. I think so." She took a final sip of wine, trying to think, to ignore the worry and questions in his eyes.

"So," he said, as he set the glass down on his nightstand with a clink. "Here's the deal. We're already going to be facing an interrogation when we get back—that's what comes from having a big nosy family around."

He cupped her hand in his big one, and his gaze bored into her. "So as long as we're already missing, we can be missing a little while longer. We can take as long as we need for you to tell me exactly what that was all about."

Chapter Twenty-seven

Jase was waiting for an answer. He deserved one—
Erinn knew that—but still the words lodged like clay in
her throat. This had been her secret for so long. A secret
between her and Detective McKindrick of the NYPD.

This was the one part of her life she'd never been
able to take control of. And she'd never quite figured
out if the visions were a weakness, a gift, or simply a
burden. But they were something that continually reminded her that Erinn Winters was not and might
never be the completely independent, in-control-of-
her-own-life adult Tiffany Erinn Stanton had worked so
hard and long to become.

Now they were getting even more out of control, not
less so. Jase had been with her during two of them. And
as she gazed at him now, she was uncomfortably aware
of the concern in his eyes—and also the implacable determination. He wasn't going to give up, not until she
told him the truth.

She could fight against telling him, refuse, delay—
but it wouldn't be easy. And when it came right down
to it, did she really want to fight him at all?

"It began the night my mother died." Her voice was low.

He didn't move. But his hand tightened around hers. Then he waited.

And so she told him. She'd opened up to him before about having witnessed her mother's suicide, but this time she explained how she'd fainted in reaction to that gruesome event. And how ever since that horrible night, some eerie monstrous door seemed to have cracked open in her soul, leading to a tunnel she didn't want to enter. It took her to places she didn't want to go, showed her things she didn't understand, or have any desire to see—visions of death and danger and darkness.

She told him how this prescient knowledge followed no pattern, but how it used to be infrequent, and had come to her nearly always as she slept. But now, since the day she'd decided to come to Wolf River, the visions had been coming more often, spaced closer together, and during her waking hours.

There'd been three visions in the past week.

Three visions of darkness and of fear, of what may have been a person locked in a coffin, entombed on the brink of death.

Heavy silence filled the old barn when she finished.

Jase released her hand and Erinn pushed herself upward from the pillows, trying to read his thoughts.

His voice when he spoke was level, making it hard to tell what he was thinking. "The last time—when you fainted outside Fortune's Way, you said, '*Is it happening now? I have to stop it.*' " he studied her. "This time it was

'*She's going to die!*' Erinn, do you remember saying those things?"

"No," she replied grimly. "But I seem to remember *thinking* them as I stared at the . . . the figure in the coffin, willing the vision to tell me more, show me more—something that could help. What good is it to have a vision if I can't *do* anything?" she asked in frustration. "I don't even know if it's already happened, or if it's happening right now, or . . ." She swallowed. "If it's going to happen soon . . . or in the future."

Her voice trailed off dejectedly. "If I said it was a woman, then . . . it must be, but . . ." Her green eyes were dark as a river in winter. "If it's happening now, Jase, I could save her, if I only knew where, and *who*."

Jase moved to the bed, sat down bside her, and took her in his arms.

"It's not your fault, Erinn." He kissed the top of her head, holding her close. "You told me yourself you don't control the visions. You have to wait it out, wait for them to show you what's out there. It seems to me there's going to be more coming, and maybe the next one—or the one after that—will reveal what you need to know. Then you'll call your friend McKindrick at the NYPD. See if he can put it all together."

She nodded against his shoulder. "Yes, you're right. As soon as I have something worth telling. Vague images won't help him," she muttered. Then she sighed and drew back, gazing at him with a troubled expression.

"I'm going to have to tell Devon. Another vision might hit me anytime—and she could be with me. It would scare her to death."

"You're right. Did Devon know about them before, when she was a little girl? You lived in the same house until she was four, didn't you?"

"Yes. But I don't think she knew. The visions used to only come at night when I was asleep. Her room was down at the other end of the hall, and she never mentioned anything to me."

She gave a start, as memory rushed back. "Speaking of Devon—"

On the words, his cell phone rang, and Erinn swore silently.

Sure enough, it was Lily.

"Forget dessert," his sister said in Jase's ear. "It's almost time for breakfast, Jase. Did you and Erinn get carried off by aliens—or was it wolves?"

"Aliens, but they've dropped us back at my place. Is Devon okay?"

"Better than okay. She had brownies and pie and now she and Pop are playing gin rummy—in the stables. I think she'd sleep in the hayloft if we'd let her."

Jase shot Erinn a reassuring smile at his sister's words. "That won't be necessary. We're on our way." He clipped the phone to his belt.

Erinn was already scrambling up, finger-combing her hair.

She was in her responsible, big-sister, carry-the-world-on-her shoulders mode again, he noticed. Her next words confirmed it.

"I can't believe I completely deserted her all this time." She hurried toward the door, muttering to herself as she yanked it open. "We never should have—"

Then she stopped herself. She didn't mean that. Just

looking at Jase made her toes curl. And that was nothing compared to what he did to the rest of her.

"Maybe we should have picked a better time," she
corrected herself as Jase threw back his head and
laughed.

"We'll have to plan it out better next time. So we
don't have to rush." He kissed her again, a warm, lingering kiss that had her melting against him.

When the kiss ended, he took a leather jacket from a
hook on the wall and draped it around her shoulders.
"We can't have you freezing to death on my account."

*There's no chance of my freezing to death when I'm any-
where near you.* Erinn thought as they went out together
into the Montana night. *I'm much more worried about
spontaneous combustion.*

Chapter Twenty-eight

Wind whipped through the craggy rocks atop Eagle Peak as Culp lay bleeding beside the rig.

It was two in the morning. The road was deserted, dark as the undercurrents of a river. If coyotes were howling, he couldn't hear them. This high up, he could only hear the wind screaming through the trees, lashing at the branches, pounding him with merciless ferocity.

As if pummeling anew his already battered body.

Its icy breath blasted through his torn and filthy shirt as he dragged himself slowly forward, blood oozing beneath him onto the road.

He didn't go far. Just a few feet from the open door of the truck.

Then a few more.

After that he simply lay there, his bloodied jaw resting against the pavement. Thinking about the beating. The knife slashing across his temple.

Then thinking about LeeAnn.

Regret filled him, every bit as painful as his broken ribs and as the bruises his assailants had inflicted across his body.

He was trying to accept the fact that he'd never get to see his sister again. Never have the chance to tell her good-bye.

Lying across that dark, lonely road, Culp wished this last hand had played out differently. He didn't cotton to throwing in his cards. Never had.

But drop by bloody drop, he knew the game was over.

Don Culpepper's lucky streak had come to an end.

Chapter Twenty-nine

Lily called the next morning as Erinn padded into the kitchen in search of coffee. She'd been hoping it would be Jase.

"I know you said last night you'd stop by the day-care center today to read to the kids." Lily spoke hurriedly. "But it's not going to work out, Erinn. I won't be there." Her voice quavered. "Would you mind if we reschedule?"

"Lily, what's wrong?" She'd never heard Lily sound this upset. Even yesterday, when they'd discussed Rawley's shooting, she hadn't sounded this unnerved.

Devon glanced up from her bowl of Frosted Flakes.

"Culp's missing." Lily choked down a sob. "He never returned from patrol this morning. No one's seen him in the bunkhouse—or anywhere. His rig's not here either."

"You tried to reach him on his cell?"

"For the past few hours. There's no answer." Lily drew a deep breath. "I'm hoping he just ran out of gas. Or the truck broke down and his cell isn't working, or—"

"I'm sure that's all it is," Erinn said quickly, but she was not sure at all. And she knew Lily wasn't either. A lick of apprehension trickled down her spine.

Culp had wanted so badly to get his hands on whoever had shot Rawley, whoever had been killing off Fortune cattle. What if he'd gotten his wish, found whoever was responsible?

Or what if *they'd* found *him*?

"We've started a search," Lily said. "My pop's out there already—so are Jase and Colton. Stitch and I are leaving now in one of the trucks. Some of our hands are searching on horseback, and Sheriff Farley's on his way with some deputies."

"What can I do?" Erinn asked. She felt Devon's gaze on her. "No, never mind," she continued before Lily could answer. "We're coming over there. At least I can make sandwiches and coffee for when you come back, and stay by the phone in case Culp calls the house. If it's okay with you," she finished.

"Erinn, that would be great." Lily's voice shook with gratitude. "Rawley will be here. He's still under doctor's orders. So you won't be alone . . ."

Her voice trailed off. Erinn realized the unspoken implication behind that statement. She wouldn't be alone at Fortune's Way—in case Culp had fallen victim to whoever had been attacking the ranch and its people; in case whoever it was brought his grudge—and the danger—to the ranch house itself.

"We'll be there soon," she promised Lily and hung up.

Quickly she filled Devon in. "You should hurry and get ready," she said, quickly rinsing her coffee cup and Devon's bowl in the sink, shoving them in the dishwasher.

"I want to tell you something first."

Erinn turned in surprise at the seriousness of Devon's tone. The girl was staring at the table, but slowly she looked up.

"I came out of the barn last night when you were on the porch at Fortune's Way talking to Lily. I heard you tell her you'd come to the day-care center today—to read to the kids."

"Yes." She bit her lip. "Devon, I meant to tell you sooner—"

"Wait," her sister interrupted. She got up awkwardly and as Erinn fell silent, the girl limped into the master bedroom. She returned with the copy of *Princess Devonshire and the Big Surprise* that Erinn had left on the dresser when she'd unpacked her suitcase.

"I already know," she said matter-of-factly. "I went to your room last night before we went to Fortune's Way. I wanted to ask you how my new clothes looked on me—but you were still in the shower. Then I saw this." She set the book on the kitchen table and Erinn could see that her hands were shaking.

"You wrote a book about Princess Devonshire," she said slowly. Pain and confusion shone in her eyes. "Why didn't you tell me?"

"I wanted to, Devon. That's why I brought the book with me when I came to Wolf River." Erinn's heart squeezed painfully in her chest. Now she understood Devon's silence in the car yesterday when they drove to Fortune's Way. She'd found the book.

"I wanted you to know that I never really stopped

thinking about you. Or caring about you. That the time we spent together when you were little was important to me. That *you* were important to me. And you still are, Devon. You always will be."

Erinn heard the quiver in her own voice as her sister gazed at her, biting her lip uncertainly. "I meant to tell you about the Princess Devonshire books sooner, but I...I never found the right moment. So much happened—with Hank and Mick, the car accident—"

"You used to make up stories." Devon's voice was a whisper. "About a mouse who was a princess—and a superhero. You named her after me."

"That's right. You always loved listening to Devonshire's adventures. Do you remember them?"

Devon nodded. "Every night there was a different one. They were always in the Emerald Forest—the animals, that is. Devonshire and all her friends. Squeaker the Squirrel," she said, her gaze fixed on Erinn. "Chunky the Chipmunk. And Devonshire's enemy— that goose. Smo...smo...."

"Smogul," Erinn murmured, her throat tight.

"Smogul always called Devonshire a rat."

"He still does, Devon."

A look of wonder crossed her sister's face. "You really didn't forget," Devon breathed. "You didn't forget about me...all those years." Her eyes were wide, tears sparkling on her pale lashes. "You really did c-call me, Tiffany? You...wrote to me, like you said?"

"Yes." Erinn didn't remember going to her, but suddenly she was touching her sister's cheek, cupping her thin face in her hands. "I did, Devon. I thought Annabeth would give you the phone messages. She was your nanny and she knew even more than your mother did how close we were. I was sure she'd see you got my letters. I tried...in the beginning...I shouldn't have stopped—"

"You really did write those books for *me*," Devon choked out suddenly, and Erinn wrapped her arms around her as the girl began to cry.

"I never knew you th...thought about me again. I thought you didn't...c-care—"

"I did, Devon. I *do*." Erinn held her tighter as her sister's shoulders shook with sobs. She felt tears spilling from her own eyes as love and sadness and pain ached from deep within her and she rocked her sister in her arms.

"I made mistakes, Devon," she whispered. "I went back one time and tried to visit you but he was horrible to me. I should have stayed, faced him down, waited there until I could see you. I know that now—but I didn't then. I ran."

Slowly Devon lifted her head, staring through tear-filmed eyes. "You...went back? Really?"

"Yes." Erinn's mouth compressed. "But I was a coward. The Great Dane tore into me and I let him get to me, I let him drive me away—"

"But you didn't *forget*," Devon whispered wonderingly. "You *tried*."

"Yes, I tried, but not hard enough." Erinn blinked back her own tears. "I wasn't as strong as I should have been. I—" She broke off, reaching for Devon, smoothing her hair as more sobs burst from her sister's throat. "I swear I'm going to make it up to you, Devon. I'm going to take care of you from now on."

"Do you...p-promise?" Erinn could barely hear Devon's choked-out words, but she saw the longing in those swollen eyes and felt a surge of hope. Hope for a second chance.

"I *promise*." She squeezed Devon's hand and kissed her wet cheek. "I won't ever let you down again," she whispered, holding the girl tight as Devon's body shook with sobs. "You can count on me, Devon. Today. Tomorrow. Always."

They were late getting to Fortune's Way. Lily had already left with Stitch by the time they arrived, but Rawley was sitting on a chair on the front porch, scowling out from beneath his Stetson.

"No word yet, Miz Winters," he told her as she and Devon came up the steps. "Lily said you're to go on inside and make yourselves comfortable."

"Can I go out to the barn and see the horses?" Devon asked, glancing hopefully back and forth between the grizzled foreman and her sister.

"It's up to Mr. Cooper."

He shoved his hat back. "I reckon I can use a little help with 'em today seein' as we're short-handed. Me and Charley are the only hands left at home right now." His eyes gleamed critically at the slight blonde-haired teenager. "You wantin' to ride or to work?"

"Both." Devon met his gaze hopefully and the foreman's harsh, sunburned face softened ever so slightly.

"Devon, don't forget, you're supposed to be careful of your ankle," Erinn reminded her, but Rawley shook his head.

"I'll take care of her, ma'am, don't you worry. She's

got a bad foot, I've got a bum arm. We'll help each other. You comin', little miss?"

He started toward the barn and Erinn watched as Devon limped after him. Her limp was less noticeable today. Already, her ankle was healing.

Inside the ranch house Erinn confronted silence. It felt strange. No voices filled the house that only last night had been brimming with a lively array of people, smells, tastes, and conversation.

And most of all, Jase wasn't here.

She closed her eyes a moment, thinking of last night, their incredible lovemaking in the barn. And the way he'd kissed her breathless just before they reentered Fortune's Way. She'd felt young and silly and as if her happiness was glowing like a beacon in her face, and she'd been sure his family must know what she was feeling, what they'd been doing when they'd disappeared for all that time. But to her relief, even Lily hadn't said a word, or cocked an eyebrow.

Did Jase sleep last night after we went our separate ways? she wondered, wandering into the living room. She hadn't—at least, not very much.

She glanced up at the painting of Anne Fortune, studying the luminous pearls around her throat, the pearls Jase's first wife had stolen from Lily. She had a feeling that Carly's betrayal of both his mother's memory and his sister had been every bit as painful to Jase as her cheating had been.

Suddenly the phone rang in the kitchen and she raced back and grabbed it from its cradle.

"Fortune residence."

"Erinn?" Jase sounded surprised. "What are you doing there? Did something happen at the cabin?" he asked tautly.

"No, I'm just holding the fort. Lily told me about Culp going missing. Please tell me you found him."

"Not yet." She could hear the tension in his voice. "But we will. Where's Lily?"

"She left to help search for him. She was gone when I got here—"

"Damn it. I told her to stay put until we know what happened to Culp," he growled. "The last thing I need to do is worry about Lily too—"

"She's with Stitch," Erinn told him quickly. "She should be there soon. She's okay, Jase. How are *you*?"

"I'd be better if Lily had listened to me. Erinn, is Devon there with you too?"

"Yes . . . well, sort of. She's in the barn with Rawley at the moment."

"Good. Stay there, both of you. Don't go back to the cabin until we figure out what's going on. Because if Wheeler is behind any or all of this, he might be a lot more angry and a lot more dangerous than we thought. And if Devon knows something—anything—not only can she help us, but . . . she could be in danger."

Erinn felt cold at his words. She turned toward the window, studying the road.

"We'll wait here until you get back. Jase—" She bit her lip. "Be careful."

"You too." His voice softened. "Stay close to the house, Erinn. Don't let your guard down, not until we know what's going on."

She shivered as she set the phone down, then busied

herself making coffee and assembling turkey-and-cheese sandwiches, which she wrapped in foil and stored on a platter in the fridge. Just as she began pacing, her stomach churning at the lack of news, she saw a flash of movement through the window.

An old Silverado was hurtling fast down the long drive. She tensed, glancing toward the stable and outbuildings. Rawley and Devon were still inside, and there was no sign of Charley or any other ranch hand about.

She stepped warily onto the porch as the pickup jerked to a stop and LeeAnn Culpepper jumped out.

"You?" LeeAnn looked astounded and none too happy to see Erinn standing on the Fortune porch. "What the hell are you doing here?"

As she came up the steps, it was clear she hadn't even taken time to brush her hair, much less put on any makeup. For once her narrow, foxlike face was pale, without a trace of blush; her eyes squinting in the sunlight looked naked without the heavy black eyeliner.

"What are you doing here?" she demanded again. "Did they find my brother yet?"

"Not that I know of. I'm waiting for news—"

"Where's Jase?" LeeAnn snapped.

Despite the woman's brusqueness, Erinn felt a wave of sympathy for her.

"He's out searching for Culp along with the rest of his family and most of the ranch hands. Why don't you come in? You look like you could use a cup of coffee—"

"I don't have time for coffee. I'm going to look for my brother." LeeAnn spun around, but in her haste stumbled on the top step and only at the last second caught herself from falling.

"Come on," Erinn said firmly. "Sit down for a minute. Lots of people are out there looking. They'll call as soon as they find him."

"I don't need the likes of you telling me what to do," LeeAnn barked, then she stiffened, her face crumpling like a child's.

"I know I'm . . . being a bitch. It's just—" Tears tumbled down her cheeks. "Donnie's the only family I got left," she grated, pressing the heels of her hands against her eyes. "If anything happens to him . . ."

"He probably got stranded and he's waiting for help . . . or else he's walking home. Someone will find him," Erinn assured her, hoping it was true.

"Yeah. They will, right?" LeeAnn had swiped away the tears, but her eyes were still red-rimmed and bleak. "Guess I will take that cup of coffee before I head out. I usually start the day with three cups, but this morning, I didn't have time. Soon as I got the news—" She broke off, swallowing hard. "Something tells me it's going to be a long day," she muttered bleakly.

In the end, Erinn made her toast as well as coffee and found herself listening as LeeAnn slumped in a chair at the kitchen table and began to unload.

"Donnie and me, we've had to depend on each other for a long time." LeeAnn took a long drink of steaming black coffee. "Our folks died in a freeway wreck when I was seventeen. Culp's three years older. He took care of both of us after that." She couldn't seem to stop chattering.

"He could have just taken off, looked after himself,

but no—he's always been there for me. The only man who ever really was," she added as she set down her mug with a thump on the table. Suddenly she seemed to recall exactly whom she was talking to.

"Jase called me this morning to let me know Culp hadn't come back from patrol." Her eyes pierced into Erinn. "I guess he must have called you too. Or—based on what I saw of you two at the barn dance—maybe he didn't have to call you at all."

The implication was clear. LeeAnn was fishing, Erinn realized. No doubt wondering if she and Jase had spent the night together in Jase's barn.

"Actually, it was Lily who called me. I was supposed to meet her today and she wanted to reschedule."

LeeAnn took another sip of coffee, then slanted a glance at her. "You're seeing him, though, aren't you?"

"I'm renting a cabin from him." Erinn had no intention of discussing her relationship with Jase with LeeAnn Culpepper. She didn't even fully understand what was going on between them herself, any more than she understood the laws of molecular physics.

"It's okay, you know. You can tell me." LeeAnn raked a hand through her messy red hair and sighed. "I'm not going to have a meltdown and scream at you about stealing my man. Jase and I are over. We've *been* over for the better part of two months now."

She threw Erinn a knowing look, her eyes narrowing. "You and he will be over soon too. Count on it. The first hint he gets that things might get the least bit serious—" She snapped her fingers. "He'll hightail it out of your life so fast you'll miss him if you blink."

Despite herself, Erinn felt pain stab her. She wasn't

surprised by LeeAnn's words. She'd been thinking much the same thing all along. She'd known about Jase's aversion to serious relationships since her first day in Wolf River. She'd known it when she kissed him, when they'd made love.

Except she'd forgotten it all in the heat of his arms, in the way he made her feel when she was with him, the way he stopped her world, and sent caution and wisdom scattering like tumbleweed.

He'd filled her mind, her soul, her heart.

Yet standing here in his home, with this woman who knew the score even better than she, a chill of reality surged through her.

"Speaking of Jase," she managed in an even tone, "why don't you call him for an update before you set out. Maybe they—"

The phone rang. LeeAnn's body went rigid as Erinn snatched it up.

"We just found Culp's rig," Jase said tersely. "He's not in it."

Acid churned in Erinn's stomach. "Was it a breakdown? He might be hiking back—"

"It doesn't look that way. There's no sign of exterior damage to the rig. I'm there now, we're checking it out."

Erinn's throat closed at the somberness of his tone. LeeAnn was watching her through those keen, red-rimmed eyes.

"Erinn, there's more. We found blood on the road," Jase said.

Blood. Oh, God, no.

"There's traces of it in several places—looks like he

must have been hurt and tried to crawl away—or else he was dragged."

She closed her eyes. She didn't want to think of Culp being hurt, dragged away...

Especially with LeeAnn here, listening to every word. "What happens now?" she asked carefully.

"The forensics team's on their way," Jase replied. "We're not calling off the search—just refocusing it. Culp may just be injured, and there's a chance he crawled somewhere of his own volition and is lying nearby, unconscious or unable to call out. We're going to fan out from here and search every inch of the road and the ridge below as well as the hillside."

"Jase, LeeAnn's here. She wants to come help you search."

There was a brief silence, then Jase spoke again, his voice calm and level. "Put her on."

Erinn expected LeeAnn to fall apart at the news, but the woman surprised her. She looked shaken, but kept her composure as she asked where the rig was found and told Jase she was on her way.

As LeeAnn started outside, Erinn ran out after her.

"Wait a minute, LeeAnn. I'm going to follow you. I just need a second," she added, sprinting toward the barn to tell Devon and Rawley she was leaving.

"Why do you care about searching for my brother? You don't even know the area—you'll get lost and we'll have to waste time searching for *you*," LeeAnn called scornfully.

"That's not going to happen." Erinn disappeared inside the barn and emerged a moment later, running to her Jeep.

"Suit yourself." LeeAnn shrugged. Her tires squealed as she turned the Silverado and spun out onto the drive even as Erinn put the Jeep in gear. Erinn had to practically floor her car to catch up, but she managed to keep the pickup in sight.

She knew she was acting impulsively, but she couldn't help it. She kept remembering the friendliness in Culp's brown eyes the day she met him, the pride with which he'd shown off the boots he'd bought after winning the poker tournament, even his offer to help her move into the cabin.

It seemed that many of Wolf River's citizens were banding together to search for him. She needed to help too.

If Culp wasn't found, wasn't with them, healthy and unharmed, by the time she and the Fortunes returned to the ranch later, she had a feeling most of those sandwiches she'd fixed would probably go to waste. No one on the ranch, including her, would feel much like eating a thing.

Chapter Thirty

It wasn't until darkness began to descend over Wolf River that the search for Culp was finally called off.

By then everyone involved was exhausted, discouraged, and worried. But no one, not even LeeAnn, objected when the decision was made to halt until daylight.

It would be useless to continue now that inky darkness was beginning to steal over the mountains. The searchers had spent more than nine hours scouring every trail, every clearing and rocky crevice within a four-mile radius of Culp's truck.

There was no trace of him.

Jase was headed for home when he spotted Erinn on a trail near the top of Eagle Mountain, working her way down.

"What the hell!" He couldn't believe his eyes. He couldn't see anyone around, and here she was, in the open, alone and vulnerable. "I thought you were staying at the ranch with Devon," he called, striding toward her.

Startled, Erinn turned to see him scowling at her. His

expression wasn't the least bit loverly. In fact, he looked mad as hell.

"Good to see you, too, Jase."

"Look, I get it that you want to help, but this isn't the way. You're all alone out here, damn it—"

He bit back the next words as Kevin Samson emerged on a ledge only a few yards below, and spotting Jase, grinned and clambered upward.

"One of the deputies paired me and Erinn up to search," the vet explained, wiping sweat from his eyes. "We've been at it all afternoon. Not that we've had any luck."

Erinn crossed her arms as Jase shot her a rueful glance. "You know, you could've at least *told* me that Kevin was with you before I made an ass out of myself," he grunted.

"You didn't give me a chance. Besides, I kind of like it when you make an ass out of yourself."

A reluctant grin broke across his face. He knew he deserved that. Still, it was all he could do to keep from blurting out what he really wanted to say to her.

That she wasn't helping him at all by being out here. That he didn't want her anywhere near the danger encircling everyone at Fortune's Way and that the sight of her out here alone had scared the hell out of him.

He needed to get a grip. To stop thinking about her so much, worrying about her so much. Unfortunately, *knowing* he ought to do that wasn't the same as *doing* it.

He'd even been thinking of suggesting that she and Devon return immediately to New York. It would be safer, for both of them. And a helluva lot less distracting for him.

It scared him how much Erinn filled his mind now, even when he wasn't with her. It had been bad enough before they made love, before he knew how deep passion flowed beneath that cool, sophisticated demeanor. But now he kept picturing the glow that lit her face and sheened her body when they made love. He kept remembering the lushness of her breasts in his hands, the heat of her lips against his when he kissed her.

But this was a woman who'd carved out a life for herself clear away on another coast. She no more belonged in Wolf River than an orchid belonged in a desert.

What the hell was he getting himself into?

"Jase, did you hear what I said?" Kevin was staring at him curiously. So was Erinn. Jase hauled his attention back to the search.

"Sorry, I was thinking about Culp," he lied. "Tell me again."

"I searched Eagle's Cave earlier before Erinn arrived," Kevin repeated, rubbing the back of his neck. "No luck. There was nothing there. The two of us also checked that ridge over there, every inch of it. So tomorrow, I guess we'll pick up right here."

The vet turned to Erinn. "The sheriff said the search resumes at 7 a.m."

"I'll be here."

Kevin nodded. "Good deal. Want an escort back to your Jeep?"

"I'll see her back," Jase said before she could reply.

As Kevin glanced at her for confirmation, Erinn nodded, but her mind felt a million miles away. She barely registered what either of them were saying.

Something strange was happening to her. She felt odd, light-headed. Almost like another vision was coming on. But instead of being separate from what was going on around her, she sensed the odd feeling floating through her was somehow related.

But related to what?

Kevin's words. They were rolling through her mind, spinning over and over again. *Eagle's Cave ... I searched Eagle's Cave ... nothing ... Eagle's Cave ... cave ... cave ...*

Her head ached. The image of a gaping cave, dark as the bowels of hell, filled her mind, throbbing like a strobe light. Eagle's Cave ...

She forced herself to focus on where she was. Kevin tipping his hat. "See you tomorrow," he said.

He was leaving. And Jase was staring at her as if she had two heads.

"What's wrong?" he asked, concern threading his words. Yet even his voice was distant, far distant from the strobe light and the image flashing, pulsing in her head.

"I don't know ... I think I just ... hate to give up," she muttered. Of its own volition, her body turned toward Eagle's Cave.

"We have to search it again. Eagle's Cave," she repeated, and started down the path.

The strobe was still flashing with brilliant violence in her head—then Jase was by her side, his arm snagging hers.

"Hold on, Erinn. You're a million miles away. What's happening? Tell me, is it another vision?" he demanded.

She ignored him, shaking loose, scrambling down

the trail, her gaze, her entire attention fixed on something she couldn't quite see.

He caught up to her, silent now, watching her as his own heartbeat raced. As she rushed down the path, it was Jase who guided her toward the cave tucked deep in the mountain wall.

"Let me go in first—" he began, but she was already brushing past him, and some instinct kept him from stopping her, from interrupting whatever—or whoever—was calling to her.

She paused ten feet into the yawning darkness and peered ahead, a cold mist seeming to obscure her vision.

Who am I looking for? Culp? Or someone else . . . a woman? . . . A coffin? . . . Who's there . . . who's calling me?

The mist shifted before her, drifting closer.

Let me see, she begged. *Let me see . . .*

With a blast, the tunnel sucked her in. She rocketed down it, her breath frozen in her throat. The tunnel was narrower, colder than ever before. It was like being sucked down a vertical pit of ice, at roller-coaster speed, wild, careening, out of control . . . and then she saw it . . . on the wall of the cave. The mist cleared for an instant . . .

A drawing. A drawing on that dark rock wall. A drawing sketched in blood.

Dark red, a horse running . . . screaming. Tail flying, hooves in midair . . . running . . . free . . . red . . . blood . . .

Screams. Filling the air. Inhuman screaming . . . stop, make it . . . stop . . .

She opened her eyes to find herself lying in Jase's arms. They were just outside the cave and he was staring down at her, his face grim beneath the brim of his hat.

"Did I . . . say anything?" she asked weakly, closing her eyes against the dizziness.

"Yeah, but that can wait. Are you all right? Can you sit up?"

She could, with his help. She leaned against him, still shivering. Twilight had deepened, the shadowy fingers of night brushed the land, and a cool wind whipped at her hair. She rested her head against Jase's shoulder and felt her muscles relax as he held her.

Suddenly, she broke from the moment of peacefulness and pulled back, peering at him. "Tell me what I said. During the vision."

"Something about a horse. A running horse."

The image flooded back. "A painting on a cave wall," she breathed. "A horse . . . running. It was outlined in blood . . . vivid red blood." She fought to keep her voice from trembling as she sat up.

Was there something else too? she wondered, grasping at the fleeting bits of memory. *What was it?*

She couldn't quite summon it . . . all she saw was the horse, the red outline of it on the cave wall, seared now in her mind. The tail flying as it ran . . .

"I guess I should call McKindrick tonight," she said slowly. "Maybe all of these pieces will mean something to him. The horse, the cave, the coffin." She stared beyond him at the sky, searching for answers in the first stars glittering amid the blackness. "None of my visions have ever been so disconnected before. And there's something else different too."

"What's that?" Her eyes looked huge in the starlight—huge and baffled and uncertain.

"The oddest feeling came over me when Kevin mentioned Eagle's Cave. I felt compelled to go in there—and that's when the vision happened. Usually they just come out of the blue—but tonight, I was drawn to that cave. And then . . . when I entered it—that prompted the vision."

"Like a trigger of sorts," Jase mused.

"I guess so. But . . . I don't know why it happened that way. Or what it means. Unless . . ." She swallowed, hesitant to even give voice to what she was thinking. But she had to tell him, in case she was right.

"Unless the vision of the cave has something to do with Culp." She scrambled to her feet and Jase followed. "Maybe what I'm seeing isn't happening somewhere else, like all the other times. Maybe it's happening *here*. In Wolf River. But . . . I still need to talk to McKindrick," she said quickly as his gaze sharpened.

"I could be wrong. I could be seeing a cave in Kentucky, or South Africa, or *anywhere*." *But I don't think I am,* she thought.

Jase studied her a moment. "You feel okay? You can walk?"

"Yes. Of course." It was true. The visions' effects always faded within a few minutes. Jase caught her hand.

"There's a flashlight in my truck but I don't want to leave you alone to get it," he said. "I'm parked less than a quarter mile away. What do you say we go get it, then come back and have a look around inside? Both of us."

"I say yes."

"One second." Her eyes were brilliant, luminous as

stars in the darkening twilight. "Sorry," he murmured, "but there's something else I have to do first."

She stared at him, puzzled. Then something cold and weary inside her dissipated as Jase drew her closer, cupped her chin, and bent his head to kiss her.

It was a soft, warm, yet oddly possessive kiss. She melted into him and suddenly didn't want to ever move away.

"It's been nearly twenty-four hours since I did that." He drew in a breath and smoothed her hair with his hand, a light caressing touch that made her tingle all over. "It feels at least twenty-three hours too long."

"Closer to twenty-four," she murmured before she realized what she'd said.

His eyes gleamed in the cool, gusty night and a grin split his face. Then he released her and put his hand at the small of her back. "Watch your step," he said in a careful neutral tone as he guided her back onto the dark twisting path of the mountain.

It was late when they returned to Fortune's Way. They'd found nothing in the cave—no drawings on the walls, no coffin, no Culp.

Nothing but rock and dirt and empty blackness.

If not this cave, Erinn thought, there must be another. She'd asked Jase if there were many caves in Montana and he'd grimly explained that the state was ripe with them. Too many to count. Too many to search—unless she could somehow narrow it down.

Clay, Lily, Devon, and Ginny were all still huddled around the dining room table when they reached

Fortune's Way. Colton had gone to Crystalville to see Sue Lynn. But LeeAnn was there, sitting listlessly at one end of the table, her eyes dull, her red hair even more windblown and tousled than it had been when she'd arrived this morning.

They'd picked at the turkey sandwiches Erinn had prepared, and at the salad Ginny had thrown together. No one had been hungry, but they'd gone through the ritual of sharing a meal, while each was lost in his or her own thoughts. Unlike the previous evening, the atmosphere in the house was dominated by a sense of gloom.

It had settled over the ranch house in the hours that the search dragged on, and only deepened after the hunt for Culp had been called off for the night.

"I hate to think of him up there now all night," Lily muttered. Then her gaze flew to LeeAnn.

"I'm sorry," she said quickly. "I know he'll be okay. Culp's tough. We'll find him in the morning and he'll...he'll give us hell for not tracking him down sooner. He's going to be so hungry..."

Her voice trailed off.

"Yeah, he will," LeeAnn said dully. "If he's...if he's...you know."

Alive. They all knew what she was thinking. They were thinking the same thing.

LeeAnn suddenly pushed back her chair and left the room.

Jase and Clay both stood at the same time. "Let me," Jase told his father and to Erinn's surprise, the older man nodded and sank down again. Jase's eyes met Erinn's briefly, then he strode after LeeAnn.

"Reckon it's a tough night for everyone—LeeAnn most of all," Clay said in his gruff tone. "Ginny, I'll follow you back home when you leave here. Jase will make sure the two of you get back okay."

"There's no need," Erinn assured him. "I can take care of myself and my sister." But when she glanced at Devon, the girl looked pale. And scared.

"Would you excuse us a moment? Devon, come with me, please."

She drew the girl into the kitchen. "What's wrong?" she asked, studying her sister's wary face. "What's frightening you?"

"I'm . . . I'm not frightened. I just want to go back to the cabin and call Hank. I need to talk to him."

"About what?"

"Stuff. Private stuff." Devon's chin jerked up defiantly.

"Listen, Devon, you need to be honest with me. Do you have *any* reason to believe that Mick Wheeler might be behind Culp's disappearance? Is it Mick you're afraid of, afraid he might come after you next? If you or Hank know something that would help us find Culp, you have to tell me now!"

"I would." Devon's lips quivered. Misery filmed her eyes. "Don't you think I would, Tiffany? Mick hates the Fortunes," she burst out, "because of some run-in he had with Colton awhile ago—and then Lily. But he doesn't really get along with anyone. And I don't see why he'd hurt Culp. I've thought about it all day."

She bit her lip and continued quickly. "He's never said anything bad about Culp, so it wouldn't make sense. Besides, the main thing he's worried about right now is that I'm going to tell you about the—" She broke off in horror, her eyes widening at the words that had slipped from her mouth.

"Go on," Erinn said quietly. "What's he worried you'll tell me?"

"Nothing! It's got nothing to do with this. Or with Culp. I want to go home now."

She flinched away and started to the door. "If you won't take me home right now I'll just have to walk—"

Erinn grabbed her arm. "Devon, we're going now, but we're going together. We can finish this conversation in the car."

For a moment there was taut silence in the kitchen. Devon's eyes mirrored resentment, tears, and something else—a lurking fear that made Erinn's own sense of dread mount.

Silently she led the way back through the dining room to say their good-byes.

"Sheriff Farley called. The search starts again at dawn," Ginny told her, gathering up the dinner dishes with her usual efficiency.

Erinn nodded. "I'll be there."

"I'll be there too," Lily said, collecting the water glasses. "But I'll have to leave for a while and put in some time at the day-care center in the afternoon— they're short-handed. When things calm down," she said to Erinn with a sigh, "I hope you'll still come and read to the kids."

"I promise I will before I go back to New York," Erinn said.

It occurred to her as she and Devon made their way down the hallway that she was getting too attached to this town. To the people in it. And especially to those who lived in this house.

It astonished her that she felt so close to all the Fortunes, to Ginny, even to Culp. Somehow or other, their lives had become so much a part of hers. Strange, since she had lived a long time in New York with few attachments.

Other than her former editor, Nancy Leonetti, and Detective McKindrick, there had been few people whose lives had become enmeshed in any serious way with hers.

And now there was this family, this town—and Jase.

She heard his deep voice, a calm reassuring rumble coming from the living room as she and Devon headed down the hall. She could hear LeeAnn, crying quietly, but couldn't make out Jase's words of comfort. She glanced into the living room as they passed and saw him seated on the sofa beside Culp's sister.

His arm was around her shoulders, her face buried against his shirt.

A deep sudden pain sliced through Erinn's heart.

It was a stupid reaction, she knew, but she couldn't help it. Rationally she knew that he was only comforting a woman whom he cared for as a friend, and that LeeAnn badly needed that comfort now. But her quick, instinctive reaction was one of dismay, jealousy, and pain.

It passed in an instant, of course, but with it came a stunning realization. Damn it, she was in over her head even more than she'd thought. If she wasn't careful, she was going to fall in love with Jase Fortune.

Or maybe she already had . . .

A tightness filled her chest. She couldn't deal with that thought. It was like thinking about falling off a cliff. A long way down, with no guarantee of a soft landing.

She had to get out of here. She had to think. To analyze all of this and figure out where she'd gone wrong and what she needed to do to get back on track.

For starters, don't sleep with him again, she thought as she yanked open the ranch house door.

But at that moment, Jase saw them. He sprang up, extricating himself from LeeAnn and striding toward them.

"You're going already?" he asked quietly when he reached her side. "Let me follow you back—"

"That's not necessary, Jase. I just need to talk to Devon—alone. It can't wait."

"No problem. I'll follow you back right now."

Erinn shook her head as Devon paused uncertainly in the hallway. "There's no need, Jase. Whatever's going on, you said yourself it's centered around Fortune's Way. It's not about me, not about Devon."

"You don't know that for certain. And neither do I. I'm coming with you." He stepped outside, closing the door with a firm thud. "Too much is happening right now. There's no way I'm letting the two of you go back to the cabin until I check it out—"

He broke off, wheeling toward the sound of a car door slamming in the driveway, cutting the silence of the night.

"Who's there?" he snapped, even as he moved in front of Erinn and Devon, blocking them with his body.

A man materialized in the darkness.

"I'm looking for LeeAnn." Frank Wells sauntered

toward the porch, a cigarette dangling from his lips. "I heard about her brother. Thought she might need a shoulder to lean on. And what do you know—her car's here at Fortune's Way."

His eyes flicked to Devon, standing still as stone. Then they settled on Erinn, slender and tense in the faint light above the porch.

"Hello, angel face. Going back to the Redrock? I'd buy you a drink, but my woman's inside and she's hurting. Another time, baby—if you ask real nice." Erinn's gaze narrowed and he smirked as he started up the steps.

He flicked the smirk in Jase's direction.

"She tell you how she came on to me that first night in town, before you showed up and got everything all wrong? Man, she was all over me. I was actually fighting her off 'cause LeeAnn was on her way—"

That was as far as he got. Jase's fist shot out and nailed him in the jaw.

Frank Wells hit the ground like a corpse.

Chapter Thirty-one

Devon gasped, clutching Erinn's arm as Jase hauled Wells to his feet.

"Glad you dropped by, Wells." He dragged the man to the side of the house and shoved him up against the wall. "I've been wanting to ask you a few questions and now you've given me the chance."

"Jase." Erinn raced to him. "What are you doing? Stop. You can't just—"

"Who says I can't?" With one hand at Wells's throat, Jase pinned him to the wall. When he glanced at her for an instant, his eyes were so hard and cold a shiver skated down her back like a blade of ice. "Go inside, Erinn. Take Devon with you. I need five minutes alone with him to get some answers."

"I'm not going anywhere," she flashed, but suddenly the front door flew open and LeeAnn appeared.

"What's all the—" She stopped dead, spotting Frank, Erinn, and Jase at the side of the house.

"Let him go, Jase," she cried, dashing down the steps. "What the hell do you think you're doing?"

"He just . . . went nuts, LeeAnn." Wells's voice sounded

hoarse and a bruise was spreading across his jaw, visible even in the ghostly light.

Jase tightened his hand around Wells's throat. The man's eyes bulged as he strained to break free and failed.

"Did you shoot my foreman, Wells? And my cattle?"

"Damn ... you ... *no*. I just came to see LeeAnn—"

"How about Culp? Did he catch you on my land last night? What'd you do to him?"

"Nothing," Wells croaked out. "I don't know nothing about Culp. Or ... any of it."

"Stop it, Jase," LeeAnn yelled, but it was Erinn's pressure on his arm that made him tear his gaze away from Wells's purpling face to focus on her tense, anxious one.

Slowly, his grip on Wells's windpipe slackened. Scowling, he let him go. "Get the hell out of here, Wells, before I change my mind."

"Frank, are you all right?" LeeAnn hovered worriedly beside the man whose hands gingerly touched his bruised throat.

"No thanks to this asshole," he rasped. "He nearly killed me." He lurched away from the wall. "I'm calling the sheriff, Fortune. Charging you with assault!"

"No, Frank. Don't." LeeAnn looked alarmed. "Everyone's just on edge—worried about my brother. Let's just go, okay? I'm beat. Will you come with me?"

"Damn straight. But we're going right to the sheriff's office. I gotta file me a report."

"Farley knows where he can find me." Jase's tone was curt. "Now get off my property. LeeAnn, you don't have to go with him. Someone will see you home."

"I *am* going with him, Jase," she retorted. She hooked her arm through Wells's. "Come on, Frank, I'll follow you in my pickup. Let's get the hell out of here."

And then they were gone, both LeeAnn and Wells, roaring off into the dark as Devon stood trembling in front of the ranch house.

"It's okay," Erinn told her, though she too felt shaken by what had just occurred. "It's all over. You don't need to worry about Frank Wells."

Yes, I do, Devon thought, trying to subdue the panic surging through her. *And so do you.*

But she couldn't tell Tiffany that, could she? Because Wells would find out—and so would Mick—and they'd come after both of them. *And it'll all be my fault . . .*

"I'm not worried. I'm just . . . tired." Suddenly, Devon looked at her sister, her eyes pleading. "Do you think . . . maybe . . . we could stay here tonight?"

"Here? At Fortune's Way?" Erinn gaped at her. "Why, Devon?"

"It's such a long drive back to the cabin—and tomorrow you're going to search again, right? So we'll just have to come right back here in the morning if you want me to hang out. If they've got room, we might as well just stay here." She glanced at Jase, her eyes hopeful. "I could sleep on a couch," she offered.

"No need for you to rough it," he said. "We have three guest bedrooms and three private baths in the east wing of the house. In addition, Colton's room is at the end of that hall—he should be back shortly. You'll be very comfortable there—and very safe."

"I could go to sleep right this minute," Devon said, and yawned.

Laying it on pretty thick, Erinn thought, studying her. "I thought you were eager to call Hank."

"He's probably asleep now. I'll call him tomorrow. Can we stay?" Devon asked.

What the hell does she know? Erinn wondered, a stone dropping into the pit of her stomach. *But it's clear she's scared. A lot more scared than she's let on.*

Devon had wanted to go home before this incident with Wells. Then he'd shown up—was *he* the one she was scared of?

But it was Wheeler Erinn had seen skulking around the cabin. *What if it was both of them? Wheeler and Wells both had grudges against the Fortunes—were they working together somehow?*

There was another possibility. Maybe Devon was so "tired" because she was trying to avoid answering any more questions tonight. She was hoping to buy herself some time.

But it will only buy her so much, Erinn thought. *Tomorrow, we're having another heart to heart.*

"All right, we can stay." Erinn turned toward Jase. "If you're sure you don't mind."

His gaze lighted on hers. "I wouldn't have it any other way."

Frank Wells lit a cigarette at four in the morning and stared at the ceiling of LeeAnn's bedroom. Beside him, she slept like the dead, thanks to a tranquilizer *and* a glass of wine.

But he was far too wound up to sleep. He was thinking. Thinking hard. Her brother's disappearance seemed like an omen.

Time for me to disappear too, he thought. Things were getting too sticky here.

There was nothing to hold him. He could do business in any town, any county in America. All he had to do was get to the money stash, take it, and leave.

Oh, yeah, one or two other things too.

Tie up all the loose ends.

Loose ends were dangerous—you could get all twisted up in them and take a fall.

Wells had no intention of taking a fall for anyone.

It was a damned good thing no one in this burg could connect him with the Wheelers. No one except Mick, his brother, and the little blonde skank.

Shouldn't be too hard to keep them quiet. And once they were safely out of the picture, Frank Wells could disappear for good.

Chapter Thirty-two

A grim mood hung over the searchers who streamed over the ledges and hillsides the following morning, wearing jackets and sweaters to protect them from the chill as a cool opal dawn shivered over the mountaintops.

Lily, bundled in a pink sweater, jeans, and boots, came across Erinn and Jase searching along a series of caves high on Buckhorn Point as she trudged toward her SUV.

"I wish I could stay, but Edna needs me. Callie called in sick and Sandra has college orientation this weekend. Edna just can't handle all the kids herself."

"There's plenty of us out here," Erinn assured her. "You have to do what you have to do."

"You know what would really help us out?" Lily asked. "I hate asking you to leave too, but if there's any way you could swing by the day-care center later this afternoon, it would be an ideal time to meet the kids and read one of your books. With only me and Edna there, anything that'll get them to sit down in one place and be quiet for a while would be a godsend."

"Sure. I'd love to. And maybe by later this afternoon, we'll have found Culp," Erinn said bracingly, trying to hold on to every ounce of hope. She glanced at Jase, but she knew time wasn't on their side, and the grimness in his eyes told her he was already fearing the worst.

Right now, every hour, every searcher counted.

"Where's your car parked?" Jase asked his sister. "I don't want you wandering all the way back to the road alone."

Lily pointed toward the road where Culp's rig had been found a day earlier. "I'm parked ten yards from Sheriff Farley's patrol car, so don't worry about it. Don't even think about walking me all the way back there. You two keep looking," she added with a worried frown between her brows. "We . . . we have to find Culp today."

Jase ignored her. "Colton," he called to his brother, searching through scrub brush along a dirt track two hundred yards away. "Walk Lily to her car!"

Colton waved an arm over his head in agreement and Lily groaned as she moved back toward the road.

"I give up," she muttered, casting an exasperated look in Erinn's direction. "Be thankful you don't have worry-wart big brothers," she grumbled.

But privately, Erinn couldn't blame Jase or Colton for being careful. If Devon hadn't been safely back at the ranch with Clay and Rawley, she wouldn't have let Devon out of her sight either.

Devon had still been asleep when she and Jase had left this morning, so there'd been no opportunity to pin her down about Mick Wheeler. *That would have to wait for later,* Erinn thought, as she turned her attention to the scrub brush skirting one of the caves, searching for a trace of blood, a scrap of material—anything that might have come from Culp and indicated he'd been there.

By noon, there was still no sign of him. Spirits were lagging when Ginny, the Saddleback's teenage waitress Amanda, Clay, and Devon all arrived with coffee and doughnuts, sandwiches, and apples for the searchers.

"Your sister made at least twenty of these BLTs," Clay informed Erinn, handing a sandwich in plastic wrap to her and another to Jase. "We're going to partner up and help you search for a while this afternoon, then we have to head back. Kevin Samson's coming to pay a little veterinary visit to Sheba. She seemed a little under the weather today."

"Sheba's the mare in foal," Devon informed Erinn.

Clay shot his son a challenging glance, as if daring Jase to try to send him packing, but Jase merely raised an eyebrow.

"Suit yourself, Pop. But don't overdo it, or I'll have Doc Stevens on the phone faster than you can shoot a snake. He can read you the riot act better than me any day, and you might actually listen."

"Don't you pay him any mind, young ladies." Clay's scowl encompassed both Devon and Erinn. "He's got a hell of a lot of nerve worrying about me. He's the one who nearly turned his mama's hair snow white when he was four and wandered out in the middle of the night looking for wild mustangs. We had the whole ranch searching for him and you know where we found him? Half a mile away, at the edge of the creek, chirping along with the frogs. He thought if he sat real still and pretended to be a frog, the wild horses might come down to drink. Damnedest thing I ever saw. His mother nearly squeezed him to death when we brought him home."

"Is that so?" Erinn glanced at Jase, a smile hovering at the corners of her lips as she tried to imagine this tall, wide-shouldered cowboy as a bold and curious four-year-old.

"Did you ever see the horses?" Devon asked. "Hank told me there's wild horses in Montana, but I've never seen any."

"There's a herd or two that live about an hour away from here near Red Horse Canyon," Jase told her. "One day I'll take you and your sister there. If we're lucky and quiet, you might get to see them."

Erinn started. *One day I'll take you and your sister there?*

Why would he say that? As if there was going to be a "one day" for the three of them to go on an outing like that. Chances were she and Devon wouldn't be staying in Wolf River much longer. If she was smart, she'd get the two of them out of here sooner rather than later. Only now she'd have to convince Devon to leave not only Hank, but the Fortune's Way horses behind.

And am I ready to leave Jase behind? she wondered. A weight settled over her heart at the prospect.

Devon's eyes had lit up at Jase's words, though, so for the moment Erinn shoved away all of her reservations. Today was about finding Culp. If they could only do that, she could sort everything else out tomorrow.

The refreshments reinvigorated everyone for the

next few hours, but as the afternoon wore on, and the search area widened, with still no sign of Culp, the mood of the search party began to change.

Discouragement set in, and people talked less, studying the land they traversed in silence, their faces grimmer as the minutes and then the hours wore on.

It was nearly three o'clock when Clay and Devon headed back to await Kevin Samson's visit. An hour later, Erinn remembered her promise to Lily.

Jase walked her to her car, parked in a long line that rimmed the road.

"Don't stop for anyone or anything," he ordered as he held the door open for her.

"Don't worry, I know the drill."

"Erinn." As she turned to him, a question in her eyes, his chest ached with unexpected pain. She looked incredibly beautiful in the late afternoon light, those gorgeous black curls fluttering delicately in the breeze, her serious eyes as vivid and intense as emeralds.

He remembered how they'd shimmered into his the other night when he was inside her and the world was exploding around them. Suddenly, he had to fight the impulse to pull her into his arms.

"Erinn," he said quickly, "you and Devon need to leave. It's time for you to go back to New York."

"I . . . know." She spoke calmly, but he had seen the look of surprise and pain that flashed for an instant across her eyes. "I've been thinking along the same lines."

"Good. You were right when you said that what's going on here centers around me and my family. And that means that you and Devon shouldn't be mixed up in it.

If there *is* any danger from Wheeler," he continued doggedly before she could interrupt him, "it'll be over once you get on a plane headed east. You've got to leave Montana."

"The same thoughts crossed my mind." She shrugged, watching his face. "So if you want us to leave, Jase, we will."

His eyes narrowed. "Hold on a minute," he said irritably. "I didn't say I want you to leave. I said I want you to be safe."

"Did you?" Her gaze searched his face. "Safe *is* important," she said softly. She tilted her head to one side, studying him. "You like being safe too, don't you, Jase?"

"What the hell is that supposed to mean?"

"This is all too complicated for you, isn't it? *I'm* too complicated," she said with a slight shrug. "So is the way we feel about each other, what we shared the other night. I understand—it's much easier to be alone, not to care. Far be it from me to mess up your perfect solitary existence." Her eyes darkened. "I wouldn't want to interfere with your perennial bachelorhood. Your endless obsession with Carly, the wife from hell—"

Jase grabbed her then, without thinking, and kissed her. A long deep powerful kiss that shook all words and thoughts right out of their heads.

When Jase finally lifted his mouth from hers, and studied her, her eyes were still closed. He waited, watching her face like a wolf watching a mouse until she opened them.

"How's that for obsessed?" he grated. "If there's anyone I'm obsessed with, Erinn or Tiffany or whatever your name is, it's *you*."

"Well, then, now we're getting somewhere," Erinn murmured. She still felt dreamy from that kiss. She smiled at him mistily, and reached up, stroking her fingers along his cheek, down his jaw, savoring the rough scrape of his five o'clock shadow against her skin.

"Yeah?" His hands moved swiftly, cradling her face. She heard his breath coming hard. "Forget I said that," he said thickly. "Forget I just kissed you. You have to leave."

"I know." Erinn smiled. She reached up on her tiptoes and pressed her lips to his. "Lily's expecting me at the day-care center," she breathed.

Just as he slanted his mouth against hers once more, Erinn heard her cell phone ring. Jase swore and let her go so she could tug the cell from her purse.

"I got your message, Erinn." It was McKindrick, returning the call she'd placed to him last night. "All about the cave, the coffin, that damned mist."

"Yes, and the horse—the horse outlined in blood," she reminded him, trying desperately to concentrate while her heartbeat was still racing and all she wanted to do was step back into Jase's arms.

"Yeah, well, none of it suggests anything to me right now," the detective complained in the flat raspy voice that came from smoking three packs a day over the last twenty years. "You're giving me too damned little to go on this time. I'm good, but not that good. Got any names, any faces for me?"

"I wish I could say I did."

"Well, get back to me when you do. I need something more substantial. Like a description of the perp or victim, you know? In the meantime, I'll keep my eyes and ears open, see what I come across. Life treating you okay these days?"

"Not too badly."

He disconnected and she put her phone back into her purse. That was about as personal as McKindrick ever got. "He's less than thrilled," she told Jase. "Not enough to go on. Hey, I really do need to get to the day-care center."

She hopped up into the Jeep before she could be tempted to change her mind. Jase seemed to know exactly what she was thinking.

"We're not finished here, Ms. Winters," he said as he slammed the door.

Erinn started the engine, her gaze locked on his. "I didn't think we were."

But as she drove away, Jase felt a surge of panic in his chest. How had he come to care for her so much? What was happening to him?

Not love, he thought, his jaw tightening. *I'm not in love with her. No way.*

Better tell her that, buddy, he thought in alarm. *Soon. Before somebody gets hurt.*

A bedraggled-looking woman in a light blue cotton pantsuit hurried from the day-care center as Erinn drove to the end of a rutted lane. The woman had shaggy light brown hair and carried a girl of about two in her arms.

Half a dozen other children about five or six years old tumbled out behind her, spilling across the front yard, laughing and shouting.

"Can I help you?" the woman asked distractedly, as the girl in her arms grabbed with chubby fingers at her eyeglasses, trying to pry them off her face. "Don't pull my glasses, Abby, I need them to see. Here, play with this."

The woman stooped and grabbed up a doll lying in the grass. The two-year-old grasped it in delight.

"You must be Edna." Erinn hurried forward as the woman nodded. "Lily asked me to come and read to the children today."

"Oh, you're the author! Well, she never said anything to me this morning." Edna looked flustered. "I had no idea."

"You mean she didn't tell you I was coming?"

"No—but she did tell me *she* was coming." The woman sighed. "She *promised*, actually. I just don't know what happened—Lily's usually so reliable."

"What . . . what did you say?" Erinn stared at her as if she hadn't heard right. "Lily isn't here?"

"Nope, not yet. She was supposed to help me out today since we're shorthanded, but she never showed up." Wearily, Edna set the little girl on her feet. As the child raced off toward the sandbox, clutching the doll, Edna blew away a wisp of hair that had fallen across her eyes. "I guess she's still out there searching for Culp. Maybe she couldn't get away, but—"

"She did get away." Erinn felt fear surging through her. "Lily left to come help you *hours* ago."

Edna stared at her, then shook her head. "I wish. There's ten more kids under the age of five inside. I've got to go back and check on them, but—she left hours ago, you said? Are you sure?" For the first time, worry deepened the creases in her narrow brow.

"Did you try calling her cell phone?" Erinn demanded.

"Two or three times. Just got her voicemail, that's all. It's so unlike her. I wonder if she had car trouble—still, you'd think she'd have called."

"I took the same route she'd have taken. I didn't see her car anywhere." Erinn felt ill. "Oh, dear God—"

Edna's eyes blinked rapidly. "You don't think?... No, who on earth would want to hurt Lily—"

"Jase—I have to call Jase." Erinn's fingers flew across the buttons on her cell phone as she turned back and scanned the rutted lane, hoping against hope to see Lily's car coming toward them.

But the lane was empty.

"Jase." Her voice was low and fast as he answered on the second ring. "Lily isn't here. She's not at the day-care center."

"What do you mean?" His voice was sharp. "Erinn, slow down. Where are you now?"

"I'm at the day-care center with Edna. She says Lily never showed up and she couldn't reach her on her cell phone. Oh, Jase—"

"Stay there. *Don't move.* I'm on my way."

She started to turn around, to look at the road once more, but instead she toppled forward, the phone tumbling from her hand as the vision swooped in without warning like a giant bird of prey and carried her off down the dark icy tunnel.

Chapter Thirty-three

Erinn awoke to find herself lying on the grass. She was cold, ice cold, shivering as violently as if it were the dead of winter and not June in the foothills of Montana.

Shakily, she tried to sit up, and saw Edna hurrying from the day-care center, a small paper cup clutched in her hands.

Lily. Something's happened to Lily. The rush of memory, of dismay and horror sickened her stomach and she took great gasping breaths.

"Now there, young lady. Don't you get sick. Here's some juice. Sit still now, and take small sips."

She obeyed, drinking apple juice from a child-size paper cup, as all around her swirled the sounds of children playing. But the calls and the laughter didn't drown out the terrified voice she still heard in her head.

He's going to kill me. I'm going to die.

It was Lily's voice.

This can't be happening, Erinn thought. She was still cold, still shivering, and fear deep as a bottomless well shuddered through her.

Rawley. Culp. Lily.

Setting the juice down on the grass she closed her eyes and tried to reconstruct the vision.

She was still trying when Jase arrived. By then, Edna had rounded up the children and herded them all inside.

She tried to get Erinn to join them, but Erinn shook her head and sat on the grass, focusing on the vision, searching her mind.

The air crackled with danger, or so it seemed to her as she sat there, staring straight ahead, seeing only the tunnel, the dark, the mist.

When Jase pulled up, her heart nearly broke at the expression on his face. His skin was gray as oatmeal, his eyes glittering with pain and fear and a quiet deadly fury all rolled together as he vaulted from the Explorer and raced to her side.

"I had . . . another vision, Jase. I saw something . . . something different this time." The words poured out of her, slowly at first, then coming faster as if she would forget them if she didn't tell him quickly enough, as if perhaps he could find something she'd missed, something that would help them save Lily.

"The mist was thicker than ever. Curling like ribbons, obscuring everything. I tried so hard to push through them—"

She shook her head in frustration, still mentally trying to penetrate the murk that had obscured her sight. "It was dark again and cold, like before. But it wasn't a cave, there was no entrance, no light. Just the darkness and the mist . . . and the box . . . wooden slats . . . a coffin . . ."

She lifted her head and tears stung her eyes as she looked into his face.

"But I saw something pink, Jase. In the coffin. And today Lily was wearing a pink—" Her voice broke, but Jase finished the sentence for her.

"A pink sweater." A boulder seemed to have lodged in his chest where his heart was supposed to be. He'd given Lily that pink sweater last Christmas.

"I know for sure now, Jase." Her voice trembled. "McKindrick can't help me figure out the visions. What I'm seeing—it's happening *here*. It's not going to be on some police blotter or in a national database or in the *New York Times*. It's happening in Wolf River, all around me. That's why they're coming so quickly, one after the other, and not just at night. The danger is close—the people in trouble are close, they're people I care about."

Jase's hand gripped hers. "Listen, Erinn, tell me everything you saw, no matter how inconsequential it seems. Lily and Culp, they have to be nearby. She . . . she wasn't dead, was she?" His voice was hoarse with fear.

"No, no, I think she's alive. I heard her voice, Jase," she cried, her heart twisting. "She said, *'He's going to kill me. I'm going to die.'*"

Jase froze. "What . . . else?" he bit out.

"Nothing. I couldn't see clearly where she was, there was all this mist, weaving like . . . like transparent string. It was like peering through shreds of clouds. But Jase," she gulped. "We have to find her—quickly. I have this feeling . . . there isn't much time."

"You're right." His hands closed for a moment on

her shoulders, his eyes suddenly dark and unfathomable. "Go inside with Edna and the kids. Lock the doors and windows and wait for Farley to get here. I called him and he's on his way, probably less then ten minutes behind me. Tell him everything, make him believe you. Be sure to tell him about the coffin and the cave."

He gave her a quick hug and started toward the Explorer.

"Wait a minute, where do you think you're going?" she demanded.

He broke into a run. "Someplace I should have gone days ago. To the Wheeler cabin."

"Not without me, you're not." Sprinting faster than she'd ever run for a taxi, Erinn raced across the packed-down earth and grass. She reached the Explorer as Jase slammed the driver-side door closed, but she flung the passenger door open and jumped in before he could protest.

"Get out, Erinn. You can't come with me."

"Who says?"

She fastened her seat belt with a loud click as if to emphasize the point and felt his eyes boring into her. But she stared right back.

"I don't have time to argue with you."

"Then don't," she told him. "Let's go search the Wheeler cabin."

Two seconds ticked by before he spoke in a hard tone. "If Wheeler's there, you stay inside this rig with the doors and windows locked," he told her, putting the Explorer in gear.

"We'll just see about that. *Drive*."

———————

Clay and Devon were playing gin rummy on the front porch when the phone call came in.

Clay listened to Sheriff Farley's voice, his face turning slowly to stone. When he pocketed his phone at last, he didn't say a word, just sank heavily back in his chair.

"Mr. Fortune—are you all right?" All of the color had gone out of his cheeks, and Devon was scared.

"Mr. Fortune?" she asked again. "What's wrong?"

He ignored her question and pushed himself out of the chair with a sharp lurching motion. "Stay here. You hear me? Stay inside." He lumbered down the steps, his shoulders stooped.

"I'm going to get Rawley to come keep you company, but I have to go."

"Where?"

He turned and stared at her. "To find my daughter."

Devon barely recognized his voice. It sounded so old suddenly, old and quavery. And there was something in his face she'd never seen there before.

Fear.

"Where is she? Did she . . . get lost?" *Like Culp?* Devon thought in horror.

"I think . . . someone took her." His eyes welled with tears and he vigorously blinked them back. "I don't know what's happening anymore. But if anyone hurts my little girl—"

Stopping short, Clay shook his head, then strode toward the barn.

Devon's cards tumbled from her fingers and she

stared at them on the floor of the porch, not really seeing them. She was thinking about Mick. And Frank Wells. They couldn't be behind this. Could they?

What if they are? she thought, a sob rising in her throat. *What if all this time, they're the ones who shot at poor Rawley, or hurt Culp? And now they've taken Lily...*

She stared at Clay Fortune's retreating back. He loved Lily so much. *And Tiffany begged and begged me to tell her about Mick, but I didn't. What if it's my fault they did something to Lily?*

"Mr. Fortune!"

He turned around ten feet from the barn as Devon limped toward him as fast as she could.

"I know something bad about Mick Wheeler—and someone else. I wouldn't tell Tiffany because I didn't think they were the ones who hurt Rawley or Culp but..." Her lips trembled. "What if one of them did? I...I wanted to tell her, just in case, but I've been too scared. Mick threatened me. He said he'd hurt me and Tiffany if I told anyone—but now I think I have to. Just in case he took Lily—"

"No one's going to hurt you, young lady." Clay glanced down, met her gaze squarely. "I'll see to that. Tell me what you know—out with it. Otherwise, people might get hurt because you're scared. That's wrong, Devon."

She knew he was right. Swallowing hard, she fought the fear that had been curled up inside her ever since she and Hank moved into the cabin. "Mick's...Mick's breaking the law. He and Frank Wells. They're in it together!"

"In what?"

"They make fake ID's. They have a computer and a scanner and a printer in the back room. They've been printing fake drivers' licenses, and passports and things, and selling them. For a long time now and—"

"Selling them to who?" he interrupted.

Devon shook her head, shaking inside because she had actually told him about Mick. "I don't know... somebody important, but I...I think they're from someplace else, part of organized crime or something. All I know is that Wells goes to Crystalville sometimes with boxes and boxes of fake ID's in his truck. They all look real. And the man pays him and he gives some money to Mick, and they hide it somewhere. I don't know anything else, I swear it."

She drew in her breath, staring at him pleadingly.

"If they find out I told you—"

"They won't. You did the right thing. Devon, thank you."

He patted her arm and then straightened. She was shocked. Though his voice was calm, his eyes had turned dark—the dark roaring blue of an angry sea, and she took a step back in spite of herself.

"Go inside now, Devon, like I said. Lock the door." He wheeled toward the barn, yanking his phone from his pocket.

"Farley!" Devon could hear his voice booming into it as she ran up the porch steps and into the house.

She didn't close the door though, just held onto it as her heart skittered in her chest and she listened to him telling the sheriff everything she'd said about Mick.

"And I'm on my way to that scummy cabin to tear the place apart, so you may just want to show up there and see if you can prove your sorry self the least bit useful. If they have my daughter or Culp there, I won't be responsible for what happens," Clay barked and snapped the phone shut.

Devon closed the door and locked it. She was glad she had done the right thing, but she was still scared. Maybe because she'd been scared for so long she didn't remember any other way to be.

She stared out the window, trying to calm her breathing, until Clay got in his rig and floored it. Still she stood there, chewing her lower lip until the only thing left in his wake was a cloud of dust.

Chapter Thirty-four

The jig was up.

Wells had heard everything. Every last filthy word the little slut had spoken. His name. She had told Clay Fortune *his name*. Linked him to the counterfeiting.

If he hadn't been planning to get rid of her before, he sure as hell was now.

He leaned against the far side of the Fortune ranch house, his eyes narrowed, and waited until Clay Fortune's rig roared off into the distance.

The brat had done just as he'd said. She'd gone inside, locked the door—he'd even heard the tiny sound of the bolt clicking into place.

A fat lot of good it'll do her, he thought, his lip curling in contempt. He'd earned his stripes breaking and entering way back in the day. Before he'd ever joined the Contello organization.

Before he'd learned everything there was to know about crime—and punishment. Before he'd struck out on his own.

He'd left LeeAnn's place while his lover girl was still

in dreamland, and had been taking care of business ever since.

Now all he had to do was tie up these final loose ends and dig up his money. Five hundred fifty-six thousand bucks. Easy money and all of it real. All of it his. Jase Fortune wasn't the only cowboy in town with piles of dough.

And once the little skank and her boyfriend are dead, Wells thought, easing his way around the back of the house, *there'll be no one left who could positively link me with the counterfeiting operation.* The girl had clearly told Clay Fortune that her sister didn't even know about it. So the old man was the only one who could connect him to Wheeler.

But his word was hearsay, nothing more. It'd never hold up in court, even if they caught him. Which they wouldn't do.

He smiled to himself as he jimmied the lock on the kitchen door. He hadn't lost his touch—he was inside in under a minute.

And he already knew there was no one else inside. Ginny Duncan had gone back to run her diner and Rawley Cooper was out in the barn.

Blondie was all alone.

Now where was she?

He moved through the house with practiced stealth, his boots making only a faint clack on the hardwood floor. *Okay, skank, where are you? Come out, come out, wherever you are.*

Then he saw her. Limping up the staircase—less than halfway up.

"Hey, blondie."

A grin spread across his face as she glanced back in panic and saw him. Saw the gun in his hand.

Those sweet melty blue eyes looked ready to pop out of her head.

"Don't make any noise, little girl, and don't try to run," he warned. "Turn around real slow and come down."

He adjusted the gun so it was pointing straight at her head. She was shaking like a mound of jelly as she inched her way down the steps.

"We're just going for a little ride." Wells grinned even wider. "I'm arranging a reunion—for you and your loser boyfriend. You can thank me later."

Chapter Thirty-five

Jase braked hard outside the shack on Whistle Road. Hank's Blazer was the only vehicle parked amid the weeds.

"Do you think Hank's inside? Could he have been released from the hospital?" Erinn asked softly.

"I doubt it." To Erinn's shock, he reached across her quickly, scooped a gun from the glove compartment, and stuck it into his belt. She wasn't sure if that made her feel better or worse.

"Mick's car looked totaled the other night," Jase muttered. "He's most likely been using the Blazer. So maybe we'll get lucky and find him inside." He glanced at her, his mouth grim.

"Here, stay inside and take the keys. If anything happens to me, get the hell out of here."

"Nice try, but did you really expect that to work? I've got a better idea. We do this together." She flung the passenger-side door open and vaulted from the SUV.

Scowling, Jase overtook her as she hurried toward the shack.

"Open up, Wheeler. Now!" he called, pounding his fist on the scarred door.

Eerie silence echoed in the clearing. Only last week Erinn had come here for the first time in search of her sister—and now it was Jase's sister who was missing.

And once again she was standing with her heart in her throat at Mick Wheeler's door.

"Wheeler!" Jase shouted again. His fist rammed against the door three more times, the sound loud as gunfire in the quiet of the late afternoon. "Get out here!"

There was only silence from inside. An odd silence. A sudden prickle skittered up Erinn's arms. "Maybe he isn't here," she murmured. "He'd be yelling by now for us to go away—not hiding. That's not Wheeler's style. Jase, this doesn't feel right."

"Yeah, something's off," he agreed. He was feeling the scarred surface of the door, his hands quickly testing the old wood. "I've got to get inside. If he's got Lily in there—"

He turned the knob and shoved against it hard. The door swung open.

Unlocked, Erinn thought. A chill skimmed across the nape of her neck. *Something definitely isn't right.*

"Jase," she began uneasily, but he was already inside, glancing sharply around, his muscular body coiled to react if Wheeler came at him.

But the main room of the shack was empty. It looked exactly as it had before when Erinn was here, except the laundry pile was even larger. And beer cans now littered the floor as well as the coffee table.

"I don't like this," she breathed as she stepped

across the threshold. Jase moved ahead, his head turning this way and that, wary and on guard. He moved toward one of the bedrooms and shoved the door open, stepped inside.

Erinn headed toward the room she'd seen Wheeler come out of the first time she'd been here. She opened the door cautiously, pushed it back, and stepped inside, braced for him to leap at her.

But Wheeler wasn't going to be leaping at anyone. Ever again.

"Jase," she said shakily. Nausea rose in her throat. "Jase, I . . . found him."

She stared in horror at Mick Wheeler. He was lying facedown on the bare pine floor, his face half submerged in a crimson pool of his own blood.

Chapter Thirty-six

Rawley Cooper swore a blue streak as Stitch Nolan battered fiercely at the locked barn door.

"Here, damn it, try this!" Thrusting a hammer at him, Rawley tried to control the rage coursing through his blood.

"Gawddammit. That little gal's alone in the house, Stitch! Break it down!"

Sweat poured down Stitch's face as he drove the hammer against the door. The wood was too thick. Too solid. He swung again. And again.

Rawley's face was rigid with worry. His arm in the sling began to throb as it hadn't in days. Clay had told them to keep an eye on the girl. They should've dropped their work and gotten to the house right away, soon as he said to.

Who the hell had locked them in here? Maybe the same bastard who'd taken a shot at him. Helpless fury tore through him.

One thing he did know was that the little gal was probably in big trouble.

"Shit. It's...not...working," Stitch panted, and Rawley

grabbed a rake and jammed it one-handed against the door.

"Somebody . . . anybody out there?" he yelled.

Silence.

He kicked at the wood as Stitch laid in with the hammer again. The thick door held. Rawley slammed the rake against the damned thing again and suddenly they heard a man's voice on the other side.

"What the hell! Who's in there?"

"Open up!" Rawley shouted through the door.

It burst open almost upon his words and he blinked against the sunlight.

Kevin Samson held a long skinny stick in one hand and Rawley realized instantly that's what had been jammed across the outside latch, barricading them inside. But the vet grasped a sheet of paper in the other hand, his vet bag forgotten on the ground.

"Clay wanted me to come by and check on Sheba," he said heavily as Rawley and Stitch bolted out of the barn. "I found this damned stick lodged across the latch. But that's not all. This was taped to the door."

Rawley grabbed the paper from him and studied it. His leathery brown face turned the color of bleached bone as he met the vet's sober eyes.

"Lord, no. We gotta call Jase," Rawley groaned. "Right away."

Stitch peered over his shoulder at the crude block letters marching across the white paper. His mouth gaped as he read the words.

If you want to see Lily again, pay up. One hundred thousand dollars cash. Don't even think about calling the law. If you do, she'll die real slow. More instructions later. This is your only chance to save her.

"Call Jase," Rawley ordered the vet, his voice thick with fear. "Fast!"

He started at a bow-kneed run for the ranch house. As Kevin yanked out his cell, Stitch bolted after Rawley.

They searched every room of the house, their boots thumping up and down hallways and stairs. They checked closets, bathtubs, under beds, every nook and cranny.

But the house was still and empty. The little blonde gal was gone.

"Hank, get your butt out here," Wells barked into his phone. "If you want to see your little girlfriend again, you'll get out of that damned hospital bed right now."

Hank could hear Devon sobbing in the background. Sweat broke out across his temples.

"Don't listen to him, Hank!" Devon shrieked, then he heard a loud slap and Devon screamed.

He bit back a yell of fury. He wanted to scream at Wells not to hurt her, but an aide was bustling about, setting down his dinner tray, sliding it closer, and putting a fresh jug of ice water alongside the applesauce, stringy chicken, and overcooked peas. He ignored her, concentrating on the smug voice in his ear.

"Where are you?" he grated as the aide headed out.

"Not far. Quarter mile east of the hospital parking lot. Hotfoot it over here, lover boy, or you're never going to see the little slut again."

Hank threw down the phone. Rage and fear for

Devon pumped through him. He'd been taking care of her ever since he met her in that shelter—and it was his fault she'd ever met Wells. His and his brother's. If he'd known what they were up to in the cabin, he'd never have brought Devon there, never insisted Mick let them stay.

This was all his fault. Devon had counted on him. It was the first time in his life anyone had ever counted on him for anything and he'd screwed it up.

He threw back the blanket and pushed himself off the bed. He was being released tomorrow, even though the doctor had warned him against too much exertion.

To hell with that though. He tore through the paper bag in the hospital closet containing the blood-spattered clothes he'd been wearing the night of the accident and pulled them on, then started for the door.

Suddenly, he turned back and grabbed the fork off his dinner tray, stuffing it into his jeans pocket.

No one stopped him as he slipped from the room and forced himself to stroll nonchalantly down the hall. By the time he ducked into the stairwell and raced down the steps, his ribs were throbbing like hell, but he ignored the pain.

Then he was outside for the first time in days. Dusk was moving in and huge gray clouds hung heavy in the sky.

He turned east and ran as fast as he could.

Chapter Thirty-seven

Sirens wailed in the distance as Clay Fortune roared down Whistle Road. He could still hear Kevin Samson's voice in his head despite the high-pitched scream of the sirens. It was enough to make his hands sweat as he clenched the steering wheel, and his heart was pumping so hard and fast he thought it was going to burst right out of his chest.

Never in his life had he been so scared. First Lily. His sweet, wild-hearted Lily. And now Devon, that pale teenager who had a way with horses like no one he'd ever seen.

All he wanted was to get his hands on whoever had touched them. Who would want to hurt two young women who'd never caused any pain to so much as a bumblebee?

He hit the brakes as he hurtled straight toward the Wheeler cabin and Jase and Erinn ran outside.

"Pop," Jase called as Clay launched himself out of the Explorer. "What are you doing here? Wheeler's dead. Murdered. Farley's on his way, but there's no sign of Lily or of Culp—"

"You sure?" Clay interrupted. As Jase nodded, Clay spun toward Erinn, guilt pummeling through him. "I'm sorry." His breath wheezed harshly in his throat. "I have to tell you—Devon's gone too."

Her mouth dropped.

"I never should have left her. Rawley called me—someone locked him and Stitch in the barn and when they got out, she was missing."

"She...can't be." Shock whitened Erinn's face. "I...left her with you...you were supposed to—"

"There's more," Clay said thickly. He told them about the ransom note for Lily.

Jase felt as if the world was crashing in on him. On all of them, crushing them beneath its weight. Erinn looked stunned, bereft of words. He could see she was trying to grasp the enormity of what his father had said.

But suddenly, concern for his father crowded out all other thoughts. Clay looked ready to collapse. His breathing was raspy, his face flushed.

"Sit down, Pop." He gripped his father's arm. "Get in my car, there's a water bottle under the seat. We'll find Devon and Lily, we'll find Culp too. But right now you need to calm down—"

"Damn it, this is partly my fault—don't tell me what to do!" Clay jerked his arm free, a muscle jerking in his neck.

"Shut up and listen to me, both of you. There's more—I know who took Devon. The reason I left her and came *here* was because she told me that Wheeler and Wells were partners in some counterfeiting operation. They did it all right there in that damned cabin," he added, jerking a thumb toward the shack where Wheeler lay dead.

The shriek of the police cars was almost upon them. Any moment they'd come tearing down Whistle Road.

"Did you find the computer equipment—printers, scanners, and such?" Clay demanded.

"No, we didn't see anything like that," Erinn muttered dazedly.

"They're there—or someone took 'em. Probably whoever killed Wheeler," Clay growled.

Erinn turned toward Jase, her throat tight with fear. She knew he was thinking the same thing she was.

It was Wells. Wells who'd kidnapped Devon. Wells who'd killed Mick. He'd taken the computer equipment. He was getting rid of all the evidence, all the witnesses—

"Hank!" she gasped. "Jase, he must be going after Hank too!"

She was interrupted by the now deafening blare of the sirens as three sheriff's vehicles and an ambulance jolted down the dirt road.

"Wheeler's inside," Jase said when the sheriff and two deputies hurried toward them. "He's in the larger of the two bedrooms—looks like he's been shot in the throat. But right now we've got bigger problems, Farley."

"What's bigger than murder?" Farley demanded. His lawman's eyes flattened in his face when Jase told him.

Five minutes later, the hospital returned the sheriff's call. Hank Wheeler had gone missing sometime this afternoon. No one knew if he'd sneaked out on his own or if someone had forcibly taken him away—but his clothes were gone, his bed was empty, and a search of the hospital had turned up nothing.

"More bad news," Farley told them. Clay had finally sat down in a dirty rusted folding chair Jase dragged from behind the shack. He'd gulped some water and his color had improved, though not his mood.

"Out with it," he ordered the sheriff as the lawman surveyed the three of them.

"No counterfeiting equipment was found inside. The deputies are going over everything in the shack again, but they didn't come across anything on first inspection. No computer, no scanner, no documents, real or fake."

"Then Wells took the evidence with him," Erinn said at once. "Just like he took my sister."

"Could be," the sheriff conceded. "But in the meantime, I'm going to need your statements. We need to speak with each of you separately. Miss Winters, you found the body. I'll question you in my vehicle. Clay, Dennis will take your statement right here, and Jase, you step inside and talk to Henry—"

"We don't have time for statements, Sheriff," Erinn flashed. "We need to search for my sister!"

"First things first, ma'am," Farley said politely, but Jase cut him off, his eyes like dark winter ice.

"Forget it, Guy. You've got all you're going to get for now."

"He's right, Farley." Clay rose like a giant from his chair. "We've got a damned killer out there and every second counts. Get every officer you can muster in the county searching, damn you."

"Hold on," the sheriff growled, then sighed in exasperation as the deputy in the shack beckoned him inside.

The moment he walked away, Jase said in an under-voice, "Pop, you stay and fill them in on as much as you can, then call Colton. Try to take it easy. I'll keep you posted."

"You'd better," Clay grunted.

Jase's eyes met Erinn's. "Let's go."

Together they ran to the Explorer, jumped in, and shot like a bullet down Whistle Road. Farley heard the screeching tires and burst out the cabin door, yelling for them to stop.

They never even slowed.

Devon couldn't stop crying. The hot tears streamed from her eyes, and little sobs quivered up and down her throat as she struggled against the rope binding her wrists behind her back.

"Shuddup already, will you?" Wells barked, half turning to glare at her in the backseat of the car. "If you don't, I'll do it for you. You want that?"

"Leave her alone," Hank snarled in the front seat.

Wells kept one hand on the steering wheel and with the other, slammed the boy across the face.

"Stop that!" Devon shrieked.

"What? You don't like your boyfriend getting hit in the face?" Wells glanced back at her again, grinning. "Well, it'll be a lot worse for both of you if you don't shut your trap."

Menace glittered in his eyes and Devon believed

him. She slumped back, trying not to cry anymore, trying not to make a sound.

Wells stomped down harder on the gas pedal and the car jolted wildly over the bumpy back roads. They were rutted and narrow, filled with stones and twisting tree roots, and Devon was jerked sideways, then forward, slamming against the back of the passenger seat.

She leaned back again, gasping, and stared out the window in dread. The countryside through which they were driving was totally unfamiliar to her. All she knew was that they were climbing upward over these rough, deserted roads.

He's taking us into the mountains, she realized.

And it would be dark soon. Grayish shadows brushed the treetops and the light was bleeding fast from the sky. Too fast.

We have to get loose, she thought desperately, rubbing her wrists against the rope. *Keep trying. Maybe Hank is trying too.*

Wells had forced her to tie Hank's hands behind his back. She'd tried not to pull the knot tight, but Wells had checked it, then shoved his gun against the side of her head and told her to make it tighter or he'd shoot her right there.

She'd done it, though her hands had been shaking so much she almost hadn't been able to pull the rope through.

Now the rope he'd wound around her own wrists chafed against her skin, and her eyes felt raw and swollen from crying.

Still, she kept trying, trying to get free . . .

All she wanted was to go back—back to the cabin

with Tiffany, or to the Fortune house. She liked both those places. She liked . . .

Tiffany, she thought, pain slicing through her heart. She liked her sister again. And she liked the Fortunes.

Not that anyone, except maybe Mr. Fortune, could guess.

Why had she been so mean to Tiffany? she wondered as she was thrown sideways again on the seat. Ever since Tiffany first showed up at the cabin and tried to take her away, she'd barely said one nice thing to her.

And Tiffany was trying hard. She was just like Devon remembered her from so long ago. Nice. Caring. Patient.

Not at all like the Great Dane . . .

And now I might never get to actually have a sister again. To be part of a real family.

Now Wells was going to . . . he was going to . . .

He's going to kill us, she thought bitterly, wincing from her scraped wrists. *He's going to kill Hank and me in the mountains where no one will ever find where we're at.*

Not if I get free, she told herself. *And if Hank gets free. If we can both fight . . .*

She'd never known how to fight back against the Great Dane. She'd never even tried. But now she was going to fight Frank Wells. With all of her strength.

Devon knew she wasn't very brave, but there was one thing she did have going for her. She repeated it over and over in her head, as pain and fear tried to envelop her, tried to make her cry and give up. One thought she clung to, because it wouldn't let her do either of those things.

I don't want to die.

Chapter Thirty-eight

LeeAnn Culpepper was searching nearly four miles from where Culp's rig was found when Jase and Erinn tracked her down. In the fading daylight she looked exhausted and hopeless. She glanced up from the scrub brush she was peering behind when they sprinted toward her and the set expression in Jase's face made her clasp her hands to her throat.

"You found Donnie," she gasped. "He's dead, isn't he?"

"We haven't found him yet, LeeAnn." Jase's eyes bored into her. "Talk to me about Frank Wells."

"Frank? You scared me half to death because of Frank Wells? Why don't you just concentrate on finding Donnie, Jase, and leave Frank the hell alone—"

"Wells kidnapped my sister." Erinn lunged forward, her nails digging into her palms. "We don't have time to explain it all, LeeAnn, so just talk. Did you know Wells was involved in a counterfeit scheme?"

"What? You're crazy." The woman turned away dismissively. "What the hell is she talking about, Jase?"

He filled her in as quickly as he could. Erinn spun away and paced the clearing, too restless to stand still.

She had no patience for LeeAnn's shock; her own was too raw and fresh. She had to find Devon. Now, tonight, before the sun went down. Wells was going to kill her—and Hank. And maybe Lily and Culp too. He was crazy. His grudge against the Fortunes had spun out of all control, and now he was after everyone who knew about the counterfeiting.

LeeAnn didn't know—that much she believed. And not only because of the woman's vehement denials. The proof was right there—LeeAnn was still alive.

Is Devon? she wondered, pain stabbing her.

Quickly she prowled toward a stand of trees, peering beyond them, looking for . . .

Looking for what?

She turned in a slow circle, then cocked her head toward the mountains towering against the gilded gold and apricot sky. Her temples throbbed and her edgy restlessness was intensifying by the moment. She couldn't seem to stop pacing.

There's something I'm missing, she thought. *What is it?*

"Erinn." Jase strode to her side, frowning. "LeeAnn doesn't know anything. She doesn't even believe what I'm telling her. And considering she's been dating Wells, she knows very little about him. He drinks, but only in moderation. He used to ride bulls. He grew up on a farm in Wyoming. She had no idea he was involved with Wheeler in any way, never saw the two of them speak. We're not going to get much more from her."

"So what do we do now, Jase? Just keep driving around? Hike up one hill, down another, looking for them? For all these years, I've been having visions of people in trouble, and now, my own sister is the one in danger, and I can't see a thing—I can't find her!"

The desperation on her face cut Jase like a knife. "You told me once you don't control the visions. That isn't how it works, remember?"

"I just feel so helpless. Devon's out there—Lily, too—they could be hurt, scared. Right now Wells could be doing God knows what to them—" She broke off suddenly and spun to her right, staring straight up again at the granite peak of the mountain.

"Are there caves up there?"

"Skeleton Peak? Yeah, a few. You keep going back to the caves, don't you?"

"I don't know why. But I can't shake the feeling that I'm missing something. I keep seeing that red drawing of the horse on the cave wall. But I don't understand it, any more than I understand the vision of the coffin and the mist."

"Let's head over to Skeleton Peak, poke around the caves, see what happens. It's not as if we have any other leads right now," Jase said grimly.

"It's worth a try."

Pressure clamped through Erinn. Her head throbbed with dull pain and her thoughts were racing. She hadn't been able to save her mother—she'd awakened too late. By the time she got to her parents' bedroom, Evangeline had the gun pressed to her head. But maybe now, there would be a way. Maybe now she wouldn't be too late to save Devon. And Lily. And Culp.

Jase knew a back-road shortcut to Skeleton Peak. But even so, the drive seemed to take forever.

"This would be quicker on horseback," he muttered as he wrested the SUV around a hairpin turn. A canyon yawned to their right, steep and jagged, and Erinn couldn't even allow herself to look down.

When they finally reached the caves, she leaped from the car. She and Jase entered several of them together, but he stood silent as she gazed around, her heart fluttering as she let the cool darkness envelop her.

Nothing . . . Nothing . . .

Panic built in her and she willed it away. Moving forward, she touched the ancient, rough walls, took a deep, long breath.

She wasn't cold, no vision rushed her down the tunnel.

Jase watched her in silence, seeing the torment in her eyes, the stiffness of her narrow shoulders.

If he ever got his hands on Wells, he'd make the bastard pay for every moment Erinn and everyone else in his family had suffered. But they couldn't stay here forever. The seconds were ticking past and darkness was moving in. Night would only hide Wells deeper, give him time to get away.

"Erinn," he said at last, reluctantly.

"I know. It's useless." Her voice was low, defeated. She started out of the cave, then stopped, trembling.

Before Jase could reach her, she was sinking, sinking to her knees.

"Erinn!"

He caught her at the last instant, before her head struck rock.

"Erinn!"

But he knew she was far away from him and couldn't hear a word.

Wells shoved his prisoners into the blackness of the cave, oblivious to their groans as they sprawled across the rock floor.

Five feet in, he hunkered down, pulled a small shovel from his duffel, and started to dig along the rocky wall.

"Don't you worry, this shouldn't take long. Then we'll get on with things," he said as he plunged the shovel into the ground.

Devon struggled to a sitting position, straining against the rope burning like fire into her wrists. Hank managed to work his way up too. As he glanced over at her she saw with horror that his lip dripped blood from where Wells had struck him.

"Sorry, Dev," he choked out. "We never should've come back to live with Mick. If I'd known what he was—"

"Shut up!" Wells glared at them. "No more talking, you two. Play time's over."

"You can still let us go," Devon said quickly. "We won't go back...or...or tell anyone. We'll just keep moving. Me and Hank were going to leave soon anyway."

"Well, where you're going now, you won't ever be coming back from," Wells told her. Then, suddenly, he gave a grunt of satisfaction, as the shovel scraped against metal.

"Paydirt." He grinned to himself.

Devon's eyes widened as he lifted a metal box from the dirt and dust, opened the latch, and started flipping through six-inch-high stacks of money inside. When he closed the box again with a loud clink and set it down, she felt terror squeeze through her, obliterating everything else from her mind.

Wells turned, eyed her and Hank. She found herself shrinking back against the opposite wall of the cave, away from the frightening glint in his oily dark eyes.

"That's it, kiddies. Time for me to be moving on. You two are taking a trip too."

"We won't tell anyone about you, Wells—let us go!" Hank bit out.

Wells seized Devon's arm and hauled her to her feet. "You must have me mixed up with someone else," he told Hank coldly. "I don't leave loose ends. Ever."

With that he yanked Hank up and pushed both of them toward the mouth of the cave.

"Keep going." He pushed at Devon's back, shoving her closer to the rim of the deep-walled canyon ten feet ahead. The gorge sloped dizzyingly downward, ending in a twisted pile of rock and scrub brush. "Which one of you losers wants to jump first?"

"It was the same vision as before." Erinn's voice shook as Jase helped her into the Explorer.

"The cave, the drawing of the horse in blood—exactly the same. But this time I remember what I couldn't recall before, Jase. I heard something—I heard it last time too, but it slipped away from me." She gripped her hands in her lap as he closed the door and sprinted to the driver's side.

"I heard screaming, Jase. Horrible screaming—it was nonhuman, bloodcurdling. All around me, these frightened, high-pitched shrieks in my head—like animals on fire—"

"Horses." Jase stared at her as realization hit him. "Wild horses—stallions—scream when they're fighting."

"They do?" Erinn's heart began to thump. Had what she heard been the screams of wild horses? It could be . . .

"You told Devon about a place where she might see wild horses—mustangs. Where was that?"

"Red Horse Canyon. It's maybe twenty miles from here." His gaze sharpened. "Erinn, there's a cave there. Red Horse Cave. Is it possible the image of the horse wasn't drawn in blood—that it was just red? Like the color *red*?"

Red. Red Horse. She blinked, seeing the cave wall yet again in her mind's eye. A quiver of recognition came from someplace deep and knowing inside.

Red Horse Cave. "Yes, that's it, Jase. I'm sure that's it!"

He had the SUV in gear before she finished the words.

"How long will it take to get there?" she asked frantically, praying she was right, praying they weren't jolting at full, crazed speed toward another dead end.

"I know a switchback up ahead; it should get us

there faster. Maybe fifteen minutes." Jase's mouth was clenched with determination as he maneuvered the SUV on the narrow twisting road.

Erinn nodded, unable to speak now, only to pray. Pray with all of her heart that they wouldn't be too late.

Chapter Thirty-nine

"You're crazy," Hank told Wells, planting his feet a few yards from the rim of the canyon, facing Wells defiantly. "I'm not jumping. And neither is she."

Tears streamed down Devon's face. But she spoke up vehemently. "He's right. N-no way."

No sooner than the words were out of her mouth than she saw something. Hank had freed himself from the rope. He was holding it in his fingers behind his back so Wells wouldn't notice.

His hands were free.

Hope flickered in her and she had to fight to keep from staring at Hank. She forced herself to look at Wells's cold, handsome face, all the while wondering what Hank was going to do, and how she could help him.

Then, with horror, she saw Wells lift the gun and point it at Hank. An instant later, wearing a thin smile, he shifted it to her.

"Back," he said. "Back up to the edge and turn around."

"I won't," Devon cried.

"Look at it this way, kiddies. If I shoot you dead,

there's nothin' you can do about it. You'll *be* dead. But if you jump . . ." He waved the gun toward the sheer canyon beyond them.

"You might survive the fall. You might get lucky, be able to crawl away. Maybe someone'll happen along and find you—though I wouldn't count on it." He chuckled and rubbed his jaw with his free hand.

"Still, it's a chance, as opposed to certain death. So what's it going to be, boys and girls? I don't have all day."

He's crazy, Devon thought. *Cruel. And crazy.* He might have read her thoughts because suddenly he frowned and waved the gun at her.

"You first, blondie. Get going. Jump."

"I won't!" Devon choked out.

She saw his finger curled on the trigger. She couldn't stop staring at it, her heart hammering so hard her whole body hurt as she waited for the gunfire to explode.

"Then you'll die just like Hank's big brother, Mick, did," Wells grunted.

Suddenly, Hank was screaming at her, launching himself at Wells.

"Run, Dev!"

Wells swerved the gun back toward him, but not in time. Gunfire roared but the shot went wide and then Hank's body hit the other man, knocking him to the ground. They both crashed to the dirt in a desperate struggle for the gun.

Devon froze for an instant. She couldn't run away, she had to help Hank. Her gaze flew frantically about for a rock or a stick—anything she could use to cut her bonds.

She spotted a branch, lying near the mouth of the cave, but even as she sprang toward it, terror roaring through her head, Hank yanked something shiny from his pocket. As she watched, before she could even reach the branch, he plunged a fork into Wells's throat.

Blood gushed like a geyser, streaming down Wells's chest, spilling onto Hank's hands. Bloodied hands and all, he yanked the fork out and Wells screamed, a gurgling, agonized sound that echoed through the clearing.

But as Hank tried to twist the gun away, Wells somehow managed to hang onto it. With a burst of strength born of adrenaline-fueled rage, Wells swung the barrel and squeezed the trigger.

What happened next left Devon screaming. Hank fell back, blood spurting from a bullet hole that went straight through his chest. Blood, bones, flesh splattered across Wells, across the clearing.

Nausea rose in Devon's throat. She swallowed back the bile, tried to run. She couldn't move.

Hank was dead, blood was everywhere. Wells had somehow staggered to his feet—he was pointing the gun at her, covered in a sea of blood.

"Your . . . turn, blondie. Say . . . good-bye—"

A gunshot exploded, cutting off his words. Devon's body flinched, buckled. She waited for the pain, for the blood, but a moment later she saw Wells topple backward into the dirt and realized he'd been shot, not her.

Wells was dead. Hank was dead. *Why am I alive?*

she wondered dazedly as hot tears, not blood, poured down her cheeks.

Then Jase was there, racing toward her, and Tiffany was a step behind, and she threw herself into her sister's arms.

"He shot Hank. Hank tried to save me—"

"It's okay, Devon, you're safe. You're going to be okay." Erinn struggled to untie the rope. Wracked with pain, Devon wept, gasping, her entire body shuddering in the bloody clearing.

Tears streamed from Erinn's eyes as well. Through them she saw Jase hunkering down beside Wells.

"He's still alive," Jase said, snapping open his phone.

"Colton, get up here to Red Horse Cave with Farley and an ambulance. Get here fast—Hank Wheeler's dead, Devon's hurt, and Wells is in bad shape. If he dies, we might never find Lily and Culp."

He disconnected before Colton could respond, and focused his attention on Wells.

The man was writhing on the ground, spitting out blood. Blood still poured from the punctures in his throat, and now also from his hand, where Jase had shot him, knocking the gun from his fingers.

"I might try to stop the bleeding, Wells, and save your filthy life," he said grimly, "but first you're going to tell me one thing. And you'd better tell me fast." He leaned closer, his gaze drilling into Wells's ghastly face.

"I don't care about your pain. I don't care if you live or die. You're going to answer me right now or I won't lift a finger to help you. *Where's Lily?*"

Chapter Forty

It was almost midnight. And still Jase had no answers.

He paced up and down the hospital corridor, past the nurse's station to the stairwell, then back again to the closed door of Frank Wells's room.

He raked both hands through his hair in frustration, and rubbed his knuckles over his eyes and called on every ounce of self-control he possessed to resist shoving the door open and taking matters into his own hands.

Tension was eating him alive from the inside out. If they didn't find Lily, his father would be destroyed. They'd all be destroyed. Farley was in there, with a doctor and two of his deputies, and they'd better break Wells down soon, get him to admit he'd been responsible for Lily's and Culp's disappearance and to confess what he'd done with them both.

Or else.

So far, the slimebag hadn't admitted to a thing. He was refusing to answer questions until he talked to a lawyer, claiming that he was innocent, that Devon and Hank had tried to kill *him,* that he knew nothing about a counterfeit operation run by Mick Wheeler, he didn't know how any of the computer equipment, the printer, or scanner got in his car. Nor did he know anything about Don Culpepper or Lily Fortune, and he wouldn't answer any more questions until his lawyer was present.

Jase wanted to flay the bastard alive, but Farley had barred him from Wells's room. Jase was all but ready to bust down the door when Erinn appeared at the end of the corridor and hurried toward him, looking exhausted and pale.

To his surprise, the sight of her calmed him. As she drew near, those beautiful eyes of hers studying him with concern, he felt some of the tightness in his chest ease. A trickle of warmth flowed through his bones for the first time since Lily's disappearance. And that both surprised and scared the hell out of him.

"Has Wells talked yet? Has he told you about Lily?"

"Not a damned thing." His face hardened. "The bastard's lucky the fork missed his larynx and arteries. He could have been dead by now. He will be, if he doesn't tell us where to find Lily and Culp."

"He will, Jase. He *has* to." Erinn's heart ached for him. She knew the torture he must be feeling. His jeans and shirt were dirty, stained with blood, his eyes were bloodshot, his powerful shoulders tense. The heavy stubble along his jaw made him look like some kind of fierce outlaw on the run. Even so, he was indescribably handsome. He looked as strong and solid as always— and still nowhere near as numb and depleted as she felt herself.

Just looking at him, being with him, made her feel so much better. Stronger.

Yet in some ways she felt worse.

Because she was leaving—with Devon—flying back to New York within the next few days. Possibly even tomorrow night.

And she had to tell him.

As soon as Sheriff Farley had reviewed her complete statement as well as Devon's, as soon as he told them they were free to go, as soon as Lily and Culp were found—and she prayed that would be within hours—she was getting Devon away from here.

It'd be so much easier for Devon to recover from the trauma she'd gone through away from the place it happened.

And Erinn needed to get away too. She'd figured that out while sitting in the ER with her hysterically sobbing sister. She'd gotten in too deep with Jase—with his entire family. She needed to pull back, leave, protect herself. And focus on Devon.

As it was, right now she was so in love with him that the thought of leaving him made her heart crack like a seashell flung against a rock. She'd fallen hard. Much harder than she'd ever thought possible.

And now she'd have to pay for it.

"Remind me again why I bothered to staunch Wells's wounds and save his worthless hide," Jase grated out.

"Because you believe in your heart that he's going to tell us where Lily is—and so do I," Erinn replied quietly, all the while praying she was right. She touched his arm. "And it's the best shot we've got."

He met her gaze bleakly. She had a knack for putting

everything in perspective, for framing things in the most positive light. A soothing quality in a woman.

It was one of the things he loved most about her . . .

Loved? His mind froze on the word. "How are you holding up?" he asked hastily, to block that unwanted, unsought-for word from his mind, even as panic lurched through him once again. "Did Devon check out all right?"

"She just has some bruises and rope burn on her wrists. They're going to release her soon. I'm taking her home—back to Fortune's Way, I mean—for tonight. She feels safer there right now than anywhere else. Then tomorrow . . ."

She moistened her lips. "Well, as soon as the sheriff's finished interviewing us and as soon as Lily and Culp are found . . ."

She hesitated, and somehow he knew what she was going to say.

"You're taking her back to New York."

Erinn nodded. "Devon needs . . . to get away from here. She associates Wolf River with Hank, and she just saw him killed. It will be easier for her to get over the shock in New York."

"I guess that makes sense." It did. But Jase was using every ounce of self-control he possessed right now to fight the impulse to take Erinn in his arms and ask her to stay. Ask her to stay for his sake, because he wanted her—not only in his town, but in his life.

The very idea stunned him. And scared the hell out of him. How had she become so necessary to him, so important? He was much too attached to this woman, much too intrigued. He knew damn well that if he asked her to stay, she'd get ideas—and who could blame her? It wouldn't be fair to stir up any ideas about love and marriage and permanence.

Love. There was that damned word again.

I don't love her, he thought angrily.

Quickly he reassured himself that he'd just gotten used to having her around. He was attracted to her beauty, that was all. To her sexy little smile. And to the way she cared about her sister. *Not to mention the way she has of kissing a man so he forgets everything but how it feels to be with her,* a troublesome voice inside him pointed out.

Jase felt sweat break out on his brow and this time it had nothing to do with his fears for Lily and Culp. He had to slow this thing down with Erinn, give both of them some space. With everything that had happened in the past few days, they were moving way too fast. Hell, *he* was moving way too fast. Letting her in too close, wanting her far more than he should. If he wasn't careful, she'd get the wrong idea, and he'd end up hurting her the same way he'd hurt LeeAnn.

And hurting her was the one thing he didn't ever want to do.

"You need to do whatever's right for Devon," he heard himself say in a voice that sounded far calmer and more rational than he was feeling at the moment.

He thought he glimpsed something sad in her eyes—but an instant later it was gone and he wondered if he'd imagined it. Especially when she straightened her shoulders and her chin edged up in that decisive gesture he had begun to recognize.

"Right." She shrugged. "Which means I should get

back to her. Your father's with her now, keeping her company, but I can't stay away for too long."

At that precise moment, a petite nurse with short dark hair appeared around the corner and bustled toward them. "Ms. Winters, Mr. Fortune said to tell you that your sister's been discharged. As soon as you return to the ER, he'll get the car."

"Thank you." Erinn turned to leave. Devon needed her. It didn't seem that Jase did. It hadn't even occurred to him to ask her to stay. And he didn't appear the least bit upset that she was planning to go. He looked weary—but as tough, sharp, and in command of himself as always.

"Where's Colton?" she asked, turning back, despite herself. "I thought he'd be keeping you company, waiting for answers. You shouldn't be here all alone."

"I sent him to head up a private party of searchers— they're branching out right now from Red Horse Cave. I figured that since Wells had all that cash hidden up there and took Devon and Hank to the cave as well, he might have Lily and Culp stashed somewhere up there too. They've got high-powered flashlights and they're combing through not only the cave, but all along the trail rimming the canyon. Then, come daylight," Jase said, grimacing, "if they haven't found anything, Farley's going to send a search party down into the canyon. In case . . ."

He paused, his eyes grim and dark. Erinn knew how the sentence ended. *In case Wells had driven Lily and Culp off the cliff as he'd tried to do to Devon and Hank. In case their broken bodies were down there, smashed against the rocks and the scrub brush.*

"Go ahead to the ranch," he told her tightly. "Get Devon into bed. She's had a helluva day. And so have you."

So have we all, Erinn thought. *Including you.*

But there was nothing more to say. He knew she intended to leave Wolf River, and he hadn't said a word to stop her.

And her sister was waiting.

"I hope there's good news by morning, Jase," she said quietly.

"You and me both."

Erinn felt his gaze on her as she hurried away. She was grateful he couldn't see her face, see the sudden, stupid tears that were blurring her vision. She wanted to chalk them up to exhaustion and stress and the aftermath of Devon's ordeal, but she knew better.

Pain poured through her. Jase had accepted her decision to leave without a word of protest or regret. Without even a blink of the eyes.

What did you expect? she asked herself bitterly, hurrying toward the ER. *He's a man. A man who's been burned—who's turned his back on any serious involvements. You've been spending too much time in the Emerald Forest. Life is not a fairy tale.*

No, her life was real. And she had to get on with it, the sooner the better—for Devon's sake and for her own.

By the time Erinn reached the still and darkened ranch house, a limp exhaustion had crept through every bone of her body. Clay Fortune escorted them personally to Devon's room, then left for his own in the main wing.

At Devon's request, Erinn slept in her sister's bedroom, sharing the queen-size bed. She awoke instantly when Devon sat up sobbing in the middle of the night, and wrapped the weeping girl in her arms.

"It's okay, honey. You're safe. It's over, it's all over. Wells is never going to hurt you again."

"Hank..." Devon wept. "I k-keep seeing Hank. He was trying to save me—"

"I know, baby. I know." Erinn could only hold her, and remind her that she was safe, just as she had when Devon was a toddler and beset by nightmares.

But now Devon had lived a nightmare. It was over though, she told the girl, reassuring her again and again throughout the night.

Tomorrow will be better.

And, she thought as at last Devon's breathing evened out beside her, and the sister she'd both lost and found escaped for a time into sleep, *it will be better for everyone—if only Wells will talk—if only Culp and Lily are found alive.*

She awoke again at ten minutes to four in the morning when she heard the slam of a car door. Fortunately, the sound didn't awaken Devon, but Erinn slipped from her bed and padded to the window in time to see Jase striding up the porch steps.

Is there news about Lily and Culp? she wondered, hurrying from the room and down the stairs—barefoot, clad only in a black camisole and white sweatpants.

Jase glanced up when he saw her, his face drawn.

"Any news?" Erinn's hopes fell as she reached the bottom of the staircase and studied his grim, gray face.

"Not a word. Wells is out for the night, doped up on painkillers. And Colton's still searching."

"Then why are you here?" she blurted, suddenly conscious of his nearness, of her sleep-tousled hair and bare feet, of the stillness of the house where the only other occupants were deep in sleep. "I mean, I know it's your house, but—"

"I just wanted to check in here first, make sure everything's under control before heading to the barn."

Under control? Hardly, she thought, studying his powerful, weary frame with inexplicable sadness. "We're fine. You look exhausted."

"I'll survive. I just hope Lily and Culp will—"

He broke off, his face bleak. More bleak than Erinn had ever seen it. She couldn't bear it. Reaching out, she touched his beard-stubbled cheek.

"They will, Jase. They'll make it. Have faith. Somehow, we need to have faith—"

She broke off suddenly as his hand encircled hers. His fingers were warm and strong. A hot sizzle of need spiked inside her like a streak of lightning.

Then Jase yanked her toward him, his face full of darkness and need and pain, and Erinn crashed against his solid chest, her heart beating in her throat. Her lips sought his as his arms clamped like iron bars around her waist.

He drank her in like a man wasting in a desert, devouring her with a violence that had Erinn's knees trembling. Her entire body burned with a craving that was beyond thought or reason.

"Jase," she gasped as they came up for air. Then his mouth drove against hers again, sucking her in still deeper, to a place of craving and raw desire. She was swallowed up by a rushing physical need more intense than any she'd ever experienced before. With it came a rush of tenderness that wracked her heart.

Then he pulled back and for an instant she felt lost. Bereft. But even as she reached for him again, he was bundling her down the hall, his breath quick and rasping in the quiet of the house.

He shoved her into his office and kicked the door shut. Erinn's heart raced at the intensity in his eyes as they drifted over her. Then she and Jase were tumbling together onto the dark brown leather sofa, kissing once more, their bodies locked together even as they struggled to undress.

Erinn's fingers fumbled over the buttons of his shirt, then flung it aside. She groped for his zipper, tugged at his jeans. Meantime he was stripping off her camisole, his mouth seeking the softness of her bare breasts beneath.

When he lowered himself onto her, Erinn opened herself to him, shaking with need, knowing only the dark musky taste of him, the scent of leather and sweat, the way he made her feel alive, like no one else ever had.

Slick with sweat, they made love. Not slow, gentle, heated love—but fierce, no-holds-barred, red-hot love. A furious joining born of heat and thunder and despair, of blinding need and emotion that swelled like a driven sea. Passion jolted between them like waves of nuclear energy that could do nothing but explode.

And when it was over they collapsed in each other's arms.

"I love you," Erinn whispered dazedly as she nuzzled his throat.

The next instant, the realization of what she'd just said hit her. And so did the silence that greeted her words.

She sat up, reeling with shock. To her horror, Jase looked equally stunned.

"Forget I . . . said that," she managed, trying hard to sound offhand. "It was . . . a mistake . . . just the aftermath . . ."

She scrambled off the sofa and lunged for her clothes, humiliation burning through her entire body. "I know that what just happened . . . we were blowing off steam. It didn't mean anything," she gulped hastily, as she yanked her camisole over her head and pulled it down to cover her breasts.

"Erinn—"

"Don't say anything," she pleaded, tugging on her thong. "I was just being stupid."

"Well, I was as stupid as you." Jase swung his feet to the floor. His hand shot up as she flung his jeans toward him, her cheeks the color of fresh roses. "Look, Erinn, we're both out of control. We've been . . . under a lot of stress."

He felt like an idiot as those eyes of hers nailed him. "I mean, it was great and everything," he said hastily, "and—"

"Shut up, Jase. Just shut up."

He could have kicked himself. Man, what was wrong with him? His brain had completely shut down. He was saying all the wrong things. *Doing* all the wrong things. He never should have laid a finger on her tonight. He'd been playing with fire.

But she'd touched his cheek and he'd just gone nuts. Dragged her down here like a Neanderthal. Not that she hadn't wanted it, all of it. As badly as he had.

Panic coursed through him. He was losing control— of everything. His life, his emotions, his senses. His entire family and his best friend were in danger and he was here with Erinn Winters, making love to her in his damned office in the middle of the night after he'd already decided to back off of her—of *them*.

"Look," he mumbled, trying not to sound as unnerved as he felt. "Don't get me wrong. This doesn't mean—"

"Anything," she finished for him, her voice tight as she yanked on her sweatpants with trembling hands. "I know that. You don't have to spell it out for me. If you say another word about it, I'll . . . I'll throw your boots at you. Just forget it. We both have to forget it."

"Right." Relief flooded him. "I agree. But Erinn—"

She was gone, though, the door gaping in her wake, the memory of her shimmering eyes, of her soft, sleek body curled against his, of the tender way she'd cried his name when they climaxed only that—a memory.

Jase sank down on the sofa again and scrubbed his hands over his face. He was too shook-up right now; it wasn't the time to think about what had happened between them. How good it was. How much he'd needed her at that moment when she'd reached out to him in the hall. Yet he couldn't *stop* thinking about it. And, he realized with a gulp of fear, he hadn't needed just any woman. He'd needed *her*.

Erinn.

Grabbing his shirt, he clutched it in his fist and stalked from the office. He let himself out of the house and headed to the barn.

Too many emotions were swirling through him. He had to shut them down. He had to focus on Lily. On Culp.

But first he had to find a way to stop thinking about Erinn.

Chapter Forty-one

The next morning, Erinn showered and dressed quickly, quietly, determined not to awaken Devon. Finding that she'd run out of clean clothes at the ranch, she pulled on the black cami and sweatpants she'd slept in, grimacing as she remembered how swiftly Jase had dispatched them from her body last night.

But she pushed that thought from her mind. She couldn't bear to remember the frenzied need of their lovemaking, or her stupidity afterward. She forced herself to think about Devon.

Devon needed clean clothes too—donning the bloody garments she'd worn yesterday would only serve to remind the girl of everything that had happened outside Red Horse Cave.

After breakfast, she thought, heading downstairs into the kitchen, *I'll drive over to the cabin and pack fresh clothes for both of us to wear today.*

She could also start packing her suitcase. This afternoon would be a good time to check out flights to New York and see what was available within a day or two.

The sooner she put some distance between herself and Jase, the better.

She made fresh coffee and poured herself a cup, noticing that Jase's Explorer was still parked outside. *He must still be asleep,* she thought. *And Colton too.*

Had the search party found Lily last night? Was she alive?

The heaviness in her heart told her they hadn't. She hoped she was wrong.

More than ever she was aware of how empty the ranch house felt. Different from the first few times she'd been here, when it resonated with warmth, life, and family.

Lily was gone—and with her went the heart and soul of the Fortune family. The house seemed to sense that its mistress was in danger now—hurt, frightened . . . possibly dead.

No, not dead, she told herself, horror coiling inside her. *She can't be dead. If she's with Culp, maybe he's protecting her . . . somehow.*

Unless Culp is dead too.

The ransom note had only mentioned Lily. Not Culp. This sent a ripple of apprehension through her. Wells had all that money from his damned counterfeiting, yet he'd tried to extort a ransom as well. Sick, sick man. His hatred of the Fortunes was only equaled by his greed.

But if he's asking a ransom for her, it means Lily's still alive, she thought, setting her cup down in the sink. But Wells hadn't counted on being captured before he could collect the money and release her—if he'd ever really intended to release her . . .

Erinn felt cold, despite the warmth of the coffee. They had to find Lily soon, or she could die of thirst or starvation or the elements. Where the hell was Wells keeping her?

A coffin, she thought. The vision of the cave was about Devon. Perhaps the coffin is where Lily is trapped . . . or Culp . . .

Could they be in a cemetery?

When the phone rang, she jumped. But it was only Deputy Ross from the sheriff's office, informing her that Farley wanted her and Devon to come in for more questioning at 11:30 a.m. No, Deputy Ross told her regretfully, Lily and Culp had not been found during the night. The search of Red Horse Canyon had commenced at daylight and he had no word yet on how that was proceeding.

Erinn's spirits sank still further as she headed outside. Spotting Rawley leading some horses out to pasture, she asked him to let Devon know when she awoke that Erinn would be back soon with fresh clothes from the cabin.

As she drove toward Black Bear Road, the brilliant sky and bright sunshine seemed to mock the nightmare they were living through. This would be the first time she'd been to the cabin alone, without Jase, since all this started. With Wells in custody there was no longer anything to fear—except that he wouldn't tell them what he'd done with Lily and Culp.

Her heart lurched as she pulled up amid the peaceful beauty of the clearing and stared at the cabin that was now so familiar, at the porch where Jase had first kissed her on a sweet rain-swept night. But all that was over. Her stay in Wolf River was over. She resolutely pushed all the memories from her mind as she went inside.

It had only been a few days since she'd last come here, but everything felt different. It was odd to see the walls she still hadn't finished painting, the garden she hadn't planted, even her laptop on the kitchen counter. She hadn't opened it in days, much less thought about Princess Devonshire.

The poor mouse. Still trapped in a spiderweb deep in the Emerald Forest. Still struggling and helpless.

Suddenly a flash of inspiration struck her—what Devonshire needed was a friend to come to her aid. Even a superheroine princess mouse needed a helping hand once in a while—or maybe a helping *beak,* she thought suddenly.

What if...

She rushed to the laptop, set it on the kitchen table, and powered up. What if Smogul the Goose showed up and broke the spiderweb apart with his beak? Turnaround was fair play, after all—Devonshire had saved his neck more than a few times. It was his turn to do her a favor—something useful, instead of calling her a rat all the time. Of course he wouldn't be able to admit he was doing it for her, he'd have to tell her he hated spiders.

Perhaps a spider had spun a web around his beak once when he was a gosling, and he hadn't been able to honk or eat until his mama helped him out. But he'd never stopped carrying a grudge against spiders—at least that's what he'd tell Devonshire. Smogul didn't want anyone to know he had a kind feather on his body . . .

Just as she'd begun typing the words *Devonshire wriggled again in desperation but the web held fast, its sticky strands binding her tiny claws. Suddenly she heard a sound* . . . Erinn heard a sound. She froze.

What was that? It sounded like . . . tapping.

She stared around the cabin, trying to identify where it was coming from, but the tapping had stopped.

Maybe she'd imagined it. Or it had come from outside.

Get back into the book, you're finally on a roll.

But she found herself standing up, glancing uneasily out the window. The yard and the road were empty, except for the full-leafed summer trees. A meadowlark flitted among the branches right outside the kitchen window.

The tapping had been her imagination—there was nothing, no one in sight.

She slipped into the kitchen chair again, stared at the words on the screen of her laptop.

Tap. Tap. Tap.

Erinn jumped up. *Tap. Tap.* The sound was faint, but steady now.

And it was practically beneath her feet.

She stared at the floor, spooked. Something was under there—probably a mouse. Or a rat. Or . . . she thought in dismay, it could be a trapped squirrel or a rabbit . . .

Then it hit her. She remembered what Jase had told her on the porch that night about the gun hidden beneath the floorboards, the trap door, the crawl space where a person could hide—

The tapping had stopped, but Erinn knelt down, began to run her fingers over the knotted pine floor in the area Jase had described. She found the groove.

It felt like a knothole, a natural indentation in the pine, but it was larger, large enough for a finger to dip in and under.

She slid her thumb beneath the hole and lifted. Her heart thudded as the trap door rose an inch off the floor, then she braced her hand under it and slowly lifted up. It ran longer than she'd anticipated—a good three feet wide, six feet long.

It's like a storage cellar, she thought, her nerves crackling as she began folding the trap door back, getting a glimpse of filmy, gloomy darkness. The walls beneath were slabs of pine, the air thick with cobwebs and dust. She could barely see through the intertwining spiderwebs and she suddenly found herself hoping it was only a small, harmless creature that had gotten trapped down here.

Suddenly ice-cold fear paralyzed her. Her vision. The cobwebs. The coffin. This cramped wood-slatted space beneath the floor *was* the coffin.

For a moment she just stared into the darkness, heart pounding, then, with fear crawling through her, she lifted the trap door, pushed it back, and leaned down, peering into the darkness.

And there was Lily.

She was strapped to a chair only a few feet below-ground, a blindfold fastened around her eyes, a gag in her mouth, her arms and legs bound. As Erinn blinked at her in shock, Lily shifted her weight on the chair and rocked forward and back. One uneven leg of the chair *tapped tapped tapped* against the rough wood floor.

Horror pummeled Erinn like a physical blow. She was squeezing through the opening in a split second and dropping down into the cold musty darkness.

"Lily!" Her fingers tore frantically at the gag. "It's Erinn. You're safe. It's going to be all right!"

"H-hurry." Lily's lips were dry and cracked, her voice so weak Erinn could scarcely make out the words. With her heart in her throat, Erinn tugged at the blindfold and flung it aside, then she attacked the rope binding Lily's arms to the chair.

"He'll be back s-soon," Lily croaked, coughing.

"No, he's not coming back. He's in the hospital, Lily. The sheriff has been questioning him, but he wouldn't tell him where you were."

"He's . . . not coming back? Oh, thank God." Lily started to weep then, tears sliding fast down her gritty face. She moaned in relief as Erinn freed her arms at last, and Lily hugged her arms to her chest as Erinn knelt to untie her legs.

"He . . . said he was going to kill me," Lily gulped. "Are you sure he's in the hospital?"

"I promise you—Jase was standing outside his door the last time I saw him. And Sheriff Farley was in with him. He's not going anywhere, Lily."

The rope fell away and Erinn scrambled up, almost afraid to touch her. Lily looked like a weak, sickly version of her former self, so wan and fragile she wrenched at Erinn's heart.

"Can you stand?" she asked gently, a lump in her

throat. "I'll help you. We'll get you out of here and then I'll call Jase—"

A man's voice spoke regretfully above them. "Sorry, ladies, but that's not going to happen."

Erinn's head flew up and Lily gave a soft scream. She clutched at Erinn's arm. But Erinn couldn't take her eyes off the man staring down at them.

"Too bad you showed up here, Erinn. Now neither of you are going anywhere," Culp said quietly. "Now I have to kill you both."

Chapter Forty-two

Jase stood beneath the hot water blasting from the shower for a good ten minutes, letting it pound over him as he sudsed up. His muscles felt like they'd been trampled by a herd of buffalo and his mind was numb.

No sleep and no good news will do that to you, he thought bleakly as he rinsed the lather from his shoulders and chest.

He'd gotten back to the barn at five in the morning, stumbled into his bed, and slept fitfully until eight. A hot shower and a thermos of coffee would have to keep him going all day. He had to get out to the canyon, had to search until he found Lily and Culp.

Stepping out of the shower and toweling off, he tried not to think about Erinn—about whether she was leaving today, or tomorrow, about whether he'd see her before she vanished from his life.

Maybe it would be better if he didn't. For both of them.

But part of him wanted to, needed to see her, even if it was for the last time.

Someone rapped at his door five, six times, hard.

Wrapping the towel around his waist, he hurried to the door, thinking that maybe it was her. But it wasn't—it was his brother.

"Did you see this?" Colton demanded tautly. His brother's bloodshot eyes bored into his as he shoved a sheet of paper at Jase. "I came to see if you were ready to ride out to Red Horse Canyon, and I found this taped to your door."

Jase took it from him without a word and scanned it with a dawning sense of dread.

It was a ransom note—the follow-up to the first one, printed with the same black block letters.

Bring 100,000 dollars in twenties and fifties to the parking lot of the Crystalville movie theater at two o'clock this afternoon. Bring it in a duffel, leave it in the dumpster. If anyone comes with you or cops are spotted within two miles, you'll never find Lily's body. But the vultures will.

"This wasn't here when I got in at five a.m." Jase said hoarsely. "Someone left it since then—that means . . ." He felt a cold sweat break out over his body. "It's not Wells, Colton—Wells didn't take Lily and Culp!"

"Then who the hell did?"

"We have to call Farley," Jase said sharply. "Where's Pop? And Erinn and Devon?"

"Erinn told Rawley she was going to the cabin to pack some clothes and stuff." Colton frowned. "Pop joined the search about an hour ago. Hey, what'd I say?"

Jase's face had drained of blood. Erinn was at the cabin. Alone. And whoever had taken Lily was still on the loose.

He was yanking on his clothes like a madman, his

mind screaming with the need to hurry. "I've got to find Erinn," he said, grabbing his gun from under the mattress. "You call Farley and tell him either Wells has another partner we don't know about—or someone else took Lily. And then *stay with Devon and Pop* until you hear from me."

He sprinted past his brother toward the Explorer, fear pumping through him. "Whatever you do," he yelled over his shoulder, "don't let Devon out of your sight!"

Erinn blinked dazedly up at the man looming over the opening above her.

"C-Culp." The word was nothing but a croaked whisper. She tried to reconcile the somber, bruised face of the man staring down at her with the handsome, easygoing ranch hand she'd spent days searching for.

"What are you talking about? Help me. We need to get Lily out of here."

But even as she said the words, a part of her knew that they were fruitless, that there was something very wrong here. She just couldn't quite bring herself to comprehend it yet.

His next words made it easier.

"That ain't going to happen, Erinn." He shook his head, sadness etched in his face. "You've seen me. So has Lily. I'm real sorry, but I can't let either one of you go."

"You said he was in the hospital," Lily whispered. Tears swam in her eyes. "You told me he couldn't get away—"

"Oh, God. I was talking about Frank Wells, Lily. I thought *Wells* kidnapped you—we all did—"

Her gaze swung back to Culp. "What did you do? Stage your own disappearance?"

"That's right." His large feet were planted firmly apart at the opening as he stared down at them. "I didn't have a choice—I had to do it. It was the only way out of some real bad trouble. See these bruises, Erinn?"

How could she miss them? Both eyes were blackened. There was a cut on his mouth, gashes and bruises on his cheeks, more on his forearms, visible below the short-sleeved T-shirt he wore. She cringed at the sight of them, and wondered what the rest of his body looked like, then realized she didn't want to know.

"Who did that to you? I know it wasn't Lily."

His face twisted into a humorless smile. "No. Lily fought when I grabbed her from behind, she fought hard and she even got my ski mask off, which was a damned shame. Otherwise," he said sadly, "I really would've let her go once Jase and Clay paid the ransom. But she isn't the one who beat the shit out of me. That was Brock Henson and Dusty Palmer. Remember, those two guys who came into the Saddleback that afternoon, the day I disappeared? Those two bastards set me up."

Erinn resisted the urge to glance around the sunken hiding place she and Lily were trapped in. Hadn't Jase told her there was a gun down here? And that it was loaded? But she didn't dare take her gaze off Culp right now to look for it; she had to keep him talking. Keep delaying the moment he would decide what he was going to do next. She had to be ready when he made his move.

"How'd they set you up, Culp? I... don't understand."

"I owed them money... big money. Seems I hit a bit of a losing streak at the Lucky Lady—the cards just turned against me. They're bound to turn around one of these days, but in the meantime, I can't seem to win a hold 'em hand to save my life." Another one of those mirthless smiles curled his lips but never touched his sad, grim eyes.

"So I nearly lost it—my life, that is. I lost ten grand to ol' Brock. Almost as much to Dusty—and then a few thousand each to some boys from Crystalville and Bridger. They got tired of waiting for me to pay up, so that day—when they came into the Saddleback while we were all sitting around talking about Rawley gettin' shot—they *knew* I was in there, and they knew I'd hightail it out real fast when I saw them. Because I wouldn't want to risk them demanding their money right in front of Colton and Ginny and Lily—all of you. They figured right," Culp added bitterly.

"So I left pretty damn quick, but when I turned the corner, they had those boys from Crystalville and Bridger waiting for me. They dragged me into the alley and lit into me pretty good. Next thing I knew, I woke up in a field five miles outside of town, right next to my rig. Vomiting, bloody, in bad shape. I was about to head over to the ER, but then I started thinking."

Lily had slumped against Erinn's side, her hand squeezing Erinn's, her breath coming fast and shallow. *I need my hands free,* Erinn thought, and slowly eased

Lily down onto the chair, her heart cracking as Lily stiffened in momentary resistance.

Who could blame her? How many hours had she
spent strapped to this chair, in darkness and fear? Erinn
had to wonder if the old vivacious, spirited Lily would
ever return, and for a moment she hated Culp with all
of her being for destroying the soaring spirit of this
buoyant, vibrant young woman.

"That's when you decided to stage your own disappearance?" she asked quickly. "So you wouldn't have
to repay your debts? Why didn't you just go to the
sheriff?"

Erinn darted another swift glance around the crawl
space, looking for some sign of the gun. But she didn't
see it . . .

Culp shrugged, and for the first time resentment replaced the regret she'd seen up until now in his expression. "Jase and Clay and Colton wouldn't have liked
that I got myself in so deep. I didn't want to hear any of
their holier-than-thou shit lectures about not betting
more than I could handle. Matter of fact, I haven't been
too pleased with Jase in a while, to tell you the truth.
Ever since he dumped my sister two months back."

"Jase . . . and LeeAnn were . . . never a couple," Lily
spoke up tremulously. "They were just friends. It . . . it
wasn't his fault LeeAnn got the . . . wrong idea."

"You stick up for him, Lily—go right ahead." Culp's
mouth thinned. "And I'll stick up for LeeAnn. Everyone
knows how fast and hard women fall for Jase. LeeAnn's
no different from any of 'em, even Erinn here." His gaze
narrowed on Erinn.

"You fell for him, didn't you?" he said, pity shining

in his eyes. "A smart, sophisticated city gal like you. And when he dumps you, which he will, you'll know just how LeeAnn felt when Jase walked out on her like she was a piece of trash."

"He didn't—" Lily cried, but Erinn raised her voice, interrupting her.

"So the shooting of the Fortune cattle—that started two months back, around the time that Jase and LeeAnn split up. Was that you, Culp? Did you shoot the cattle because you were mad at Jase?"

"I knew you were smart as well as pretty." He shrugged. "I was just letting off steam that time. Jase treated my sister like shit, so I killed a couple of his cows. Did it a few more times too, so what? He can afford it. But I didn't shoot Rawley," he said sharply. "That must've been Wheeler or Wells, just like everyone thought. I never would've hurt Rawley, especially in a lowdown ambush."

Damn it, there's no gun down here, Erinn thought in despair, as her gaze flicked one last time through the dust and cobwebs. Only the chair, the rough pine walls, the ropes and blindfold she'd removed from Lily.

"You looking for this?" Culp smiled at her then, a stiff, glassy smile that was so different from his usual engaging grin. He pulled a gun from his waistband and pointed it at her with careless ease.

"This is Jase's gun. One of 'em anyway. I knew he always kept one hidden in here. I helped him build this cabin for him and Carly, did he ever tell you that?"

Erinn nodded, her heart sinking. There was no weapon here for her to use. That meant she had to get Culp down here somehow, on their level. She had to get the gun away from him—somehow she and Lily had to overpower him—

"What did you think you were going to do with the ransom money, Culp?" she asked. "You know you won't ever be able to show your face in Wolf River again."

"Yeah, I know that—I'm not stupid," he snapped in sudden annoyance. "I'm going to Vegas, baby." He chuckled suddenly. "I'm starting over, all over. It'll be a cinch winning some major dough once I hit Caesar's with a hundred-thousand-dollar stake in my pocket. Only thing I regret is that you saw my face, Lily," he said ruefully. "I swear, if you hadn't fought me I'd have let you go right after Jase paid the ransom. It's your own fault in a way, for pulling off my mask."

Lily's voice shook with fury. "I only stopped in the middle of the road because I saw your hat lying there. And I was so worried about you I never once thought it was a trap. You grabbed me from behind when I picked it up," she cried. "Did you really think I wouldn't fight? You should have known the Fortunes better than that."

"Yeah, well, look where it got you, Lily." He made a *tsk*ing sound with his tongue. "You and Erinn sure are making this a lot harder than it had to be. You think I want to kill you? I never planned on that. I don't have a choice now. You won't suffer though—I'll shoot you both before I lock you down there again. You won't have to starve or anything—it'll be quick and as painless as I can make it."

"Right, you'll kill us just like the Fortune cattle," Erinn muttered, her heart pounding.

He took a step forward, right to the edge of the opening. "*This* isn't my fault. It wasn't supposed to turn out like this!"

His gaze swung to Lily, slumped weakly in the chair, and regret glistened in his eyes.

"Lily, I took care of you all this time, didn't I? Tell her. You had food. Water. I even let you go to the bathroom upstairs—I untied you whenever I could."

"I suppose for that I should . . . kiss your feet?" Lily shot back shakily, for the first time a glint of fire glowing in her eyes.

Feet.

Erinn stared at Culp's booted feet, his toes less than an inch from the opening. The trap door was just a few feet higher than her head. She edged forward, closer to where he stood looking down—looking at Lily, she realized, as if searching for some sort of understanding from her. He was only a few feet away . . .

"I know you're mad, Lily," he said miserably. "I can't really see as I blame you. But I tried to do this all as gently as I could. I don't have a choice, can't you see that?"

"You have lots of choices, Culp," the girl argued. "Make a . . . a different one. No one else needs to get hurt. Not you, not me . . . not Erinn—I'll tell Jase you didn't hurt me and he'll—"

"Shut up about Jase." Culp gripped the gun tighter, his brown eyes narrowing on her. "He's *never* finding out what I did—"

Erinn leaped forward to the edge of the opening and in one frantic movement reached up, locked both hands around his ankle, and yanked his foot forward with all of her strength.

Culp shouted and fell backward, sliding down on his back, into the hole. As he tumbled down beside Erinn, the gun flew from his hand and skittered wildly across the floor, slamming into the wall.

"Get the gun, Lily!" Erinn screamed.

Then everything happened in a blur. Lily hurtled off the chair and dove for the gun. Culp was already grunting, scrambling to his feet, but Erinn seized the chair and swung it at him. The impact knocked him into the wall.

"I've ... got ... it," Lily panted, but even as she started to whirl with the gun clenched in both hands, Culp lunged at Erinn. His fist slammed into her jaw and sent her reeling to the floor.

Vivid red lights danced before her eyes and a hard, weird buzzing clamored in her ears. Through it all, she felt pain crunching through her face.

An instant later, he hauled her up, clamping her against him as a shield as Lily swung the gun toward him with shaking hands.

"The slug has to go through her to get to me, Lily. I'm betting you're not willing to do that. Drop the gun!"

"Let her go, Culp!" Lily's face was white, but she was holding onto the gun for dear life. "Let her go!"

His breathing ragged, he tightened his grasp. Erinn cried out in pain as he twisted her arm behind her back. "I'll snap it in two," he snarled in Erinn's ear. "Unless she drops that gun! Tell her to drop it."

Agony shot through Erinn. Every nerve shrieked in pain, bringing tears to her eyes. "Don't ... do it ... Lily," she gasped, her knees giving out as Culp twisted harder.

"Stop!" Lily screamed. The gun was shaking in her hands. "Stop it, Culp!"

Erinn could barely think. But through the red haze of unspeakable pain, she lifted her foot and slammed her heel down on Culp's instep as hard as she could.

He yelped and for a split second his grip faltered. She jerked free, flinging herself away from him—and Lily pulled the trigger. She hit him in the shoulder, but instead of stopping him, it made him scream in rage and sent him diving toward her and the gun.

Then a big dark blur shot past Erinn's dazed vision. A man's body dove into the hole, slamming into Culp like a linebacker, smashing him to the ground.

Jase's arm drew back. His fist bashed Culp's face. The ranch hand screamed, and Jase hit him again. And again.

"Jase—he's unconscious," Erinn cried. She flew to his side, clutched at his arm as he drew it back yet again. She'd never seen such cold deadly fury before and her heart thumped wildly in her chest.

"Jase, you have to stop. It's over—we have to get Lily out of here!"

His arm froze in midair. He stared into her face, that beautiful, fine-boned face, streaked with dust and tears, her hair full of cobwebs. She was *alive*. Lily was *alive*. His sister sat huddled on the floor, still holding the gun, staring at him like a wild-eyed stranger. Her face was gray and she looked too weak to move.

But she was alive.

He heaved himself to his feet, staring down at Culp's prone form as Erinn gasped in relief beside him.

He wrapped her in his arms and held her close. The entire way here, he'd thought about the possibility of never seeing her again. As she buried her face against his neck, and he felt the tremors running through her body, a powerful emotion rushed through him, rocking him to his core.

"Hey." Lily had lowered the gun. She was limping toward them, stiff and wobbly, but there was a wan smile on her face. "Can we hug later and . . . and get out of here first? I really have the creeps down here. I want to see . . . the sun . . ."

Jase swept her into his embrace too.

And then the sound of tires screeching down the drive filled the air—there were car doors slamming, shouts, boots pounding across the threshold of the cabin.

The cavalry had arrived.

Chapter Forty-three

Erinn sipped her morning coffee at Fortune's Way for the last time. Standing at the kitchen window, she watched as Clay boosted Devon up into Peaches's saddle.

Her sister's smile sparkled every bit as brightly as the Montana sun as the horse started forward at a walk. It was the first time she'd seen Devon smile since the nightmare with Wells at Red Horse Cave.

It wasn't surprising that a horseback ride on Peaches, with Clay Fortune about to ride along beside her, had brought it on. Somehow, Jase's father had become her little sister's new best friend.

Well, we won't have Clay there, but we can see about riding lessons in New York, she told herself, as Jase's father swung into the saddle of a buckskin gelding and the two horses trotted off across the pasture. *If horses are Devon's passion, we'll find a way for her to ride as much as she wants.*

But as she gazed out at the grand beauty of the mountains, at riotous wildflowers and open land, she knew in her heart that for Devon, riding in the city wouldn't be at all like what she'd found here at the Fortune ranch. And as for herself. . . . Nothing in New York City would ever compare to what *she'd* found here. Friends, a sense of belonging. Love.

She felt a pang as she remembered what Devon had asked her this morning before she hurried out for her ride.

"Do we really have to leave Wolf River, Tiffany? So soon?" Hopefulness had shone in her eyes as she'd pulled on the new riding boots Clay had bought her in town. The question had ripped at Erinn's heart.

"I thought you'd want to leave. It must be hard staying here, with all the memories of Hank . . . and everything else that's happened."

Yesterday, after all, had been the funeral for Mick and Hank Wheeler. There'd been no members of the Wheeler family attending—Mick and Hank *had* no living family as far as anyone knew. And few people from Wolf River had bothered to come.

Only the Fortunes, Ginny, Devon and Erinn, and a handful of ranch hands from the Hanging J had shown up for the brief, impersonal service under a cloudy sky—and those who'd come had made it clear they came only for Hank, not for Mick.

Red Drummond had confessed to the sheriff during the investigation that Mick hadn't really been working with him on the afternoon of Rawley's shooting. He'd admitted that Mick had been gone for several hours that day and that he'd asked Red to cover for him.

Word had later gotten out that Mick Wheeler shot Rawley Cooper due to his grudge against Jase Fortune, and this had done nothing to increase his popularity.

No one shed a tear for Mick as the caskets were lowered into the ground, but men bowed their heads, hats in hand, when Hank's name was mentioned, and Devon wept for him, and clung to Erinn as her sister led her away from the fresh grave.

"It's going to be hard anywhere, for a while," Devon had replied, biting her lip. "But at least here, I know people and . . . and I think some of them even like me. Ginny and Colton do . . . and that waitress, Amanda, at the Saddleback, she's a junior at the high school and she said if I stay and go to school, she'd introduce me to some other girls. And Mr. Fortune—he was telling me about some riding competitions they have in Billings, and he said that if I practice real hard and get good enough, I could ride in some—"

"Devon—"

"And if we stayed here I could see Peaches and Diego and Sheba and Wild Eye all the time! Sheba's going to foal next spring and I was thinking, if I got a job at the Saddleback or something, like Amanda, maybe I could even save up enough money to buy her foal and—"

The hope faded from her eyes as she saw the expression on Erinn's face.

"I know. You really want us to go back to New York, don't you?" the girl said quietly.

"I want us to . . . to be a family again and to start fresh and to make some good memories together. I think we need to get away from here to do that."

Or do you just need to get away from Jase? a little voice inside Erinn asked. *To get away from the memory of his kisses, his voice, the way he looks at you when he speaks your name? And the way he was silent when you told him you loved him.*

She brushed the voice aside. "Maybe we'll spend the fall and winter in New York and then, if you still want to, we could visit Fortune's Way next spring when Sheba's foal is born."

When you've forgotten about Jase. About that drafty barn, his bed, the sofa that's just the right size for making love . . .

Devon's gaze had dropped. She hadn't argued, or sulked, or done anything to show her disappointment, but Erinn had seen it in her eyes as she turned toward the bedroom door.

Now, gazing out the window at the brilliant summer day, watching her sister on horseback, galloping across the pasture, Erinn's heart twisted with regret.

Nothing about her stay in Wolf River had turned out as she'd expected. And nothing about her life felt right now that she was leaving.

It had been three days since she found Lily, three days since Hank and his brother had been killed. Three days since Culp and Wells had been arrested, each charged with separate counts of kidnapping, assault, and murder.

She and Devon were flying home to New York that afternoon. They'd have left sooner if Sheriff Farley hadn't needed to question and requestion everyone involved in the case for hours on end, two whole days in a row.

Now they were finally free. At least until Culp and Wells came to trial.

But Erinn would worry about that later. She didn't

want to think about having to return to Wolf River, about having to see Jase again, not now. Not when it was taking all of her determination just to leave him.

She'd scarcely seen him since he'd rescued her and Lily in the cabin. Instead of spacing all of his police interviews over the two-day period, as she and Devon and Lily had, Jase had endured his grilling straight through, insisting on staying at the sheriff's department the first day for hours on end until he was finished.

Then he'd made himself scarce. She hadn't seen him at breakfast or dinner at Fortune's Way, she hadn't seen him in town when she went to the Saddleback to have coffee with Ginny, and she hadn't asked a soul where he was.

She refused to ask. Obviously Jase was trying to keep his distance, to make the break easier on both of them, and she wasn't about to look like a lovelorn idiot by asking his family members or friends why he wasn't around.

He'd been plenty busy with his ranch and his business before she'd arrived in Wolf River, and now he was plenty busy again. End of story.

"Penny for your thoughts." Lily had entered the kitchen behind her, and Erinn turned with a smile.

"You don't really want to know."

"Try me."

"I'm thinking how much Devon will miss it here. The horses, her visits with your father—and I'll miss you, Lily. Promise you'll come to New York and visit us."

"Really? New York?" Lily's face lit and Erinn was delighted to see a measure of color and life had returned to her cheeks. "Just try to keep me away!" she exclaimed.

But her smile was nowhere near as vibrant as it had been the day Erinn first met her. There were shadows haunting Lily's eyes that had never been there before. She'd seen the darker side of life too young, just as Devon had.

"You're doing it again," Lily said, one slim eyebrow lifting as she reached for the box of Frosted Flakes on the kitchen table. "Daydreaming. Only—it doesn't look like you're dreaming of anything pleasant. Are you still thinking about . . . you know . . . Culp?" she said in a low tone.

"Not any more than I need to. What about you?"

"Well, I'm very much looking forward to testifying at his trial." Lily pursed her lips as she poured milk into her cereal bowl and slipped into a chair. "I do feel sorry for LeeAnn, but if I have anything to say about it, her brother's going away for a very long time."

The front door slammed and boots thumped toward the kitchen. Erinn tensed, thinking it might be Jase, but it was Colton, looking like a handsome rodeo rider who'd just won a grand prize.

"Pop says you and Devon are leaving today. You're going back to New York."

She forced a light smile. "I'm all packed except for the things still at the cabin. Including my laptop," she added with a rueful glance at Lily. "At least now that I know how Princess Devonshire gets free of that nasty spider web, I may even have a chance to write the next two or three chapters on the plane."

"How about some company going back to the

cabin?" Lily offered, only a trace of hesitation in her voice. "I'll go with you, if you'd like—it might be too upsetting walking back in there alone, after everything that happened."

"It will be more upsetting for you," Erinn said quietly.

Colton quickly agreed.

"Well, then," Lily mused, still troubled, "why doesn't Colton go with you?" She gazed at her brother, obviously expecting him to volunteer. "Or better yet, Erinn can give you a list of what to pack and then she wouldn't even have to be there at all."

"Well...I guess I could do that." Colton looked startled—and reluctant. "It's just that I'm so behind on everything, and...and I have so much to do. I need to go into town for supplies and stuff. And I have a date with Sue Lynn later," he remembered suddenly. He glanced apologetically at Erinn. "She gets really offended when people run late."

"Of course. Don't worry about it, Colton."

Lily shot her brother an irritated glance, but Erinn shook her head.

"I'm perfectly capable of doing this myself," she said firmly.

And she was. Oddly enough, she was almost glad of this opportunity to say good-bye to the cabin on Black Bear Road in her own way.

The good and the bad.

The bad was all about the dark hole where Lily had been held. The good was...everything else. The half-painted living room, the kitchen table where Devon had eaten Oreos for breakfast that first morning, the porch where . . .

Never mind the porch, she thought as she grabbed her purse and went outside. She never saw Colton's widening grin as he watched her head out to the Jeep, or the way he shrugged his shoulders and tried to look innocent when Lily demanded to know why he looked so pleased with himself.

She had no suspicion of what lay ahead of her, and as she made the drive from Fortune's Way to the cabin for the last time, the ache in her heart deepened.

She tried to tell herself she was happy that she didn't have to face saying good-bye to Jase. But part of her was mad as hell that he hadn't even cared enough to see her one last time before she left.

But you have no reason to be mad, do you? It's not as if he wasn't up front about everything. You knew that falling in love—with you, with anyone—was simply not in his game plan.

And yet, knowing all that, you let him into your heart. You told him you loved him.

It was her own stupid fault. The first time he kissed her, she should have pushed him away. Or slapped him. Or run like hell.

Instead, she'd thrown herself into his arms and thrown caution to the winds.

This is the way it should be then, she thought as she turned onto Black Bear Road for the last time. *It's better that he didn't show up to say good-bye. Better to end this on a note of dignity and self-respect and maturity.*

Then she slammed on her brakes.

Jase's silver Explorer was parked in front of the

cabin. And he was leaning against the porch rail, wearing a white T-shirt and jeans, his hat shading his eyes and a can of root beer in his hand.

For a wild moment, Erinn considered backing down the road, leaving her laptop, leaving everything.

Then she told herself to grow up. So what if Jase was here? It was his property, wasn't it? He had every right to be here.

And she had every right to retrieve her belongings.

But since he'd avoided her all this time, you'd think he could have stayed away until she was on a plane back East, she thought grimly.

She eased onto the gas pedal and drove forward, her mouth set. *Get in, and get out,* she told herself.

"I'll be out of your way in a minute," she said as naturally as she could manage, slamming the door of the Jeep and starting toward the steps with no intention of pausing to chat.

"What makes you think you're in my way?" he asked, deliberately stepping into hers as she reached the porch.

"Don't be a smart ass," she muttered. "I'm sure you didn't plan on being here at the same time anymore than I did. It's awkward for both of us and—"

"I *did* plan on being here the same time as you," he corrected. "And it *is* rather awkward, but I'm hoping we can fix that."

"You ... *what*?" She stared at him incredulously. "You've been nowhere to be found for the past three days and now you're telling me you *planned* to be here right when I'm coming to pack my stuff? How in the world would you know when that was going to be?"

"I've been spending a lot of time here anyway, but Colton did his part—he called me as soon as you left and told me you were on your way over."

She blinked. Colton—who had refused to come here with her. He'd *known* she wouldn't be at the cabin alone. He'd known that Jase was waiting for her.

Why?

"It was all part of my plan," Jase said, and smiled at her, but behind the smile, she saw a question in his eyes. A hint of uncertainty.

"What plan would that be?"

"I'll tell you in a minute. But first, come inside. There's something I want you to see."

She hesitated as he moved out of her way. Then she took a deep breath and walked through the door. She expected to see the trap door still open, to see everything as it had looked three days ago when she left here—after Culp had nearly killed her and Lily.

But . . .

The hole was gone. The trap door *was* open, but the wood-slatted space beneath the floor had been filled with poured concrete.

She whirled toward Jase in astonishment.

"I filled it in. That's part of what I've been doing the past few days. I didn't want you to ever think about that hole again when you came into this house."

"I probably won't be back in this house after today," she pointed out.

His eyes held hers. "That's what I want to talk to you about."

Erinn felt a tiny, primitive seed of hope take root in her heart. She drew a breath. "So talk."

"I'm planning to put in an all-new floor," he said, pinning her gaze, his eyes steady and searching on hers. "No more knotted pine. Something completely different. Hardwood or tile or granite or—"

"Why, Jase?"

"So that if we get married and you want to live here you won't have any bad memories of what was beneath the old floor."

She went very still. She couldn't have spoken a word if she'd tried.

Jase reached her in two swift strides. The easygoing confidence faded from his face. "That wasn't how I meant to say it," he said quickly. "Come outside. Let's talk on the porch." On the words, he snagged her hand and pulled her with him.

"I know that didn't come out sounding romantic," he apologized, catching both of her hands in his. "But I wanted to get that out of the way first—the floor, I mean. And the hole. And the bad memories . . . but if you still don't want to live in the cabin, that's fine. I understand. We can live in the barn . . . my barn. I can add on to it, a room for Devon, for a baby . . . whatever you want. Or we could live in Fortune's Way, or I could build a new house—or if you want to stay in New York, we'll work that out too—"

"Jase," she interrupted, stifling a crazed hysterical urge to laugh. "What are you talking about?"

"About us." He pulled her closer suddenly and his arms wrapped around her, tight and warm and strong.

"I didn't know there *was* an 'us' anymore. I haven't even seen you lately."

"About that . . ." He smiled into her eyes. "I can explain." And he kissed her. By the time he finished, she felt so dizzy and warm she could barely concentrate on his words.

"I had a lot of thinking to do. And then something happened—I had a vision."

Erinn narrowed her eyes at him. "A vision? I believe you're making fun of me, Jase Fortune."

"Never." He touched her lips with his thumb, tracing their lush outline as she drew in her breath. "I definitely had a vision. A vision of you and me. Naked. Hot and heavy. Making love. Every night. Every afternoon."

This time when he kissed her, the kiss was long, deep, and hungry. "Every morning too," he added, brushing his lips against her throat.

"Is that . . . so?" Erinn's hands fluttered up, smoothed through his thick hair. Her heart was beating so fast she thought she'd pass out, but she didn't want to miss anything.

"Yep. That's so. But that's not all." Slowly, Jase backed her against the wall of the cabin, just as he had that rainy night. His eyes gleamed into hers and he leaned closer until his mouth was only one tempting inch away from hers.

"In my vision, we had a baby. Two babies. No . . . make that three." He grinned. "That's all I can see for now. But there could be more."

Babies. With Jase.

Erinn smiled, her heart lifting, soaring. "That sounds lovely, but there's something that has to happen before we can have babies," she murmured, her eyes locked on his.

"We have to make love? Again and again?"

"Besides that."

"Oh." Jase nodded knowingly, as he nuzzled at her lips. "You mean getting married. And before that— engaged."

"Even before that," she informed him. She clasped her hands around his neck, nestling closer. "There's usually some words that are said. I can't quite remember what they are, but they do usually precede everything else—"

"I love you, Erinn."

Her heart soared. "It took you long enough."

He grinned ruefully. "I tried to fight it. The other night . . . I was an idiot. But it wore off. Think you can forgive me?"

"I think I'll manage." A smile bloomed across her face. "Because I happen to love you too." Suddenly, tears began to slip down her cheeks, and then she was laughing and crying all at the same time. Jase held her and kissed each of her tears away.

Then to her astonishment, he let her go and dropped down on one knee right on the porch.

"Pouring cement beneath the floor is only part of what I've been doing. I did a little shopping as well."

"I . . . I guess you did." She could only gape at the small box he fished from his pocket. It was a blue velvet box. A Tiffany & Co. box.

"Last time I looked, there wasn't a jewelry store in Wolf River," she gasped.

"I had to do a little traveling," he acknowledged. He lifted the lid of the box to reveal a staggering three-carat diamond ring set in platinum. It glittered so brilliantly

in the morning sunlight that it snatched her breath
away.

Jase looked pleased as he studied the shock on her
face.

"Will you marry me, Erinn?"

"I . . . I do believe I will."

He slipped the ring onto her finger and she dropped
to her knees, throwing her arms around him and kissing him.

"I take it that means you're canceling your flight today?" he murmured against her lips.

She smiled into his eyes and saw everything she
wished for in their depths. Including her future. And
Devon's future. Right here in Wolf River.

"There's no reason to go anywhere, Jase," she said
simply, touching his face. "I love you. And I'm already
home."